Also by Stephen Swartz

FLU SEASON
The Book of Mom

A Novel

Stephen Swartz

MYRDDIN PUBLISHING GROUP

UNITED STATES ✦ UNITED KINGDOM ✦ AUSTRALIA

ISBN-13: 978-1-68063-073-2

ISBN-10: 1-68063-073-3

www.myrddinpublishing.com

Cover design by Iris Schaeffer

NOTE

This is a work of imagination created for entertainment purposes and is not intended to convey any medical advice or provide health care information for readers.

What characters may state on the pages is solely a product of their fictional personalities and should not to be construed as the Author's own views on any particular facts and opinions whether accepted or contested.

"A boy's best friend is his mother."

—Norman Bates, *Psycho* (1960)

PART 1

JOURNEY

1

IN WHICH MOM GOES TO THE BEACH

Mom told me she named me Sandy because she was lounging on a beach when I was conceived. I got only bits and pieces of the story until I was a teenager. Then one night, half-drunk with sorrow at yet another pandemic spreading over us, she held me close, like I was still her baby, and gave up the whole tale.

She was laying on a big towel on a beach one bright sunny afternoon. She had gone with a friend down to the nude part of the beach – the section designated as 'clothing optional' – and they were excited to stroll down the beach without a stitch of swimsuit on. Then, having done that without sufficient fanfare from other nudists, they decided to lie down, stretch out, and work on their tans.

At some point, Mom's friend got up and went for a swim. Mom continued sunbathing. She lay on her back, knees bent up, feet flat on the towel, when a shadow fell over her. When her eyes opened at the dimming of sunlight, there stood a handsome man twice her age, as nude as she was. His smile was quite enticing as he knelt at her feet.

Speaking to her in a seductive voice, he took her knees in his hands and moved them apart. He scooted up to her and with some teasing strokes, pushed forward. Mom never held back the details and her tone was clinical, using proper terms rather than slang.

When he finished, he thanked her for her gift. He said he felt blessed she would allow him to enjoy her. The flowery language he used let her know she was special. And she liked feeling special because, other than on that beach, she wasn't. He was welcomed that afternoon because she wanted to and because she knew her father didn't want her to.

Behind him, she saw, was another man watching curiously.

As the first man stood and stepped aside, he stayed by her as the second man took his place. He followed through as the first man watched, smiling as he caressed her hair, telling her how beautiful she was. Behind them, down the slope, a pair of young men gazed at their activity. The first man saw them looking and waved them up. When the second man finished, these two were ready.

That first man took the role of moderator, a kind of master of ceremonies. He directed the new men while he remained beside her, speaking his seductive words to her. He knelt beside her and she could've done more for him if she'd wanted to, but he didn't insist on more. It was enough that the third and fourth men took their turns. They treated her gently and departed.

The first two men remained with her, the older man sitting cross-legged next to her head, the younger man kneeling between her outstretched legs. They had a conversation about what had just transpired. Mom said they were friendly, concerned for her well-being, inquired how she felt, if anything hurt, how they could make her more comfortable. She only told me the first man was too handsome to ignore. The others she never really noticed, being fixated on the first man.

She eventually returned home. Her gal pal came back to the towels with a new boy in tow. In the weeks to come, Mom noticed she was pregnant. It was a shock to her parents, a mark against them in the high society reputation ledger. She was sent to live with her grandparents for a few months. At the same time, her friend married the boy she met and they had kids, moved away, and that was that. When I was born, Mom thought back to that day on the beach and told the nurse my name should be Sandy.

"I met your father at the beach," she told me when I was a little boy. "I met a few men at the beach," she admitted later. "So I don't know who your father was. Does it really matter?"

It didn't seem to matter at the time, but I continued to wonder who he might be.

When she noticed how I'd become aroused by the story, she paused. "Does it excite you hearing about the men who fucked your mother?"

I shook my head, my face frozen. I knew nothing of sorrow or shame even on the cusp of adulthood. Mom took care of me, protected me. She always had. That's all I knew.

"It's how life happens," she said. "Nothing to feel ashamed of. I'm happy to have you here."

She moved beside me, gazing down at my lap, at the bulge there, and laid her hand there. She urged me to slip my trousers down and I did, afraid to refuse.

"When the world ends," she said with a grin as another siren wailed outside, "we might be the only two people left. What should we do then?"

I had no response, listening to the sirens outside fade. "Call for help?"

"What if all communication's stopped? So we have to rely on ourselves?"

"Right." I remained confused.

Mom gave me a wink, removed her hand. "It may be up to you and me to repopulate the world."

As a young man, it felt odd she would suggest that scenario to me. She had to know how a young man would respond, how any male would take the suggestion. I flew into a full-fledged panic. The fact that it would be Mom and me saving the world was uncomfortable. Yet I tended to consider things in logical terms, seldom caught up in emotion. First, she was attractive at her age, probably able to have a baby. Second, I worried – like any young man might – whether I could please her. I worried if she would still love me, take care of me, if I didn't please her. She teased me with the idea many times. She would stiffen me with an off-hand remark about how beautiful our children would be, even more beautiful as the last remaining couple on this planet.

And then, thinking through future possibilities, long before anything could actually happen, she might get old and pass away, perhaps taken by the latest virus threat digging through her until she was only a husk and glad to die. I'd have the responsibility of assuring she looked her best for viewing by friends and colleagues she collected during her time here. Over the years I'd heard some of them call her 'a real pistol' as well as 'slut', 'rebel', 'hippie chick', 'that bitch', and 'cunt'. I couldn't be sure if any of them might've ever been a lover. They hadn't known her name on that beach long ago so they couldn't have followed her life as a musician nor recognize her in an obituary.

I imagined putting her in the ground, under the shade of a tall oak tree, not far from the office I would have once the pandemic ended and I finished college, started my own career. I would often stop there, going to and from my job, have a brief chat or a long silence, leave her a pretty flower, wondering what could've been if we were to be the last people.

"Sandy?" Mom called. "You daydreaming again?"

✳ ✳ ✳

And then there was the tuba. The *damn* tuba! Once so silvery bright, now dull gray. Once smooth as ice, now pock-marked with indentations great and small. However, Mom loved that machine – slightly more than me, I guessed. She'd sit on her wooden stool, a small pillow to support the beast, and blow out her lungs into that coiled metal, producing as much cacophony as possible or on occasion a mournful tune that sailed down the street, punching neighbors in their ears. That would often produce a neighborly response. "Shut up, ya blowhard!" was a common one. She loved provoking responses.

I was a response to her going to a nude beach at the age of sixteen and letting her friend chicken out and sneak away. I was a response to her waking each day with nothing to do but complain about her life. Once everyone agreed that the next pandemic wave had arrived, she complained more. Individual freedom versus the common good was her everyday rant. That made a good motif for her music; always new tunes written down for later. When the Symphony's concert season was cancelled she had little to do but blow away her troubles. When it became obvious that the way to survive was to leave the rat trap cities, she insisted on taking that tuba.

"What good is that thing going to be?" I asked.

"We might need to signal for help," she replied. I couldn't ever tell whether she was being serious or speaking sarcasm. I had no sense for that, being a special kid.

"More likely we would be signaling the bad guys as much as any help." Had to think logically, or at least recite my side of the script.

"But I can't bear to leave him."

Him – like he was my big brother. So it was me that would *bear* him mile after mile on my back, its flared bell above my head. I imagined us stopping for the night, and she would play a melancholy tune in the darkness. Strangers would appear, sitting close but not too close, listening. When she finished, they would slink away, back into the shadows, satisfied.

She taught me how to play it in my younger days but I'd forgotten my lessons. She didn't really want me to be a tubist, much less a musician, not in these times. She taught me because I asked her to and she reluctantly conveyed the basics.

I'm almost certain she never meant for her musical ways to corrupt my childhood, yet they did. Hanging around Mom's workplaces – the rehearsal hall or on campus – I couldn't help but make the acquaintance of trumpeters, hornists, trombonics, and a host of percussionistas, as well as select saxophonians and the occasional clarinettos and flautists. She never dallied with double-reed folks, however. That would've been too much, she advised. String players? There was only one as I recall, a blonde female cellist, as curvaceous as her instrument, who may have taught Mom a thing or two about *pizzicato*. They all served as surrogate parent to me. They seemed to pity me, called me 'gifted' but with tension in their voices like it was sarcasm.

Mom would remind me every week, sometimes more often, I wasn't supposed to become a musician. In the post-apocalyptic world, no tribe would want to feed the musicians. Learn a useful skill, she encouraged. That meant nothing that was book-learning, nothing in the Arts, and certainly not philosophy or psychology which were, to her, the keys to the lock on the door to the passage to Hell's lower basement.

Mom thought it would be good to learn practical skills, and give her some time away from me, so I joined the Scouts. By that time, the 'Boy Scouts' had disbanded after too much hassle over gender bias. Troops tried to stave off elimination by allowing females to join, then faded further over the years as boys exited and the identification of trees became difficult as trees vanished. Tying knots was too bondage-triggering. Merit badges were marks of narcissism. Everyone was equal, we were told – except those more equal than us. Even uniforms of scarves and shorts smacked of silliness, too sissy for boys yet too patriarchal for girls. In the end we dispensed with uniforms altogether in the name of equity – ignorantly posing in an aura of simulated sameness, where boys and girls and others could hike, camp, and hone our outdoor skills together as a tribe of naked persons, fully nondescript as anything so individualistic could be. We were inspected daily for outward blemish that might distinguish one from another. Uniformity was the goal.

Mom predicted there soon would be no more music, not even the folksy tunes we sang around Scout campfires. They would be banned, too controversial: rousing marches or patriotic anthems of the ruling class! I was inspired by those songs and sang along. Mom didn't want me to waste my time on what she'd wasted her time on. She learned that much about music and was passing on that lesson to me. Oh, she enjoyed music as much as ever, dared to play it in my presence, took me to rehearsals and concerts. From my seat in the center of the auditorium I would raise my hand, give a thumbs-up to let her know it sounded good. Being a music critic seemed all right with her, though; music should be criticized. Everything was criticized in those days. Critic was a job for which there were always positions available, Mom noted.

The limitations on music was the first sign of our decay, looking back, my first indication that all was not well with what we liked to call 'society'. There were other names for it: the 'vast right-wing conspiracy' or the 'deep state' or the 'left-hand of justice' or the 'swamp' or the 'new world's order of burgers and fries' – many names for the collection of humans, groups of them in competition more than cooperation. Always in groups, never as individuals.

I wondered what it was about groups that drew people so eagerly into them. After all, I was fine being alone, or with Mom. In those days official reports constantly reminded us how groups were pulling apart 'society', for lack of a better word. For lack of a better world, Mom would echo, checking what I was reading. She encouraged me to read everything I could, even if she didn't agree with it.

When the first newscast mentioned the contagion, few of us paid attention. It was yet another blather among other blathers designed to maintain fear, Mom pointed out. A fearful populace was easier to control. I thought back to my Scout experiences, nervous and afraid of what would happen next, and I knew it was true. I hated conflict. I shrank from a fight. Easier to go along, blend in, keep my head down, and never volunteer for anything. I learned a lot in Scouts.

But Scouts was not 'real life' – what blue checkers tagged as 'RL' – a realm that oppressed them to the point of causing them to prefer staying home in front of a screen, managing their actions from keyboards, wielding VR joysticks like professional engineers. To them, RL was a menace, a jungle of toxic predators and two-way mirrors, body shaming and face paint products, and their latest dinner. Before the pandemic came, they had to show their vacations.

"It's all a ruse," Mom would remind me, seeing me staring at pretty people in exotic locations on the screen and slipping into my dream land. "Don't waste your time trying to be like them."

"I'm not." But I wondered why I couldn't be like them. Even

then I wondered whether I was normal, why Mom always kept her eye on me. She promised to take me away someday, let me enjoy a nice place for a while. One time we went up to the mountains and camped out under the trees.

As time went by and everyone was urged to stay indoors, safe from the pandemic, those 'influencers' couldn't go to any vacation destinations. We pondered how the lucky few were able to get out, skip the lockdowns and fly to faraway places, have parties and lounge on beaches. Then a newscast told us how they were fake. Sent to check that they were actually staying indoors – they were – their fabulous vacation destinations were revealed as nothing but manufactured illusion. Some famous scenery prostitutes were rounded up and sentenced to four square walls and two meals a day with no access to make-up or stylists.

"Told you," Mom intoned.

So much for RL. Better to remain at home and stay inside a scene of my own design. I invented a concert hall, put virtual musicians in it – but Mom found it and deleted it.

"RL is unpleasant," said Mom, face in full scowl as though she'd uncovered a log history of sex sites, "but RL is what we must learn to operate in. There is no substitute. None but for the insane who live inside their heads."

I sat stunned, contemplating her words. I actually liked living inside my head.

"Then what is there for me to do?" I asked her.

The way the world was disrupted by the pandemic, I wasn't going to school. Instead, I sat on the study chair, face turned to the screen, plugs in my ears to bring in approved audio from both human and AI teachers. My mind tended to drift away from the lesson, hearing phantom music wafting through my ear buds and recalling encounters with horners and flautists in the meadows of my mind. Electric shocks would hit me whenever I was unfocused too long. I snapped back to attention, seeing the stern face of my teacher or red eyes of the AI figure. Six hours a day. Five days a week. Forty weeks of the year. For two years. Then I graduated.

The ceremony looked like a recording of a ceremony from the

past because there were crowds of people, unmasked and smiling, proud music blaring, colorful flags waving, with uplifting speeches spoken from unmasked authority figures. I got my diploma by electronic messenger, a file with my name on it. Mom was so delighted. She kissed me all over and, at her age, it felt odd.

I made plans to start college in the fall – a virtual campus, again, but one which we hoped would soon welcome students to set foot there. How long could a pandemic last, anyway? Mom described her college days: studying on the grass under the shade of trees, or tucked away in the corner of the library – which all sounded good to me. I liked being by myself, studying something without interruption. Like normal, like the traditions of long ago, not like the 'new normal' they kept talking about now.

That was when everything went south.

2

IN WHICH THE WORLD GOES MAD

One bright sunny morning, as I prepared to go off to virtual school at the desk in the back room, loudspeakers passing by outside announced new restrictions. Usually I ignored them. But this time I listened. There would be meat only on Tuesdays, bread only on Mondays, fruit of some kind only on Saturdays, a new medicine ration every other Thursday, and every third Thursday for some items, with no more paper products until the end of the year. Furthermore, health credentials would now be scanned at any time by any officer, not just when entering buildings or traveling outside our neighborhood. Also, penalties for non-compliance were again raised. Several detainees had died in quarantine camps, it was reported. But we shouldn't worry. Our government people were working hard, safe in a sterile environment.

I was about to call Mom, to ask if she heard it, but she was standing behind me, fresh from her weekly shower's allotment of water. The worsening water quality left her with a chlorine scent.

She leaned down and kissed my cheek.

"I heard," she said, "though I try not to listen."

"What are we going to do?"

Her smile was encouraging; she never faked it.

"Do?" Her smile widened, teeth gleaming. "We do what we always do. Keep busy. We can survive anything. It won't last much longer. Pandemics always die out – when enough people have died. We simply must be the ones who don't."

She kissed the top of my head, stood up behind me as I logged on my teaching machine, tapped to the first class, saw the small faces of my classmates in a grid and the AI figure in the corner.

"Greetings, students," the robotic voice said.

We gave the official hand sign, demonstrating our compliance.

The AI figure glared at me, my picture square flashing red.

"Parents and guardians must exit the study space," the AI figure commanded.

Mom waved a finger at the AI figure.

"You must keep a brave face," Mom reminded me every day. "You never know who's looking, taking notes, clicking red flags to your file."

"I know, Mom."

She stepped back, her towel slipping as she turned away from the view of my machine's camera. Gasps from my classmates.

The AI instructor paused, its eyes flashing red.

All the faces of my classmates went away and the AI face filled the screen. A stern lecture about morality ensued, and I sat with a serious face on.

"It was an accident," I responded when allowed to speak. I felt an electric shock. "You taught us about gravity. Things fall."

More lecture from the AI instructor, then the faces of my classmates appeared on the screen. They seemed as dismayed as me. Perhaps they'd also been caught and chastised for some minor infraction.

The day's lesson continued.

The new history of the present era. We began with a lecture on why old history needed to be restricted, with much of it completely removed or replaced with different sets of facts and the approved interpretation.

Many acts of aggression had been perpetrated upon many innocent people, our AI instructor intoned, as maps and charts flowed across the screen interspersed with images of violence. But now we have peace and justice for everyone. Oppressors are now the oppressed. The world is right again. Obedience is a virtue. We need to forget the past; it's done and gone, lessons which are best forgotten. New lessons will teach all we need to know. Compliance is a virtue. We are not to be considered individuals but members of groups, like spokes on a wheel. Spokes alone cannot go far. Think no thoughts that are not the thoughts of others. Look to the government for answers. And never ask questions. Questioning is not a virtue.

The screen went blank as another loudspeaker blared a new message outside. Apparently, the government had fallen. The last cabinet secretary had succumbed to the pandemic. There was no one in charge now – not until some appropriate person could be appointed. We were urged not to panic. We were reminded to be kind to each other. We were all in this together. But stay apart. Wear approved hazmat gear when outdoors. And most of all, do not go outdoors. Penalties are further increased.

"Oh dear," Mom moaned. "It's finally happened."

I turned to regard her. I had never seen that look on her face before.

"Sandy," she said, "go pack a bag. Pack like you're going on a Scouting weekend."

I saw how serious she was so I did what she said, but I took a while deciding what clothes to bring. Clothing for the kind of weather we had now or also for later when it gets cold? A suitcase would be too heavy, but had wheels. Backpack would be better. I stuffed clothing into the pack, not folding any of them. I counted out plenty of undies and socks.

By dinner time I was finished packing. I went to check on Mom. She opened the fridge, found the power had been out. Inside was warm. Half the food was bad. She pulled out the last piece of fruit and a bag of salad. She grabbed a plate from the cabinet.

The only light that was on flickered, then went out.

"Better leave your electronics behind," she said.

I went into my dark bedroom to feel for anything else I might need. It wasn't like my room was full of camping gear ready to go. But it was where I slept, where I leafed through paper magazines – I was accused of being an 'old soul', a spirit from long ago trapped in a freshly born body. I did not disagree.

And then I heard, wafting up through the stale darkness, the mournful moan of Mom's tuba. She played her own tune, a lament for better days now gone by, deep and rich, touching my heart, making me just sit back and listen. She often would pick up the instrument and play out her mood, no lyrics required. Tonight was no different.

✳   ✳   ✳

We slipped out before dawn, quietly left our home on the second floor of that apartment building where we'd lived since I started school. Before I was born, Mom lived with her parents – who were disappointed in her becoming pregnant at a young age. Yet they loved her, I guessed, and did their best to deal with the situation. I visited them during the summers in my childhood. Now we were headed to their house in the country.

Mom's car was a lower-priced automobile of ten years and still ran on gasoline but had a battery, too, what they called a hybrid. Mom kept the tank full during these worrisome days. Stations ran out soon enough. Extra cans of gasoline sat in the trunk. Mom calculated we could get to my grandparents' house before we used it all.

She slid the tuba into its soft-side case, which had shoulder straps. The case was scarred from hauling it around campus during her student days. As a professional, she used a hard-side case but kept it in her office in the Music building, only used if the orchestra traveled. The hard case weighed as much as the tuba; the softy not so much, but it wouldn't protect the instrument from serious bumps.

"You're bringing Timmy?" I asked as we loaded.

"Have to." She gave me a look, like she wondered why I would ask that. "He's been in the family for generations. Your grandfather's grandfather Louie – Ludwig – he brought it from the old country."

"But it's no loss. It's already old. Are you gonna trade it in for something later?"

"I won't trade," she said with a rebutive face. "Not unless it's to save your life."

I nodded, pursed my lips, hating whenever she got serious; it scared me. I shouldn't have suggested that. Timmy was her first love, her first boy, before me.

"Besides, I need to play him to feel at peace."

"Okay, then." There was no arguing with Mom.

And we were off.

In our neighborhood nobody seemed alarmed. The streets were quiet, deserted as usual. We didn't see anyone and we wondered if they already departed or were dead. A few blocks over, we met other vehicles, half in normal use and half it seemed starting a trip like us. We didn't glance at people in other vehicles; that was no longer allowed. Meeting eyes was rude, as though making accusations about their health choices, whether they wore a full hazmat suit and headgear or something less uncomfortable.

Inside a vehicle, with windows sealed, they should've been able to disrobe safely, being in their own bubble. But, with the inconvenience of removing the suit while sitting inside then donning it again when going out, it was a lot of trouble. Better to leave it on all the time, ready to exit the vehicle or to open the door at a quarantine checkpoint. It didn't take long for clothing companies to start producing more decorative hazmats for the upwardly infectious.

It seemed other people had the same idea as us: leave the city, make a new life in the rural areas. Gradually the roads became congested. Mom, looking worried, exited the highway, took to the suburban streets. They began to clog, too.

Going block by block, stopping at every intersection – none of the traffic lights worked – made the trip longer. Every time we stopped, we might be attacked by people wanting a ride, wanting to steal from us, or in the worst case wanting to make a meal of us. I'd heard reports of people going mad, attacking and eating other people. There were always discussions of the side effects of the vaccines – before the airways and the internet went down.

We eventually got to the outer suburbs and found almost no

traffic. A few groups of people walked along the roads, one group pulling a cart, another pushing a grocery basket. We kept going, Mom focused on the road, with her eyes open looking for other vehicles or roadblocks or checkpoints.

She didn't drive fast, keeping aware of hazards appearing in the road. We passed unhindered through checkpoints at major intersections at the edge of the city, both unmanned. Possibly the personnel were needed elsewhere, or they also had died.

Mom checked the fuel gauge: "Still good." It had been a few hours but it seemed we hadn't gotten very far.

I sat beside her, glanced at her from time to time. She was confident, ready to take control – although she often played the chill parent or flirty colleague or precocious teen. She would take my hand, pull me up, and twirl me into a dance. We would shake our booties in uninhibited fashion, hugging cheek to cheek, bow and dip, and swing each other around the room to a polka she played on her tuba and recorded for posterity.

I thought of that tune as we started through the country, farmland on each side of the road, no animals in sight. Horses were the obvious substitute for a vehicle. I doubted very many knew how to ride a horse. I had a lesson at Scout camp. Perhaps they were hitched to a wagon. No more sheep or goats either – probably taken for food. Same for pigs. Cows were the first to disappear. The houses and barns we passed looked abandoned. One house stood only as burned lumber on a stone foundation. Same for a barn further along.

"I hope Grandma and Grampa are okay," I said and Mom gave a nod, kept her eyes on the road.

Another few miles in silence.

Mom reached in the side pocket of the car door and grabbed a disk, slid it into the slot on the dashboard and music filled the car. Mahler, I knew, the 10th Symphony, completed posthumously by one of his students. The rich somber notes of the famous tuba solo. Mom's performance, one of the last they played before the pandemic closed concert venues. I listened, watching the road chewed up before us, and felt both sad and hopeful.

The music continued: deep strains of desperation unfolding into chords of angelic light. The rough bass giving way to airy flutes. The sorrow only fuel for a fire of joy, layer upon layer, building to a glorious climax of heavenly beauty. We reached the very doorstep of God's palace. Then the disk ended, popped out. She left it there, driving on – driving on toward night.

We stopped at an old motel along the road, got out and checked that we were alone. The motel wasn't in operation. Mom had me try a few doors to see if any were unlocked, perhaps with beds inside. Maybe the showers would work. We were still fresh enough, but eight hours in a car added some scent.

Mom went over into the shadows of the eaves and squatted, peed out a good stream. I stood in a different shadow, eyes on the car, and eliminated mine, too. Then we had dinner of what snacks we'd brought. We talked, always keeping ears and eyes trained on our surrounding area.

"We'll have to leave the car behind eventually," said Mom. "Our gasoline will be used up. We wasted too much going slow through the city instead of the highway. The highway would've been worse with all that congestion. We may not get all the way before it runs out. I'm just warning you."

"Warning? Why?" I asked.

"Because then we walk. We'll have to carry things. But I know we can't carry it all so, of course, we'll have to choose what's most important."

"Enough to get us to Grandma and Grampa's? They have food there. They have supplies."

"Let's hope so." She held up her phone. "Still no service. Out here I expected that. Seems that all communication is down."

I checked my cell, too, confirming her assessment. Turning it on would've alerted authorities searching for us, Mom liked to remind me – not that we were wanted for anything, unless leaving the city was against the rules. They added new rules every week. But the cell was dead anyway, no signal out, no signal in. We were alone in the empty parking lot of the run-down motel. Perhaps it hadn't been used since the first pandemic, when everyone was ordered to stay home for only a couple weeks so hospitals wouldn't be overrun with patients, yet that stretched into months, then years. Travel was restricted for most of us. Tourism died. Only people providing essential needs, like truck drivers bringing food into the city. But the trucks were fewer as years went by.

"Guess we'll sleep in the car tonight," said Mom. "Windows up, doors locked." She looked down, patted her hip where her pistol rested. "Locked and loaded."

"You have a pistol?" I was surprised. Mom had always been a carefree type, outwardly opposed to guns, for free love, all that. I knew her grandfather had been a Marine a long time ago and fought in a war.

"For protection."

I nodded. It was all I could do.

"I know you've never shot one before, Sandy," she said, "but I'd rather not waste any bullets letting you practice." Her grimace made me pay attention. "Just aim for center mass, at the chest, and pull the trigger two or three times, holding your hand steady with your other hand. You've seen cop dramas on streaming. And never assume you stopped him with the first bullet."

I pursed my lips. "Got it, Mom."

"Let us hope we don't need to use it."

3

IN WHICH DECISIONS ARE MADE

The night was calm. We lay on the hood of the car, gazing up at the stars. That was nice. Mom telling stories of her childhood. I loved having Mom beside me. When the bright twinkles overhead began to look like millions of viruses, we decided it was time to go to sleep.

We drove slowly the next morning, not because of any traffic but to be careful of obstacles we might encounter on these country roads. My vivid imagination wreaked havoc with my senses, ever alert to hungry vagrants out to get us. Roving bands of savages made mad by their harsh existence – or by overdoing the vaccines and booster shots, like some did, thinking they could never get enough jabs. People went crazy. At every intersection we might be stopped, either by something laid across the road or by other vehicles or, if we stopped at a stop sign, set upon by a band of lunatics. I held the gun in my lap, as Mom instructed.

We passed only a few vehicles on these country roads, but whenever the road went close enough to the state highway, we could see how packed it was, vehicles going nowhere. In some places, people had gotten out of their vehicles, waiting their turn to move, or they were arguing or complaining or fighting, or some just ruminating on their fate.

"I'll bet they've run out of gas, blocking everyone that's behind them," Mom explained. "Someone's going to die for it."

Everyone talked about fate like it was some giant hand that

sprouted from the ground and grabbed their ankles, squeezing until circulation was restricted enough to get their attention. I felt it, too. Mom seemed unaffected, plotting her next move and I was just along for the ride. But others?

Lots of reports of the municipal madness spreading through the city – through the countryside, too, and around the world. Eventually we lost news reports from distant places. It wasn't enough that we were locked in our homes. Some didn't have homes. Others dared leave and were shot dead like they were rabid dogs. The newscasters in their shiny suits announced with painted smiles the number of 'dogs' that had been removed from the streets on a given day. Those of us with the privilege of being able to maintain a semi-normal life at home were the audience for those news reports. We felt safe, reassured we were cared for by our leaders. I often felt Mom's sarcastic tone wandering through me, lounging in my head, and when I thought or spoke, there she was dictating words to me.

According to Mom, we'd done everything right: followed the rules, worked hard, paid taxes, smiled when appropriate, frowned at other times – like the poem I learned in school about the 'perfect citizen' who was forgotten when he died, one among many, a nameless cog in an endless machine. But Mom's profession was different. They managed to put concerts online, each musician playing in a small box lined up on the screen that viewers could see – free music for a while, until the bills needed to be paid, food purchased, medicine collected. But nobody had money for music so the concerts ended. It was mostly to keep people's spirits up.

We got our emergency pay like most families. Mom did; I lost my delivery job. It was only an after-school thing. When the situation got worse, my boss apologized for letting me go. Not enough delivery orders. The big chains had the financial backing to keep going but not the mom-and-pop stores. Months later he closed. Weeks after that, he died – a few days after his wife died. Because of gathering rules, their adult children couldn't tend to them or have a funeral. Cremation and deposit in a mass grave. Mom played a funeral march on her tuba – online.

I thought of that march, heard it in my head, but realized Mom was humming it beside me as we drove.

Withered fields stretched away from each side of the road. I hoped for a normal scene of happy farms: blissful cows, satisfied horses, tractor in operation, corn shoulder-high. We tried to forget city life. I was looking forward to seeing Grandma's and Grampa's farm. I had memories of chasing chickens, feeding pigs, riding horses, and herding sheep.

We weren't able to contact them after phone lines went down and the internet went off. Then the cell towers stopped working – whether intentionally or from some malfunction we didn't know. They had to control the flow of information, Mom said. Even the postal service closed because of lack of staff. You could get things delivered within the city, if you could afford the fee from private delivery companies, but out of the city not a chance.

It was a long day's drive under normal conditions – if Mom could've sped along the highway. But going slower on the back roads, we still would get there soon, she kept assuring me like I was twelve again. She smiled as she drove, humming tunes, in no hurry it seemed.

Mom always pushed me to read books or online versions. Texts were constantly being eliminated, other works put into disrepute, some criminalized. The list was constantly updated. New texts were always coming out, labeled 'official edition', replacing the corrupt originals. Everything had to be remade. Every update was a softer, gentler version of the story, with every offensive thing reduced or removed. Mom never bought into that; offensive books were the best ones, she told me.

So I read old paperbacks in Grampa's collection. A lot of what were called 'science fiction' – stories about space travel, mostly. He'd always wanted to be a rocket scientist. I had a little of that in me, too. As a young boy I wanted to study music like Mom, but she insisted I not and pushed me into science. Other stories were about the future, about the way society was changed from what Mom knew when she was growing up. It was always a worse society, never a better one. Even the ones that seemed better on the surface were bad underneath. Others were bad from the start and got worse; people tried to escape. In most books everyday life was normal but there was an underlying threat, a sense of doom, a vague dread that permeated everything. Like now: what may seem like a pleasant country drive is actually an escape from the pandemic-ravaged city.

Perhaps that's the reason our situation didn't alarm me very much. I'd already read about these things happening in Grampa's books. I knew what to do. I'd gained some perspective: this isn't so bad, not like in this or that sci-fi novel. Even a viral pandemic was nothing special; I'd already been practicing for it via those books. Same with the videos I saw. We got used to bad things happening, because that made a more interesting story. Nobody wanted to see a movie about Mary Sue playing with her dolls on the front porch on a sunny day. Better story if her creepy uncle is leering at her from around the corner, planning how to groom her to be his sex slave. But Mom snatched that book away from me before I got to the middle.

Back to science books, not as stories but as textbooks. School pushed those on us. Did they really expect us to learn enough to save ourselves? To learn exactly what we needed to know? Was that the plan to educate each generation? One generation fucks things up, the next fixes it, quoting Mom. Or was it only a way to pass the time while we matured into adulthood, prepared to join our fellow cogs in the social machine? I could feel both. Mom made sure I maxed out learning, never letting me have a free moment – unless it was to 'go out and get some fresh air' while a friend of hers visited.

As Mom slowed to make the turn off the road to the gravel drive up to the house, we both saw it at the same time.

The house and farm looked abandoned. Besides the animal skeletons in the yard, almost completely eaten, stripped of flesh, it was clear that a fire had burned part of the house. Although it still stood, the blackened roof on one side showed that the fire had likely started around the chimney.

Mom rolled up to the front porch, shut off the engine, gazing at the fuel gauge.

"We have about a hundred more miles, I calculate." She turned to me. "Bring the spare gas cans inside."

"Inside?" I gasped, nodding at the house. "Is that safe?"

"Don't want them stolen." Mom got out of the car, stretched her back. "Unpack the car."

"Shouldn't we go check on Grandma and Grampa?"

"Go ahead." She waved me on and went to the rear of the car, opened the trunk.

"Me?" I blanched. "I don't wanna go in by myself."

She grinned. "Oh, you want your mommy to go with you?"

I didn't think she was funny. "No...."

So I went up the steps, calling out. I wanted them to come out and greet us, like previous visits. I wanted to see they were all right, unaffected by the chaos in the city.

The handle was intact, the door shut tight. I raised my hand and knocked. With no response, I tested the door.

"It's locked," I called.

"Go around back," said Mom.

So I went around the side of the house to the back.

There on the porch, sitting in lounge chairs were Grandma and Grampa, dressed nice like for dinner, the fancy clothing they always wore. Grandma had her sewing. Grampa had his fishing magazine open in his lap, the pages waving in the breeze. They regarded each other across the gap between the chairs, close enough to hold hands. But their arms had grown tired, fallen, hanging limp from their shoulders. The gun had dropped from Grampa's hand and rested on the porch now.

I took the tarp off the table on the porch and tossed it over Grandma and pulled a towel off the nearby clothesline to put over Grampa's head. Nothing could cover the blood on the porch; only rain could wash it away.

I'd read about scenes like this in books. I'd seen people do the same thing in videos. When things get too bad and you don't want to face it, don't want to suffer through it, then.... Apparently as planned, he aimed that pistol at Grandma's head then put it to his own head. They chose to depart from the catastrophe coming their way.

"Mom...?" I shouted from the backyard.

*　*　*

Mom stood in the yard, hands on hips, looking from Grandma to Grampa. Although I'd covered them she could see the blood on the porch. She saw the pistol caught on Grampa's finger by the trigger guard. She nodded several times.

"There were other options," she muttered, stepping onto the porch. "If you'd just held on a little longer. Then you'd see the options. You could've made it."

She seemed on the verge of crying but sniffled back the urge as she mounted the porch.

"We're going to have to bury them," she spoke as she gazed up and down the bodies, folded in the chairs. "Go find a shovel. Two, if you can."

I left for the other side of the house. Probably there would be shovels in the barn rather than the garage. The barn was scarier. In childhood, I was frightened by the animals there, most larger than me, with strange smells and sounds. Picture books did not prepare me for the immensity of a cow or horse. But I went, feeling like I had to grow up and be a man for Mom, even though I was by official measurements already an adult.

Lots of tools in the empty barn. They had reduced the farm year after year until there were few animals. No animals alive or dead inside the barn, just their musky scent. The farming tools hung from hooks along a wall. The useful tools seemed to have been stolen. I didn't see any shovels.

Probably passing vagabonds had slaughtered the animals out front, taken as food. Then they, or someone else, had camped in the house and lit a small fire that got out of hand. They tried to put it out, but not before the walls were damaged and the ceiling and roof blackened. Maybe it was Grandma and Grandpa who'd made the fire to cook their dinner, with all the electricity being off like in the city.

The room smelled like someone had been cooking. With closed windows it had gotten worse. I shook my head at the sight of the framed family photos in a pile on the floor. Grandma's souvenir collection, all the trinkets collected from around the country that she displayed, a miniature museum of her adventures, now lay destroyed by vagrants – like they were deliberately smashed.

The rest of the house seemed intact, undisturbed, although everything had a layer of dust and a mildew odor, left unused, unrefreshed for weeks. It was tempting to stop and examine each item that had memories attached to it and each piece of furniture – one chair had been broken apart, its legs missing, perhaps used as fuel for the fire.

I heard Mom calling, so I returned to the backyard, closing the side door leading to the patio. The best I could find was a garden trowel.

Mom was further out in the backyard, already at work. She had found a shovel. She paused to call again but saw I was coming toward her. She snorted at my trowel. It could be used later for smoothing the sides of the grave, I suggested.

Mom swung the shovel hard. She'd marked off the dimensions of a double-wide site, then began removing dirt. When she was down a foot, she paused and pulled off her sweaty shirt and resumed her work. I sat on the grass watching. Two feet down. She halted, breathing hard. I begged her to rest while I worked the trowel around the sides to make sure they were straight.

I pulled off my shirt and instead took my turn with the shovel as Mom went to the porch to prepare the bodies.

She laid them on the tarp and dragged them, their faces now plainly revealed, across the lawn to the grave site. I continued as she stood over them, gazing down, unmoved by the violence shown on their faces, and spoke softly. I couldn't hear her words clearly but they seemed like funeral words.

When we'd gotten the grave down four feet we pulled them to the edge, let them slip into the pit. First went Grampa, Mom straightening him as best she could, then Grandma, who mostly lay atop of him but had some of her own space alongside. Laying face up, their grim facades summed up their lives: always waiting for Mom to come home, expecting her to do this or that, to stop playing with those boys, to give a damn – all the anecdotes Mom told me over the years.

They'd never gotten along very well, I understood from what Mom told me. It wasn't until I was about five or six that she first welcomed them to be my grandparents – so she could go off and do whatever she needed to do. Some was pure mischief and she needed a babysitter. Her adventures were legitimate, depending on how she spun it. For example, she toured with a band: The Tubafonics, her rock music group featuring two tubas and a euphonium as well as electric guitar, keyboard, and drums. Mom was the 'topless tubist'. I'd seen a few photos of her on stage previously, tuba swinging from a strap as she blasted notes into the crowd, strutting back and forth. Maybe if Grandma and Grampa had the chance to see her in concert, hear her music, they might've appreciated her more.

"I wish they waited for us," I mumbled, standing over the mound we had fashioned with the dirt.

"They never wanted to wait," said Mom with a huff. "For anything. Even without this pandemic, probably would've done the same thing one of these days. They had a lot of baggage to carry."

"If only the phone lines were working. We could've called and let them know we were on our way."

"Not calling them was better, I think." She gave me a hard look. "Like old times. Me on the road, not giving them a call. And they not giving a fuck about me. But they loved you." She gave a snort, amused. "Good they had you to entertain them."

I grinned, knowing she was right. She was always right.

Gazing at sweaty, bare-chested Mom, I wanted to give her a hug, to show my sympathy. I started toward her and she seemed to recognize what I wanted. She held up a hand.

"Huh-uh," she said in a husky voice. "I'm too fucked up for a hug." But seeing my sad face, she relented.

While maintaining her frown, she took the towel I first tossed over Grampa's face and wiped off sweat from her neck, under her arms, then between her breasts, and down over her belly until she was satisfied.

"Mom," I said, insistent, "you need a hug."

She dropped the soiled towel on the grass, held her arms out for me. I stepped up against her, wrapped my arms around her warm body, feeling like a baby again, her arms closing tightly around me.

"I'm all right," she said, "but you may need a hug."

I nodded, my cheek pressed to her neck. Then I turned my face and we regarded the grave mound.

So many times I visited their farm and I became more like their child than grandchild. They pampered me like they never wanted me to leave. But soon Mom would return and take me away. They got in the habit of sending me birthday cards and Christmas cards. Later, when I was a teen, I visited less often but I helped with the farm during the summers. Mom stayed just long enough to be polite, then left – and returned, staying long enough to be polite, and took me home.

I understood how Mom could be so unmoved about seeing her parents this way, how she could handle the burial tasks without shedding a tear. She did seem to choke up but didn't let it go too far. She did what had to be done: get them in the ground before they decayed too much. Just a series of steps. Like cleaning all the pipes and valves of a tuba.

Later, as the sun was setting, the yard in darkness, orange glow over the horizon, Mom sat on the mound and pulled her tuba to her lap and played. Nothing I recognized. Perhaps it was a tune of her own invention, something that mirrored her heart's mood. A mournful wailing filled the yard and made the earth shake. She let the instrument grunt, sing, moan, growl in 5/8 time, and soar with C-major joy, as though she called their spirits to rise and fly up to heaven. When the music ceased, I wanted more, asked for more, but she shook her head and released water from the spit valve.

Everything in the car had been unloaded into the house. And although much of the interior was a little disturbing, a bit icky, we made camp there. Mom took her parents' room, slept on their bed with fresh sheets from the closet, and I took my usual guest room, likely untouched since my last visit a few years earlier.

I stretched out on the small bed for children. My crude school artwork hung on the walls. On the nightstand a framed picture of me and Mom got my attention: me about nine and Mom always a perfect twenty-six, her arm draped around my shoulders, smiling proudly like she'd won me in a school carnival raffle. I tried to think back to that moment, wondering if that younger me could've ever imagined returning here to escape a deadly virus. I recalled that moment, before everything went bad, and felt peace. Mom was close, and the din of crickets filled the night.

4

IN WHICH SHIT HITS THE FAN

There was no running water to the house so I got by with a few pumps of well water for a quick wash out back before bed. Mom did, too. She splashed some water at me for fun, like when I was little. Also, there was no electricity. So no A/C. No fans either. And better not open any windows for fresh air, Mom warned, or we might invite some roving band to stop by.

I lay on the small bed, stripped to my undies, sweating in the room's warmth. I hovered on the edge of sleep for a long time then tossed and turned. The image of my grandparents stayed with me, and the bits of memories throughout my childhood played in my head. I had questions that prevented me from relaxing.

So I got up and stepped to the open door across the hallway.

"Mom?" I called softly.

It was dark but, as she rolled over, I could see she was naked, as usual, dealing with the heat.

"What is it?" she called sleepily.

"It's too warm. I can't sleep."

"Not my problem," she said.

I stepped into the room, sat on the side of the bed.

"I keep thinking about Grandma and Grampa."

"What about them?" she asked gruffly. She pushed herself up on an elbow, facing me in the darkness, and yawned.

"I wanna know why you never got along with them. I mean, they're your parents. You had both a mom and a dad."

"Now stop that," she said with a groan, laying back. "You got along with them just fine. Right? That's all that matters."

"Maybe so. But they're gone now, so what does it matter if you tell me?"

"Yes, what does it matter now?"

"What happened to make you guys so...uh...."

"Estranged?" She turned to face me again, grimace showing in the sliver of moonlight that cut through the window. "You mean besides me getting pregnant at sixteen?"

"Well, yeah."

"And me going to too many parties *with boys* at fifteen? Or was it fourteen? I was rebellious. What can I say? Like any teen girl with too-strict parents. More rebellious than my sisters. Laura was so prim and proper, raised to be a society elite and marry well. Jackie...a little less well-bred, a kind of bridge between Laura and me. Plus our age gap — ten years between Laura and me. So my parents were older when I came along."

"It was just the age gap?" I asked in the darkness, keeping my voice low like we were telling secrets and someone might hear us.

"Yes, the age gap." She repressed a chuckle. "They always harped on the age gap. Men...too much older.... Too much age gap between a girl and her father, too." She grinned at me. "Not like you and me, huh, Sandy?"

My eyes shifted to her face. "What do you mean, Mom?"

She took a long breath, the old bed shaking under us.

"I mean, sometimes you don't get to choose what happens. You are chosen. Sometimes there are no options. Decisions are made for you and you do the best you can. It's like being tossed into a lake and you suddenly have to figure out how to swim. Or else you drown. You don't want to be tossed into the lake, but there you go. Just have to figure it out. To survive."

"They tossed you in a lake?"

"No, Sandy. It's a metaphor." She sighed, frustrated with me. "When they discovered I was pregnant with you and they sent me away to Nana's for a few months." She chuckled. "Grandfather teaching me to use a knife like a commando, despite me having a big belly." She stared at me in the dark, a frown on her face. "'Oh, Polly's just visiting her grandparents,' they happily told everyone. Everyone knew what that meant. No one was fooled. I missed graduation – a dead give-away. Couldn't bring a baby to that."

I cleared my throat. "So you hated them because they made you miss your graduation?"

"Not only that."

"Then what?"

"Probably that time when I was thirteen. Maybe still twelve. On a night like tonight: warm...too warm to sleep. And then the door opens and in sneaks your grandpa." A moment of silence. "I suppose it was because your grandma kicked him out again. He was a creep. She was done with him, his cheating, his abuse. So he went to the only other female in the house. You see, Laura and Jackie were away in college by then. They never had to put up with his attention."

I gasped. "Grampa did that?" Suddenly I glanced around the room, their bedroom, as though looking for clues.

She shook her head in the dark. "Not here. The house back in the city. They bought this farm later, a place to retire."

"Oh."

"So I was quite the little slut when I went to 'boy parties', as my mother called them. I wanted him to know how I was turning out. A rebellious girl, for sure. That I wasn't his."

"Not his...?"

She went on, her voice sounded strained, holding her head up. "It wasn't difficult to go to the beach with my friend that day. Too bad she ran off like she did. Well, you can't predict the past. And here you are."

"Oh, Mom." I wanted to cry but I was too tired for that kind of emotion. "I'm sorry. I'm sorry I asked."

"No, you should ask those questions." She sighed, concerned, and shifted toward me. "And learn from the answers you get. Especially now that you're an adult. You have to make your own decisions, or else decisions will be made for you. Hard times demand hard questions – and hard answers. And we are living in hard times now."

I felt her hand on my back, a touch that comforted me, as though I'd been the one who broke down.

"Makes me wonder about his patients," Mom went on after a while. "He was an Ob/Gyn, you know. He liked his work. It paid for the beach house—"

"I just wanted to know, that's all. I heard some stuff over the years...." I checked my emotions, like I was supposed to if I was to be a man. But in the darkness I could let them slip a bit. "I don't blame you." Thoughts boiled in my head. "And I guess I don't like Grampa so much now. Or Grandma. She let it go on, right?"

"Why're you so concerned about all that?" asked Mom, rolling on her side. "It doesn't make you any less valued."

I responded by stretching out beside her. My hand went to her arm, feeling the hot moisture on her skin.

"I don't know...."

Her hand went to my shoulder, patted it. "Sad?"

"Yes." I let out a whimper, wanting to sleep but wanting more to be at peace with no questions needing to be asked or answered. "Can I sleep here tonight?"

"It's already too warm." She pressed against me then, slid her arm around me. "Aw, there's my little baby boy." She hugged me.

I held her tight as her fingers combed through my hair. Tears filled my eyes. Her breath caressed my cheek, tickled my ear. Her soft, warm body against me. In her arms, I could fall asleep.

✳ ✳ ✳

We awoke at dawn to breaking glass. Right below us in the living room. A window smashed. Male voices mumbling. They climbed through, stumbled inside.

Mom sat up, a bit of sunrise lighting the room, put a finger to my mouth as I opened my eyes. She pointed to her suitcase, made the shape of a pistol with her hand. She gestured for me to get up slowly, not let the bed squeak.

She rolled off the bed, stood naked beside it, a cave woman

protecting her child from an encroaching cave bear. Bending down to retrieve the pistol, she brought it up to her chest. Her eyes went to the door, open to the hallway.

We listened to the vagrants downstairs, counting three by their voices. They seemed to discuss whether or not to check the rest of the house, to see if it was abandoned – or if there might be people asleep upstairs.

"Not after you broke that window," grumbled one of them.

"Okay, I go check," another responded.

Mom threw the door shut, a little too loud, and locked it. That noise was enough. The footsteps on the stairs slowed.

She motioned for me to get in the closet and I made a face, refusing.

The footsteps got louder, closer. Then a hand on the door, rattling the knob.

"Wakee wakee," said the vagrant. "Anybody home?"

Pressing against the door. A shoulder push. Again, harder.

Mom stood firm, both hands holding up the pistol, aiming at the door. She jerked her shoulder toward the closet, ordering me there. She moved to center herself in front of the closed door.

The door knob rattled again, then another push—

Bang!

Mom had pulled the trigger. The shot went through the door. I guess it must've gone straight into the vagrant on the other side.

"Ahhhh! Ah, shit! Shit, shit, shit. *Shiiiiiiiit.*" A big weight hit the door then slid down it with a hard thump on the floor.

Footsteps pounding up the stairs.

I rushed into the closet, pulled the twin doors closed. Half a second later Mom joined me. We crouched in opposite corners, letting the hanging clothes cover us. Inside we couldn't make out what they were saying in the hallway, but I could imagine their confusion at finding their buddy shot dead. Someone was at home, they had to understand.

And the bedroom door was locked.

They tested it again, kicked at the door. After a few kicks, they broke it open and let the door swing free. Looking around, they could see someone had been sleeping on the bed. But where was that person? Look under the bed.... Nope.

A suitcase was open on the floor, women's clothing in it. And a tuba in a soft-side case in the corner. Mom would hate anyone touching Timmy.

She fidgeted as we listened to them talking. They didn't seem too sad their buddy was shot. Knowing the resident had a gun slowed their search for valuables. One man nudged the bed, made it squeak. The other laughed, said a crude joke.

The next thing happened too fast: the closet doors were thrown open, hands rifling through the clothes, finding Mom, pulling her up and out of the closet by her arms. In a single motion the man tossed her against the bed. She fell to her knees there.

"Well, looky here," said the closet opener. "A naked lady. And not bad lookin neither. I guess she bin waitin for us."

He took her by the arm, jerked her up, threw her on the bed.

"Stop," said Mom firmly, righting herself on her knees. "You're not supposed to be here. Leave now!"

"Leave?" the guy laughed.

"Mouthy bitch, ain't she?"

"This is my house. You all get out," she growled.

I heard a slap to her face. The bed squeaked again.

"She shot Lucky," the second man reminded him.

"Yeah, we can deal with that later," said the other man. "His luck done run out. First things first."

The bed squeaked more as the second man cursed at the first one. Both men cursed at Mom. She fought them, hands slapping and feet kicking. The man on top shouted for her to stop fighting or he would make the situation worse. But she didn't let up.

I didn't know what to do. What if they had a gun? I could rush out and bowl one of them over but the other would still be hurting Mom. Maybe my presence would scare them off.

Extending my leg in the closet, my toe touched the metal of the pistol on the floor of the closet. I took it in my hand, carefully got up, doors already apart, and looked out through the clothing.

The man on top of Mom was grabbing her arms as the second

man stood at the foot of the bed, trying to hold her feet down.

"Come on now, bitch," said the man on top.

I burst from the closet, shouting "She's not a bitch!" as my finger squeezed off two shots, one at each man. The man on top, hit in the ribs, rolled off her, spilled off the side of the bed by the wall. The man holding her feet fell back, hit in the belly. His head banged against the wall, hands going to his wound. He howled in pain as he slumped on the floor.

"You okay?" I called to Mom.

She got up, wrung her hands like they were covered with dirt and she wanted to shake it off. Her lip was bleeding.

The belly-shot man moaned, sitting on the floor, back against the wall, Mom directed me to pack up. She took the pistol and stood guard. The man who fell off the other side of the bed, tried to get up, reaching for and grabbing the sheet, but slid off the bed.

"He's done," said Mom.

She handed me back the pistol then selected clothes from the suitcase.

"I'm sorry, Mom," I cried. "I'm really sorry."

"For what? You didn't do anything."

"I didn't do anything! And they hurt you."

Mom took a breath, shaking her head. "No time to talk about that now. We need to leave. No telling who else may be around here."

"To where?" I was too upset to think straight.

"Someplace else."

"I'm sorry, I'm sorry," I muttered like the whole bad night had been my fault. If only I'd acted sooner.

She stopped getting dressed, muttered "Hell," and threw the dress into the suitcase. She kept an eye on the belly-shot man. He was bleeding, ruining the carpet.

"We need to leave." She ripped the sheet off the bed and wiped her body down. "No telling what they might have. Bastards broke our bubble. Don't want to waste a fresh outfit before I can wash off. Damn clothes hold the virus." She glared at me. "You packed yet?"

✳ ✳ ✳

On the road again, hauling ass, she kept looking over at me. The sunrise showed she had a scratch on her cheek. Her lip was cut. She never said a word in complaint. I wanted to cry inside but I needed Mom to know I was strong for her.

I should have fired sooner. But I hesitated, thinking of laws and penalties, judges and juries. The world went in slow-mo. In a sane world, law and order makes sense. In this new kind of world there was no law and no order, and nothing made sense. I had no training for this kind of world.

"You did good," said Mom, like she had to say it to calm me, based on a script written long ago. Mothers always know what to say – or what they're supposed to say – for every situation. As a kid, I learned to wait for Mom to say the words; only then would I know how to feel and, maybe, what to say.

My face flushed, embarrassed for my actions.

"Hard times require hard decisions," she said.

She slowed as we came to an intersection on this country road. A four-way stop. But she didn't stop, just looked both directions and continued.

"They say hard times make strong men. Strong men make easy times, but easy times make weak men. And weak men cause hard times."

I remained agitated, fearing for my mom. I almost lost her. I didn't act fast enough and she got hurt by those men. I'd never be able to forget how I let my mom down.

"Where are we going?" I asked, hesitant to break the silence. I could sense her plotting her next move.

"Anywhere else," Mom muttered, then cleared her throat.

I looked out. "I think we've been on this road before."

"We're just tricking trackers." She gave a little snicker. "Every vehicle has a tracker. Doubling back can trick it."

"But what about the gas?"

"Better to take the long way than get intercepted."

"Intercepted?"

"Too many questions, Sandy," she barked. "Because we left the city, crossed out of our health zone. They could be tracking us now and we wouldn't know. And we...."

"We what?"

A mile of silence.

"They're the bad guys," Mom responded, "and you did the right thing. But, who knows, maybe some cop may think differently. You never know. So we're not going straight to our destination. Detour. Got it?"

After a while, Mom had me take over driving duties. I'd offered to drive from the start but she'd refused, preferring to manage the road herself.

She tilted the seat back, resting. No doubt her mind was full of plans, worrying what to do about me. That made me feel bad.

"I need to wash off," she said suddenly. "He was coughing all over me."

Regarding her, I knew she was serious. The virus could be anywhere. People in the city wore face masks and plastic shields. Others went out in full hazmat suits, breathing canned air through a tube. Mom wasn't superstitious. She insisted on making her body strong. If you've put your mouth to enough old brass instruments over the years, she often told me, you're immune from anything.

Then she cursed, withdrawing her hand from between her legs and staring at her fingertips. "He got me."

Shaking her head, she glanced out the side window, as though a clinic or pharmacy would be right there on the corner, but there was nothing out this far, only farms.

I hadn't noticed as she wiped herself down at the house. Good enough for now, she said. Better to get on the road and leave this place as fast as we could. She didn't bother to get dressed.

"There." She pointed to a pond near the road. It was another farm. "Pull over."

I eased the car off the road, rolling to a stop. Mom jumped out before I shut off the engine. She shuffled over to the fence and climbed over with unusual grace, and jogged to the pond.

She waded right in, arms held out, and crouched down so the water came up to her chin. She dunked her face under, swept her hands through her hair.

I prepared the medicine as she bathed in the pond.

When she returned to the car, dripping wet, hair in tangles, I was ready for her.

I checked the road in each direction. Of course, others might be escaping by car on this road like us. More likely, they would be opportunists preying on escapees. That worried me. A young man traveling with his mother was a target. Even if she hid, just one young man alone could be seen as an easy score. Suddenly the world felt different, more dangerous than I could imagine.

"What're we gonna do?" I wailed.

Mom told me to be quiet and spray her down with disinfectant. Then she dug out some clothes and got dressed.

I handed her the small bottle of medicine. She quaffed it down, choked a bit, almost spit it up. Bending over, she maintained her dignity. The medicine wasn't officially approved but a lot of people said it killed the virus. It wasn't fun, however. Most places sold out as soon as it came on the market.

"I'm going to have to be sick for a while," said Mom, "so bear with me." She straightened up, leaned against the car. Waves of nausea would sweep through her. She might vomit but had to try to keep it down for it to work.

She held up the bottle, reading the label – like she hadn't read it many times before.

"I doubt there's any drug store around," she said, glancing in each direction along the road. "Looted by now, if there are any. What a wonderful time to be alive."

"Are you gonna be okay, Mom?"

She sighed and swung herself down into the driver's seat as I stood by the open door.

"This is not a good time to get raped." She took a very deep breath. "I didn't think he could get it done so quick. I was fighting him. Premature, for sure." She gazed at me. "I think I was able to wash it out. But who knows?"

I just stared at her. My mother, attacked, and I didn't act fast enough. I hated myself.

"Are you okay?" I asked in a wimpy voice.

"Who can ever be *okay* after getting assaulted?"

"I'm sorry." Tears collected again. "I should've acted quicker. I'll be ready next time."

"Next time?" Shaking her head, she pouted.

"Maybe it won't work. You know, because of the virus. Or the boosters. Maybe he's sterile."

"We shall see, Sandy." She forced a grin. "Maybe I'm too old. Maybe my body will reject it due to my stress. Right? That's how nature works, they say."

"I hope so."

"Listen, Sandy." She took my hand. "You acted the right way. Don't think about it. Don't keep wondering what-if, okay? You did good. It's those vagrants who were wrong."

"But I could've—"

"Stop." She squeezed my hand. "You're my little boy, love of my life. If I had to, to save you, I would've let them do whatever they wanted with me if you would be safe. Hear me?"

I nodded, tears in my eyes.

"I'm your mother. I have responsibilities. I do my best. Sure, I know I'm not always right or do the best but I try like hell. I try. Understand?"

"Yes." But I couldn't keep from whimpering.

"Stop that," said Mom. "You're a man now. You acted right."

I wiped my eyes. "I'm sorry."

She stood, wobbled a moment, put her hand to her throat as if to check for the likelihood of vomiting but erupted in a coughing fit instead. Her pale face gave away her concern.

"Better get me the other bottle," said Mom.

I went to the back of the car, the trunk still open, and dug in a box for her bottle, the real medicine. She liked a swig of whiskey once in a while "just to clear the palate," she liked to say.

"Want some?" asked Mom, offering the bottle.

"Oh, no," I said. "Someone has to drive."

We started off again, me at the wheel, Mom sitting beside me. I drove at a reasonable speed, trying to hypermile to save gas.

"Thanks," she said, lowering the bottle. "That'll probably make me puke. Be ready to pull over."

I nodded. "Where should we go now?"

Mom remained silent, rummaging through her memories.

"Might as well head to your Aunt Laura's. She's the closest. It's been long enough. Maybe she's ready to apologize."

5

IN WHICH MUSIC WILL SAVE US

I awoke with a start, thinking I was driving and fell asleep at the wheel. But it was Mom who was driving. She gave me a quick look and laughed at my consternation, the way I jerked like I needed to swerve to avoid another car.

"You okay?" she asked.

I pulled myself up, swimming back to consciousness. "I had a dream. We were running away from a catastrophe. Like a volcano erupting. Trying to outrun the lava flow."

"No volcanos here," said Mom, smirk hanging on her lips like an old cigarette. "Just viruses."

I reached for the radio buttons on the dash. Only static. I ran through the stations. Nothing but a weak station from the city broadcasting the same repeated emergency announcement: Stay home, close your doors and windows, take your anti-virus meds, pray. Power and water will be restored soon. Food and fuel are on the way. Obey authorities.

"They always say to obey," Mom snarked. "That's the most important thing."

Looking around, I found we were no longer in farmland but going through a forested area. The land was hilly, the country road curving left and right every half-mile or so. The sunlight had shifted. We seemed to be going north.

I remembered Mom mentioning Aunt Laura from time to time. She lived in a town to the north. According to Mom, Laura had married a rich man, a lawyer or doctor, and had five kids, all younger than me. Mom liked to point out the youngest daughter had the first child in the family. Mom liked that status. But Mom was trash to Laura's family and not welcome. No bother; Mom had a music career and me as her entertainment.

Music filled the car and I startled. I knew it: Mom playing the Vaughan Williams tuba concerto with the Symphony about six years ago, before the pandemic started. She was proud of that performance, except for the final movement when one of the clarinets blew a reed and squeaked in the middle of the quiet section. She had it on a thumb drive, all her great performances, plugged into the dash. But she always stopped before the clarinet could squeak again and switched to another piece of music, a symphonic work I didn't recognize, something light and cheerful.

"Like it?" asked Mom after a while.

"It's all right, I guess."

"I wrote this for the chamber orchestra. Before you were in school. Lots of time to compose with you playing in your little play yard. Remember your play yard?"

"Yes, I remember." Always bringing up the past!

"And they said a tubist couldn't compose a decent piece for strings." She glanced at me like she dared me to disagree. "You know we had to learn all the instruments. I'm actually not too bad on the viola."

We listened to the four-movement piece, thirty-two minutes total, all strings with some woodwinds – no tuba. I asked why.

"Because I didn't want to play," she replied. "I just wanted to sit back and listen."

Mom explained how she composed the piece, and by extension how music was made in general. There are always a lot of choices, options, which way the musical line can go. But once you head down a chosen line it's difficult to return and try again if it doesn't work. It sounds faked that way. Thus it requires planning.

"Kind of like society. Every instrument playing its part and, because of that, they all come together in beautiful harmony. But then some composers have to try to see how discombobulated they can make the music, pitting instruments against each other, just for show. Discord. Noise. So ridiculous. Music is meant to unite – it's the very definition of unity – not meant to produce conflict. They've forgotten. That's why there are no symphonies today."

"But there's all kinds of music today," I recited my lines on our script, "different styles, different—"

"Yes, but it's rather narcissistic. I mean, they seem more for the pleasure of the singer than for audience."

I had to be careful or I'd push Mom into one of her musical rants. "Okay...." But I'd already gone too far.

"Music is a perfect model of diverse elements coming together as one, regardless of their individual properties. One musician, choosing to suppress her own talent, her innate urge to stand up and play a solo, in order to mix with the group, to join the mix for the sake of the experience, to share and share alike rather than overrule the others."

She cleared her throat like she had a lot more yet to say.

"One musician may be singing. Maybe she sounds good, but others may refuse to join in – which is one option. Or they may not know the song. Or they don't want to hear it and they beat up the singer to make her stop. This is our world today. Too many soloists, and the off-key ones the loudest. We need more chamber ensembles. I kept telling my students we'd have a much better society if everyone learned music, took up an instrument, joined a band or orchestra, but...."

I'd heard it all before. Of course, the world hadn't listened to her. The world never does. So Mom had to play her tuba alone, late at night, on the balcony, out where everyone could hear her – and shouted at her to be quiet, which would enrage her and make her slip into polka tunes for a little longer.

"But they cut Music from school budgets." She gave me her standard frown. "Art, too. Then added all the political crap."

The string piece ended and I felt a void in my gut.

We drove on in silence, the autumn afternoon waning. The leaves were colorful here, at higher elevation and more north. The road straightened, the forest fell away, small clusters of buildings here and there looking as abandoned as the towns we passed. We went through a village as quiet as a mountain meadow, empty storefronts looking like no one had shopped there for a few years.

Mom slowed at a gas station, gave it a long look. When gas ran out we could go on electric for as long as the battery held. It could charge as we drove on gas. But it was an old battery and wouldn't take us far. There wouldn't be any places to charge the battery once we were out of gas.

"I think we can make it to Laura's before we're on battery," said Mom in a cheery voice, probably trying to keep my spirits up after the troubles we'd had.

We hadn't passed any other vehicles since I awoke and the drive was becoming eerie, as though we really were the only people left. Abandoned vehicles sat every so often, like the drivers and passengers had parked, gotten out, and walked away. We had heard of that happening. People with the virus couldn't go on, had to pull over, then weakly slunk out, crawling over the ground, dying somewhere out of sight.

Over the hill ahead came an old pickup barreling down the road like a bat out of hell, chased by two blue and white police cars, lights flashing, sirens wailing. They zipped past us so fast Mom barely had time to swerve off the road. They were way past us before she could come to a complete stop, so she just veered back onto the road and kept going.

A third car appeared over the next hill, coming at us. This one, all brown, with lights and siren off, slowed. Suddenly the lights flashed on as the car turned across the road ahead of us to block our way. Mom hit the brakes.

"What's this guy doing?" Mom muttered, slowing to a stop and pulling onto the shoulder.

The police car straightened, drove right up to us, facing us bumper to bumper. Inside the vehicle was a rotund man with a buzz haircut. Dark glasses and a surly scowl. He sat there a while, watching us.

Mom focused on him through the windshield, her hands on the top of the steering wheel.

"Get your cards out," said Mom.

I was confused. "Aren't they on our phones?"

"No phone service."

"Oh."

If the towers were still active we would likely only get official announcements and out-of-service messages. No room for idle chat on private apps. They had blocked ordinary citizens, non-essential phone users before. Calling in food deliveries was allowed, but people sent a list which was quicker. Otherwise, they would be happy to collect our chats to add to their databases, to sort us into good and bad. That was how they determined who'd spread the virus, sector by sector, then sent health police to detain the bad ones and reward the good ones. Mom said it was a racket.

I dug in my wallet.

"What's he doing?" she mumbled. "Border check?"

"Maybe they found the bodies...?"

That broke her concentration. She turned and glared at me. "Don't you say anything."

"I won't."

"Anyway, it was justified."

I looked at the cards from my wallet. Some of the ink had smeared, probably from the heat of being in my wallet, stuffed in my pocket.

Identification and medical history cards were required, more important than even a driver license. In the city they were strict about showing proof of clean status when going into any venue, from a concert hall to a corner grocery. Every place had a guard at the door, checking cards or phones. In fact, there was a growing industry of people who had cards and went inside to get things for people without cards waiting outside. Mom did that gig for a while when schools first closed, not even charging them for the service. She thought it was the right thing to do.

"It's messed up," I said, referring to my paper cards.

She glanced over. "Blow on it, let it dry again."

The police car's door opened. The beefy man climbed out. He had a canvas mask on his face that matched his khaki uniform and blue latex gloves on his hands. He was taking his time, eyes scanning us. Then he stepped toward us, pistol drawn.

The policeman tapped on my window, the passenger side, off the road, rather than going around to the road side for Mom.

"Got face masks?" he shouted from outside my closed window.

I turned to Mom. We had some old ones in the glove box. Did she want me to get them out?

"We are bubble buddies so we don't need masks while we're driving," Mom responded.

"Get some masks on," ordered the policeman.

I pulled out our pack of medical-grade masks and handed one to Mom, but she didn't put it on. I left mine in my lap.

Instead, she hit the button that lowered my window.

"What's the problem, Officer?" asked Mom, leaning across me. She pasted on one of her fake smiles. "Now I know for sure we weren't going too fast. See, we're hypermiling. To maximize fuel economy. Just like the President said."

The man just looked us over, his pistol held up.

"You ain't from these parts," he said, leaning heavy against the car.

"No, we're going to my sister's," Mom responded.

"Put yer masks on," he repeated.

Mom complied. I put mine on, too.

Officer Tanner – from the name tag over his pocket – asked all sorts of questions, most not relevant to any good reason to stop us. As Mom suggested at previous incidents getting stopped, he was just messing with us, part of his day's fun. It was something we ordinary citizens had to endure.

"Okay now, lemme see yer passes," he demanded.

"You know the towers are down," said Mom, "so our phones don't work." She glanced at me. "We got the old paper ones."

She handed hers across me to the officer. I handed mine, too.

He waited until Mom's arm started to get tired, then took her cards. I lowered my hand, holding my cards.

He looked over Mom's cards, flipping them on the back, then to the front again, like he was trying to figure out what the words meant. Then he scratched at the stamp on the card.

"Hmm," he grunted. "This looks fake."

"They're just old," Mom countered. "It's been stuck in my purse a few years. Same with my son's. His have been in his wallet just as long."

She urged me to offer my cards to him. He snatched them from my hand like he was disgusted by our lies. But we hadn't lied. Our cards were legit. We got all the required shots, took the prescribed meds, stayed home (mostly) and away from family, friends, and neighbors, followed all the government mandates, and we even smiled through it all. Our disdain for the way life was changing was entirely private – we thought.

He put his thumbnail to my cards, then studied the ink that rubbed off on his thumb.

"Ma'am," he said, bending down a little and looking across me to Mom, "could you step outta the car, please?"

"Me, too?" I asked, concerned.

"Naw, just yer mama."

Mom opened her door and got out, glancing up and down the road for other vehicles that might be coming but saw none. She took a second to adjust her sleeveless blouse, and shook out her knee-length skirt with the leafy pattern, one of her favorites. Closing the door, she stepped around the rear of the car, paused by the rear passenger door and faced the officer.

"What's the problem? Why did you stop us?"

He straightened up, a wry grin on his face – like Mom had said the wrong thing. He glanced down at me, gave me a wink.

"Me n yer mama's gonna have us li'l chat."

"About what?" asked Mom.

He directed her to stand against the car. From my seat I could see her in the side mirror. He began searching her, having her put her arms up and out to the sides as he patted her down. In that position, he was happy to grope her, grinning as he did. Mom endured it. Her lips pinched tighter with every "Nice" the officer uttered. Then he made a show of patting her hips, swept a hand between her legs. Mom's jaw clenched.

"Mom?" I called, looking back out the window. "You okay?"

"Yeah, she okay. Now you mind yer own bidness, boy."

"What about the laws?" asked Mom in a measured voice. "I mean, don't you have to tell me the reason you stopped us?"

"Don't hafta tell ya squat, girly." He paused from feeling Mom to scratch his nose through his mask. "I think yer cards look fake. That's against the law."

"You wouldn't have seen them if you hadn't stopped us—"

"You know it, but maybe you're tryna get way wit sumthin. Yeah, I kin turn y'all in. But way too much hassle. Big hassle for you, specially. Maybe jail time. Ya know what kin happen ta gals in the slammer."

"But we haven't done anything illegal, as far as I know."

He held up one card. "Is this your real address?"

"Of course it is."

"Well, might not be if these're fake cards."

"But they're real. We got them before they had digital cards for phones."

"Look fake to me."

"But they're not."

"Ya gonna quibble with me? Anyways, you're way too far from this here address. Without authorization. You could be spreading. Prolly I need to call in some health official to check out you n yer boy. Could be a real uncomf'able experience."

"So what're you saying?" Mom was breathing harder. "We have some money, if that's what you're implying."

He chuckled, his belly rolling like ocean waves.

"No, no, girly. Money's no good these days, don'tcha know? But you're lookin mighty fine, so let's just settle this matter the ol' fashion way, awrighty?"

"What do you mean?"

He shoved his pistol into its holster and placed his porkchop hands on Mom's shoulders. His thick arms pushed her down to the ground, on her knees before him. Then he opened his trousers.

"You sure you want to put your willie in a strange opening? No telling what kind of virus you might find in there."

He paused, thinking. Then gave her cheek a slap.

"Open up."

"Mom?" I could see only the top of her head in the mirror.

"You be quiet now, boy, and y'all be on yer way," said Officer Tanner. He looked down at Mom. "There ain't no law now, girly. We kin do whatever th' hell we want. Way too easy to throw you in the slammer fer just about anythin. Or just shoot ya, leave you on the side here. Nobody cares. Nobody gonna ask questions, see. So you best do what I say or else you n yer boy maybe get hurt."

I saw Mom's head bobbing in the mirror – and I had to act.

"Officer," I called from next to his head, Mom's pistol pushed to his ear.

He froze, mask slipping down off his nose.

Mom jumped up and grabbed the pistol out of his holster. She stepped back with the .45 service pistol trained on him.

"Sleazy bastard," Mom growled, then spit on the ground.

"You all right?" I called to Mom.

"Don't worry. Nothing a little whiskey can't fix."

"What're you gonna do?" asked Officer Tanner, now a few sizes smaller.

His face was red, slick with sweat. He probably knew just how crazy people could get when they were stopped for no good reason then assaulted.

"Awrighty now, we kin jus let it be, no harm, okay?"

"What should we do with this bag of shit?" asked Mom. She showed an evil grin and the cop shivered. "If we let him go he'll damn sure report us. Then every cop from every jurisdiction will be after us."

"No, no, I swear! I won't tell nobody." He laughed. "I won't tell cuz I shore wouldn't want the guys to *heh heh* know I got played by a nice lady such as yourself and her fine son here." He shifted his gaze to me. "Ain't that right?"

"I don't believe you," I responded. To Mom: "I don't believe him. He's the type that'll call as soon as he can grab the radio."

"Yes, I think so, too." Mom narrowed her eyes as the man wet his trousers. "You wanna do it? Or should I be the one?"

"Be the one?" the man quizzed.

"Off with your clothes," Mom commanded. She aimed her pistol at his groin. "All of it. Right down to your tighty whities."

"What are you doing?" I asked her, still holding the pistol aimed at his head. I stepped back as he started begging for his life. "Are we going to shoot him?"

"Depends."

"On what?"

"On whether or not this bag of shit obeys." She pointed her pistol at his face. "What a day! But you stopped the wrong bitch today. Now disrobe, you piece of shit. Now. Fucking mask, too. And gloves. Everything. Make like the sorry day you were born."

"Oh, God, lady," he cried. "Please, no. I got family. Wife and two young'uns. I-I'm not a bad fella."

"Well bless your heart. Why do you call God? He doesn't have a gun aimed at your nuts." She lowered her aim more. "Maybe we should call your wife and tell her what a sack of shit you are. But I'll bet she already knows."

"But the towers are down, Mom."

"It's a figure of speech," she responded, as stern as I'd ever seen her. "From now on, things like that will be figures of speech."

The gunshot startled me. I really thought she was bluffing, only make him strip to embarrass him. Maybe take his uniform so he'd remain naked and be further embarrassed when his police buddies found him. That would be all, enough for what he'd done or tried to do.

The man screamed, putting his hands to his groin. With Mom keeping a pistol on him, she ordered me to tie him up. There was rope in the trunk of our car. I got it and did as she instructed, putting the man's thick arms behind his back as he fought against me removing his hands from his groin.

"Good." Mom stood over him, opened her mouth, let drop a big glob of spit which landed on the man's face.

She turned to me. "Put his stuff in the trunk. Then lock up the patrol car, keys inside."

We watched the man moaning, rolling in the bloody gravel at

the side of the road. With a foot to his hip, Mom gave a push and he rolled down the gravelly slope into the drainage ditch. He landed face up and continued to cry like a baby, no longer begging for his life but sad at his poor choices. He tried to be a soloist.

"Bring me the empty gas can." She went to the police car. "Let me get rid of that awful taste with some siphoning – if I remember how to do it. We can refill the can."

Mom put her blouse in place, and released the fuel cap from inside the car, went around the car and squatted. I tossed her the length of rubber hose from the trunk of our car. She sucked up the gasoline, let it drain into the empty can. I filled up our car from the can and she refilled the can from the police car.

When she was finished, she rummaged through the police car's trunk, took the shotgun and a couple boxes of shells she found there.

"You never know what you'll need in the future," said Mom in a rough, disappointed voice. "Never know what kind of mess you need to clean up."

6

IN WHICH MOM COMES CLEAN

"As I was saying...." Mom gripped the wheel tightly as we sped along just under the speed limit. "When you choose to take the melody up the scale, let's say, or down, you must keep going with instruments that play in that register. Those are the choices you make as a composer. Do you start with a good melody – like the life force inside each of us? Or do you begin with a harmonic progression – like the world we happen to find ourselves in? Or maybe you start with a rhythmic motif – like the vibrations of the cosmos. Decisions, decisions. And you must choose, not knowing if you'll make a good choice or not. Because, unlike the score sheet and your pencil eraser, you can't easily change what happens after you make your choice."

"Mom...?" I tried to cut in, unsuccessfully.

She kept on talking, nervously it seemed, all about how she'd composed another piece, a concerto for tuba and woodwind choir, even singing some of the melodies. By the end of her talk she seemed happy.

"Mom, we're in big trouble."

"Trouble?" She made a face. "How? You mean that incident back there? When that officer broke the law? And we showed him the righteous path? You mean that?"

I shut up, had to think how Mom was dealing with it. How she must be feeling, being assaulted like that. And twice in the same day. She had to be pissed. In an instant things went south. How many other times in her life had some man come along and forced her to do something, like had his way with her? Or even tried? My gut tightened more.

"Where are we going?" I asked after she'd continued her music lecture and eventually fell silent.

She smiled like it hurt. "To your Aunt Laura's. Like I said. That's the plan."

"Tell me about my cousins." I thought that would get her mind off the assault. "What are they like?"

"Laura's kids?" She had to think. "Well, there's Sammy and Tammy, the twins. They should be in high school by now – virtual school like you. Then there's Kevin or Karen or something. Don't know for sure. We lost touch then. I think the toddler had some stupid name that wasn't a name, you know, like Cooty or Cobbler, something like that. The baby had some goofy name, like Bootsy, I remember her saying. I pretended to be happy for her. Sisters, you know. She was well-put with her rich husband so she stayed home with the kids. He was CEO of some manufacturing concern, made parts for rockets, I think. Never liked him much. Oh, he was a good provider. Not that I've ever cared much for good providers. I can bring home my own venison, you know? Anyway, never really met him. He answered Laura's phone a few times. My last visit was...let's see, nine years ago? Yes, you played with your cousins then. You remember any of that visit?"

I shook my head. Honestly, none of what she said matched my memories. I was blank. "You sure I visited them?"

"Of course." She seemed to be calmer now, her grip on the wheel softer, her speed slower. "Pretty sure. I'm not *that* old."

"That's not what I mean...."

"But she's such a smug bitch, that Laura. Always thought of me as the slut of the family. Ah! How about that gardener she employed, huh? I'm sure that Bootsy, whatever the name is, has a resemblance to him. She should be five by now. Hmm, maybe she divorced Henry to run away with José. You think? But would she take the older kids with her or leave them with Henry? She's that kind of woman. She should've been the one stopped by our Officer

60

Tanner back there. She could handle that situation, pouting and fuming to get her way, putting on airs."

Mom fell silent suddenly, staring ahead. We were entering a town. There was no by-pass, no way to avoid going straight into the town, down Main Street.

Ahead a few blocks was a crowd of people, a whole lot more than we'd seen since leaving the city. They seemed to be divided into two groups, each consisting of all kinds of people, men and women, teens, older people, everyone going at it, fighting the opposite group with fists, tools like shovels and hammers, wooden boards, iron bars, whatever they could find.

"How about we take a left?" said Mom, and turned the car at the intersection without any extra attention to the conflict ahead.

We went down the street a few blocks. Mom slowed at each intersection to have a look down the side street. After a few, she chose one and we went up it, a street like a canyon between tall brick buildings that formed its sides. Warehouse district. Vehicles sat abandoned along the street, wrecked, burnt, tires missing, glass broken, metal dented. Trash filled the street, bags of it, and much more distributed everywhere by rats and dogs that ripped into the bags for whatever they could find.

"This is where Laura lives?" I asked.

"No," said Mom curtly, maneuvering the car through the street debris. "Other side of town. In the ritzy neighborhood."

"Doesn't look like anybody's ritzy now."

"And you would be correct."

"What do you think those people are fighting over?"

Mom pulled the car into an open-air parking garage, found a spot between two parked cars that didn't seem damaged. She shut off the engine.

"We'll wait here, out of sight, for a bit." She gave me a hard look. "Anything could happen, so be alert." She forced a smile to reassure me, like I was still five. "Listen to me, Sandy. If anything bad happens, I want you to forget about me and save yourself. Just run as fast and as far as you can. You hear me?"

My eyes burned with tears, but I nodded. "Okay."

Mom pulled out a folded map from the glove box, opened it, and studied it. I dared not interrupt her. She traced a route with her finger. She looked up at the rear-view mirror every minute, checking behind us.

"Get down," she whispered.

We both slunk down, hiding. "Somebody coming?"

She put her finger to her lips.

Footsteps echoed through the parking garage, boots splashing puddles, kicking loose debris. Two people strolling through it like they had no place to be, killing time. Thankfully, they didn't seem to stop to take a look inside the cars, to see if anything valuable could be taken from them. Then the noises stopped.

One guy called to the other, drawing his attention to one of the cars, three cars over. They shook the door handles. Cursing, one of them banged his fist on the window, then cursed at the pain in his fist. The other laughed and they walked on.

"That was close," I mumbled.

Mom slid up, peering over the dashboard.

"Remember what I said."

"About running?"

"Yes." She pulled herself all the way up, ready to turn on the engine. "No matter what happens, you save yourself. No matter what anybody's doing to me. Okay? Don't worry about me, just you go. Got it?"

"Yes, Mom." But I didn't. I could never leave her. I could never see her getting attacked and just run away. I knew I'd have to save her – even if we both died. She was my mom.

"Swear it," she insisted, her face stern.

"I swear it," but I knew I was lying.

"Good." She glanced around outside. "Let's get out of here."

She started the engine, backed out of the space, slowly rolled around to the exit. She looked in each direction.

Pulling onto the street, we saw streams of people fleeing from something. Sirens wailed, echoed down the streets. Police trucks rumbled by a couple blocks down. Mom slammed the brakes. We heard rapid-fire shots in that direction. More people running right to left across the street ahead. Mom made a tight U-turn, drove back the way we'd come, turned down another street, more turns, zigzagging through the town, keeping away from both the police vehicles and the agitated pedestrian crowd.

Finally we drove on a wide avenue with small trees down the median strip. Vehicles sat here and there along the avenue as it bent away from the town center, all empty, damaged, abandoned.

Mom stayed sharp as she took us further from danger. I felt better being away from that town. Had to admire her, always knowing what to do, never panicking, getting us out of dangerous situations. I figured she must've been through things like this before. No wonder she was tough.

"How'd you learn to be so cool?" I asked her.

The parkway led to the highway but Mom, uttering a curse, saw the traffic jam there and veered away, not interested. We turned onto another road with a rough surface and quickly lost any signs of civilization.

"Cool?" she asked, steering the car around a hill and down a long slope.

"Yeah, you know. Not panicking."

"Oh, that." She didn't smile, concentrating on the road. "There is actually a class for that. Some call it kindergarten. It's where they teach the really important things."

"No way. I went to kindergarten but I didn't hardly learn any of that."

Mom laughed. It was good to hear. She needed a break from the stress of our journey.

The road wound among hills on the west side of the city, trees blocking the view and when there was a gap in the trees we could see the congested highway to our left going nowhere and on our right the burning business district with columns of black smoke rising from a few places.

We passed suburban enclaves: nice homes with big yards. The neighborhoods were surrounded by walls or fences. They seemed to be doing all right, unaffected by the chaos outside. I thought they must've stockpiled supplies, enough to last for years – until the madness faded and normal life could resume.

In front of one suburban house, a family of four was packing their truck like they were just going weekend camping – but the weekend would never end. Mom waved and the dad waved back as we passed.

I turned and watched them out the rear window as Mom drove on. The older daughter was good looking: blond hair in a ponytail, athletic legs, wearing shorts and a sweatshirt. I wished we could stop. After all, I hadn't seen many girls my age – not up close, not in the past few years.

"What was that back there?" I asked after a silence. We were well out into the country by then.

"In town?" Mom shook her head, brushed hair from her face. "Don't know, don't care. The world going crazy over there. Hey, I made a rhyme. You hear that?"

"People were fighting each other. Then police came to break it up. So who was right?"

"Right? Maybe left. Who knows? There's certainly no middle anymore. If there are two sides, then likely both were disobeying local ordinances, emergency mandates, whatever new laws were put in effect. Or simply breaking protocol. You know how crowds can be, especially when they're free again after being locked down for too long. They want to storm and savage – to feel alive once more: make their mark, like they actually have power. But it's only an illusion. Yep, they have all the power that's granted to them by a bigger power. But power is a dangerous thing – having it or, worse, not having it but wanting it. Better to stay away from power of all kinds."

A smile crossed her face.

"You know not to stick a fork into a wall socket, don't you?"

"Of course. I never even thought of doing that."

"Then I taught you right."

I fiddled with the radio, no broadcasts. I hoped for news about the riot we witnessed. But Mom assessed it correctly: any mass of people will divide into factions and the factions will battle for supremacy, forcing the others to conform, obey, then serve. I got that much from my Sociology class. She said similar things many times during my life. On the playground, the park, the shopping mall, her campus, the same thing.

"Yes, you taught me right," I conceded.

* * *

When I was little we had a dog, a Schnauzer named Whiskers, salt and pepper coat, ears cropped, tail docked, like the Kennel Club required. I pondered the cruel choice to mutilate a dog that way. As a boy without siblings or friends, I simply loved having someone to play with, but I regretted having to clean up after him. Mom thought a dog would be good for teaching me responsibility.

We hadn't enjoyed our relationship too long before I took him to a park one day. I decided to release him from the leash, let him run free through the field. He took off like the wind. He found a rabbit to chase, then a squirrel. He ran and ran and I could see how happy he was to be free. But then it was time to go home.

I called him but he continued running. Thinking he might not return to me, I panicked. I ran after him but he thought it was a game and ran further. Getting angry, I demanded that he come to me. Waving the leash probably didn't help. I needed to take back control, make him obey, and be in charge once more.

I had finally convinced him to come to me, after he got tired of running. As he took the long way to me, he padded into the street and a car coming right then slammed on its brakes and the tires screeched and Whiskers lay dead.

Shrieking in horror, I dropped beside him, crying. The driver said the dog came out of nowhere. If only Whiskers obeyed me, come at my call, given in to my control.... If only he'd kept to the leash, he would be alive.

I imagined people in government thinking the same way: If only citizens obeyed, did their tasks, didn't ask questions. Then everything would be better for us, the leaders of society.

The car hit a bump as we drove along the country road and I was jolted from the memory. We never got another dog.

"Mom?" I asked, turning to her as she drove.

"Yes, Sandy?"

"Are you okay?"

"What do you mean?"

"I mean the assault back there." I sensed the changing mood. "And the attack at Grandma and Grampa's house. Are you okay?"

Her lips tightened. "I'm okay."

"You sure?"

She gave me a hard look.

"Mom, I'm serious. Why aren't you more upset?"

She hit the brakes, throwing me forward.

"Just how am I supposed to feel?"

I was so shocked by her reaction that tears started bubbling up into my eyes, clouding my view.

"He hurt me, okay?" she barked. "So am I'm going to stay hurt forever? Fuck no. That's not what I want."

She hit the accelerator and we charged ahead, me mumbling apologies.

After a few miles Mom cleared her throat. "Did you know the first instrument we could call a tuba was patented in 1835 by two gentlemen named Wilhelm Friedrich Wieprecht and Johann Gottfried Moritz? It was Prussian patent number nineteen for a 'basstuba' in F – but with 'tuba' being the Latin name for trumpet, actually 'bass-trumpet'. The newly designed instrument included piston valves, which allowed the playing of the full range of notes – rather than being limited to only the harmonic pitches like the unvalved trumpets and horns were. Then valves were added to trumpets and horns. Of course, the trombones could produce the full range of notes by adjusting the slide and so they didn't need any valves."

"Mom, why're you telling me this?"

"You may think the ophicleide came sooner, but it wasn't a true tuba. More a glorified saxophone – woodwind-style valves on a curved brass body. A trumpet mouthpiece, not reeds. Similar to what they called the 'serpent'. You've seen pictures of it. Got to play one while I was in college. Went to Germany on a band tour."

"Mom, stop talking tuba."

"In fact, it was the ophicleide that Berlioz was writing for in his *Sinfonie Fantastique*, not a tuba. The part is rather high – works for an ophicleide but a stretch for a modern tuba. A lot of tubists play it on an F tuba – which is cheating, as far as I'm concerned. But I've played it on an F, a C, and a B-flat tuba. Because I'm that good." She glanced at me. "See these lips? I can hit those high notes."

"Mom, I don't wanna hear anything more about the history of tubas. I wanna know why you aren't angry at being raped."

She stopped her rant, glared at me almost too long before turning her eyes back on the road.

"I've been through that before, Sandy. It's like a car wreck. When it happens, it happens, and you handle it as best you can. But it doesn't keep you from driving again. You have to drive, even knowing you may get into another wreck someday. It hurts – same as a car wreck – but because you didn't ask the other car to crash into you, you have double the pain – physical, but just as much mental, spiritual. Because the integrity of your car has been assaulted, the wholeness broken apart, purity dirtied, innocence smashed. It's a whole process."

I felt bad for pressing her to answer. "Sorry, Mom."

"I've been through it before." She inhaled a long time, exhaled just as long. Her voice got darker: "You get toughened up by that kind of experience. But I don't mean you should set up that kind of experience just so it'll toughen you. In fact, if it's artificial, it won't work. You have to actually be assaulted – and fight like hell through it, not allow it to defeat you. It's just...."

I waited for her to continue but she didn't. After a short time I told her she could go ahead and tell me about tubas, if she still wanted to.

"It's just an act. Then it's done. And you can dwell on how it hurts you or you can vow to go on. But being a damn victim won't get you to the next day, not like being a fighter does. I mean—"

"Really, it's okay, Mom. I wanna hear more about tubas."

"I do care. But I won't shed a tear. No, I won't. You hear me?"

She glanced over as she put a finger to her lower eyelid and pulled it down. "Never a tear." She released her finger and her eyelid snapped back. "They didn't break me. Hurt me, maybe, but never destroyed me. Never. I'm still here."

"I'm sorry, Mom."

"Bullets. They're like little miracles, you know?" She laughed, an ominous sound I'd never heard. "We had a song called 'Bullets' with the Tubafonics. First line was 'Bullets over Babylon and the Gods fell down....' Get it? Instead of spears and whatever. If the poor agrarians'd had bullets then. Then they could've killed their gods a lot sooner and gotten on with the destruction of the world they'd been mapping out since the day they were slapped together from all that red dirt." She laughed more. "At the end of that line I played *ba-ba-ba-bow! ba-ba-ba-bow!* You know, like a machine gun. High E-flat. It was great. Then the big *glissando* from low G up three octaves to the high B-flat and let it wail on. You really need a tuba in a rock band, let me tell you."

"Okay," I said to cut her off. "So tell me about that Sax guy."

"Adolphe Sax? Inventor of the Saxophone? Well, not much to say...other than his obsession with families of instruments – soprano down to bass – did lead to the reign of the 'saxhorns' and the rise in popularity of the brass band all over England and Germany. And the wind ensemble was born! As opposed to the traditional orchestra with mostly string instruments. And in the United States eventually. Perfect timing for John Philip Sousa to twist the tuba into a Sousaphone so we could carry it marching."

Then she hummed *The Thunderer* as we drove on.

✳   ✳   ✳

Mom suddenly slowed and I fell forward, catching myself. We had come to an intersection with a few services. A gas station. A drug store. Three fast food restaurants. Nothing was open.

"Why are we stopping here?" I asked Mom.

She gazed out the front window into the dark opening where doors and window panels had been smashed out.

"I wonder if there's anything left." She shut off the engine, sat a moment. Then she opened the door and climbed out.

"Wait, Mom."

"Stay in the car," she said gruffly, leaning down to the window. "If anything happens, drive on. Like I told you. Save yourself."

"But Mom...."

She took the pistol she got from Officer Tanner and made sure a bullet was in the chamber. Stepping around piles of trash, she paused at the entrance, studying the territory, then entered. I could see her for a while, then she moved out of view.

Turning my head to survey each direction, I sat nervously in the driver's seat, ready to escape. A car might get the attention of vagrants. They might surround the car, demand a ride, or kill us for the car. I watched the nearby treeline, deciding if the shadows were actually moving or not. I kept an eye out for anyone coming around the sides of the store. I would honk the horn if any danger appeared.

A sigh of relief came when I saw Mom exiting the store with a few items in her arms.

"Not much left," she said through the window. "Of course they took the drugs. Like that's going to save them. But the big, bad thugs left a lot of the feminine stuff, thankfully."

Mom had a few bottles of vitamins and a first aid kit. She held up a small box.

"They missed one, Just what I was hoping for." She tossed it to me. I picked up the small box from my lap, read the label. "It was on the floor under the cash register. Besides, it's nothing a man would take."

"This?" I gasped. "A pregnancy test?"

"No." She waved me to move over.

I climbed across to the passenger seat and she got in.

"Have to be prepared. No pregnancy tests left. That box is a morning-after pill. Just in case."

"But it's way past morning, Mom."

"Better late than pregnant."

I read the package. "Says you have to take it within seventy-two hours."

She flashed a smile. "I think we'll make it."

Reaching in the back seat, she grabbed a bottle of water from the cooler. She took a swallow, then tore open the box, squeezed the pill out of its wrapper. She held it up like a shiny gold coin.

"Sometimes it's a blessing," she said, making a sour face. "Like when you came into my life. Other times, it can be a curse. Can't be bothered with nine months of infirmary, not in a pandemic, not to mention eighteen years of on-going responsibilities." She turned to me with her accusing smirk. "What're you, nineteen now?"

"Yes." I felt ashamed to have her still looking after me. But I also looked after her. We were a team, she constantly reminded me. Especially now. We had to be a team. Who else could we trust but each other?

"I just hope it didn't take," she muttered.

"That'll stop it, right?"

"That's the plan." She chuckled like a thankful woman in a TV commercial.

With a dramatic wave of her hands she plopped the pill in her mouth, drank down the rest of the bottle of water.

I read the package insert as she sat back resting. I read aloud the parts I thought she'd want to know: how she would feel during the next few days, how her period would be different, and so on.

She made an ugly face.

"Taste bad?" I asked.

"Not too bad. They should consider making them in chocolate."

I took over the driving, coming around the rear of the car to the driver's side. Mom rested.

We continued down the road. At Mom's direction, I kept the speed down, always aware of anything off the road that could be trouble. The sun was lower and we would be in darkness soon, a bad time to travel. We didn't want to turn on headlights; they would alert vagrants that we were approaching.

Mom said she felt nauseous, probably from that pill. But we also hadn't eaten much in the past 24 hours. I pulled over when we came to a wide grassy area and a gravel road turn-off. I drove us down the gravel path to a flat, shaded area, where trees hid us from the road. There was a farm house ahead along the gravel path but it appeared abandoned like so many others. No lights on, no smoke from the chimney.

"Should we see if anybody's home?" I asked.

"More likely they want what we have more than we want what they have."

"If nobody lives there now, we could break in and have a place to sleep, at least."

"I don't trust it."

Digging out some of our supplies, I made her eat. We were starting to run low. Who can live on jerky and dried fruit and nuts for very long? The big can of caramel popcorn remained unopened. The sugar cookies were the first to go, then oatmeal-raisins. Tubes of potato chips half-empty. The crackers were stale. A few old apples remained.

"The package says if you throw up you'll need to take it again, so keep it down. Okay, Mom?"

I watched her fighting her stomach.

"Maybe we should stop here, not drive any more today. No telling what's ahead. And you should eat."

She nodded and laid her head back. "Okay."

7

IN WHICH MOM LIGHTENS THE DARKNESS

"How are you feeling?" I asked a couple hours later.

Mom had dozed off in the back seat, which made me stay more alert. I kept an eye out for trouble as the orange sun set and the woods darkened. I had Mom's pistol close by. Officer Tanner's .45 pistol was near Mom so she could use it if necessary. We also had Grampa's .38 revolver, but we couldn't find any more bullets – two left in it. Mom's pistol used 9mm.

The evening remained calm, so calm that I stayed on edge, so certain something was about to happen. Every rustle of leaves, every snap of twig, every chit of some little woodland creature set my nerves firing, my finger tighter against the pistol's trigger.

"I'm fine," said Mom softly. "Relax, will you?"

"I can't relax. I gotta protect you."

"Aw, what a sweet boy." She sat up lazily, stretching out her arms. "Such a loving boy." She leaned forward and kissed my head. "I'm glad you're here. No one else I can trust to watch over me while I sleep."

That made me blush. When Mom was affectionate that way I was thrown back to my childhood when it was permissible to show affection. Now that I was a grown man, it felt odd but was never unwanted. Tears came to my eyes. I sniffled them back.

"What's that?" asked Mom.

She pushed herself up more, stretching over the top of the seat to wrap her arms around me. Right then I happened to turn my head to look at her and our lips met, just brushed randomly, but instead of it feeling awkward, I wanted more.

With a grin, Mom dropped back, leaving me unfulfilled.

"I taste gasoline," I said, pondering the softness of her lips.

"Well, that's better than Officer Tanner's sweaty dick."

"Mom!" I snapped. "Don't talk like that. Yuck!"

"Like what?" She laughed like a little girl. "Really it's not so different from you." She teased me about certain incidents in my childhood, others in my teen years.

"Stop it, Mom."

She sat frowning, her face grim. The fun was over.

I hadn't intend to upset her. She'd been through a lot on this trip – not to mention the years we've already endured: one threat after another from disease, and imprisonment in our homes by a slew of government edicts. Stay home. You can go out. Stay home again. People will go crazy that way, Mom said. But she always remained calm and took it all in stride. She often joked about government repression, saying it was a lot like sitting through an orchestra rehearsal when she only had three notes to play in the last movement.

Maybe I wouldn't make it through the pandemic without her guiding me and taking care of me. She'd always guided me and taken care of me. That wasn't going to change. What's a mother's job, anyway? It must be true: a boy's best friend is his mother.

"Remember that weekend when I didn't come home? Back in the first year of lockdowns?" She regarded me until she had my complete attention. "You didn't know where I was. And I couldn't call you. And you panicked?"

I nodded, not sure where she was going with it. "I was a lot younger then."

"Yes, you were." She narrowed her eyes. "The reason was, like I told you when I finally got home, I was in jail. Remember? The whole ridiculous mask thing. And cops liked having new excuses to grab people, throw them in jail – and you can't complain, file charges, or even call a lawyer, because it's pandemic time."

"You told me they were mean to you."

"Yes, they were." She took a big breath, held it a while then released it slowly. "But I didn't say *how* they were mean to me. Mostly I worried about you, about what you'd do without me, how you would survive by yourself. They—"

"Mom, stop. You don't have to say anymore."

"Okay, I won't. Just know that I didn't like what they did, so I don't like cops – especially the ones that like to force themselves on innocent people."

"I get it, Mom." But I didn't, not really. Who would want to hurt my mom? She's a good person. She'd never hurt anybody. I couldn't imagine how she was treated while she was in jail over that weekend.

Mom groaned, her hand going to her belly. "Oh!"

"What's wrong?"

She opened the door and got out, bent over as the contents of her stomach erupted and spilled down her shirt, dropping onto the ground. Another purge. Another. She squatted, caught her breath.

"Dammit," she muttered. She took deep breaths.

I handed her a bottle of water.

"Damn," she said, then groaned, wiping her mouth with the back of her hand. "A waste of food." She coughed, spit. "And that pill. That was it. I don't have another one."

"Maybe it worked enough while it was in you."

Mom shook her head. "Doubtful."

She got to her feet, regarded her soiled shirt. With both hands she took the bottom hem and tore the shirt upward, removing it over her head. Tossing it to the ground, she stood bare-chested in the darkness, moonlight not yet shining on us.

Mom never wore bras. She cupped her breasts like she was weighing them. She nodded approvingly.

"How about these puppies? I still got it, vomit and all." She glanced at me, turning to give me a good look. "What do you think? Is your mom still hot?"

She was, but I couldn't say that.

"Stop it, Mom. You're embarrassing yourself."

"Embarrassing *you*." She laughed. Pinching one nipple then

the other, she grinned. "Remember sucking on these?"

"Mom!"

"I used to be known as the 'topless tubist' back when I was performing with the Tubafonics. I told you that before. Sometimes I had to wear pasties if the venue's rules required. But they had tassels."

"Okay, I can imagine that."

"Maybe I should've nursed you longer. They'd sag more, look more motherly. Then you'd appreciate my sacrifice."

I had to wonder, unable to recall her nursing me, but I'd seen plenty of pictures of naked girls online. Mom's pair was still top-grade, like she insisted. But I didn't feel like being teased.

"I'm sorry, Mom."

"I can't deal with a baby now. Not in the middle of a pandemic. After, maybe okay. But not a rapist's baby. When we are post-pandemic and ready to build a new society, and it's someone I love, then maybe." She gazed up at the stars coming out. "When we get past this, uh, situation. Post-pandemic. Post-plague. Post-apocalypse. Post-normal. Then we'll need to make babies. Lots of them. You know?" She grinned at me, a seductive glimmer in her eye. "As I told you before. We might need to repopulate the world, you and me."

She playfully covered her breasts with her hands, playing peek-a-boo and dancing shyly with a swing of her hips.

"I don't want to think about that," I said.

"But I'm sure you've thought of it." She cocked her head. "Not even a little?"

"No, never."

"I bet you have. You have a few pictures on your phone."

"Not of you, Mom."

"But they're women my age."

She sure had a way of putting me in my place, making me feel ashamed, and in that one way I hated her. She kept me on edge, first teasing me like I was still a child but then just as quickly building me up, treating me like a man she might sleep with only to say or do something that took me straight back to my childhood when she was holding me in her arms, pushing her fat nipples at me as she hummed a lullaby—

"Mom...? Why are there no people around?"

I deliberately looked away as the moonlight finally shone.

"I mean, except for the riot in that town. We don't see hardly any people. Not even dead bodies laying everywhere. Where did they all go?"

She gazed at me, wiping between her breasts with a rag from the car. "Go?"

I waved my arms around. The world seemed empty. This farm was abandoned. Grandma and Grampa had checked out but their bodies remained. I knew people got the virus and died, but there should be bodies everywhere.

"That's your concern?" asked Mom.

"It doesn't make sense."

She came up to me, gave a glance down to her chest to be sure it was clean now, then hugged me.

"What were you studying in school? Biology?"

"Sociology, actually. I just declared my major."

"The first pandemic killed off a lot of people. Then came wars that had nothing to do with the pandemic. Just settling old scores. I didn't want them taking my sweet boy, sending him overseas to die. Then came the second pandemic, when nature's angry mother decided the first one didn't work as well as intended and sent us the big plague. A lot more died. And, of course, more war – police actions, whatever they called them – protests against everything. Then the *next* pandemic, now that we're down and almost out. The mop-up pandemic—"

"But they're all just corona viruses. Like a common cold. The seasonal flu. We studied plenty about those in school. They're just a lot weirder, like they're tuned in to our particular genes. What's the word, 'targeted'? Is that it? I mean beyond what they were doing in the labs, them scientists playing around like kids putting Lego blocks together, building a better bug. And they denied it for so long—"

"Like they had no idea what they were doing, huh? Like they

couldn't guess what would happen."

"Yeah, but now?" I looked around. "Shouldn't there be more bodies that dropped everywhere?"

"Well, we haven't been in many population centers. Look back there on the highway. I bet a lot of those stopped vehicles contain dead bodies. Keeping the windows up seals them inside so they don't drain away."

I made a disgusted face. "Yeah, we studied that. A little. The late-stage effect, when the bodies fill up with disgusting fluids and spill out every orifice."

"This one isn't like back then, not like the first pandemic, when everybody tried to pretend it wasn't a big deal. The second one was more on target, sufficiently tweaked, got the ones the first pandemic missed. More efficient. Little fucking creatures. Hate'em."

"Actually plants. Bacteria are animals but viruses are plants. Just a tiny speck of material, like a grain of pollen. It's like.... There are millions of coronaviruses. But only a few of them cause us any harm. For millions of years we survived."

I paused, had to run calculations in my head. We'd never had several pandemics so close together like we did now. It seemed like they had a schedule to follow. And each seemed determined to get certain people the previous viruses missed.

"Yes...? Go on, Sandy."

"I mean, how is it we are still alive?"

"We stayed home, as we were told. Right? And we became suspicious of other people, like we were supposed to, shunned them like they shunned us. And we covered ourselves up and washed obsessively. Made our own bubble and stayed in it. And then there's our good genes."

"But lots of people still died. They died doing what we're doing. Even people who went out in hazmats died. Even the people who got every vaccine they came up with, plus boosters – they still died. Some people died after they *got* the vaccine, right? The side effects they never expected. Like the red rash thing."

"No, that was from getting too many vaccines. You know some

people just couldn't get enough and over-vaxxed, thinking it made them stronger."

"But they died from their enthusiasm...."

"There's all kinds of people in the world, Sandy. We're good at different things – like instruments in an orchestra. Each of us is protected from some dangers but not from others. Depends where you live, too. Where your people lived long ago. Where you're from, the make-up inside."

Her stomach rumbled, wanting to be full again. I handed her the tube of potato chips.

"They never studied the people who were living through it, the survivors, never tried to find out why they didn't die." She nibbled on a chip. "Instead, they just kept churning out more shots that didn't improve the mortality stats."

"So...are we special? We got the vaccines. They worked on us."

"Well...." She fell silent, started counting the stars overhead. "You're half right, I suppose."

"We got the vaccine," I insisted, wanting to believe. "Right? I remember going to the clinic. And we got the cards – first time, codes on our phones the next time."

Mom pursed her lips. "Actually, I took us to a clinic where a friend of mine worked. The dad of one of my students. He thinks like us – like me, anyway. People who ignore the official stories. So you and I got what they call a 'saline solution' instead of the vaccine. Both times."

"What?" I erupted, my body suddenly feeling inflamed, cells ready to burst in anger. The virus was sitting on me, in me, just waiting for the confession from Mom before it would launch its attack. "How could you? You risked our lives!"

"Risked our lives? Look at us. We're alive. We're perfectly fine – and others died."

That stopped me. I froze in mid-rage, angry words storming through my head. "But how?"

"Too many reports...." She had to take a deep breath. "I heard too many reports of people having bad reactions, side effects from taking the vaccines. You know we were ordered to stay home, so we did. Stayed away from people, the sick ones, so no reason to rush the shot. We waited. First vaccine, everyone was so happy, eager to line up for it. We really were not in any hurry, you and me, being comfortable at home. You had your virtual school and so did I, teaching those brass players and the music theory classes. No reason for us to go out and stand in line – even six feet apart."

She checked her hands, clean enough, then rubbed her face with them and gazed up at me.

"Remember that old woman who boasted she was staying nine feet apart from us, like that made her morally superior?"

"Yeah, I remember." I had to laugh.

"It's impossible, you know," she said. "You can't be making one thing that's supposed to treat different people and not see some of them having bad reactions. We're not all the same. Like I said, we have different backgrounds, different make-up. It's Biology 101, isn't it?"

"But Mom...."

"That's what's happening now. Another pandemic, another vaccine. They don't mix and match quite like they believe they do. You heard some of the reports, right?" She shook her head, sadly. "Like those people whose organs liquify inside and they literally drown inside their own skin – pink sludge when it breaks through their flesh. But, of course, the authorities covered that up. 'Keep taking the newest vaccines we produce, whatever it is. *Ka-ching*, profits go up. Everything will be all right. *Ka-ching*. Almost as profitable as war materiel. Don't pay attention to the man behind the curtain. Some people made a lot of money from vaccines. Others profited from the virus itself. Lots of stocks trading hands. While lab assistants died – the first Guinea pigs!"

My whole body tensed. "Mom, that can't be true."

"It is. I heard it straight from my doctor friend. He kept his mouth shut to keep his job, but he talked to me. I tutored his kid, another budding tubist. But the dad, an epidemiologist, saw first-hand what happened to patients in the ICUs."

"But Mom...."

"Now you've got me upset! I can't think about that any longer.

I need to play Timmy."

She popped up and went to the car, pulled out the soft-side tuba case, unzipped her favorite toy.

"So...we have...special genes?" I asked as she sat down on the grass and pulled the tuba into her lap.

She didn't answer, started playing. A few warm-up licks, then launched into a sonata she'd often played at home. And the notes filled the grove, echoing among the pines, returning to my ears as a church organ that called angels to come dance with us, to pray with us. Mournful yet vaguely hopeful.

Then, as she finished the second section and started the final one, I noticed movement in the darkness.

"Uh...Mom...?"

She kept playing as two figures emerged from the pines — stepping forward cautiously. The man had a long beard, clothes that were ragged and dirty. The woman beside him was a mess in ripped leggings and dirty dress, multiple sweaters and a scarf, as though that was her entire wardrobe. Her feet were stuffed into snow boots though it was only autumn. She was probably about Mom's age but looked older in her state of disarray. The man might be younger than he appeared.

Standing side by side, keeping a polite distance, they listened.

Mom finished that piece, switched to Gershwin's *Rhapsody in Blue*, playing the opening *glissando* from the basement of her range to the wailing high notes, three octaves up, as agile as the original clarinet version, but Mom could do it.

"That's mighty fine playin," the man said when Mom held the final note that an orchestra would've been playing, then stopped. She noticed them as she'd played, but she was more concerned with finishing the song.

Having finished, she regarded the dirty couple.

"We're not crazy," said the man.

He took the woman's hand in his, dipped his head in greeting.

So Mom played another piece.

8

IN WHICH MOM LISTENS FOR ONCE

"It's Vaughan Williams," said Mom, cross-legged on the cool grass, Timmy resting across her lap after finishing the piece. "*Concerto for Tuba and Orchestra*. But without the orchestra obviously. You can imagine the orchestra part if you've heard it before."

"Yes ma'am, you play real nice," said the man.

"Thank you." She glanced at me, smiling, always enjoying appreciation. "I've performed it a dozen times. It's rather folk tunesy. People love that. They're writing more for tuba these days, thankfully – well, they *were*, before the pandemic. It really fucked up everything."

The man nodded, chuckled. The forlorn pair stayed at the edge of our space. not threatening. We were conditioned to measure the distance between ourselves. The suggestions to stand apart had evolved into directives, into orders, becoming customs. You never dared approach within six steps of other people. That was rude. Some people would kill you if you got within their bubble.

After a minute they sat down and we talked quictly among the moonlit pines.

"I'm Jimmy," he said as though proud of the name, "and this is Claire." He smiled at the disheveled woman. "She don't talk much on account of her getting hit on the head."

"Sorry for that," said Mom.

"Ain't yer fault," Jimmy responded. "It was a gang of vaxxers, tryna jab her, and she fighting them."

"I'm sorry that it happened to your...wife."

"Oh, she and me...." Jimmy paused. "We ain't what you might say a couple, except for these circumstances. See, I lost my wife in the first pandemic and Claire, well, she lost her husband, too. But then we found each other during the next pandemic. Yep, we both walked out the same damn hospital the same time. Looked round and said 'Wanna get a cup o joe?' And off we went."

"You were infected?" asked Mom.

"Got some symptoms, yeah, but we's getting better on our own. Somebody called the health police to pick us up – same thing for Claire. Everybody ratting out neighbors and co-workers, anybody they didn't like. Got home and everything was gone, cleaned out. Had to steal clothes because cain't go round in hospital gowns."

"They do feel comfortable – if you're not in a hospital," said Mom with a laugh.

Jimmy raised his voice to cut her off: "Later some vagrants hyped up on vax beat her, left her for dead, thought they saved the world, I reckon. Raped her pretty bad, though. I been nursing her back to health, and I think maybe we're gonna make it. We been staying in that house down there – not ours, but we're living there. Then we hear music." He glanced at Claire. She nodded.

Again Mom thanked him, offered to play another.

"Mom, how about putting on a shirt?" I suggested, speaking in a low voice. She ignored me. I went to the car and found a t-shirt of hers, brought it over to her. "Here, Mom."

"I'm all right," she said with an edge of defiance. "The cool air feels good."

Undeterred, I took off my long-sleeved flannel shirt, wrapped it around her shoulders. I wore a t-shirt under it anyway.

"You want to button it up, Mom?"

"No, it's okay."

"Just button a few."

She continued talking with our guests, so I knelt behind her and reached around to pull the edges of the shirt together, began buttoning it. At the second button, Mom put her hand over my hand, pressed my hand against her breast, trapping it there.

"See how my boy takes care of me?"

"Mom...," I whined.

When I finished the task, getting three buttoned, Mom took up her tuba again and played. It was a short lullaby kind of song – I think she was improvising, pouring out her mood like a warm breeze that touched thorny flowers and manure-rich dirt and pond scum alike yet it sounded sweet.

They listened patiently.

As soon as she finished, Jimmy launched into his story like he'd been holding it inside for years waiting for sympathetic ears:

"They called it a weird kinda flu, then gave it some official name like it was a new grandchild. They declared it a pandemic and the madness began. As it ravaged through city after city we called it the scourge. God's retribution. Our due."

He coughed and we all froze until he continued.

"Yep, everything was fine when I went south on business. I sold my parents' house, see. They died. Natural causes, not the pandemic, advanced age. I stayed in a hotel near the shore I knew was damaged by hurricane couple years before. I figured it was properly renovated. I did my business, met with people, signed here, there, got a fine seafood dinner, returned to my hotel. When I entered the room, after I turned off the A/C for the whole day, I noticed right away th' awful smell and immediately flicked th' A/C on. I recognized th' odor as mold, pretty common after hurricane if the walls ain't properly dried and treated. Thought of asking for a new room but the new room might be worse. I was leaving in the morning anyway so I simply lowered the temp and stayed."

He glanced around our circle, daring each of us to guess what happened next.

"Next morning, had a cough. Just some phlegm down in my throat. I cleared it, prepared to leave. Checked out, put my bag in the truck, drove home. I coughed once in a while. By then I was guessing I done picked up something so I could anticipate a full-blown cold by the time I got home."

Mom nodded with the rhythm of his voice.

"When I got home, I was sick. Went straight to bed, coughing and feeling hot. As it turned out, I stayed in bed for three days, too damn exhausted to move. Felt no hunger and made no meals, not even snacks. Fever came. I sweated up the bed, then chills shook me, then fever. Head swoll like gonna explode, pounding. Coughing fits made headaches worse. Even so, I just thought it's ordinary flu."

He had to take a long breath, choked up at the memory.

"I was surprised I didn't have no other symptoms I usually get with cold or flu. Nose was fine, didn't run and no sneezing. My eyes didn't feel itchy or watery. Throat wasn't sore, but muscles in my throat got sore from the damn coughing. I kept coughing gunk from my lungs, had to spit it out. Years before, when I got same kind o' coughing, doctor called it pneumonia. Little sacks in my lungs, where air I breath in gave its oxygen to my bloodstream, they was filled up with gunk so I couldn't breathe. Had to put all my strength into coughing to clear enough little sacks so I could breathe good enough to get some rest. You know, I immediately blamed the mold in that room."

He began acting out his misery, hands to his head.

"Once fever lifted and headaches went away, I got up to try and make dinner. Hadn't eaten for three days. Found I had no appetite but forced myself to eat. Had to regain my strength, see. Even though it was my favorite foods, I couldn't eat more than half my usual amount. My brain gave me a signal the food no longer tasted good. Didn't really have any taste. This continued with everything I tried to eat over the next week. It had no taste. Got to the point I stopped eating. Lost lots of weight. I did regain my strength yet the coughing continued at a nagging level for another month. There was still gunk in my lungs had to get out, specially to sleep. I slept on my belly and could breathe better."

He took several sympathetic breaths.

"I tried going into work and everyone asked how I was. Got to demonstrate my coughing fits. Coworkers weren't impressed. Boss sent me home. Yeah, stayed home a few days, but didn't improve, so I went to a neighborhood ER. Doc gave me a shot and couple prescriptions. Still thought it was mold. That's the story I told."

He chuckled a bit, shaking his head, amused.

"I was ready to return to work again but I had to go back south to finish up the sale. So I drove down, coughing. Took some antihistamine to reduce coughing urge and thin mucus. Held together enough to get through the signing and was about to leave town when damn coughing fit overcame me in the lobby of, you betcha, a different hotel. Fit zapped all my strength. I passed out. People called the ambulance and I woke up in a hospital bed. In fact, it was an ICU bed and the doctors wore coveralls and plastic hoods. Gave me strong medication through an IV to kill th' infection in my lungs. After two nights in ICU they moved me to a regular room, where I stayed five more nights. They asked me if there was anyone to pick me up and I said no, I'm alone in this city. So they kept me another two days until one of my sons could fly down and get me, drive us back north."

He got quiet for a moment, remembering.

"So, finally back in my own place, I thought I was getting back to normal but the damn fatigue left me as energetic as a wooden board. Didn't have no more cough, got my appetite back. Regained ten of the pounds I lost. Out from work so long, I began thinking of other projects I could get done to fill the time but whenever I started something, I felt too tired and just pulled myself into bed again. Eventually, I was feeling back to normal, took myself out to see a few movies, grab some good food at nice restaurants before I used up my sick leave. Then I returned to work."

I let out a long exhale which sounded like a sigh, thinking he was done. Mom flashed a grin, both of us hoping he was finished.

"But couple months later," he went on, "everyone was catching same damn infection."

Mom shifted Timmy off her lap, laid him on the grass. She leaned back on her arms, stretching the shirt tight.

"So you were the first to get it," said Mom. "That makes you famous."

"Didn't put it all together then," said Jimmy, "not till it was serious enough everybody's talking about it, everybody sharing their symptoms. See, this new disease matched what I got. Except

I didn't die. Now lots of people were. I felt a few times like I was *gonna* die, but I fought it, pushed myself back from th' edge. But other folks, specially elderly and ones already got some medical problems, they didn't make it. Funny how TV news announced the latest death totals each night – like they was counting gold coins!"

He nodded at each of us.

"I began to worry," Jimmy continued. "Wondered if I should tell th' authorities my experience. Like, maybe I was Patient Zero, so maybe I could give'em some advice. Guess it wasn't mold, after all. Something left by another guest that housekeeping never got clean? Or it was a sick housekeeper. Didn't know what to do, but as long as I was over it, didn't really care."

I took more breaths, watching how attentive Mom was to his tale, being polite.

"Then the rashes began – on other people, not me – hair and teeth falling out. They were giving vaccines by then. Some folks got no side effects, but others.... Well, hit or miss, mild or severe, ya know? No telling what you would get, which one you would be. The cure worse than the disease, huh?"

"Sure," I responded. Mom glanced at me.

"But I was fine, good to go," said Jimmy. "Figured I didn't have th' infection long enough for those late-stage symptoms to develop. I never got their vaccine – rushed into public clinics like it was a new soft drink flavor. Emergency approval, they said. As reporters on TV tried covering their blemishes! Wondered what the hell was happening. They reported outbreaks in other countries, made lots of excuses, confirmed it couldn't come here, then accepted it did come here, with all the global travel. Gave lots of explanations, got official people to speak from big podiums, just to let people feel reassured and to be a little more comfortable."

I could remember back then, but I was too young to really understand what was happening.

"Yeah, I saw it beginning," he said with a righteous laugh. "Restrictions! For our own good. Starts the same damn way every time. I read history books, and I seen plenty of movies about the same thing – called them science-fiction. Again I thought of telling my story to authorities, but by then I was afraid of being forced into one of their quarantine camps that was popping up outside hospitals and treated like a lab rat. Might be better to leave the city, go on a road trip and forget all I seen. Yeah, I could visit my sons, see my wife again. Ex-wife. I stopped by work, stocked up on supplies, headed south."

Then Jimmy got angry, shook his hands.

"But she tells me not to come. Still had phone service then. They got the scourge. Better I stay away. Then my wife, she was taken to the hospital by my sons. They got admitted, too. Never heard from any of them ever again. So...I gotta think they didn't make it. Part of the purge. Trimming the herd. Mother Nature getting even with us."

Mom was transfixed, giving him serious attention, alarmed by his story. We hadn't experienced the pandemics so directly as this Jimmy had. We stayed home.

"Sounds awful," Mom offered. "We didn't know things like that were happening." She pointed to me. "I tried to keep my son away from the news. Tried to stay in our own bubble and just live."

"But finally we had to go," I spoke up. "Now we're on our way to my aunt's."

"You best call and see they're still alive," he said with a wink.

"No cell signal," I responded.

Jimmy laughed, shaking his head. "I remember the face of that hot news anchor Jessica Hunt, wiping tears from the corner of her eye, opposite side of her face red and lumpy with the rash that no cosmetics could cover. What a shame. She whimpered all through her announcement. She apologized for her appearance and the poor signal, then recited the official statements one by one – cautions for people to heed, suggestions for obtaining medical care or providing the basic daily needs. She paused between each item to suck air from a canister she held. In late stages, the virus corrupted the lining of the lungs, made it hard to breathe. She was resigned to her fate, faking calm like a pro. Whoever operated the camera chuckled – a dry, raspy sound, broke into a coughing fit. Then Jessica fell over, hit her head on the desk, loud thump.

Camera operator zoomed in on the crown of her head, focused on the bald spot where her hair'd fallen out, her rash exposed to the whole world."

Jimmy chewed his lip, head dipping in quiet condolence.

"Damn, I loved her smile – before her teeth fell out, two by two – and her bright green eyes – before the left one turned too red to be usable and th' other yellowed. Ah, her voice was a love song that kept me going during those days. When I thought what to do now my family was gone."

He paused and we thought he was done now, but he began laughing.

"The camera guy let the lens slip too low and I saw the bodies of other studio staff slumped on the floor in front of the broadcast desk. A pair of rats'd come, scavenging their dinner. On camera. Then – this is funny – as the image faded, the camera guy stepped in front of the camera. He crawled to the pile of bodies in his blue hazmat coveralls and white mask, took his place among them. Gave a thumbs-up to the camera audience and collapsed. Camera projected that image until power ran out and the damn picture dissolved into night."

Mom had gradually lowered her head but looked up when he fell silent.

"Look at these pines, standing tall around us," she said. "If not for knowing where we've come from, we wouldn't know anything bad was happening. It's fine out here."

"You're right," said Jimmy. Claire took his hand in hers.

Mom pulled Timmy to her lap, played something bittersweet, making up the song. As she played, other weary figures emerged from the darkness, forming a circle, sitting and listening to the free concert.

9

IN WHICH MOM LEARNS THE TRUTH

"What're we gonna do?" I asked Mom after her concert, five tunes of uplifting spirit, life-affirming, but nothing too lively, nothing vulgar given our collective sorrow for the loss of good times past and caution for an uncertain future.

Mom sat back on the grass.

"You called everyone out of the darkness," I explained. "You're right. Music calls people and calms, brings people together."

Mom smiled. "As long as we like the same music."

In the ring of listeners were men and women of all ages, a few children both young and teens, and elderly – twenty-two of them. The start of a village. I immediately felt more comfortable. Safety in numbers. After years of seeing a crowd only on screen, mostly when rioting, looting, or protesting in news reports, it seemed like a weird kind of dream. I had no fear. They sat and listened.

A tall man named Gibbons spoke to everyone of the need to form our own town, with everyone contributing to the needs of the many. A portly man named Jones argued that Gibbons would take it all for himself, make himself the chief of their tribe. Another man named Baker got up, tried to intercede, but calm speaking turned to shouting until their wives shouted them down.

"We're like an orchestra," Mom spoke when the arguing ended, "each with its own part to play. Together we sound good, together in harmony."

"And what part do you play?" asked Gibbons.

"I play tuba, of course."

"No, I mean in our new society."

"Oh, I...I suppose I'd be the music teacher."

"Really don't need no music teacher," he said, "not 'til our basic needs are taken care of."

"I have some survival skills, too," said Mom. "I learned them from my grandfather. He was a commando in the Marines way back. So I could guard the town."

"And be the police?" He made a nasty face, spit on the ground. A few in the crowd applauded.

"We don't need any cops," Jones confirmed.

"I'm not suggesting I'd be any kind of judge and jury, mister. I only said I could act as a guard for the town. Watching for cops." She frowned at them. "I've had my own encounters with bad cops."

"There must be laws," said Baker, "before anything. We gonna be a free town or not?"

"Ya cain't have laws n be free," said an older woman they called Mrs. Hobbes. "We studied that in school before school went viral – I mean virtual." She giggled at her error.

"Laws that protect our freedoms," Gibbons clarified.

"Laws never stopped tanks from rolling over yer border," cried someone from the back, "like the war few years ago!"

"Okay," Mom raised her voice. "First things first: food and water. Have you got that?"

They stood perplexed, like she'd spoken a foreign language. They began discussing the resources of the area. A stream ran nearby. A pond over there. The old house up the road had a small garden that could be expanded. Plenty of pasture for livestock. Did anyone have livestock?

I remember Mom saying 'we' at the beginning, but now she used 'you'. I scanned her face, saw her intent. Hands on hips, chest out. She should be mayor of this play village. It would take a lot of work. They had to build a fence or a wall for security.

I looked around, didn't see any girls my age. Only mothers with young kids. But, as Mom always said, when the time came we'd have to pull together, without hang-ups over who matches with who, to remake civilization – maybe have to repopulate the world. I regarded the prettiest young mother, possibly twenty-five; she had a toddler beside her and a baby in her arms. She looked scared.

I waved my hand at them, caught the baby's attention and the baby goo-goo'd. The mother managed a smile.

"Lots of good pine round us here," said Jimmy.

Everyone turned and stared at him and Claire.

"Them two's crazy," said Mrs. Hobbes, pointing.

"How?" asked Mom.

"Not crazy but...diseased," Baker explained.

"Not diseased no more," said Jimmy, anger in his voice. "We just wanna be part of this here village y'all are making. I don't mind work. Dirty work is okay. I'll take out the garbage if that's what it takes to be a member."

"Membership, huh?" Gibbons chortled. "Citizens. Free citizens in our own damn country."

"Better put up a sign to let people know," said Jones. "Ain't nobody allowed in here without voting."

"You mean vetting," Mom corrected him.

"No, I mean vetting then voting if they can be members."

The crowd agreed. Already laws were being made – laws that everyone would need to agree on. A village was forming. I saw Mom smiling at the developments.

I went up to Mom, spoke softly to her: "Maybe we should stay with these people. You know? Safety in numbers."

Mom gave a nod, still looking forward, not at me, focused on the group. "We are getting that 'safety in numbers' by going to your aunt's house."

"But that's still far away."

"Not much. About twenty more miles."

"Only twenty? Then why did we stop here?"

"I needed a break. Don't you remember?"

"You needed to play out your emotions," I offered, and put my hand on her shoulder. She put her hand up over my hand, patted it. I flashed back to times as a boy when I'd rubbed her back with my little hands and she moaned with satisfaction.

Mom turned slightly, started to tell me how things were likely to go from here on. What she meant was the collapse of society. We only saw the beginning – not counting the years of lockdowns by state authorities accepted by too many people as necessary in order to survive the pandemic. It's for the common good, they said. But it never ended. Even when the virus death counts dropped to almost nothing the rules remained, the repression increasing. Most people continued accepting it as a 'new normal'. But not for Mom – and so here we were, in a pine forest in the dark of night, finding our souls.

"What you two chomping about?" asked Gibbons.

Mom broke away from me. "We were discussing the general situation. The way things are likely to go from here on."

"And what's that?"

She cleared her throat. "How people die – how they will die. Not from the virus, which is mostly eradicated now, but from common health problems. When hospitals close, when pharmacies run out, when doctors flee the cities, people will die from ordinary things."

"What're you talking about?" asked Jones.

"For example, aren't there a few million people who have diabetes and require medication? Without it they'll die, sooner rather than later. And the people who haven't been diagnosed – they won't be now. People with Type I need insulin every day. No insulin and they will be dead in a week or so. Everyone like that will die, their bodies in houses, in cars, not always outdoors where we can see them—"

"So that's why we don't see bodies laying around," I exclaimed.

"Not just getting insulin but even manufacturing it in the first place. How's that going to happen? Is this little village going to be able to ramp up production soon? How about the raw materials? It's hopeless for anyone with underlying health problems. How about asthmatics? Kidney disease? People who need dialysis? Not to mention cancer patients. People with heart problems? Gone. People in nursing homes left with no care. Then children with no parents. They're gone. All of them. That's thirty to fifty million people...gone. Like that!"

She snapped her fingers and the grove had fallen so silent the sound echoed among the pines.

"Just leaves more for the survivors," Gibbons spoke up for the group. "We are the healthy ones. Else we'd be dead, like you said." He looked around them. "That's why we can make a decent town, all of us working together—"

"And you in charge?" snarled Jones, giving a big thumbs-down.

They were back to arguing.

Mom spoke to me: "We're going to Laura's in the morning."

As the leaders of the group argued, Mom and I stepped back, leaving the group.

Jimmy and Claire stood behind us, blocking our way.

"So it was a horrible week," Jimmy started again, "I felt weak, see, could barely eat anything, but no longer felt any pain in my lungs or coughed up anything. Worst coughing I ever had, like I had to stuff a lung back down my throat."

"I'm sorry to hear that," said Mom.

"Eventually my boss called, asked if I was ready to come back. I didn't feel hundred percent but not too bad. So I gave it a try. Six weeks after initial symptoms, I was at work listening to everyone tease me about my vacation. But I explained what happened, got sympathy."

"Well, that's good," said Mom, trying to bow out.

"Yeah, I remember it was holiday season, cold but no snow. News reports said a virus was coming, TV showed people toppling over. So they gave it a name, all scientific-like. Made it sound serious, to scare people—"

"Yes, well, that was a long time ago—"

"January, after everyone returned to work, more news came. With air routes everywhere, plenty of infected people spreading it. News reports alarming us as the number of cases overwhelmed medical facilities around the world. Death count rose." He gazed skyward as if reading an airplane banner. "Authorities begged people to stay home to reduce the spread. But many went about their usual affairs, no care in the world, 'til they got the cough from hell and couldn't catch a breath."

"I remember...."

Jimmy paused to take a deep breath. "I wondered why I had it so easy. I took care of myself, got medicine at my local drug store, put myself to bed. I recovered. I thought it must be something different. But reports listing the symptoms and progress matched what I experienced. Before anybody even named it. I recovered. Those that didn't recover by the stage I had it, they went into a whole new set of symptoms. So sad."

"A lot of sadness then...."

"But I per...priss...press...."

"Persevered."

"Yeah, that. I felt fine, couldn't fake it any longer, so I had to return to work. Since I was fully recovered – got sneers from my supervisor still not believing me – I was given hard labor by my supervisor, a young asshole liked to lord over me. I was stuck in back unpacking merchandise. Loads of pallets arriving every day from trucks. Never seemed to let up. He kept complaining, like it was God's wish to make our lives harder."

"It's been nice talking with you," said Mom.

"But as the virus arrived and workers called in sick, more work fell to me. Finally that asshole was out. Got it. Half our workers were coughing, half them calling in and not coming in. I stayed, got plenty overtime, made section leader. Couple weeks later, I had his job. He died. Lungs filled with fluid 'til he couldn't breathe."

"Sounds like your lucky day."

Mom took my hand, started to walk us away.

"Every day's a lucky day now, ma'am. Every day I wake up. I guess God's lookin out fer me."

10

IN WHICH MOM SEEKS AN APOLOGY

I awoke at the sound of Mom trying to start the car, the engine making a low growl but not turning over. She cursed under her breath, slapped the steering wheel.

It was a cloudy dawn outside, a hint of rain coming. The crowd from the previous night was gone, disappearing to wherever they lived among the pines.

"Mom? Where are we going?" I asked sleepily.

"Your Aunt Laura's." Her voice was rough, like she hadn't slept all night. Everything was packed in the car. She had moved Timmy over, turned him upright so I could put my seat back. But then she couldn't put her seat back.

I yawned. "But why so early?"

"Just want to get away before everyone wakes up. Before they ask more questions. Or tell more stories." She groaned. "But that last can of gasoline was bad, I think."

"Can we go on battery?"

"Yes, but I wanted to save that for after we run out of gas. The final miles of this trip."

She got out and opened the trunk quietly, then poured the remaining gasoline from the last canister into the fuel tank.

"Do we have enough?" I asked as she got back in the car.

"We'll see."

As Mom got the engine to start with an unhappy growl and sat back with a loud sigh, a big hand slammed against my window. A grizzled face pressed against the glass. It was that guy, Jimmy. Claire stood behind him a few steps.

"Take us with you," he moaned. "Please!"

Mom backed the car away, flashing a farewell smile. Jimmy jogged with us. Claire stood forlornly back where we had parked. Her hand went to her face, wiping away tears as Jimmy tried to hold on to our car. He eventually slipped and fell as Mom backed the car up the gravel drive to the road.

"We don't have room for them," said Mom. "They can see that. Besides, they'll do fine with the village."

Late in the evening the group had decided to name their new village Pineville.

"But, Mom...."

Of course, she was right. Better for them to stay in that group than try to get along with Mom.

We drove slowly, staying on the back country roads, with Mom watching for hidden dangers. Now it would be not only vagrants roaming the country looking for food and sex, but law enforcement looking for escapees to abuse and vagrants to shoot dead. It had begun, Mom said to the windshield but with me listening: the beginning of the end.

It was enough we endured those years in the city, with the increasing restrictions until we became prisoners in our own home – then no services, which forced us to flee. Get out before the rush, Mom said, like when a movie was coming to the end. You get up and skip the final credits. Now the real life movie was ending and we had left early.

Mom was right. Only thirty minutes driving and we came over a hill and saw the next town. It was aflame.

"Obviously, that's where your aunt lives," Mom quipped.

"What's burning?" I asked, genuinely alarmed.

"Looks like fires set by rioters and looters most likely. Then catches other buildings on fire. It's not from the factories."

Black smoke rose straight up on this calm morning as a few drops of rain spotted the windows.

"But we're not going into town," said Mom. "They live in a nice estate north of the town. Too nice for us. But we're going there anyway."

Like before, Mom found a forgotten road that skirted the town, slowing but not stopping at each intersection. Abandoned vehicles along the way. Some had bodies inside, sitting up in the driver's position, others with masked faces pressed against the windows. Mom paused to take a look. Blank faces, foam dried around their mouths, soaking through their masks. Bodies were strewn on the ground, bloated or burst, red with rash. No coyotes or ravens would dare eat them.

"Happy now?" asked Mom at my consternation.

"What?"

"You were asking why there weren't any bodies."

I shook my head. I guess it took time for people to die. A few days. Now they were everywhere. Like they'd all died at the same time. Airborne, maybe. I checked that my window was tight. Mom closed the vents. The car got warm. I wondered if we should put on the hazmat suits we had in the trunk.

"There it is," said Mom as we turned onto a smooth avenue that seemed more country lane than county highway.

A big iron gate announced that this property was owned by a wealthy family. The wrought iron arch spelled out *Ironwood*. We drove under the arch and up to the mansion. I vaguely recognized it from my childhood.

"I wonder if anyone's home," I said absently, then shivered at the thought of finding a similar situation as at my grandparents' farm.

We pulled up in front of the main entrance, a wide circular drive with a fountain in the middle, now off, surrounded by wilted flowers. The front of the house looked good, not run-down like so many places these days. Two tall columns held up a roof over the portico, flanked by overgrown bushes.

Mom scanned the windows. I watched behind us.

"She might recognize the car if she's looking out."

Mom got out, stood looking up at the windows. The house was neat, with rows of identical windows like a French palace.

"Should I ring the doorbell?" Mom was talking to herself, not me. "Knock on the door? Shout for her?" She turned to me. "Maybe we should go around back and have a look. Maybe she'll be there, her and her husband, lovers for eternity."

"Stop it, Mom. No more kidding."

"We have to lighten the mood. It's a form of resistance."

I got out of the car. "Resistance to what?"

"To everything happening." She told me to get the shotgun from the trunk, and some shells. "Never know what's behind door number two."

Mom wouldn't be caught unprepared. Checking the shotgun, she glanced back at me to make sure I had the pistol ready. I held it up, but not pointing it, and gave a nod. Satisfied, she proceeded to the front doors, up the stone steps to the portico.

I looked left and right, expecting vagrants to come rushing at us from the ends of the building but the morning was calm, sky gray with few birds daring to sing.

Mom tested the doors, found them locked. She pressed against them, banged the knockers softly then with louder raps, and stood back waiting.

We both listened, heard nothing inside the house.

Mom waved for me to go around the side of the mansion to the back. She would go around the other side and we would meet in the backyard. I really hoped we wouldn't find any bodies there.

I held up the pistol like I learned from cop streams before the pandemic. Mom corrected my form.

As I went, the house seemed unoccupied – but why would they go away, to escape the coming chaos, when they had such a nice house to stay in? I looked up at the windows, identical curtains neatly folded to the sides. I was impressed, never believing I had a rich aunt and uncle. This big house was like a fortress, protected from the world. Meanwhile, Mom and I lived in a less-secure two-bedroom apartment in the city, near the campus. It was a good neighborhood but a few blocks in any direction was dangerous.

Aunt Laura's family lived in luxury. I couldn't imagine them taking off as we had done, leaving their home behind to seek a safer place. So they must have died. I pondered what I'd find as I turned the corner and gazed into the backyard. A wide veranda ran along the back of the house. An empty pool. A tennis court. Beyond the wooden slat fence was a pasture with a small barn, enough for a pair of horses. But the pasture was empty.

I saw Mom round the other end of the house, shotgun held up, ready. Seeing me, she lowered the gun. We met at the steps to the veranda.

"The pool hasn't been cleaned in months," Mom remarked.

"No horses in the pasture," I added.

"Perhaps they ate them," said Mom with a snicker.

She tested the French doors there on the veranda: locked. She pounded her fist on them, shook her hand, then shouted up at the windows:

"Laura! It's me, your baby sister!"

We waited a moment, about ready to leave, when we heard a window crack open above us. It must've been a long time since it was opened because it took a while to get it up enough for a woman to poke her head out.

"What are you doing here?" called the woman.

"Came to check on you," said Mom. She threw her arm at me. "You remember Sandy? He's all grown up now. And just in time – I mean for a world like this. Not a moment too soon."

The woman stared down at us. "Wait a minute."

Yes, all grown up. A couple inches taller than Mom now.

Someone came to the French doors, unlocked them, held one open for us. It was a girl, looking maybe five. She hid behind the open door. As we passed through the doorway, she retreated as if in fear. Her dirty shirt and shorts seemed to have been worn for a while, her dark hair unwashed and unbrushed, her dark eyes suspicious over the top of her facemask. She made sure to stay six feet away from us.

Inside, the rooms were bare, no furniture. Pieces of furniture were stacked beside the fireplace. There were no signs of looting, only the organized, intentional arrangement of the disassembled items. Dusty paintings remained on the walls, vases intact, a fern in the corner wilted, a large Persian carpet curling at the corners. I looked through the large room to the front doors and could see our car outside through the frosted glass.

We stepped further into the large hall and came to a wide curving staircase, like something from a movie where the heiress mocks her lowly guests at the start of the evening's festivities, then descends to their level for the debauchery – Mom would say. But it's not debauchery if it's on a beach under a summer sun.

"Well, well, well," said the lady of the house, posing at the top of the staircase. A facemask hung from one ear, and she raised it over her face and hooked it on the other ear. Thus protected, she descended the elegant stairs, step by slow step, as if timing her descent so we might depart before she had to deal with us. "Lost everything, I'm supposing. Come for our crumbs, have you?"

Aunt Laura was well-dressed – or tried to look it. She held herself regally; I understood how Mom had grown apart from her. Laura wore a silky red and black dressing gown.

"No masks?" asked Aunt Laura.

"We're not infected," Mom responded.

"So you say...."

Mom waited until her sister was on the same level as us.

"You look well," said Mom, standing without a mask. "How are the kids? You doing all right? And Henry?"

Aunt Laura sneered at the questions.

"I need a drink."

"As usual," Mom muttered.

"It's not what you think," said Laura, being snippy. "I quit. Yes, actually quit. But these times demand it."

"I do quite agree," Mom replied, a little Southern slipping out, like she had worked hard to keep it hidden all her life.

Aunt Laura went to the glass-doored liquor cabinet at the side of the grand hall and prepared herself a cocktail. The clinking echoed through the empty room. She raised a bottle to Mom, asking if she wanted refreshment. Mom shook her head.

"No, I stopped drinking completely by the time my Bootsy started kindergarten," said Laura, pouring slowly. "The other parents, well, let's say they strongly urged me to stop for the sake of my child." I could hear the honey in her voice.

The girl who'd opened the French doors came out of hiding at the sound of her name. Her facemask had slipped down. Laura gave the nervous girl a dismissive glance.

"Don't mind her. She's got the autism. Can't be helped. Now there's no school for such children. What a pity. Now I must mind her myself – keep her out of trouble. But trouble seems to come every day." She looked up, her eyes focused on me. "And your boy? Is he normal?"

"I'm normal," I spoke up, stepping forward. "In fact, I was in college, studying Sociology, when this latest wave started." Then I remembered there was a pistol in my hand, so I made sure to lower it. "We just came to see if you were okay."

"We're fine, dear," said Laura. She shifted her robe, which had fallen open a bit, showing skin.

"Where are the others?" asked Mom.

Laura swung her head back, fluffed her hair with her hand. "Others? You must mean the twins, Sammy and Tammy. They were sent to boarding school, naturally – different schools, one for biological girls and one for biological boys. Last I heard they were both doing well, developing their proper identities, with Sammy accepting his gayness, showing an inclination to transition. And Tammy becoming a fine lesbian, rather more a dyke than fem, her teachers report. After all, it's the focus of the curriculum. Many families today are urging their teens to transition. Not everyone is born into the right body, you know. Unfortunately. Strange how you and I were. Perhaps it's the virus. Ah! But of course you know that already, what with you being at a college."

She was gazing up at the ceiling by then, mask hanging from only one ear again. Mom and I looked up, too, and noted the large Baroque painting of angels and cherubs.

"Anyways, haven't heard from either for quite some time, nor from school administrators. Who knows what's been happening to them. No grade reports yet from last term. Postal issues, I'm sure. And the email is off. Everything's broken. Communication is quite impossible now."

"I'm sure they're both fine," said Mom, gazing once more at her sister. "The schools would be sure to protect students. Different for us. We've been at home with virtual school, all classes online." Mom grinned at me. "It's hard enough to keep this boy on task—"

"Some dirty men caught her," Laura said, lowering her glass. She chinned at the sad-looking girl. "Hasn't been the same since. Refuses to wash or wear fresh clothes. Of course, no way to report it. Police won't do anything."

Mom showed alarm. "What? She was attacked?"

"Playing outside. You know how men are." Laura glared at me like a challenge. "Especially now. No law to temper their actions. Do as they please." She rubbed her tearless eyes. "We all have to submit to the violence put upon us now. Submit and live or fight and die. It's all much too dramatic for my tastes."

I watched Mom soften and go to her sister, hesitate. It took a moment but they hugged – an awkward dance, trying to find a comfortable position. Laura cried into Mom's shoulder.

As the sisters held each other, I stepped back to give them space. I looked at the messy girl and pitied her. Her fearful eyes studied me, probably determining if I were friend or foe. I set the pistol on the floor and dropped down, sitting cross-legged, leaning back on my hands. I looked up, admiring the fancy molding and the ceiling's artwork, then back to the girl.

"Are you Bootsy?" I called in a gentle voice.

She hid behind the door, peeking into the room.

"I'm Sandy. I'm your cousin. I guess we never met before. How old are you?"

She held up her hand, counting fingers, deciding on all five. A smile flickered across her face.

"Five? That's great. I'm nineteen. Too much for using fingers." I pointed to my mother. "That's my mom. My mom and your mom are sisters. So me and you are related."

The girl nodded, either understanding me or just being a good girl and going along with whatever I was saying.

"You got any brothers and sisters?" I asked, too innocently.

Mom said there were five kids.

She thought over my question and her face became upset.

"I'm sorry." Maybe my question brought up bad memories.

She rubbed her eyes and ran away.

"Let her be," said Laura from the other side of the room. They had parted but stood holding hands. "She's traumatized." Laura turned to Mom. "We lost Kenneth. And Cutler."

"Kenneth? I thought his name was Kevin. Sorry."

"Cutler was taken by her father. After Kenneth...died. He insisted it was for the best. He *implied* she didn't belong with me, her own mother." She sniffled back tears, acting like it was rude to cry in front of guests. "Cutler always insisted she was female so I tried to use the right pronouns: *she* and *her*. Poor dear, too young to know what gender *she* truly should be. We had a discussion, you might say. I tried to appeal to her father's sense of justice. I supported all the movements, did my part, after all. Yet he gave me no choice. I couldn't fight him—"

"Henry?"

Laura lowered her head. "Of course."

When she looked up, she sniffled and pulled a folded tissue from the pocket of her robe, dabbed her nose.

"Way things are now, Cutler's likely in a better situation than if she'd stayed here."

"And Kenneth?" asked Mom. "Virus?"

Laura froze, her teary face a compilation of seven emotions.

"Kenneth...." She sobbed for a minute, hands covering her face. "He was killed...by a gang of zombies."

"Zombies...?" Mom made a quizzical face. "Oh, you can't mean actual zombies."

"I call them zombies. Brain-dead animals certainly. Acting like animals. Just seeking food. Don't even care about sex. I...I tried to get them to let him be. I offered myself to them to save him. But they didn't want that. They wanted food. But I didn't have any. So they took him...out there, to the yard there, and they...killed him. Butchered him—"

"Oh my god, Laura!"

"Stabbed him, then cut him apart. Like a hog. They made a fire and put pieces over the flame. Had a feast. Like a bunch of cavemen around a camp fire. Is that what you wanted to hear? I couldn't watch, couldn't listen to them eating...."

She fell to her knees, threw her hands to her face.

"But this pandemic hasn't been going on for too long," said Mom, kneeling beside her sister. "I mean, they couldn't have been affected that way so fast, turning into monsters."

"It's been going on longer out here." Laura sobbed. "We had some of the first cases. Different areas got different strains. And different vaccines, too. Had different effects. They said it was the vaccines, something wrong with them, made people go insane, turn them into crazed monsters. Yes, like zombies! Not risen from death perhaps, yet walking mindless like corpses. No thinking, no reasoning, no sense of morality. Only hunger."

Laura broke into loud sobs, crying for a while as Mom held her, brushed her hair with her hand.

"Mom?" I called gently. "Should I unload the car?"

She nodded, so I went out the front doors to the car, glad to be away from that scene.

11

IN WHICH MOM DOESN'T GET AN APOLOGY

I unloaded the car, setting everything inside the front doors. Mom looked over as I gently set down Timmy, turning the tuba on its bell and leaning it against a wall. Then Mom took her older sister by the hand and they went up the big staircase, leaving me alone with the little girl.

"You ever see a tuba?" I asked the girl. She didn't react.

I unzipped the soft case and pulled out Timmy. I gave a few wipes to the metal and brought it into my lap as I sat on the floor. Sticking the mouthpiece in place, I hesitated. It had been a while since Mom had taught me anything. I pressed my lips against the cold metal and blew a long stream of air through the beast. Mom had the lungs to fill Timmy, but not me. I tried a quiet note, hoping Mom wouldn't hear.

The girl came out from behind the door, sat on the floor the required distance from me. She didn't smile yet seemed calm and interested. Her mask with cartoon characters dropped off of her nose. I played a few notes. The first startled her. I played a scale slowly and she leaned in with delight. I played a grunt in the low register and she scooted away in fright.

"Sorry." I tried again, just a simple song, and my effort was rewarded with a slight grin.

Gradually my concert elicited clapping, not as applause but in spontaneous thrill. I wondered if she'd ever heard music in this house, a place so grim, filled with disappointment, streaked with violence.

I stopped mid-song when I saw Mom descending the staircase. When she stood beside the banister at the bottom, one hand on the scroll, she gave me an approving nod.

"Nicely done," she said. "Of course you're clearly in need of practice. But I'm glad you remember your lessons."

I regarded the girl. "Just wanted to entertain my cousin."

"That was a kind gesture. I've clearly raised you well. A good man."

"Mom...," I moaned, like I did whenever she praised me.

She waved at me to set Timmy aside, like we had to talk. I turned him upside-down on the bell, leaning against the wall again. Bootsy remained in her spot but as Mom and I talked she got up and wandered off.

"Your aunt's had a rough time of it."

Mom explained in a low voice how Laura's husband Henry had been trapped in the first lockdown with his secretary. He and Laura were in phone contact, but neither could leave where they were – which for Henry was the secretary's apartment. She often heard the sounds of sex whenever he answered her calls. But she was already dabbling with the gardener. Mom rolled her eyes, like it was a typical story. They were separated long enough for Bootsy to be born – in a hospital, after the lockdown ended, and where she got the first vaccine, though she skipped the second and, more importantly, the third, which had the bad side-effects.

Henry never returned. Oh, he came for his things a few times, but it was arranged that she wouldn't be home then. He refused the vaccine, even after his secretary, Amber-Faye, got the virus and had a difficult time. With her weak for months, he left her for Bonnie, his new secretary, as manufacturing at the plant slowed with the lockdowns. Had to lay off hundreds of workers.

"She hasn't heard from him for more than a year. Thinks he's probably dead. Doesn't matter with the whole world crumbling. She's made a life here."

"So...umm...did you get your apology?" I asked Mom when she paused. "What you said she did...."

Mom shook her head. "That didn't come up." She changed her face, got even darker. "Listen to me. This isn't a good place for us to stay, not like I thought. In fact, it's worse than I ever could've imagined. We need to keep moving."

"But where?"

"I guess to your Aunt Jackie's."

"Your other sister? Where do they live?"

"Up north."

"Is that where the beach is?"

Suddenly Laura stood at the entrance to the great hall, her face messy from crying, glaring at Mom.

"That beach!" Laura stammered. "Such a curse."

"I only went there for fun — to try out the nude beach for the first time. And I took a friend — though she didn't follow through with our plan. Then everybody blamed me for all the shit that happened after. But I have this wonderful young man."

I smiled at her remark.

"You think you're so innocent," cawed Laura. "But you're not. You started it — everything." She turned to me, as though I was the jury. "You see, your mother got pregnant, but we all thought it was because of Dad — not a random man on the beach. That she was just lying to cover for Dad, making up a story. So we hated Dad." She glared at Mom. "We all hated him. It was your selfish, silly behavior that brought ruin to our family!"

Mom sat sullen on the floor, then put her hand to her face.

"So I shall never apologize," said Laura sternly.

Mom looked up at her. "And I'll never ask for an apology."

A moment of silent tension.

"So we're good now?" I spoke. "Everything back in balance?"

Mom cracked a grin, but Laura spun around, stalked off.

"I still say people wouldn't go zombie so fast," Mom started, "not like in movies. This virus doesn't do that. Nor the vaccines. Make you die, sure, but not turn you into a zombie. No, the ones that attacked Kenneth must've been plain ol' hungry vagrants not caring about laws or morality, just acting on animal instinct after who knows how long being on their own while society collapses into chaos. I mean, how long will it be without grocery stores or fast-food before you kill a child for dinner? This is the new normal, as they like to say. Every man...and woman, child, dog or cat...for themselves."

"There's no fear of arrest anymore," I added.

"And there's no respect for authority. Which may be a good thing, the way authority has changed." She pushed herself up. "Anyway, we need to go."

"But I just unloaded the car."

"That's fine. We'll stay the night. Maybe another. Need to bring in the things that might get stolen, anyway. Need to be smart. Stay alert, Sandy."

Mom had a look in her eyes, like she was already locked and loaded.

"I think there may be some gas in her car. Big gas-guzzler like hers, the kind that are banned, has lots of gas. She never drives. Let's see if it's still good."

The girl popped in, looking around the door, displaying a smile she waited for us to notice. I waved her to join us and she did. She really needed a bath. And food.

"So this one," said Mom, gazing down at the forlorn child, "definitely has the look of José, the gardener. Who's the family whore now?"

"Mom, be nice. It's not her fault. I mean Bootsy."

"Of course." She lowered her voice, tried to sound gentle for the sake of the child. "But I just can't stand how uppity she is. She was the ringleader in getting everyone to turn against me. I've tried to forgive her – especially since I've done well despite them."

"Mom, they're family. Our family." I regarded her with warm eyes, really wanting her to reconcile with her sister. We were in hard times now. We needed each other, even with our flaws. "Please make things right with your sister. It's the right thing to do."

"Right thing, huh?"

I nodded.

"We can't take them with us. No room in the car."

"There's room." I took a deep breath. "There's room if we leave Timmy behind."

* * *

Laura remained upstairs and I could hear her sobs as she and Mom discussed everything from the past. I tried to ignore them as I played with Bootsy, making up games in which one of us hid and the other seeked. She smiled as she chased me. I was happy to help her have some fun to break up her miserable existence.

There was a knock at the front doors and I turned to see two dark figures through the frosted glass. They stood like they were invited guests waiting for a butler to let them in.

Bootsy froze, stared at the doors, and ran away.

The figures seemed to know someone was at home. Like they came by often. They didn't try to break in.

I got up, thought of getting the pistol, and stood before the doors, half-expecting them to be kicked in at any moment.

Down the grand staircase hurriedly stepped Aunt Laura. Mom followed with less urgency.

"Don't answer," Laura cautioned me.

That made sense. No telling who these two were, or what they might do. But I was mistaken.

Laura wanted to open the doors herself.

"Don't worry," said Laura, pulling on her facemask. "I know these two. They bring us food."

Mom stood behind Laura as she opened the doors.

Two men wearing homemade cloth masks greeted her like they were delivery men, calling her "Ma'am". The older one, with a beer belly, thick arms, and a scraggily beard sprouting out from the sides of his mask, held out a sack. The younger one was taller and thinner, carrying a sack that looked heavy.

"This is all we could get fer ya," said the older man, offering the sack, "but it's all fresh. Set it aside myself."

The younger man set down his sack, adjusted his mask, as the older man glanced at Mom, then at me, back to Laura. She picked up the cloth sack, opened it, gazed inside. The second sack had rolls of toilet paper sitting at the top.

"Sure hope it's enough," said the older man, eyes blinking over the top of his mask. "Ya know...fer us ta go upstairs and all." He gave Mom a quick look.

Laura appeared nervous, not because of these men visiting but that Mom and I witnessed their transaction.

"Yes, looks quite good," said Laura. She lowered her mask enough to sniff the contents of the sack. "Quite good."

She handed the sack to Mom, then took the older man by the hand before he could straighten his mask. She led him up the grand staircase, neither hurrying or hesitating.

We watched them ascend to heaven and out of sight. The young man fixed his mask securely as he stood by the doors. After a minute, he sat down on the floor to wait.

It was a large house but mostly empty so every sound echoed through the rooms and hallways. We could hear the legs of a bed upstairs scooting against the floor, the noise of the headboard banging against the wall. Mom made a face, not quite angry but definitely not happy.

"I must play," she announced, and went to Timmy.

She sat on the floor and played a few warm-up flourishes, running scales around the circle of fifths.

"How about a little Gordon Jacobs?"

She played Jacobs' *Tuba Suite* with the piano accompaniment only in her head.

I leaned against the entryway to the great hall for a while, not interested in any small talk with this other young man. By the third movement, I had taken a seat on the floor, too, my gaze switching between Mom and this other man. Dressed in jeans and button shirt, fit for the fall season. I guessed the older man was his father, or uncle, or his boss. He grinned whenever our eyes happened to meet, like he had a secret he wanted to share. Maybe he wondered if I was vaccinated. Or he was considering if that was what I was wondering about him. Or if I'd made a delivery earlier.

Just as Mom concluded the suite, Laura appeared, descended the grand staircase, her gown flowing behind and not quite closed in front. The man she'd entertained stepped awkwardly behind her, struggling to put on his mask. At the bottom, mask in place, he thanked her, gave a little bow, straightened up and tucked in his shirt tails.

"And...I was hoping," he stammered, "maybe you could see to my boy?" He gave Mom another glance like he was seeking her approval. Mom hid her scowl behind Timmy's wide bell. "He's of age now...and...we'll be bringing ya even better food next time, ma'am."

Laura seemed to purse her lips beneath her mask, nodding ever so slightly. She took the young man's hand, tugging him up the staircase as if trying to get him out of sight before Mom could offer an amused smirk. Soon came noise from above. Mom started a new piece of music.

"She's a real darlin," said the beefy man, pointing his chin up the staircase. "Such a sweetie."

"And you bring her food?" I asked, so obvious.

"Yessir." He tried to hold back a smile. "Since the pandemic started. It's purely bizness arrangement. We're essential workers. But money ain't got no value now. So we gotta barter."

I nodded, understanding this new economy better than I could have learned it in college. As I watched Mom playing Timmy, I calculated how much a song might be worth today. You could buy a song download online for a few cents now. How would I get food after our supplies ran out? I had no practical skills to offer in exchange and nothing to sell but my ability to work, to labor for someone else.

Mom kept playing even after Laura and her young partner returned to the front doors, posed with awkward grins, happy at the day's activities. She thanked them for the sacks of food and supplies. They thanked her for the intimacy.

After she saw them out, locking the doors behind them, Aunt Laura turned to Mom, found her hiding behind Timmy.

"This isn't for you," said Laura in a rather harsh voice, eyes on me. "It's barely enough for me. And Bootsy. She doesn't eat much."

"I figured," I replied.

"They didn't know you were here, so.... Besides, it may be they couldn't bring more. The store is always short of goods, shelves bare, but they set aside some of the best for me. And we have a certain arrangement." She became weepy, letting her gown fall open more. "Please don't think badly of me."

"I don't, Aunt Laura."

"Thank you."

Then she drew her gown closed, put a hand to her face and realized she'd forgotten her mask. She hurried up the stairs.

Mom came to the end of the song, held the final note a bit, until her breath ran out in a poorly formed whimper.

Setting Timmy gently aside, she regarded me, as if saying 'So that's your aunt' with a dismissive chuckle.

"We have to take her with us," I spoke up after a moment. "I don't think she'll survive if she stays. Eventually someone's not gonna be able to give her food but they'll still want her, umm, services."

"Services," Mom echoed, nodding to herself. "Yes, I suppose that's what it'll come to. Eventually. We have no more credit cards to use, not even the old cash, nor collections of rare coins, much less a gold coin or two. You can't eat gold. Not to mention all the electronic currency everyone was crazy for a few years ago then lost it all with the war crash."

She wiped off Timmy, found a smudge on the metal from her moist grip and massaged it away.

"What are we gonna do?" I waited a moment, let Mom clean Timmy, feeling the silence of the house. "Pretty soon, there won't be any signs of civilization, like groceries or pharmacies, gas stations or...anything. Just us. And your damn tuba."

"It's not a *damn* tuba," Mom grumbled. "It's the last vestige of civilization. A reminder than we used to be better – a lot better: we could make music. And that's important. It's a way to make music. A demonstration of the arts and crafts of a human society, that values a lot more than simply the next crumb of bread. It's a demonstration of thinking beyond chaos, of planning a future – of *making* a future! This thing will play music! Who would think to make such a thing? We will have music in the future. And we will dance and sing because we won't want for anything, and now we have the time to sing and dance. That's what Timmy means!"

12

IN WHICH MOM SEES THE FUTURE

"Years from now," Mom continued her high and mighty diatribe, "people will look at this old tuba and ponder what it could've been used for, what meaning it might've had, why people in the past bothered to craft such a device, and perhaps they will try to make sounds with it. Figuring out the purpose of the valves, they may learn how to play different notes. They might put different notes together and invent their own songs, and find delight in making music. They may discover pages covered in strange marks which are instructions for how to play a piece of music. In working out the marks they may enjoy more music. And, yes, play it on this strange artifact they've found: this once-silver tuba, now dull-gray but holding its mellow tone in full, from years past and for many years into the future."

The rest of us were eating from a meager ration of snacks for our dinner. Laura had half a roast chicken, no longer warm when it was delivered but still edible. A hunk of dry bread, cube of cheese, and an old apple. She divided all of it between her and Bootsy but gave Mom a drumstick. She gave one side of the drumstick to me. The fresh meat tasted so good after all the jerky we'd been living on.

"We could fit them in somehow," I said, wiping my lips. "We can't just leave them here."

Mom rolled her eyes, glanced at Bootsy, who was playing with her food: a small box of cereal she had dumped on the floor. She had already downed a tiny carton of milk, making a face like it tasted funny but finished it anyway at her mother's insistence. Even bad food was better than no food, explained Laura. And she had worked for it, we all knew. In that way, this small offering was indeed an offering on the altar of pragmatism – doing what had to be done just to survive.

"It's not far, is it?" I asked Mom. "We could stuff the car full of everything if it's just a short distance. Don't need to worry about comfort. Bootsy can sit on my lap."

Laura got up from the floor, stood poised as though she was making a big pronouncement.

"If your plan is to go to Jackie's, I'm not interested," said Laura with a straight face. "We've not spoken in years."

Mom rolled her eyes again. So much drama in our family, she seemed to suggest.

"Laura," said Mom, "you may be getting by for now but it won't stay like this. Everything is going to get much worse, not better. Real soon, too. Likely not until after our lifetime will it ever be better again. And, I'm sure you know.... Well, let's face it, at your age, your looks will be fading. Then will you still be able to barter your 'services' for food? Will you want to keep doing that?"

"You're such a smug bitch," said Laura, using her honey voice. "It's what I learned from you: how to be a whore. I suppose we've all had a new normal to deal with. I mean this economy – without money, banks, or any system of commerce. Just a barter system." She chewed her lip. "You see my degree in Economics paid off."

"Yes, you're prepared. You were always destined to be a rich man's wife, helping run his business as best you can but mostly staying home and raising kids. And you've done that, haven't you? Well done, Laura."

"Fuck you, as the essential workers say. But for us, I'll say 'bless your little heart'."

Laura gathered up Bootsy, crying as they left the last few cereal pieces on the floor, and departed up the grand staircase.

Mom started to roll her eyes again but stopped.

I understood: pride would help them survive, make them

stand tough and never give in. Laura was ten years older than Mom, used to being pampered but forced to find ways to survive.

"I feel for Bootsy," said Mom, "but I can't see Laura being any more than a burden."

"Burden? She's your big sister."

"Sandy, listen. We have to think strategically. This isn't a field trip, or a vacation at Grandma and Grampa's. It's a journey to somewhere we can live, where we can survive this long flu season. To wait out the worst of this pandemic. If she's not able to help with that, maybe it's better to let her do her own thing. She's already chosen that."

"But Mom...."

"Did you hear me? You and I have skills. We can survive. But not her. She'd starve if not for her willingness to spread her legs. Is that a life? Wake up each day hoping for a delivery of food? At least I can be entertaining, play tunes on Timmy. For practical purposes, I also can hunt and fish given the right equipment. My grandfather taught me that."

"But I don't have any of those skills. I'm just a college boy." I chuckled but sadly. "I was learning about groups of people and their interactions. It's called Sociology."

"That's perfect." Mom frowned. "A boy who shies away from crowds wants to study groups of people. It makes sense. Face your fears. That's why I wanted you to stay with hard science."

"Like I can mix chemicals out here?"

"Someday, yes."

A new knock on the door startled us. It was dark outside so we were suddenly frightened. Mom moved across the floor to get Officer Tanner's pistol and I got the other pistol. More knocks on the door. Without any power, the house was dark. No sign of being occupied – except our car out front. But we had made a small fire in the fireplace which lit the room enough. Did they see our light and come for something?

Mom stood up before the doors, pistol aimed.

"Who's there?" she called.

A flutter of slippers shuffling down the staircase: my aunt, her gown flowing, waving her hands to shoo Mom away.

Laura looked out through the side glass, got a hand wave, and unlocked the doors, swung one open. In stepped another man. She hugged him, then spun him around, keeping her arm on his waist.

"This is Earl," she announced brightly.

"Howdy." He gave a flick of his hand in greeting.

The man was about Laura's age and wore his clean, pressed prison guard uniform, brown with yellow badges, an employee of the local corrections institute. His big belly made the buttons work hard. His red beard was trimmed but his head was balding.

"This is my baby sister," Aunt Laura said to Earl, "and her son. From out west. Ignore the godawful tuba."

Before Mom could say anything, Laura ushered the beefy man upstairs. Half-way up she paused, sent him on up to a room he apparently was already familiar with. She gazed defiantly down at us.

"Earl's my beau," she said. "He protects me – if that's what you're worried about. I'm fine. I'll *be* fine. He doesn't need to bring me anything either. If y'all know what I mean."

Then she disappeared. Mom set down her pistol and took up her tuba, playing a series of laments. The noise above required accompaniment. Bootsy appeared and sat listening.

In the morning, Earl stumbled down the stairs and drove his van away.

✳ ✳ ✳

More thoughts and prayers for the missing. Another day full of pondering, planning, discussions. In the evening they ate their food and Mom and I ate ours. Occasionally smiles passed between us like we were one happy family with plenty to eat. Later, when it was dark, we had nothing to do but go to sleep. I tried to sleep, but with Mom talking with her sister long into the night, and me waking at every rattle of the doors when the wind blew, thinking someone was breaking in, I really couldn't. It was a rough few nights, but finally we were ready to leave.

"Goodbye for now," I said, closing the doors behind us after we loaded the car. The sunrise painted the house pink through the rear patio doors. I hated to leave. I wanted to get to know my aunt better and play more with my cousin. But Mom insisted it was best to depart before they awoke.

Mom started the car, checked the gauges. We rolled around the driveway and out to the road.

On this cool morning patches of low-lying fog spotted the fields we passed.

"We're almost on battery," Mom announced miles down the road. "I prefer to save gas for emergency."

"We can make it to Aunt Jackie's?"

"Should."

It felt strange to be on the road again. Though it lacked the vestiges of a wealthy country house, I felt comfortable there. It seemed like a family home, even with all the arguments between my mom and my aunt. The road, however, was full of dangers.

At any moment we might come to a roadblock, forced to stop, then be overrun by vagrants. Or another officer of the law might want to see what he could get from an odd vehicle passing by. We had to stay alert, be ready for anything. Mom liked to say there weren't any more laws to protect us; we were on our own. I kept the pistol ready.

"I hope Aunt Jackie's better off than Aunt Laura," I said after a lengthy silence. "I only remember you telling me about how lucky she was, living in the big house with the horses. I think you were jealous. At least back then."

"Well, Sandy, I was living in a cheap two-bedroom flat with a nosey son who liked to dream of living in a big house with horses." She gave a sideways glance, let a smirk burst upon her face. "I got you a dog instead. That lasted...how many months?"

"Sorry, Mom." I looked out my window, the trees and fields flying by as we picked up speed. "Aunt Jackie's still the same, isn't she?"

"She has a more modest life," said Mom, eyes on the road. "You know how the life of a painter goes. Always scrambling for art supplies. Sometimes you do some modeling to pay for supplies. Nude modeling." She laughed. "Similar to Laura. A kind of barter system."

Mom cringed suddenly. I turned to look out the windshield but saw nothing alarming. Mom had a distressed face, put her hand to her belly. She quickly pulled the car over to the side of the road, a spot with trees to offer shade.

"Thank the goddesses," she cried, tumbling out of the car.

She grabbed tissues from her pack in the back seat. Forgetting me, she turned, dropped her pants and swabbed between her legs. The used tissues she dropped to the ground were red.

"I've never been so glad to see blood before. See it, Sandy? Menstrual blood. I'm not pregnant."

She seemed ready to dance in celebration.

"Get my pack. There's a box of tampons that Laura gave me — only she doesn't know she gave them to me."

I had to smile. Mom was such a badass baby sister.

"So I'm guessing that, for women, tampons come right after air, water, and food on that hierarchy of needs."

"You need air every few seconds, water every day, food every few days, but tampons or napkins each month. You're almost right. In the old days — and future days — women stuffed cloth up their vaginas and just washed the cloth out every day. We've been around a long, long time, and so has Aunt Flo."

"Aunt Flo? You have another sister?"

"The worst one. It's 'flow' as in F-L-O-W."

"Oh." Always teasing me. No wonder I've grown up bent. "I get it. Hah hah."

Mom shook her head as she dealt with her issue in front of me. I'd never watched her do that. When I was a little kid she would prance around the apartment with no clothes on, and do whatever she wanted to do without worrying about me seeing her. Then she went conservative and covered up while I went through puberty. As I reached adulthood, she loosened her rules.

I was an adult and wouldn't care if I saw her naked or putting in a tampon beside the car on the side of the road. It was early morning in a brave new world.

"That sleazebag is off the hook," she muttered.

I stared at her, hitching up her pants, what she called yoga pants though I'd never seen her do yoga.

I thought of what she said, felt an ache in my gut.

"Actually he's dead. I shot him."

My words were neither proud or sad, just a fact.

"You're a good boy." She fixed her pants, adjusted her shirt.

"I don't wanna be that kind of boy. I keep thinking about it."

Mom looked up, focused on me. "And without you doing what you did, your mother might be pregnant with a vagrant's baby, or else be dead. You did good."

"But Mom...."

"Remember what I said?" Her eyes narrowed. "Save yourself. Always. Leave me behind. I know we didn't work that out when you had to act, but now that we understand each other, you know what to do. You got it? Leave me. Like we left Laura and Bootsy behind. If you come to save me we both might die – and that's not good for either of us. Then there's no chance of us going onward in the world, seeing the next sunrise. Better to save one than none. Got it?"

I nodded, feeling ashamed for thinking like a kid. Got to be tough. Cold and cruel. Just to survive.

"I won't be around forever." She winked. "You have to be able to take care of yourself eventually anyway, so you might as well toughen up. Like my grandfather always liked to say: 'You make your own path and some idiot will follow now that a path's been made.'"

She paused a minute to reminisce.

"Yes, he really said that – mostly when we had to break our way through brush to get to his favorite fishing spot. He was a good man. Not like now, with all the sex-crazed bastards running amok and no law keeping them in check – as if laws *would* keep them in check, instilling fear of prison time – yes, TV and three-a-days – like that was a deterrent for a determined criminal."

She saw I was stunned by her words. I could get scared easily when she talked in a serious tone. She recognized my vulnerable side, what my teachers pointed out before my school went virtual. I had to take some tests to confirm it. Mom said I was special but in a good way. I just needed some extra guidance, that's all. It had nothing to do with my intelligence. It was more about getting the social graces right.

"You're wrong, Mom." I stopped, realizing I'd spoken out too boldly and she might get upset even though supposedly I was an adult. "You're so negative. I know there are good men — just as there are bad women. You can't just say that about the whole society. We're all individuals."

"I know that, Sandy."

"There are good men out there. Like Earl. He wasn't mean, not a criminal. Maybe not the cleanest or most polite guy but he loves Aunt Laura, I think. And she loves him."

"And you, Sandy. You're one of those good men, but there are fewer of your kind with every passing day. People get desperate, slip down to their base instincts eventually, their social training falling away."

"We know right from wrong. We act for good, not for selfish or temporary, or spontaneous reasons — like animals, you say. In this new normal that kind of men *and women* act and react on a primitive level — I studied that in my Sociology class — and go first after food then go after reproduction. It's nature forcing them to pass on their genes before they die."

"Yep. We're all just DNA couriers in the end. No, Sandy. I doubt those we've encountered are thinking of genetics."

"There are bad ones in every group," I said, "but probably most are good."

"Okay, I get it. We've just been unfortunate to run into the bad ones. It's our bad luck. Could be worse if we went on the highway and got stuck in a jam, or drove into the center of town seeking men to help us." She fake-cried. "Oh, a poor helpless woman and her poor young son! Let's offer assistance. She can pay us in the usual way. And the youth? He can join our gang and do what we do, or else we'll cut him up for barbeque—"

"Stop it!"

"Sandy, I know all that."

She smiled at me, trying to reassure me, but I couldn't meet her eyes.

"The good ones we don't need to worry about. We can't act as though every man we meet is good. Aside from how he dresses or acts, how can we tell which kind he is? Even the saintly Officer Tanner acted professional for five minutes."

✳ ✳ ✳

Mom took the long way, it seemed, despite being threatened with having to go on battery. She never wanted to make things simple.

We were discussing what to do about Aunt Laura and Bootsy, and that there would be room in the car if she'd taken Freddy, the smaller F tuba, instead of Timmy, the large B-flat tuba. Mom said Timmy was more valuable, an heirloom, and the F tuba was only for high register compositions – for cheaters – but they didn't have a good low register that most music required of tubas.

Mom wasn't comfortable sitting up so we switched drivers and she took the opportunity to lay back. Soon after, we mounted a steep hill. Mom always cautioned to slow approaching the crest, not knowing what might be on the other side. We were talking about Bootsy, comparing her level of autism with mine. Mom said we'd see what the situation was like at Jackie's, then decide to go back for her. Mom would give Aunt Laura another chance.

At the top of the hill we could see a cop car on the side of the road ahead, doors open on both sides. Lights off, no siren. Mom and I looked at each other. I hit the brakes as we came up to it.

"Pull over." Mom craned her neck. "Maybe there's something we can use."

I pulled over in front of the car, backed up to it.

Mom got out.

The sheriff's car wasn't old, hadn't been in a wreck. The open doors made it seem like a patrol stop was active. But there wasn't anyone around. I waited in the driver's seat with the engine off, scanning the road ahead and behind, and the forest across from us, as Mom taught me to do.

"Oh my god!" Mom was at the edge of the slope falling away from the road. "Get away!" she shouted and ran down the slope, waving her arms.

I saw a coyote dash away.

Getting out of the car, I rushed down to Mom. Someone in a sheriff's deputy uniform lay in the grass, clearly wounded. When I got there I saw it was a woman – a female trooper. She seemed barely alive.

"Don't look," said Mom, dropping to her knees in the grass. She searched for what to do, examining the wounds.

I wouldn't know what to do either for such serious injuries. The female deputy lay on her back, in shock, eyes darting around, arms and legs not moving. Her uniform shirt had been ripped open, her bra cut apart, chest exposed. Her trousers were down at her ankles, caught on her boots. I knew what happened and had to turn away.

Her assailants had cut her open from her sternum down to her groin, skin folded back to each side, leaving her guts open to the air. And some woodland creature had nibbled on her intestines, leaving toothy gaps where the contents leaked out.

I knew she wouldn't survive. Where was a hospital? Would they be open and operating? Could she survive the trip there?

Mom saw the bruising below, where she'd been raped. That's what Mom didn't want me to see. She ordered me back to the car for supplies – and the pistol, which I was supposed to carry with me when I left the car. I brought the first aid kit and a towel. It was probably useless.

"What's your name?" asked Mom.

Gurgles. Mom held the woman's head up to clear her throat.

"A—lice...."

I saw the name tag on her uniform shirt: Alton.

"They wouldn't even let a woman have her authority," Mom muttered.

She brushed the woman's hair. Her skull appeared out of joint, like she'd been bashed by a hard object. I could imagine the scene: stopping for a routine check, swarmed by a gang, assaulted and left for dead.

Mom gazed into her eyes.

"My dear, I don't think there's anything we can do."

"A—lice...." she repeated, her last thought.

"Nothing we can do but end the pain for you."

Mom had me crush up some sleeping pills. She fed them to the woman bit by bit, then offered water. The woman tried to shake her head but stopped with a flash of pain. She couldn't swallow.

"Do you want something quicker?" asked Mom.

Alice Alton nodded as best she could. A line of tears ran from her eyes.

"Okay – got it."

Mom reached back for the pistol. I gave it to her and she stood. She aimed at Alice Alton's temple, and fired.

Standing over her a while, Mom gazed down, sniffling back tears. I took Mom's free hand and she squeezed my hand so tight I wanted to pull away. But I let her have my hand as she mourned this fresh sign of the new normal, a society gone mad, with its savages unleashed.

"I remember reading," said Mom softly, "about the war over in Bosnia – Yugoslavia, in southeast Europe, back before you were born – where a couple from different ethnic groups dare go out on a nice date. They were trying to show how they could unite and get along. A romantic evening. But the customs required them to be modest. Just dinner and a simple dance. None of that jumping into bed, not even a goodnight kiss. The next day war is declared and so instead of dating the nice neighborhood girl and going through the steps of courtship, he can just take her, lock her up in the new military command center, and fuck her as much as he wants. She's coy one day, the next day she's his sex slave. Only by the declaration of war. Law, the rules, customs all come to an end in a flash. Replaced by barbarity. And what is it that a man can do to hurt a woman most who makes him wait? or rejects him?"

She turned to me, one of the good men.

"This."

I pointed to Mom's shirt, covered in the woman's blood. Mom shook her head, as though a bloody shirt was the least of her worries. She pulled off the shirt over her head, let it flutter to the grass. She looked at me, her face tear-streaked, and wiped her eyes. Then she saw her hands were bloody and now the blood was on her face.

Seeing a farm pond further on, she slipped off her pants and shoes, jogged down to it, stepping straight in without hesitation. Maybe it was cold this morning, but that wouldn't have mattered to her. She had to wash off the blood, make herself clean again.

After several minutes standing dutifully by the pond, my eyes on Mom but giving regular glances back at our car, she walked out of the pond, her body sleek with water, wet hair in tangles.

Shivering, I held out the towel and Mom walked up into it and I wrapped it around her. I held her in that embrace. I rubbed her back and shoulders through the towel, drying her. She kept her arms around me.

"You see what to do?" she whispered in my ear, stretching up on her toes. "When it's my turn? You make it quick." A sniffle. "Promise me."

"I promise." My voice was weak, choked.

She hugged me tighter and I pulled her into me.

"I love that you're a good boy, one of the good men, Sandy. But someday.... Someday you must, *must* be a bad man, and do what needs to be done."

"I will, Mom."

13

IN WHICH MOM GETS REAL

"Turn right up ahead," said Mom after a long silence. She sat back wiping her eyes. The situation with Alice Alton upset her, broke her mask of toughness. I was afraid to speak. Nothing could be said that was worth saying.

We only had a small folding shovel to dig a grave but we did our best. We covered her body with a blanket from the patrol car, then piled dirt over her to make a mound. Her wallet had an ID card, so we thought of notifying her next-of-kin and letting them handle the rest of whatever needed to be done.

Mom worked on that task before she came back to our car and pulled out fresh clothes: jeans and a sweatshirt. She used another tampon; it was a heavy flow day, she said. She didn't want to ruin other clothing from her limited supply. Eventually, she sat down on the passenger side, door open wide, and caught her breath.

She alternated wiping her eyes and scraping dirt from under her nails as she gazed at the mound we made.

"I want to play," she said, exhaling a weary breath, "but I can't think of anything that fits. A funeral dirge? Chopin? No.... Some Mahler? No.... I don't even have a tune in my head."

I told her it didn't matter. She would find a good melody and it would be just right.

As we drove on, I thought of Mom's words to me. I'm one of the good men, she said. I wouldn't have even had the thought to treat a woman – or any person – so cruelly. Fear of being caught and put in prison keeps most people from committing bad acts, but others don't care. They don't think that far ahead.

Maybe it was my shyness that kept me safe. In school it was enough to get any response from a girl if I only said "Hello". That would light up my heart. And if she ignored me, well, I would be sad, maybe angry, but I sure wouldn't think of hurting her. I would swallow my feelings and go on. Nobody taught me that. It just seemed right.

Others wouldn't take 'no' for an answer. They grew bold, took what they wanted, not caring how the other person felt, ignoring customs, laws, and morality for a moment of pure lust, or hatred, or making their mark on the world, to let everyone know they existed. I read about that. A primal scream in the wilderness. I exist! That was the difference.

"Here?" I confirmed, coming to an intersection and slowing.

She nodded, flashed a meager smile.

I made the turn and continued up the new road, which wound through fields and patches of woodland, bathed in autumn colors as the sun warmed us, a perfect day except for the violence we'd witnessed. The narrow winding road, worn and broken in spots, took us to a small town which, like the others, looked abandoned, swept clean of people – although a few bodies lay among piles of debris here and there.

"This is the back way into town," said Mom, sitting up. "We'll come to an apartment complex. Used to be beige with brown trim. Newly built – back then, ten years ago. She moved there with the kids after her husband was an asshole."

We turned as the road curved, other roads intersecting it, and rolled through without stopping at stop signs or at the one traffic light which no longer blinked.

"Here," said Mom, leaning forward to look out the window.

Despite living in a high-rise apartment in the city, I'd seen suburban apartment complexes before: long buildings divided into separate units, only two floors high, with individual entrances and parking directly in front of the entrances like at a motel. Not like our building of six floors with an elevator, one entrance from the street, all of us packed in. But we had a balcony for Mom to sit out on and play her tuba.

The apartment buildings were forest green with off-white trim now but needed a fresh coat.

Mom pointed to a unit. Plenty of vehicles sat in the spaces of the long parking lot, but no people were outside. I pulled into an empty space in front of the unit Mom indicated.

I shut off the engine.

Mom did not immediately get out.

"This is Jackie's place?" I asked.

"I think so." She looked around. "I've only been here a couple times. First was to help her move in."

"And that was when?"

"About ten years ago."

"Did you bring me?"

She glared at me. "Of course. Can't be away from my little boy. You don't remember?"

"No. Doesn't look familiar to me."

"You were too busy playing with your cousins."

"More cousins," I groaned.

We scanned the apartments, looking for danger. But all was quiet on this sunny noontide. That's the scariest situation, Mom often said, because you feel relaxed and safe. Then you're caught unaware, attacked from behind. I studied our surroundings. There were no trees of suitable size to hide a criminal, no bushes either.

"People should be home. They left a lot of cars and trucks," I said after a while. "Maybe there's another lockdown."

"They could've died inside the apartments," said Mom. "Never calling for help. Your Aunt Jackie is the quiet type. She wouldn't want to bother anyone, not even to call for help."

"So not like you...."

Mom gave a chuckle. "No, not at all like me. She worked retail – art supplies – then opened a boutique-slash-gallery of her own in the mall. Opposite end of town, across from the SuperMart. She had a full gallery sometime later. She painted a lot of landscapes, like that TV painter. That was before she got married."

"You never talk about her." I regarded Mom, saw her calm face as blank as fresh canvas. "You like her? More than Aunt Laura?"

"Neutral." Mom continued staring out at the front door of the apartment. "Well, I shouldn't say that. She was protective. But in a quiet way. Kept me away from family drama. She was always good to me when I was little. Laura, however, she was a pain."

"But she's your sister. And closer in age than Aunt Laura."

"Two years closer. What difference does that make? You and I are sixteen years apart."

That shut me up. I had no right to press her for information. Mom had her own life before me, plenty of memories to sort out. At least with us arriving here, her mind might switch to Jackie and forget about Alice Alton.

"Jackie married Peter," Mom began, settling back with a huff, continuing to survey the neighborhood. "He was manager of the store where she worked, so they had that in common. She stayed out of family drama, never caused trouble. A quiet girl. Everyone liked her. She had four kids, last I recall. There's a girl about two years younger than you. When you were seven and she was five you two shared a bath while we were visiting. That was why they married, okay? She got pregnant. Once I broke the seal, Jackie got in the family way as fast as she could. Laura went off to college as planned. Jackie had another girl, so no college. Then another girl and a boy. From all accounts they were a good family. Never were in the newspapers."

"Or online?" I needed to update Mom on technology.

"No, not even online news reports. A nice family."

I watched Mom fight through a storm of emotions.

"It's good they were a good family," I offered.

"*Are* a good family," Mom corrected. "I hope they still are...a good family. Then her husband...."

Her thought trailed off. For a moment, I expected her to get out of the car and stomp up to the door. She sat still, gazing at the apartment as though deciding whether she really wanted to meet her sister. I wondered if she had the correct address.

She put her fingers to her eyes, rubbed them.

"You okay, Mom?"

"Yes, okay." She gave me a hard look, then turned and took my face in her hands. "I've always loved you, Sandy. My little baby boy. My sweet boy."

"Mom....," I whined.

She held me firmly between her hands. "You're all I've got. The only thing more precious than Timmy. Remember that, will you?"

"You sure you're okay?" I studied her eyes: genuine sorrow in them. "Still thinking of Alice Alton, aren't you?"

She gave a nod, then released my face, looked away. "I'm not sure I did the right thing. Ending her pain that way. Who am I to do that?"

"You did the right thing, Mom." I patted her leg. "We live in hard times. Have to be tough, make hard decisions. And you did."

Mom had pulled out the deputy's ID, held it in her hands, a small card with the woman's photo, a thumb print, zebra code on the back. She looked pretty, hair pulled back, uniform crisp. Mom read her address, thinking aloud whether we should find her next-of-kin, then deciding we might be blamed for what happened. So better not to get involved.

Mom let out a sigh, handed the ID card to me.

"Okay...."

She got out of the car, stood beside it, stretching. With a scan in each direction, she closed the door, keeping Officer Tanner's pistol in her hand.

"Wait here," she said. "Keep your gun ready. Keep an eye open for anyone coming out. I'll signal you to join me."

Mom went up the walk to the apartment's stoop, tried to look in the window in the door. She held the pistol by her hip.

I continued checking the area on this sunny afternoon on an ordinary day. Nothing strange. No, wait. A few doors down there was a body, looking like the man had been sitting on the steps of his apartment, mulling his fate, and just keeled over on his face and knees, frozen in that sitting position.

Further down an older woman in a tattered dress lay flat on

her back, sprawled in the yard. A man in a company uniform sat upright in a truck four spaces away, windows up, blood in lines running from his eyes and nose. In the rear view mirror I saw a small dog trotting by carrying a hand. The hand was missing a thumb. Two other dogs chased after—

I heard a gunshot and spun around, saw Mom crouched on the stoop. In the half-open doorway was an old woman in full hazmat suit, holding a .22 rifle in her hands, muzzle lowered now that Mom was down.

"Don't want any, whatever yer sellin," the woman growled. "And why ain'tcha wearing masks? You know it's the law. Been the law going on five years now – even ya got all the jabs."

Mom got to her feet, holding the pistol away. Setting the gun down, she raised her hands to signal submission.

"Sorry, ma'am," said Mom in a calm voice. "Guess we're in new territory. Back where we're from masks are optional. If you're sneezing or coughing you wear it. Otherwise, not really necessary – vaxxed or not. Anyway, I'm looking for my sister. She used to live here."

"Don't know no sisters." The woman raised the rifle, resting it on her hip. "Back away, you anti-vaxxer trash!"

"I'm not—"

Mom was waving frantically at me.

"Bring the masks," she called.

I got out of the car, standard medical-grade masks in hand. I donned mine, handed the other to Mom, and stepped back.

Standing several steps behind Mom, I saw the woman posed just inside the doorway, covered in full yellow plastic hazmat gear from head to feet.

"She says the family that used to live here," Mom called to me, "they moved out about three years ago. These apartments are only for vaxxed people now."

"Then why wear these masks?" I was confused. We had the same laws in the city. "If the vaccines work."

"She won't talk to me unless I'm wearing one." Mom gave a shrug. We knew how crazy vaxxers could be – the side effects of too many boosters, Mom explained previously.

"There's dead bodies out here," I reported to her as casually as if I were giving a weather report.

"Don't mind them," said the woman. "They come through here spraying something awful every night." The old woman cackled. "Unvaxxed folks cain't stand it. Keeps'em away. Shoulda listened. It's for the common good, don't they know?"

Mom nodded. "Common good is good. So is common sense."

"They're spraying something bad intentionally?" I asked as I came up beside Mom.

Mom elbowed me. "I'm sure it must be a lawful mandate. Or something. Thinning the herd, they say."

"They got curfew at dusk, you should know," the woman said. "Besides the spraying, they'll shoot anybody's out. Just warning ya. Gotta stay home. Only allowed to be out between ten and two on weekdays. Nobody allowed out on weekends. Not even for going to church. You gotta pray for salvation at home."

"Is anything open?" asked Mom, pointing in the direction of the town center. "Any grocery stores?"

"Most places are, but not a lot to buy. The Food Mart's got a truck that makes a run every week, brings back what they can get. But prices way up."

"Oh, that's good. We need to replenish our supplies."

"Then you best keep yer masks on. They prefer full suits if you're gonna be in the store fer long." The woman paused to think of more advice. "And they don't take cash."

"Right," said Mom in a jaunty voice. "Sure can't have anyone passing around those filthy bills, everybody touching them."

"You pay wit yer phone. A pay app, what the young'uns call it," said the woman.

"So there's phone service here?" asked Mom.

I immediately went to the car and got my phone, powered up. Mom waited for me to check it. I gave a thumbs up when my phone got a signal. I had some messages, too!

"Okay, thanks for your help. Sorry to bother you."

Back to the car, Mom pulled off her mask.

"I have no idea where they'd go." She stood by the driver's side, door open, me in the passenger seat. "Maybe the beach house." She sighed. "Of course, they might have sold it, who knows?"

"I guess you didn't keep in touch."

"Not hardly."

Mom counted the bodies up and down the parking lot. I was reading my messages. She pointed at two bodies sitting up in cars, stiff as statues.

"Three years ago, hmmm. That would be between the second and third waves. She could handle the first one okay – we all did – but freak out when the second one came. Then the third came."

Mom pondered the situation as a parade of clouds marched overhead, blocking the sunshine.

"I think she would seek shelter, find a safe location. If I were her, I'd go as far as I could, find some isolated place where I didn't have to worry about hordes of virus carriers coming for me."

"And...?"

"Let's go to the beach. That's where I'd go."

I read through my messages, mostly school friends asking how I was doing, where I was at, and saying how they were and where they were at. It seemed most had stayed in the city, some now suffering for that choice but others doing all right. A few said they or a family member were heading to a clinic – then no messages. No messages from anyone in the past week, when we left the city – like they were unable to send more.

"But first let's go into town and restock our food," Mom was saying. "Better get our suits out, though."

I put down my phone and got out.

Opening the trunk, I retrieved our hazmat suits, unpacked them. I took one around to Mom. She slipped it on over her clothes as I got dressed in mine then climbed back into the car.

"Do we really need these?" I asked through the plastic face window. "I mean, the full suit?"

"It's not to protect us," Mom responded, "it's so we blend in. We don't want to cause alarm. Don't want anyone to point at us and the crowd attacks us."

136

"Got it."

She started the engine.

"At least people here are maintaining a society," said Mom, "at least trying, even with mandates. You saw the other places we passed. People had given up, gone wild. Like your grandparents: they gave up. Others are making their own way – like jackals, roaming and scavenging. You saw them. The world is reverting to a prehistoric lifestyle. We just need some caves."

She grinned like she'd said something clever.

"Let's see what they've got here."

14

IN WHICH MOM GETS THE GOODS

We paused to look at a few bodies fallen on the lawn as we rolled through the parking lot. We were at the edge of town; heading up the avenue would take us to its center. At least no columns of smoke rose from the business district.

Mom went slowly, looking at the dashboard.

"We need to get gas, then recharge the battery," she said. "Not like the old days when you could drive a while on just the battery. No more charging stations, and eventually there won't be any gas. Better to invest in a horse if you want to go somewhere in a post-apocalypse world."

"So we're okay?" I stared at the yellow light on the dash. It looked serious. But I knew Mom had a plan. "How far can we go?"

We sat at the end of the parking lot, ready to pull out onto the street. The yellow light on the dash blinked. Mom stared at it.

"I remember there's a grocery. I don't remember if it has any gas pumps." Then she turned to me, grinning. "It's six blocks to the Food Mart, we have twenty-five percent battery, and we're wearing hazmat suits."

Mom hit the pedal and we charged into the street.

She seemed confident, but I stayed ready, holding the pistol on my knees as she drove up the street at a slow speed.

"It's still a bit unsettling seeing bodies here and there."

"I'm sure someone will pick them up eventually." She stared ahead as we rolled along. "Just don't touch any of them."

No other vehicles moved on the street but several were parked on the sides.

"I have a bad feeling...."

"Shhh! Just remember: we fit in. Probably nobody will ask any questions because we look the part: suited up and grim like them. Act forlorn."

"Okay, Mom. If you say so."

"We're just getting some food. I hope they still have some gas. Probably no new gas has been delivered for some time so it might not be good anyway."

The street was lined with tall trees, their shade covering the street. Behind them stood stately homes of an older style yet in good condition, but the yards were overgrown. No one sat out on those grand verandas or gazed down from a turret. None strolled the sidewalks. But as the old woman at the apartment said, they had lockdown for most of the day and all night. I checked the time on my phone – no new messages had come in.

These were long blocks. Mom paused at each intersection as though a cop car was sitting nearby in the shadows waiting to pull us over. And just as likely there might be a vehicle, ignoring the stop sign and speeding through. At one intersection, Mom stopped and a car on the cross street stopped, too, then gave us a wave to go ahead. Like it was a normal day.

Down another block, ahead on the right was a building with some activity. A dozen people gathered around the open back end of a box truck, unloading supplies, carrying them into the store.

"I count a hundred-and-twenty percent masked," I said. "Some are double-masked." All of them wore full hazmat suits with clear plastic head bubbles. I'd never seen so many people in hazmats before – not away from hospitals.

Mom had a smirk. "I saw those advertised a couple years ago but never saw many people wearing them. Not so fashionable. But then—"

A honk behind us made Mom drive on through the intersection and turn into the parking lot of the Alton Food Mart.

We parked at the far end of the small lot. This grocery was

only a neighborhood store but it seemed a shipment of goods had arrived and employees – and citizen-customers – were helping to unload it, taking boxes and bags inside through the double doors of the store which were propped open.

"You were right about the grocery," I said, "but I don't see any gas pumps."

"Me, neither." Mom stretched, scanned down the street we'd been on. "I see a sign a few blocks down. But do they have any gas left there?"

"So are we going in? In our suits?"

"I guess we should. Everyone is wearing full suits."

"Does that mean there's something in the air? Or, as you keep saying, they're just complying?"

"Hard to say. Dear Leader says being outdoors is safest. The breeze supposedly keeps the little critters from sticking to us. Yet they insisted soon enough that we shouldn't go out at all. Then it was okay to go out. Then it wasn't. They keep opening and closing the windows. Not sure what the rule is for today."

She continued sizing up the situation. Nobody had noticed us, or cared that we arrived. We had out-of-state tags.

"I doubt we need full suits, but...."

I watched her studying the store. "But what?"

"But we better blend in." She opened the car door a crack as if testing the air. "You wait here. Keep an eye on things. I'll go in and get what we need."

"Wait, Mom." I gathered my breath. "Why can't I go in? I can get what we need. You never let me do anything."

She smiled warmly. "Because I know what to get."

"Because you think I'll do something wrong, isn't it? Like say something that gets us in trouble. Then we'll be caught."

"Caught? We haven't done anything." She pursed her lips.

Looking at the people carrying in boxes, she nodded inside her bubble hood.

"I knew it," I grumbled, pouting.

"Yes, Sandy. I do worry. But it's not your fault. I sheltered you, maybe too much. I wanted to keep the horrors of the world away from you. To protect you."

"But I'm an adult now. I can handle it. I promise I won't have a meltdown."

"I know, I know." Then she looked at me with her wet eyes, a tear running down the plastic window of her bubble. "I just fear for you. Always."

"But I shot men for you. I've killed for you. Okay, I was slow to act but I acted."

"Yes, you did." She lifted her bubble, put her hand inside and wiped her eyes.

"I won't say anything stupid. Promise." I felt both nervous and proud at the same time. "I'll just get what we need. I got the pay app on my phone. It should cover what we need. My treat."

Mom gave a nod and listed items to get, with variations if the item wasn't available, and specifications for some items as though I was going into the giant SuperMart where they had everything we could possibly want. That was when I'd have a meltdown: too many choices. She asked if I could remember all she said. I joked I'd already forgotten half, which didn't amuse her.

"If you're not back in a reasonable time, I'm coming in," she said, placing her hand on my thigh. "Leave the pistol here. They'll be alarmed if they see it."

"Got it, Mom."

"And get another box of tampons, same brand and size as the box I have."

"Won't that look suspicious? Me getting tampons?"

"Which is the reason I was going to go in. You just say they're for your mother. Or sister. Wife. Whatever. Improvise."

"Okay, Mom."

It was awkward climbing out of the car in the full hazmat suit. I stood a moment beside the door as I adjusted the suit. I looked like a bio-scientist heading into a level-4 virology lab to play God — hoping there wasn't a tear in my suit that would let in the deadly pathogen that would not only kill me but spread around the world killing millions of other people, then mutate to kill millions more with each wave.

Turning on the suit's ventilator, hearing its hum, I took a deep breath, filled my lungs. I proceeded to the front entrance of the store, noting the words on the long sign that ran down the side of the building, wondering if there was any connection between this Alton Food Mart and the Deputy Alton we had left far up the road under a mound of dirt.

I approached the open doors. A man in a suit called to me. We smiled at each other through our plastic windows. I raised my hand in greeting. He asked if I wouldn't mind taking in a bundle since I was going inside anyway.

"Sure," I said, raising my voice inside the hood.

I went to the back of the truck and grabbed a box — a case of precious toilet paper rolls — and carried it on inside. Another guy checked what I had, pointed down the aisle.

"Can I buy some things or are you closed?" I asked the guy with the checklist.

"You can get whatever you need, but you can see a lot's not unpacked yet. Better come back tomorrow."

"I just need a few things. Can I take a look?"

"Go ahead, have a look-see."

I strolled the aisles. I had to step back against the shelves a few times when a guy needed to pass with a box to deliver to its spot. I grabbed handfuls of food items, nothing different than we'd been surviving on the past week: sausages and jerky, crackers and cookies, chips, granola bars, dried fruit, nuts, chocolate. I went by the cooler and took a few cans and bottles. I juggled everything in my arms.

Tottering toward the check-out counter I dropped a few items.

"Whoa, mister," the checklist guy called. "Need all that?"

This was where Mom would say the right thing, I realized, a remark that was mildly sarcastic, disarming words that would let her get her way. But I had no response as I set everything on the counter and went back to pick up what I'd dropped.

"We're on a ration basis here," the guy explained.

"Well, this isn't real food," I said, forcing a chuckle. I knew it sounded fake. "But it's what Mom wants."

"Yer mama sent you?" He grinned, amused.

"Oh, yeah. That reminds me. She needs something else."

"And what's that?" He got serious again.

"Lady stuff." I grinned through the plastic window.

"We ain't got much of that. Gals've snatched'em up long time ago. Hard to get now."

He pointed to an aisle and I went down it, searching for what Mom wanted. I found the spot but only a bare shelf space where the item used to be, price tag still up, costing a lot.

Remembering Mom saying she'd found her B-pill on the floor under the cashier station, I got down and poked under the bottom shelf but found nothing there but lint. I knew a little about girly products; Mom never shied from teaching me about her monthly needs. Like it was all my fault. So I looked around the shelves. Napkins? There was a box so I grabbed it, not even caring if it was the right brand or size for her.

"I have a pay app," I said, coming to the checkout, holding up my phone to the man at the front.

"Good. We don't take cash no more," he said, moving behind the counter and giving my phone screen a look. I wondered then what they'd do when the electronic banking system went down, like it did in our city. How would people buy anything? Or would they be forced to barter?

He added up my items, gave me a total on his handheld device and I held my phone up to it. Beeps. The wrong kind. I looked at my phone. It was rejecting my purchase. Probably it was rejected because we were out of district, a leftover mandate to limit travel.

"You got any money in your account?" he asked.

"There should be plenty. Back home the cell towers were off so no way to buy anything."

I stopped myself. In a flash I realized that was the exact kind of stupid thing I would say that Mom wouldn't.

"I mean, when I got a signal here, I thought: 'Oh, good, now I can get some food' – you know?"

"Only works on one bank system: *ViralPay*." He glared at me through his plastic window. "You ain't from around here, huh?"

Stupid or not, feeling my chest tighten I had to respond. "No, we're on our way to my aunt's place. She lives here."

"Is that so?" He looked sideways at me through the hazmat hood. "Y'all out-of-towners, huh?" He let out a sigh. "Hey, I wanna help ya, but we gotta keep supplies for ourselves, for our folks."

"But I'm buying them."

"Don't look like it, son."

Son! Geez. I was nothing more than somebody's son. Still my Mom's little boy, just taller now. Not my own adult. I could feel pressure building in me.

"My mom's outside, waiting. She probably has more apps on her phone. Let me get her."

I went outside, breathing hard but walking at a confident pace down the parking lot to our car.

Mom smiled, then narrowed her eyes as I arrived.

"No groceries?"

I explained the situation, had to apologize. Mom didn't rub it in, but I felt bad that I wasn't able to complete the mission myself. At least I held off a meltdown.

Mom went in the store. I waited in the car. A few minutes later she returned with a bag. Without a word, she dropped the bag in back and got in. She gave my leg a loving pat.

"Unfortunately, I have a dozen bank apps. At least one of them worked. So we're good for now." She turned in her seat, watched the men unloading the truck. "It won't be long before the banks go offline. Then we exchange seashells."

She shook her head, reached for the bag behind her, retrieved a can of beer. She popped the tab and broke the bubble seal to lift the can up under her hood and drank it down.

"Ah, so good," she sighed, closing her bubble.

I laughed. "Yeah, guess so."

"Looks like we're on battery now," she said, setting the can in the center console. "We can go full speed for a few miles if we have to get away. Then the battery's done. The man said there's a gas station across from the SuperMart. It's fabulously expensive, no matter what bank app we use."

"Mom...." My voice was weak, defeated. She turned to meet my eyes. "I'm sorry."

"You said that already. It's done."

"But...I almost had a meltdown."

"I know. But you didn't. That's good."

She didn't want to start the car before we decided where to go.

"Maybe we should go by their house, see if anyone's home. If Peter moved out then maybe Jackie and the kids moved back in. Who knows? Anyway, we need a place for tonight."

As she started the car, I watched the men working: carrying heavy things, using their muscles, breaking their backs. Not at a desk pushing papers, reading e-books on tablets. I wasn't ready for this new normal. I'd shot a gun, killed men, sure, but I wasn't ready to protect my mother. I couldn't even find her some damn tampons. But I got napkins.

"You know those are dinner napkins, not the feminine kind," she had to say as we drove up the street, "don't you?"

15

IN WHICH MOM GETS GAS

Two blocks up the street Mom started breathing hard. She pulled over, jumped the curb, shut off the engine. Ripping off her bubble hood and her gloves, her hands went to her face. Tears ran down her cheeks, even as she tried to hide them with her hands.

"Mom...?" I called softly. "What's wrong?"

She regarded me with wet eyes. "You saw the sign? On the store?"

"Yes, of course. Alton Food Mart."

"When you were inside, did you see a poster on the plexiglass divider up front? By the app reader?"

"Didn't really notice. I was—"

"It had a picture on it." She tried to control her emotions. "It read *Alice Alton, Sheriff's Deputy.* The store owner's daughter. It must've been her graduation picture from the academy. So proud of her he put it up in his store. I didn't say anything. I couldn't."

"But Mom...."

"I shouldn't have shot her. Even to end her pain."

"There was no way she would ever survive a trip into town – if a hospital was even open."

"But it wasn't for me...not for me to decide."

"You did the right thing. It was those guys that attacked her that were wrong. The bad guys. Like you said. Nothing you could do for her – except what you did: end her pain."

Mom wept for several minutes.

"I really want to like this town," she spoke, "banding together to help each other. I want to be part of this. We've been taught – conditioned – for so damn long to keep away from each other, to be suspicious and shun strangers. But we're the strangers now. And he...he let me take the food, no charge. The bank app didn't work. Signal, yes, but not the app. The same out-of-district shit: we're restricted. So I was, like you said, caught."

"Caught? Not being local?" I swallowed hard. "Are you okay? Did they say anything? Call anyone about us?"

"No, I think we're safe." She sniffled back tears. "He was just being kind to a mother and her son."

"Yeah, he was nice to me, too."

"It's about the common good." Mom pursed her lips. "You know history? They can make people do anything if they say it's for the common good. If we all work together. Remember the 'We're all in this together' slogan? That was no lie – but they wanted us to stay apart, hah."

"We had to—"

"You want to help the poor, don't you? Well, how about a tax on your income? You can spare some. Or are you a greedy robber-baron? You want to help people who don't have jobs, don't you? How about new government programs that give some of your income to them? Thatta girl. Do your part. Be kind, rewind. You want to help the war effort, don't you? Give your fair share. You want to stop the war, don't you? Come protest with us. Donate. Volunteer. Be pro-active. Do your part. Give your fair share. Co-exist. We have to make society a level playing field – no matter what circumstances each of us has that makes life a crapshoot. So how about this new regulation? Policy? New bills to give us more power over you? It's for your own good. We know best what's good for you. And a few mandates thrown in for good measure. You want to help out your fellow citizens, don't you? Then obey us. You want to be a good citizen, don't you? We'll decide the way society should be and you'll like it. If you don't, we'll make you like it. We have ways of making you like anything. You'll go along with our plan or we'll ruin you, make you disappear. Yes, put up all those new devices in your homes, so we can watch and listen, make sure you're thinking correctly, with only the approved views. Not good enough? Why not produce a virus? Or a virus hoax? Or better yet a virus panic but call it a *pandemic*. A few people always die, so we'll say they died of this virus. That'll destroy the economy. You don't need anything anyway. Then let's add a war just for fun, and more profits. Then you'll need us to save you—"

"Mom, stop it!"

"I'm not for any side. I'm *for* authorities being truthful with the people who put them in office." She shook her head slowly, weary from her anger. "We're not ignorant children. They treat us like we are. Because, for the powers that be, it's not deciding what to say or not say, it's whatever will give them their best hold on power. It's not about what the science actually shows, it's how can they spin it to benefit themselves."

In school we were tasught how to respond whenever we heard anti-government statements – even if it was my own mom saying it. "That's not approved speech" was what we were instructed to say as our initial response. Some of my classmates boasted they'd turned in one or both of their parents. Even got rewarded.

I felt a punch to my gut. "You're upset, Mom." I took a long breath. "Okay, I know that's what I'm supposed to say. We drilled responses so much. My classes taught us to be vigilant, and pay attention to what our parents said and did."

"Thanks for not turning me in." She wiped her eyes. "We have to get back to music. All of us. Notes are not political. They're uniting." She glanced back at Timmy. "I want to play."

"How about we see if they have any gas first?"

She sniffled. "Okay."

With a glance for other vehicles, we pulled out into the street, continuing at school-crossing speed, the engine making a weird humming/grinding noise.

We got to the gas station by the Supermart, found three cars lined up at the two pumps. They had been abandoned.

"How rude," Mom cursed, sizing up the situation. She could pull around and get close to a pump, see if the hose would stretch far enough. "Or they did it intentionally. You know, to discourage the Mad Max types."

I didn't get the reference so Mom explained it: In the post-apocalyptic future everyone drove monster trucks and suped-up muscle cars, somehow always having plenty of high-octane fuel even though they were in a desert, fighting over what resources remained. We weren't there yet, I knew. We didn't have any fuel.

"We should've gotten one of those fully electric cars," I said, looking up at the sign giving the price: $38.99 per gallon. Likely it hadn't been changed in over a year. An electric charge back in the city was almost as much. "Or were they too expensive?"

Mom maneuvered the car as close as possible. "And just where do you think the electricity to charge them comes from?"

I paused to think. "From...lightning?" That was meant to be a joke, but Mom didn't smile. "No, the power plants? Or, uh, the windmills? Solar panels?"

Mom sighed. "Power plant is correct.

"Knew it."

"And how does the electricity get from the power plant to your car's battery?"

Okay, she was going to make me feel stupid again. Might as well get it over with. "By power lines?"

She smiled in a condescending way. "That's right. You park your electric car in your garage and plug your car into your house. That adds to your home's electric consumption. Electricity to the house is produced by turbines turning around...in power plants, which are made to turn by...guess what? Coal? Oil? Natural gas? Or nuclear energy. If you're lucky maybe by hydro, like when they dam a river and water is forced through turbines."

"Yeah, like that." I felt better, knowing something.

"So how does that electricity get to your charging station?"

I pouted, getting annoyed. "Geez, Mom, I dunno. Why don't you tell me?"

"Most charging stations are run by diesel engines. Powered by petroleum. That's what makes your electricity."

She stared at the gas pump. "No gas means no electricity."

"We've been on battery for a few blocks."

"Yes, and now we're done. It's not meant to run on just the battery for too long. The gasoline engine charges the battery; the battery runs the car. That's how it's fuel-efficient. But this old car doesn't hold a charge very well."

"That's so fucked up."

"Watch your mouth, Sandy."

"Sorry." I shook my head as Mom climbed out. "We're running away from chaos and you complain about a bad word?"

She ducked her head inside. "The last vestige of a civilization is being fucking polite."

After a minute of checking the pump, she opened the trunk of the car, brought out the empty gas cans. She said a little gas remained but she was saving it for an emergency, like when we really needed to get away.

"Hey! Hey!" someone called. "Stop! No gas! Gone!"

An old man wearing a bathrobe and nothing else, no mask or hazmat suit, long white hair flung in the breeze, stumbled toward us, waving his hands like a warning.

"No gas!" he shouted. "All gone. We gone to war for that."

Mom watched him carefully, prepared for danger.

"All the wars, just over gas," he continued, coming closer.

I got out to help, keeping Mom's pistol in my hand.

"Stay back," I called out, holding up the pistol.

"All gone," he said mournfully. Overcome, he stopped. "Damn wars! For nothing. No more gas. We tried. But we failed."

"Okay, I get it, " I said to the man. He looked confused, like he wasn't sure where he was. "We'll be on our way in a minute."

"So many boys died fighting for oil," he ranted, "when we got plenty here." He opened his robe, showed his wounds. The ugly scars suggested horrific surgery. "I did my part. And they patched me up."

Mom tried the pump, found it turned off. Same for the others. No station attendant to complain to. She grumbled, slapped the car, slapped the pump.

The old man laughed at her frustration.

With a slew of curse words, Mom poured in the last of our gas from the last can.

"This will get us to the house."

"You said they live on the other end of town?"

"If Jackie went there, that's where the house is."

"Can't wait to meet all my cousins," I said, trying to muster some enthusiasm.

* * *

The house was exactly as Mom had said: a modest ranch, urine-yellow trimmed in fecal-brown, with a front yard that hadn't been kept trimmed, bald spots of football-scraped dirt. A lot of yards were like that; no gas for mowers. An old-model car was parked in the driveway, so Mom parked on the other side. She immediately shut off the engine, not wanting to waste our last portion of fuel.

I looked up, studied the front of the house. It was possible they no longer lived here, had moved on to another place Mom didn't know about and couldn't guess. That was like Jackie, she said, always the odd one, avoiding family drama, hiding or running away, keeping quiet. Doing her art. Living in her head as much as possible, everyone shut out.

"Stay alert," said Mom, her hazmat suit crinkling. "Keep the pistol ready." She gazed at the front door. "If somebody else lives here now, they may not like having visitors. Move over and be ready to start the engine and go."

"But if they're here...?"

"Then I guess I'll have to play nice."

Mom gave me a reassuring grin through her face window. She went to the front door, hazmat suit swishing. She reached her gloved hand out and pushed the doorbell, only then remembering the house probably wouldn't have electricity for a bell to ring. She knocked hard on the door a few times. As she waited, she opened the front of her hazmat hood so they could see her face better.

After a minute that seemed longer, the door opened partly.

I could see a teenage girl. She stayed behind the door, only her face showing, dark hair framing it. She held a mask up to her face like she'd just grabbed it to answer the knock.

"I'm your aunt," said Mom. They talked for a minute, running through a checklist of questions to determine health status. Mom waved at me to join her.

As I got to the door, Mom was already going inside. I followed with my hazmat suit swishing. I felt stupid dressed like that. We weren't handling any hazardous materials.

Inside, Mom removed her hood and began slipping out of the suit. I did, too, thankfully. I wanted to take a deep breath but I worried what I might breathe in. The place smelled dusty, with a hint of lemon-scented air spray.

The girl watched us suspiciously, as though she was checking for signs of contagion. She had hooked the mask on her ears and wore old jeans, faded with knees torn open, and a too-small t-shirt sporting anime characters. She stood barefoot in the living room, among the old, upholstered furniture.

"Wait here," said the girl solemnly. "I'll get Mother."

When she left the room, Mom turned to me, folding her suit in her arms. "That's your cousin Hannah."

"She's pretty," I said automatically, feeling a pulse of heat run through me. I realized how my comment must have sounded. I felt embarrassed.

Actually, I didn't notice her much, afraid to look at her. As we learned in my classes, I didn't want to be accused of 'male-gazing' or, worse, 'preying'. I had no desire to make her uncomfortable. So I only let myself notice her face and her hair. We were taught the signs to look for if a person might be infected. The remainder of my impression was only superficial: slender body, maybe too thin, probably not eating well in these hard times.

A shuffling rose and we looked where the hall joined the living room. Hannah and two other people appeared. The woman limped stiffly, held up by Hannah. A boy of about nine followed.

The woman halted, her face registering shock. She held on to her daughter's arm.

"Well!" the woman exclaimed. "Polly!" She seemed unable to

speak more, too stunned, mouth agape.

"It's good to see you again, Jackie," said Mom. She studied her sister with the same seriousness as she did for a music score. Her face softened. "Are you okay? How are you holding up?"

She waited for a response, got none.

The boy brought a chair in from the dining room and Hannah helped her mother sit. Aunt Jackie continued to register surprise at having visitors. The girl gazed at us with a look of sadness.

"We had to leave the city," said Mom. "We had to get away. It was getting too dangerous there."

Mom explained about our visit to Grandma and Grampa's but skipped the part about the intruders. Describing our visit with Aunt Laura, she left out the part about her delivery men. She told about stopping by the apartment on the edge of town, not finding her there, getting an update on the town's latest rules, stopping at the Food Mart, and now checking the 'old house'.

"If you weren't here," said Mom, "I guess we'd head on out to the beach house."

"The b-beach...," Aunt Jackie gurgled.

"But we need gas first—"

"B-beach...."

Hannah shook her head, eyes turned down to her mother as if apologizing for her condition.

"H-house," Jackie finished.

"Are you all right?" asked Mom, narrowing her eyes. "What's happened? Is Peter around?"

"She's been this way for a while," Hannah spoke. She kept her arm around her mother's shoulders. "It's difficult for her to talk. Head trauma. And, no, Dad isn't here."

"What happened?" asked Mom. "Can you talk about it?"

Hannah looked down, thinking of an answer. "Not really."

"W-went into town...." Jackie suddenly spoke up but much too loudly, voice suddenly full of rage.

Hannah patted her mother's hand, knelt on the floor beside the chair, leaning on an arm. "She's been like this for more than a year. I try to take care of her."

Aunt Jackie started to speak, tried but sputtered, so Hannah explained everything.

Early in the pandemic, during one of the lockdowns, Peter, who had come back to the family at the first sign of trouble, and second-daughter Kristin had gone out to get food. It was not too strict in those days. Everyone thought it would only be a minor inconvenience – just two weeks, so hospitals wouldn't be overrun with cases.

"Not at all like the apocalyptic event it turned out to be," said Hannah in a dark tone. "You were allowed to go out for food, and there was enough. And plenty of delivery people, but they decided to go get food themselves, like a chance to get out and see what all was happening in town. I was over with my friends, so he took Kristen with him."

But they never returned.

Hannah's face reddened as she got emotional.

Eventually they got the call that Peter had been admitted to a hospital, determined to be infected. He had no symptoms when he left home. No idea how someone decided he was infected when all they were doing was going to a grocery store. Possibly medical checkpoints, testing at the entrance or else you couldn't go in.

They didn't know what happened to Kristin. She had gone to the hospital, gathered up with Peter. They knew that much, but sometime during the next couple of days she disappeared, couldn't be found in the hospital, so no one could say where she went. Did she just walk out? Or had she been taken out by force or lured out? Had she been found to be infected and gotten lost among the patients in the hospital?

"Nobody knows." Hannah wiped her eyes.

Jackie, beside her, was a mess of tears reliving the events.

They believed Peter died in the hospital, after being given all kinds of drug cocktails, a tube shoved down his throat, and put into a coma 'for his own good'. When his body gave out, it was put in one of the mass graves they were making. And no record of his stay. A lot of records kept on electronic systems were lost in the various power grid crashes.

"N-never...never came b-back...." Jackie burst into loud sobs.

"I'm so sorry," said Mom, and went to her sister.

Hannah pointed to the boy, sitting quietly in the corner. "This is Nathan. My brother." She blushed, a beautiful splash of pink across her cheeks. "Obviously."

"Hi," I responded to both of them.

"Are you gonna stay here?" asked Hannah.

That caught me by surprise. Mom hadn't said for certain. We needed a place to stay for tonight. It was already too late to travel.

"I guess so."

Her face remained solemn. "Then let me show you around."

"Okay, thanks." I turned to Mom as I got up from the floor. "Should I unload the car?"

Mom, hugging her sister, gave a nod.

"I think it's okay outside," I said to my cousin. "These suits are just for show. So we can blend in and nobody asks any questions."

"Yeah, they're kinda strict here," said Hannah. Her laugh was kind of flat but I appreciated her attempt. "Mother won't let me go out. Doesn't wanna lose me."

16

IN WHICH MOM FINDS GOD

"I always wanted to play an instrument," said Hannah, giving a cheerful gasp as I pulled Timmy from the car.

I explained about the heirloom tuba.

She smiled beneath her mask. "I tried to get Mother to let me try trumpet, but she said we didn't have money for that, or for the lessons. Then she wouldn't get me a guitar, neither."

"That's too bad. Mom taught me some."

"Anyways, I like to sing. Singing's free. You like to sing? I like singing to online vids – yeah, before the internet went off. You know Red Velvet or Viral Sludge? How about Perfectly Sane? Or JuJu Beans? They're the best bands, I think. You can dance to their songs. I really like the Coronas, too. You know they add a new member for every new variant. They're up to Kappa – second time. I had a super crush on Dirk Danger for a while, but he died – drug overdose, not from the virus. And Callie Odem. So sad. And Jewel Rhee. She died too – suicide by wrist slash. And I like Chi bands, too, like Wu Crew and Wuhan Wave. And Wang-Chang. Davy Lee was so hot. Lots of band members died in the last wave. Like that old guitar player from Rolling Stoners. He finally died. Car crash. I'm gonna sing their songs anyway, just to remember them and because it takes my mind from Mother's problems, and our troubles, ya know? That's really what's good about music."

I was overwhelmed by her rush of words and could only smile behind my mask. She was like one of the virtual class girls I had a crush on, sitting in a square beside me on the screen, but she was real and right here.

"That's great," I muttered, feeling tongue-tied.

"I don't listen to any songs from before the pandemic. They're not relevant. Lots of happy shit. So fake." She started singing: "'Oh, the whole world is so fudged / Wanna lick it down and eat it out....' That's Buddy D's song. It's really about sex, but don't tell your mother. My mother thinks it's about ice cream. My brother thinks I sound bad, ha-ha, but I think my voice is pretty good. What d'you think? Wanna hear more? I know like a hundred-fifty songs."

It was great seeing her in the full light of day, her natural voice speaking her mind as free as a bird soaring high – as though none of the problems her family had faced affected her. She was happy to have someone to talk to, someone her age who might understand her. In that moment, seeing her sad face brighten as she spoke of her favorite bands and how she liked to sing, I first fell in love with my cousin.

Dear Hannah, daughter of my mother's sister, so slender and mousy, pure and innocent, unspoiled by the chaos of these hard times, so ready to repopulate the world!

Shaking my head to clear my thoughts, I carried in the tuba, set it down inside the door and went back for more.

Hannah helped carry in some of our things. When we finished unloading she showed me to our bedroom. Mom and I could share it; Hannah had her own room. This was a girly room, lots of pink and lavender, twin beds pushed against opposite walls, just as it had been the last time Kristin and Julia slept there. I accepted new sheets and pillowcases from Hannah. She helped me make up the beds, pulling the sheet ends to the corners of the mattresses.

"You told about Kristin," I said, pausing with the pillow in my hands, she holding the pillowcase open, "but then nobody said any more. Mom said there were three girls in your family."

"Oh," said Hannah as her face went pale.

"You, Kristin, and...?"

"Julia." Her face tightened. She turned away. "We don't talk about her."

"No...? Why not?"

"Mother says to pretend she was never born."

Then I guessed that something bad must've happened. I didn't want to force her to tell, so I waved it off.

"It's not that I can't tell you," she said as I tried to push the pillow into the pillowcase she held, "but Mother would freak out if she heard." A quick glance out the door, then back to me. "She's gone insane, you probably guessed."

"I really don't know what insane looks like." I tried to laugh.

"If you wanna know...." She came close to me, right up to me, closer than anybody but Mom had ever come to me. Her mask slipped off her nose. In a whisper so soft I couldn't understand so she had to repeat it, she said: "Raped and murdered."

Although I was expecting something like that, the words cut into me, especially coming from this sweet young woman. I was stunned to hear her say it the way she did, so matter-of-fact, like it was too common. Then, already standing close, Hannah hugged me – like she'd waited her whole life for someone to hug, to really hug tight. I couldn't breathe.

"I'm sorry," I mumbled, hugging her. Her tears hit my neck. "I shouldn't have asked."

"No, it's okay. Not what happened, course, but asking about it. We miss her, obviously. Mother tries to say she was never born. Just a bad dream she had. It's easier that way. So don't forget to not say anything about...Julia."

Julia, I mouthed against her forehead, my mask slipping.

I thought of Mom's story about that war in Bosnia long ago, how the innocent neighbor girl was suddenly a spoil of war. Was that what happened to Julia? Out walking one day and grabbed by vagrants? Because nothing would be done to them? Somebody had their eye on her and then one day it was possible to grab her? Only my thoughts, not spoken, yet Hannah seemed to know what I was thinking and she cried against my shoulder.

"We watched them carry her away," she whimpered, "nothing we could do. Mother tried to stop them, got hit in the head. That's probably part of her problems now. Like her loss of balance."

"That's terrible," I said, still holding her.

"Men from a camp behind the SuperMart. They said they'd bring her back when they were done with her. And they did, but she was about dead then. They dropped her in the yard."

"What? Just took her? Like that?" I wanted to hunt them down and blast them with the shotgun we got from Officer Tanner's patrol car, blast them into little pieces and let the wind disperse them across the countryside like pollen.

"Yeah, like that." Sniffles. "We begged them not to, but...they just laughed. They said as long as they wore masks they could do anything – burn and loot, steal, take young girls. Wearing masks was the only rule being enforced. Two cops quit, two were killed. The others just guard the town hall and banks now."

I pulled her tighter against me. She was shaking in my arms.

"That was horrible. I'm sorry."

"You don't have to be sorry." She pulled off her mask, flashed a smile just for show. "Mother made me hide in a closet, to be safe. Men with guns went after them, shot them all dead. They weren't police, just some men that thought it was a crime – and didn't want the same thing to happen to their daughters."

Now I was shaking, imagining myself part of that posse, going after criminals.

"They had to arrest somebody for it," she continued, "so Mister Bernardi volunteered, because he was already old."

I held her away, letting our eyes meet. Hers were red, teary. I think mine were, too. She lifted my mask strings from my ears, let it fall to the floor.

"You have good memories of her, I'm sure. You have to keep her alive in your memories." The rest of Mom's speech echoed in my head. "It's the only thing to do. You have to remember her in the good times."

"I know," said Hannah, sniffling back tears. "I do."

Suddenly she kissed me! Right on my lips! My lips pressed against hers. It was magic. My whole body shook with electricity, like I was an EV getting a charge up.

"You kids doing all right?" Mom called as she came down the hallway.

We immediately broke from our embrace, stood apart.

"Got the beds made," I said as Mom ducked into the room.

"Great," said Mom. "Looks nice."

I glanced at Hannah. She grinned, fumbled with her mask.

"Yes, nice," I said. "Thanks."

"Thanks...?" asked Mom.

"Yes. Hannah helped with the beds."

"I better check on Mother," said Hannah. With a flirty glance back at me, she rushed out.

Mom gave me a long look – like she had watched the whole episode and knew exactly what happened between my cousin and me. I couldn't keep a straight face. So I thought of Julia and wiped my eyes.

"She told me about Julia," I said to Mom. "This is their room: Kristin's and Julia's. Doesn't it feel weird to be sleeping here?"

Mom spoke in a quiet voice: "Listen, Sandy, your aunt isn't in the best condition. Her mind is gone, so we have to be gentle with her. She may have brain injury." She sighed like she had no other choice. "So much trauma. Over a damn virus. We should take her with us. For the kids. They won't survive with her the way she is."

"Okay," I said, smiling inside. I wouldn't mind if Hannah came with us. "We can move Timmy behind the driver's seat, turn him upright. We can all fit in the car."

"No, we're out of gas...remember?"

"Oh – yeah."

Mom glanced back at the doorway. "But their other car – the one in the garage – has a full tank. That will get us to the beach house easily. I would feel a lot safer if we were on an island. Then we can burn the bridge behind us and let the world go mad."

"Sounds good to me." I was too cheery for apocalyptic talk and Mom noticed.

"You're all right with the plan?" she asked, her voice mocking.

"It sounds like the right thing to do," I responded. "Wasn't that the plan all along? To go to the beach house?"

Mom nodded away her suspicions. "The *plan* was to hang out with your grandparents."

I lost my cheeriness, feeling the weight of the world press on me. "But here we are...."

"Right." Mom grinned like I said a joke. "We'll rest tonight – maybe tomorrow, too – then we'll get out of here. We can make the bridge by afternoon. I hope it's still intact. We'll be lazing on the beach by sunset. Got the keys to the house from your aunt. They haven't been there since summer before last – tried to escape the miseries of the pandemic with a short vacation, but it didn't take. Should be in good shape, though."

"That's great."

"You can start getting to know your cousins. They'll be your siblings from now on."

✷ ✷ ✷

Sitting in the wild-grown backyard with my cousins, gazing at the old swing set, broken seat chain, and the wilted flower garden beyond, the world felt somewhat normal – like we were visiting here in better times. Easy to forget what had been happening the past few years. We pondered what we could've been doing if not for a pandemic destroying everything.

My cousin Nathan skipped around the yard like he was in a game, playing every position. Hannah had pulled on a sweater and slipped her bare feet into unzipped boots to sit with me on the small porch. She wore a facemask. To be polite I put on mine.

"It looks weird," she said, staring across the yard.

"I know...." But I could only guess what she meant.

At the far end of the yard a line of trees blocked the view of the next house's backyard, a wire fence separating yards. I wondered about the neighbors. Were other people there? Were these houses occupied but the people were following the orders to stay inside? We sat outside enjoying an autumn afternoon: royal blue sky and white clouds drifting by under a golden sun.

"Those are the Jorgensens," said Hannah, seeing the direction

162

of my gaze. "They got a daughter maybe thirteen, a boy about six. Haven't seen them for months." She pointed to other houses: the Wilsons, the Cordells, the Parkers, the Nelsons, the Garcias. All had kids, none seen in weeks. "I know the mother got killed. By vagrants trying to rape her right out in the street. The father arrested for shooting them, kids taken away." She pointed to the Jorgenson house. "About the same time Julia was...you know."

I expressed concern. "And the other families?"

"They maybe left. Or something bad happened, like getting the virus. Yeah, they could all be dead inside the house and nobody would know."

"They could decay there all winter and nobody find them until spring."

Hannah sucked in the cool air. "About the same weather now as in the springtime."

"I get that."

"It happened in the spring," she said after a while. "There was a little snow on the ground that day. I hate snow."

I lowered my head. "When Julia died."

"Yeah." She breathed deeply. "I miss her.... I miss Kristin, too. And Dad." She turned to me, sad face showing. "I didn't have anybody to talk to till you came." She flashed a smile. "And I miss Mother. She hasn't been the same since Julia died. And different after Dad died, too. And there's no telling where Kristin is. I have less thoughts of her each day. Fading away. I spend all my time taking care of Mother and Nathan. It's really exhausting."

Thinking of what Mom reported, I could only nod. I couldn't imagine what I'd do without my mother. She had literally been with me almost every day of my life.

"I'm sorry for your loss." That sounded insincere, I knew, but it was better than silence. And I really meant it. "Mom didn't tell me much about my aunts, and less about my cousins."

"You know about our Brewer cousins?" I asked cautiously.

She stared at me like I said a bad word. "Do I want to?"

"They're family so...umm. Maybe you should."

"Aunt Laura, Uncle Henry? They got divorced is all I know."

So I told her about our aunt, and about Sammy and Tammy, Kenneth and Cutler, what happened to them, and then mentioned Bootsy.

Hannah listened patiently but she had music in her head. "It's like that song 'Petty Grooves' by the Wu Crew. You heard it?" She softly sang the line from the song: 'Do what you want / Just don't be a cunt / Mama says come home / But you came already / Lying with your Steady' – although I'd never heard it before. Mom never liked pandemic pop.

Hannah wiped her eyes when she finished.

"That was good," I said. "You do have a good voice."

"Yeah, I coulda been a singer.... If this shit didn't happen."

"Yeah...."

"Mother hates when I curse."

"Mine, too."

"But it feels right now, don't you think? Lots to curse at."

"Yeah, it's...."

"Let's say it. Say it together."

So we did, a bit louder than we should have: "It's fucked up."

That made us laugh for a minute.

"Language," Nathan called out.

We laughed again.

"So you're Sandy," said Hannah, shaking her hair loose and looking at me through a few of the strands. Her mask slipped off her nose. Annoyed, she removed it. "Short for Alexander? I've only heard you called Sandy. When Mother talked about my aunts."

"No, it's not short for anything. Mom named me Sandy, just Sandy, because of...well, how I was...umm, conceived."

"Oh, yeah?" She gave me a wry smile.

"It's true."

I told her the story of Mom going to the nude beach on the island, meeting the debonair gentleman who seduced her on the sand – key detail – then encouraged other guys there, so I didn't know for sure which one was actually my father.

"Yeah, guess she really was a slut." Hannah giggled. "Like my mother always said. Gotta get attention somehow."

"But she's not like that—"

"Do you look like one of them? Has your mother ever said?"

"Good question." I thought of rushing inside, finding a mirror. Last I checked, I could see some features Mom had. Maybe it was impossible to determine which of the men Mom might see in my face. I never thought to ask her.

"I knew your mother played tuba, so I imagined her being big. Like a wrestler. I gotta wonder how she could be attractive. But as a teenager she could've been sexy. Now she's like a battle bitch, buff and badass. Like the War Chix. You ever see them? They like to fight on stage during their concerts."

"I think she knows how to fight, but...."

"But what?"

"She had to fight not long ago, when we were at the farm. I couldn't help her fast enough."

"What happened?"

So, just as she shared with me, I told her about the assault and me shooting the men. Now we were even.

"Fuck, you killed them?" My cousin was amazed.

"Had to." The way she looked at me, I felt proud. My chest puffed out a bit. I took off my mask.

"It's just like in those post-apocalypse movies."

"Post-apocalyptic movies, huh?"

"Yeah, after the apocalypse...whatever that is."

"It's a word for the future when everything's all fucked up."

"...fucked up," she echoed, joining me.

I honestly hadn't seen any movies like those. Mom limited my exposure to 'decadent hallucinations', as she called them. I heard lots of talk about this pandemic being the apocalypse, or the start of it. Maybe that was what Mom meant about repopulating the world – because so many people died.

"But she's not." My cousin blushed. "Not big and brutish. She seems kind. Yeah, not too different from my mother – before."

"She's shorter than me but she's strong. I guess she might be stronger than me. But we never, you know, wrestled or anything. Probably it's from carrying around that tuba."

"No, she's pretty. Thinking of her years ago and I can see her on a beach getting admirers coming up to her."

"Well, it was a nudist beach," I had to clarify.

"But that don't mean you hafta have sex."

Remembering that kiss in the bedroom, I regarded my sweet and sad cousin. Was a kiss a sex act?

"I'm sorry you had to go through those things." My chest felt tight and I had to take a breath. "Hannah?"

"Sandy," she teased.

"Honestly, I was surprised you kissed me. I mean...telling me about...*her*...then kissing...?"

"Yeah, I know. I guess I just wanted to. Sorry for that. Sorry for dropping my mask." She pursed her lips. "Just my reaction to somebody being here. Didn't wanna make you feel uncomfortable, okay? My school's big on getting consent – forgot to, sorry."

"That's okay. Don't worry. I won't tell anyone." The cool air was drying my lips. The mask held in moisture from my nose and mouth – helping bacteria grow within the mask's material. "I just wanted to be sure we're in agreement."

"Agreement? About what?"

"About us being cousins."

"But we *are* cousins." Her eyes fluttered.

"I mean.... We kissed. Like we were a couple."

"What's wrong with being cousins?" She seemed upset, maybe offended.

"Nothing. I mean, it's our relationship. You know cousins can't be couples."

"Who said that?" Her face tensed, eyes serious. "We're in the same bubble now. Bubble buddies. We can do whatever the fuck we wanna."

I tried to laugh, to break the tension. "Mom keeps teasing me that we might have to repopulate the world. Like if everyone dies and it's just us left. That's all. Sorry. I didn't wanna say anything that...that makes you feel bad, or weird."

"Geez, Sandy, I'm only sixteen. Okay, almost seventeen. In a couple months. Not that anybody cares about laws like that now.

Julia was only ten. Mother keeps me at home, safe from the world. But I gotta get out and run free. 'Got to fly high, girl / Soar, dip, dance and whirl.' Like an eagle. Ya know? 'Gotta soar high / Gotta at least try.' That part's not in their song. I made it up."

"Eagle, huh? I would've guessed some kind of songbird." I had to grin, but not in a pervy way. I didn't know what to do with my face when my mask was off. "I'm nineteen. Okay, I just turned nineteen. Well, about four months ago. So we're really just two years apart."

"Does it matter?"

She regarded me a long minute, smile hiding in the corner of her mouth, afraid to come out. She closed her eyes, as though letting the dream die. Her long exhale moved the dry leaves over the grass.

"I'm not gonna have sex with anybody. It's not worth it. The world is too crazy, too fucked up, for me to bring a child into it. That would be cruel."

"But the world won't always be this way," I insisted, fully believing it. I reached for her hand. "It'll get better."

"But it'll get worse before it ever gets better. *If* it gets better. 'No time like the present / to dream of revenants.' That's Maddy Fink and the Pink Lezzos. You ever hear them? They dress like vampires. I saw a vid—"

"And if it all goes horribly wrong, then we really do have to, maybe, ya know, repopulate the world. Like Mom keeps saying, then...."

"Fuck, Sandy." Her voice was sharp. "Your mom is strange." She gazed at me a moment. "Would you? With your mother?"

I shook my head like I was busy thinking of a good answer, dismissing each option in turn. Then I switched to counting Mom's age, putting the years up against her window of opportunity. That provided a loophole.

"She's not gonna be able to get pregnant very soon anyway, so no problem. At best she's only got a couple years, I guess, before she hits the menopause."

"Really? Isn't she, like, thirty-five or six?"

"Yeah."

"I think menopause comes at around fifty."

"Fifty?"

"It's forty-five, I'm pretty sure." Hannah tilted her head. "Or forty...-two? Anyway, starts with a bunch of hot flashes. Mother had'em. But it was a hot summer."

"Okay, I guess I didn't pay attention in Biology."

I smiled at her, waited until she smiled back. It took a minute. I'd always been good at observing people, getting a sense of them from a face tic or glimmer in an eye. I notice all of it, but never could match them with what a person was thinking. Maybe it was the reason I was so awkward and weird around people.

"But you have a lot of years ahead of you," I blurted out. "And no pressure but, if we have to...really have to, like it's only us left to save humanity, then...I would be truly honored to join with you. You know, for the express purpose of repopulating the world. It's purely business, I promise."

Nathan came up to us, holding out a softball. "You guys done flirting?"

Hannah giggled. "We weren't flirting."

Her brother invited me to play catch. Taking the opportunity to escape the awkward situation, I accepted the ball and tossed it to him. He threw it back to me. Back and forth. Between throws, I saw that Hannah had gone in.

After a while we were called in for dinner and sat around the kitchen table, said Grace, passing around a plate of bologna cold cuts grilled in a pan, mashed potatoes that were not quite mashed enough, and dry bread from a bag. A can of off-brand cream soda was divided among us, just enough to get the taste. Dessert was one wintergreen mint a piece.

17

IN WHICH MOM PLAYS HER FINAL SONG

The dulcet tones of Mom's tuba wafted from an open window a couple days later. I didn't recognize the music. It could've been a bassoon sonata; that was all the music available for tubists to play before 1835. Or cello pieces. Mom played plenty of those over the years. But this music was new to me, a melancholy song in late Romantic style, lots of *largo* and *lontano*, a lamentation I guessed was meant to comfort Aunt Jackie.

Feeling sad, Hannah and I eventually went inside. We listened to songs on her player, one bud in my ear and the other bud in her ear, the cord connecting us. She took my hand as we focused on the music. We sat on 'my' bed – the one Kristin had slept on – side by side, backs against the wall. We heard each other breathing in the darkness, could feel our hearts beating as the growling tones of Mom's tuba surged over our music then softened to nothing.

"They turn off the power at seven," Hannah reminded me. "It's on seven to nine in the mornings and again from five to seven. Enough for people to get breakfast and dinner done. Can't waste it on TV or computers. But I recharge my MP3 player. We gotta get used to the darkness with winter coming soon."

"Yeah," was all I could say.

The music stopped, battery down but enough for six songs.

Hannah squeezed my hand, tilted her head to my shoulder.

"I'm glad you're here. You're easy to talk to." She patted my arm, like she was thanking me for being a good listener. "Mother is glad, too. I can tell. She likes your mom's music, she said. Even tuba. When they were girls, she said, she always encouraged your mother to play, and never teased her about the tuba."

"That's good to know," I said. "Thanks."

We heard the shower running in the next room.

"She makes it sound good. Like God is singing. You know? A big bass voice that's comforting yet demanding."

"That's Mom, all right."

"Mother told me about the day your mother first saw that old silver tuba their great-grandfather brought from Europe. Such a big thing, and shiny, so she was attracted to it. Yeah, as a baby, crawling over to it, pushing the valves. She was trying to blow on it from age five."

A burst of sweet laughter from an angel. I smiled. Mom seldom told such stories.

"She actually made sounds at age six, started sounding good at ten, played in school band at twelve. She played in all kinds of groups – till she had to go live with her grandparents. You know? The grandfather that was a Marine. Because you were gonna be born, of course."

She pursed her lips, blinked. Her breathing got louder.

"But they blamed her for breaking up the family, Mother said. She always gets sad telling that part, about when your mother was sent away. So I never knew Aunt Polly, just heard stories, mostly making fun of her. Or complaining. Family reputation and all that shit. Fucking grown-ups! So sick of them."

Then her voice brightened: "I heard she won awards. Like at music competitions, trophies, stuff like that. They're on the hutch at Grandma and Grampa's. Did you see them?"

My voice choked. They'd been smashed by vagrants.

"Yeah, I saw them."

Hannah leaned against me, her legs stretched across the twin bed. "I'm glad you're here."

"I'm glad to be here."

At that instant, wrapping my arm around her seemed the best thing to do. I never did that before. It felt so good having Hannah against me, her body so warm. Her breath tickled my neck. When I turned to her, probably to say something stupid, her lips were right there, parted slightly as if waiting for mine, as if expecting a kiss. So I had to kiss her.

Mom came in, flicking on the light as she entered.

We quickly leaned apart like we couldn't stand being together but were forced to share the bed.

Laughing, Mom stood in the doorway with a towel wrapped around her hips and nothing covering her top.

"You kids!" She grinned at our response.

"What?" I reminded her about saving electricity.

"It'll go off soon anyway," said Hannah.

Mom stood with her hands on her hips, like she was going to give us a lecture, her boobs just hanging out for the world to see. I guessed Hannah was embarrassed.

"Ooo, what a brisk shower. No hot water." Mom shivered for dramatic effect. "But good enough."

I didn't know how to respond.

"Geez!" Hannah jumped up from beside me on the bed, exited stage right.

"Flighty girl, isn't she?" said Mom.

"Can you put something on?" I said.

"Just taking a shower. Everyone does it. So get over yourself. Besides, you know I sleep nude. Nothing to get upset about."

I shook my head. "Mom, we don't wanna make anybody feel uncomfortable while we're here."

"And I'm the one making everyone uncomfortable?"

"Yes, I think so." Her sour expression shut me up.

She went to her bag and dropped the towel, bent over to dig out a pair of panties from her suitcase.

The electricity went off with a flicker then a snap, like a big switch had been thrown.

The silence of the darkness was unsettling.

"So we're going to the beach house...." I waited for her to settle on the opposite bed, pull up the sheet, straighten the blanket.

"That seems the best plan," she replied.

"And what is that exactly? A beach house?"

"A house on the beach. Well, near the beach. No, technically, we could say it's on the beach. The street's in front, the beach in back. Business in the front, party in the back. The surf's about fifty yards from the back porch."

"But did you ever live there? Like full time?"

"It's for vacations. Spent summers there when I was little, but, as I grew up, less and less. After that summer you were conceived, I never got many chances to return – even when the rest of the family did. Especially when they went. They didn't want to have to answer questions about the little boy I had. So I stayed with my grandparents."

"Mom...," I whined in the dark.

"That's what happened. Can't wash away the facts. They were embarrassed. Besides, I didn't want to be reminded of the place."

"Yet we're going there."

"Yes, Sandy. But it's not for the nostalgia. It's...."

She paused and the evening was suddenly so silent that my heart shook. I listened for a window breaking.

"It may be the only safe place left," she continued, lowering her voice to a whisper. "Dad always said it's the safest place to be because you could only get on the island by a bridge or the ferry. He was thinking of a bank robber. They couldn't get away because it's be too easy to catch them on the road or at the ferry landing."

"Makes sense. But how about now?"

"Now? Well, I guess we'll have to see. Probably the ferry isn't running anymore. I'm guessing there's no more groceries in the store there. People liked to grow flowers in their yards – like tropical jungles – so we could grow food. And we could certainly catch fish. We can survive there. Better there than here."

"Okay, Mom. I believe you."

I wanted to turn over and go on to sleep, but she kept talking, mostly about responsibility – to me, then me to my cousins, and especially to my cousin Hannah, the precious vessel of our family tree, to be protected at all costs, even more than Mom. I heard her, but she repeated that. And circled around again to it. We also had responsibility to the world, she explained, to the community we might find ourselves a part of or that we started for ourselves, and then by extension to the greater community of humanity, the whole of society and the civilization wrapped around it, to all that remained post-pandemic.

"...to whatever remains," was the last thing I heard before I slipped away into dreams.

I ran barefoot through grass, hand in hand with Hannah, her toes wiggling, bare legs smooth, her long, dark hair caught in the breeze, as we found a good spot beneath shade trees. I looked up and found her already among the branches, having climbed up, but up there she had no clothes on, sitting on a thick limb, legs dangling. Her long hair covered her body, blocking my view. Then she swept her hair back and her breasts were like something in a comic book, pointed and perfect, and above them her grin, and her eyes calling me. Yet as I climbed up to join her, trying not to fall, I tripped and fell. Her hand caught me – caught me by my erection. In pulling me up, she accidently made me go—

I awoke in the night, wetness in my shorts. With a groan of frustration, I got up and felt my way to the bathroom, cleaned myself in the dark, returned to bed. I could smell it in the room.

Shipwrecked on a desert isle, I mused, laying back and trying to fall asleep but wary of finding Hannah in my dreams again. Just the two of us, trying to survive, never wanting to be rescued. I liked the idea. But Mom's voice arrived like an angel watching over us: Can you trust each other? Can you rely on each other? Will you love each other for as long as you both shall live?

＊　＊　＊

I awoke the next day with this thought in my head: If not for a deadly virus spreading around the world making things get so bad that Mom and I had to escape from the city, I never would have met Hannah. So that was a good thing.

Mom put on her hazmat suit and drove down to the Food Mart where she used Aunt Jackie's phone with its bank app to get more food. We lived the life of small town pandemic for a few days, each the same. Mostly we sat around staring at each other. Sometimes we talked, but other times we just sensed each other's thoughts. We put together whatever food we had for at least one meal a day, generally the evening one with a snack for breakfast.

We tried to talk, to go to happy places that we could recall but we always circled down into the abyss of lost words. Mom played more songs, half from her repertoire, half her own design. I held Hannah's hand a lot; she liked that. Nathan would play on his own but would invite me to join him and I often did. I liked being the big brother.

And the sun rose and set; nights cold, days still warm. It was starting to feel like home.

Finally it was time to leave.

Never flicking the switch off the previous night, the light came on by itself when power was restored in the morning. I hid under my pillow but Mom got up with a loud yawn and a few sniffs. It happened again.

"Good morning," she said, snicker added for my benefit. "Good dreams?"

I rolled over to face the wall.

"Got to get ready to leave," she reminded me.

She dressed and went out as I pulled myself to wakefulness. I put on new shorts, got into a fresh pair of jeans and a button shirt. I wanted to look nice for Hannah. I packed my bag, took it to the front door. Two suitcases already sat there.

There was a bustle in the kitchen. I found my cousins making toaster pastries while the power was on. Hannah's MP3 player was charging, too.

I drank some water from the tap and sat at the table.

Hannah turned, dressed exactly as she was in my dream: blue shorts and a white pullover that couldn't be warm enough for the morning chill. I saw goosebumps on her skinny arms. I stared a bit too long and she spun away.

"She's dead," said Hannah, sitting at the table, plate of pastry in front of her, voice sticky like an old drop of syrup.

"What?" I asked, not sure what I heard.

"She won't wake up."

Hannah looked down at her pastry.

Nathan was sniffling, acting brave, as he entered.

I got up to get a pastry from the toaster, returned to the table.

"What? Who?" I asked stupidly.

Hannah raised her eyes to mine. "Mother."

I listened to the word repeating in my head. Nothing wrong with Aunt Jackie, I thought, just grief, depression maybe, which wasn't a strange diagnosis in these times.

"I checked on her in the night," said Hannah, her face pale and expressionless. "I made sure her bag was packed."

"Oh," I said, words catching in my throat. "I'm so sorry."

"I know," she responded, then picked up her pastry, took a bite and studied the indentation she'd made.

I did the same. We put our hands on the tabletop. Our fingers touched, grappled then clasped as Nathan broke into uninhibited weeping. I called him over and gave him a hug.

Mom came into the kitchen, a stately march.

"Aunt Jackie's...." I started to say.

"Yes, I know." She went to the open box on the countertop and pulled out the last pastry, put it in the toaster. She watched the pastry a moment. "It's what she wanted. It's how she wanted it."

The toaster dinged and she took the pastry out. Swiping the frosting with her fingertip, she plopped her finger in her mouth.

"She wanted to die?" asked Hannah in a harsh voice. "How do you know that?"

Mom sat at the table with us. "We've had time to catch up. We talked every night. Made some things clear. We talked last night, too. She told me what she wanted. I told her there were other options but she wouldn't change her mind. She was in too much pain. So I promised I would look after you two."

Mom looked at Hannah, then me, back to Hannah.

"She couldn't go on. She was struggling to stay in reality only for you two. Insisted it was her duty. Painful duty. She couldn't keep going. When I came.... Well, she knew it was time. She could finally let go."

"But you had no right to take her from us!" Hannah cried.

"She was in pain," Mom responded. "She couldn't deal with it any longer."

Hannah left the kitchen and Mom followed.

"She wanted me to help her, so I did. We're sisters. We know each other."

"You haven't had any contact in years," Hannah snapped back, spinning around to face Mom in the living room.

"We had contact. More importantly, we grew up together. And that's when you really get to know someone. She asked me to play for her, so I did. She was at peace. I even played her favorite: *Lamentations on the Occasion of a Stillbirth* by Stefan Schweiz, my professor from college – the original, unfinished version with the extended tuba solo. Twenty-seven minutes. The string players usually go out for a smoke break. Longest cadenza ever written – a wailing of pure aural pain. Well, you heard it."

Mom had to take a breath, worked up as she was.

"I helped her drink the 'medicine' she wanted. It was her plan. She went peacefully. She's no longer in pain."

"But now *I'm* in pain," Hannah shouted, burst into sobs.

"You will get over it eventually."

I followed them into the living room, worried at the intensity of their discussion.

"Mom, you...you helped her commit suicide?"

She lowered her head. With a cough to clear her throat, she looked up, met our eyes. "I did what she wanted. Exactly what she wanted." Mom turned to Hannah. "She left a note. I wrote what she wanted me to write, as she said it. It's on the nightstand."

Hannah rushed out, heading to her mother's room.

Mom regarded me. My face must've shown shock. I'd seen how Aunt Jackie was, but I never thought she would give up. We were going to a better place. She had to stick around for that, the new normal or a newer one, at least, who knows? She just wanted to get there first.

Then I began crying.

Mom came to me, held out her arms as if deciding whether to go ahead and hug me. She decided I didn't want that, dropped her arms. But I did want it, so I threw my arms around her and wept against her shoulder, wept like a baby, like the little boy she had tried to raise to be strong – but who in the end wasn't.

We left the city in a hurry, like we had to get ahead of the crowd, escaping the lawlessness that made society crash, and the shortages that made life impossible. But here people had stayed yet still got lawlessness. A small town wasn't any safer. No matter where you went criminals would be waiting for you, taking from you all you had, leaving your flesh for crows and rats to finish. Nothing more of you would exist, no memories of you or what you did in your life or the people you loved – or hated, or didn't know. All that gone in a cruel, brutal moment of violence – as though it was the only reason you were born: to be a morality lesson for a dumb thing that could never understand. That was all you were meant for.

18

IN WHICH MOM STOPS FOR ONCE

"Will it ever end?" Nathan moaned from the back seat, an hour into our drive.

The big car that was parked in Aunt Jackie's garage held all of us and her tuba comfortably, but it used a lot more gas. Mom calculated how far we could go. If the bridge was out, by storm or vandalism, we would need to drive to the ferry landing and hope they might be in operation. If not, then we would need to drive further to find a shelter. With all the detours we could run out of gas where there wasn't any to buy or steal.

"Everything ends," Hannah grumbled, pouting beside Nathan, her arms crossed, angry face showing in the rear view mirror.

Mom took a circuitous route to throw off anyone tracking us, her paranoia ratcheting up another notch. The rural route was open, free of other vehicles, although a few were parked in front of lonely houses here and there. Farms and fields were also barren. Trees moved under a warm wind, sea breezes that smelled of salt. I began to get excited, eager to reach that bridge and cross it.

Mom pulled up to a stop sign, stopping for once, looked both ways, then proceeded through the intersection.

She began the trip muttering whether she should've buried her sister but feared someone seeing her digging and becoming suspicious. So she left Aunt Jackie on her bed, covered in several blankets, not expecting to return to the house. That led her to a discussion of fate, our duties to humanity, and inevitably to music as a metaphor for life.

"There's notes in front of you," Mom was saying. "Which will you choose? Then the next note? You have to make choices and live with them, play with them, fear them sometimes. Music is like life. It *is* Life. In fact, everything in your life *and* Life itself is a vast musical plane with notes and rests that you have at your beck and call, to mix and match, for purposes of creation – like you're Tubal-Cain smithing that horn into primal existence just because you must blow notes into the void to make your presence known. Or you're Jubal, the very God of Music, waving sounds into existence, arranging them as you please. Another musical experience to conjure emotions, to prompt memories to unfold, to provide comfort, to warn us sometimes and sometimes as nothing more than neutral entertainment, the pure joy of notes flying past you, not touching each other yet touching you—"

Then the truck hit us.

*　*　*

Mom sat in the driver's seat, left hand on the steering wheel, right hand conducting her speech, index finger extending whenever she thought she made a good point. In the passenger seat, I tried not to look at her, knowing that Hannah, who sat behind me, couldn't care less what Mom was saying. Shooting daggers at me through the back of my seat, she sat with her arms crossed, scowl on her face. Next to her sat Nathan, who also didn't care about Mom's music speech, just wishing to get somewhere so he could pee. Mom told him to wait, that he should've gone before we left. He raised his voice every so often complaining of his discomfort. Beside him, behind Mom, stood Timmy, leaning against the door, bell end up.

It was one of those big-engined Hemi trucks with a crew cab, hard shell over the bed. All black but with a rough finish, muddy, no company logo on the doors. It must've come from the side, not stopping at the stop sign, not even slowing to look. Their front end hit our rear quarter panel, behind the rear wheel on Timmy's side. The impact spun us around so that in an instant we were facing the way we'd come.

Mom grabbed the wheel, trying to get control, but we turned and turned before hitting the stop sign, bending it, rumbling down the slope and coming to rest against a thick oak trunk. The front of the car smashed into the tree, sending painful rattles through all of us and challenging our seatbelts. Bags blew out for Mom and me, slapping us before we knew what happened.

"Anyone hurt?" I called out as the bag deflated. I pushed the bags away and looked for Mom, saw her eyes open. Nobody was saying anything. I unsnapped my seatbelt, reached over for Mom. She saw me, closed her eyes. "You okay?"

She gave a nod, then raised her hand and rubbed her head.

I stretched up to look behind my seat. "Hannah? Nathan? You okay?"

"My head hurts," Nathan whimpered.

"Hannah?" I called again.

"I'm here," she said at last. "What happened?"

"We got hit by a truck." I straightened myself in the seat. I pushed the bag away. A tree branch had cracked the windshield, could've come on through if given a little more momentum.

Thank goodness we had this big car from Aunt Jackie. If we'd been in Mom's small car, we probably would've been killed.

My heart was racing as I kicked the door open. It wouldn't go easily at first. I slid out, dropped to the ground, split by decisions. Mom or Hannah? Who do I get out first? In a bleep of cursing, I grabbed the door handle in front of me, jerking Hannah's door open. I reached inside, and took hold of her arm and tugged. She helped, tumbling out on the ground. I left her and hurried around the rear of the car to get Mom.

She had already forced her door open. She squeezed through the gap, her shirt ripped down from her neck as she freed herself. With a huff she stood, hands on hips, glaring at the car as though it was at fault. She grabbed Timmy's door next and got it open, gently lifting out the tuba in its soft-side case and set it on the ground leaning against the car. She unzipped the case and gasped at the dent and the bend of the bell.

"We're all okay," I told her, seeing her worry about the damn tuba. "I said we're okay. No injuries."

"I heard you," she muttered, checking her beloved instrument.

Hannah came around the rear of the car to join us. Nathan followed, crying, pee stain darkening his pants. Hannah put her arm around him and he wept against her, half embarrassed to be crying, half shook up by the trauma.

"Well, this car's crap now," said Mom, surveying it.

"Hey, looky here," a man's voice called out.

We turned to see two men in dirty clothes coming toward us. Behind them was the truck that crashed into us, left in better condition than our car. The closer man had a long mustache but not much beard, ball cap pushed back on his head covering long brown hair. His get-up was country mechanic: worn-out cowboy boots and a black leather vest. His partner, following quickly, was better dressed but still dirty with oil and mud, cowboy hat in his hands, fixing it, then squeezing it down on his head as he caught up to his buddy.

"Hey, bitch, you shoulda stopped at that there stop sign," said moustache man. "What the hell kinda driver you anyway? Coulda killt somebody."

"No masks?" I warned them. We weren't wearing any mask, of course, because we were all in the same bubble. These guys were strangers. If they were going to come closer to us, they'd better put on facemasks.

"Masks?" asked the man with the cowboy hat.

"We don't need no stinkin masks!" the mustache man cursed. "Maybe if'n y'all weren't so blind by yer effing masks y'all woulda stopped."

I stood tall, puffed out my chest to make myself look older, stronger. "You're the ones that ran the stop sign."

"Zat so?" said the mustache man, sending a glob of spit to the ground.

"Yes. We stopped, then went on. But you didn't," I roared at them, forgetting my usual polite nature. "You guys never slowed, just charged on through the intersection."

"Hey, nobody was killt so yer lucky. Shut up!"

"Looky there, Bo," said the man with the cowboy hat, standing a little behind his buddy. "Two women. Mom and daughter. Which you want?"

"Shut the fuck up, Larry," the mustache man snapped. "We ain't like that no more, ya dumbass horndog. Man, y'ain't learnt nothin. You want more jail time?"

"Ain't no law out here—"

"So...we exchange insurance cards?" I asked, quite serious. I learned that in my driving class.

Mom had come up beside me, looking tough, a woman they'd have trouble with if they tried to wrestle her to the ground. She was shorter than all three of us men.

"I doubt there's any insurance company to take our claim," she said. "No tow truck to take our car to the nearest town for repairs, either. If we could even make a call." She glanced back at the car. "And if it could even be repaired."

"So what are we gonna do?" I asked her, knowing the answer as soon as I spoke: walk.

"Okay, sorry y'all got hit," said Bo, pulling his cap down, giving his mustache a tug, "but y'all gotta 'cept part o' the blame. If'n you'da looked both ways fore crossin."

"That there daughter's lookin mighty fine, Bo," said his creepy buddy, Larry. "Ah like them skinny ones."

Bo turned to Larry, lowered his voice. "Get a grip, man."

"Oh, man, but she just my type: young."

"Be cool, man."

I looked at Hannah, on the other side of the car, arm around Nathan who was still whimpering. My gut was tight. I glanced at Mom and saw in her eyes the same idea. Without any gesture, I knew to get the pistol from the car. As I took a step, I realized the shotgun from Officer Tanner's car was in the trunk, moved from our car as we packed to leave. But the crash made the trunk pop open. I stepped around the rear of the car as the two men talked to each other, deciding what to do.

I saw the shotgun laying there, the box of shells beside it. In a flash I wondered if I could load it and fire quick enough to do any good. But the pistol was loaded, just needed to flick off the safety. So I continued around to where I'd been sitting, reached in for the weapon, scooped it off the floor and got it in my hand.

I heard a scream then and looked up to see Larry grabbing my cousin. She slapped at his hands, tore away from his clutch, ran into the field. He chased her, tackled her.

Nathan was frozen with fear. Mom was fighting Bo, boxing him, a good punch to his face that made him pause.

I raised the pistol, decided not to shoot in the air to get their attention, not to waste any bullets, so I shouted: "Stop!"

They didn't.

I shouted again, aiming my voice at the one farther away, now sitting on top of Hannah as she squirmed in the grass.

"Get off her!"

He didn't acknowledge me. I stepped away from the car, gave a glance back at Mom, who seemed to be holding her own, punching poor Bo. Blood ran from his nose.

I ran through the grass, right up to Larry and pressed the end of the barrel to his temple. "I said stop. Now."

"Heh-heh now, sonny, just having some fun with yer sis," he laughed. "Just some play time. No big deal. She likes it."

"No, she doesn't."

I pushed the barrel harder against his head. "Get. Off. Her."

"Easy now, sonny. You know that could go off if'n yer not payin tention."

And it did. Straight through his head. My finger, nervous on the trigger, squeezed ever so slightly as I shifted the pistol in my grip, and it went off. My whole body went slack, then became a knot of muscle. I never expected that, never wanted to kill anyone.

No time to feel traumatized. I swung the pistol around at Bo. Mom was too close. He was paying attention now. The gunshot got his attention. Mom gave him a kick between his legs that dropped him to the ground.

Hannah was quiet as she got to her feet, her face stony. She stood away from me, probably afraid of the pistol going off again. I hadn't shot it so much as let it go off. An accident. It was done. I thought she would rush to me, throw her arms around me.

"Here," said Mom, her arm extended to me. "Give me the gun."

"Please, ma'am," begged Bo, crumpled on the ground. "Didn't mean no harm. I'm sorry, real sorry. Honest."

"I believe you're sorry." Mom got righteous. "In these times? All you can think of in these difficult times is how to satisfy your lust? And for what? Nothing, that's what. Do something useful for goodness sake! How about making something? Or gathering food? Help people, dammit. You might get some thanks for that. Then a woman might think you're worth being with, maybe help you start over, you and other families working together. Ever think that?"

Piled on the ground, Bo gazed up forlornly at Mom – and the business end of the pistol pointed down at him.

"Yes ma'am, I thought o' alla that. Honest. But, see, Larry, he don't think that way."

"You're both pieces of shit," Mom snarled, then sniffed the air.

I sniffed, too: gasoline. A leak from our car.

"Get up," she ordered and Bo stood shaky, off-balance. "Is your truck still working?"

He swung his head around, thumbed at the truck. "Well, it's purdy banged up but s'pose it's drivable."

"Great, we will." Mom narrowed her eyes. "I won't shoot you. But we're taking your truck. First, you can transfer our bags over. It's a nice thing to do. And give me the keys."

He pointed to the truck. "They're in the ignition." He went to retrieve them, Mom following close with her pistol to make sure there were no tricks. "I'm gonna need some o' those to get in my house, okay?"

He pulled off the keys for the truck, handed them over.

"Now go get the things from our car and put them in the back of your truck. Be useful—"

"Mom!" I exclaimed. Remembering the shotgun and shells in the trunk, I hurried to the car and retrieved them. "Okay, he can get the rest."

A moment after taking the last things from the car over to the truck, the car burst into flames. Fire quickly engulfed it, the grass burning beside it. The entire vehicle was being consumed. We rushed behind the truck, hiding, expecting the car to explode.

Mom grabbed her tuba in its soft-side case, either for comfort or to protect it.

"Whew!" said Bo, crouched down with us. "Shore was close."

I looked around for Hannah.

After I shot the guy on top of her, she'd stood up, looking unharmed but frightened. Then I got busy with other business. She wasn't with us behind the truck. Now that the car was done, I got up and rushed over to the flaming mess.

Mom called out there could be more explosions, but I ignored her as I rushed into the field beyond. I scanned the grass like she might've hidden there, maybe slid into a hole to keep away from me, from Mom, from the whole world determined to attack her.

"Hannah?" I called out, turning around in the tall grass.

Then I saw her. She was up among the branches of a tree, legs dangling like in my dream. I went to the base of the tree.

"It's all over," I called up. "You can come down now. It's safe."

It took a while to convince her, but she eventually climbed on down. When she was back on the ground, shaking and teary, she came to me but stopped short. Looking down, she acted as though she wanted a hug, or to hug me, but she hesitated.

I reached out and put my hand on her shoulder to reassure her that I would take care of her, but she shook my hand off.

"Don't touch me!"

"I'm sorry," I said, my voice choked up. "I'll never leave you. I'll always protect you."

"I can take care of myself," she growled.

She stomped through the grass to the truck and I followed.

Mom had already settled into the driver's seat, the engine on, checking gauges. Nathan was buckled in. We climbed in.

Bo raised his hand in farewell as we drove off.

19

IN WHICH MOM COMES CLEAN

The road Mom was tearing down was full of pot holes that left our teeth rattling and our stomachs bouncing.

"Mom!" I shouted, trying to get her to slow down.

She wasn't good at dodging the holes, many of them filled with puddles, the road slick with mud from overnight rain. The truck handled the terrain despite her abuse. She hoped this back road would be safe, skirting the main roads to avoid other traffic and hide from the phantom cops she believed were chasing us. Maybe someone heard the gunshot or saw the car in flames. Or they were tracking us, like they did now with devices hidden in vehicles.

"Mom, stop!"

Hannah and Nathan, sitting behind, cried and complained.

"Just for a few minutes. Please. We can't take it any more."

She eased up on the gas, let the truck hit a few more holes at slower speed, not that it mattered much. We rolled to a stop off the road, coming to rest on the muddy shoulder. Before we could catch our breaths, she turned the truck down the slope from the road into a field, the sea of tall grass spreading to a line of trees that acted as a windbreak, separating a lonely farmstead from the State right-of-way.

When the truck halted, Mom shut off the engine.

We sat back a moment, catching our breaths, letting stomachs settle. Mine was ready to vomit but there wasn't a lot in it. I dry-heaved as I baled out my door, falling on my knees in the grass.

Mom remained in her seat, annoyed we had to pause. Hannah got out of the truck, stood like a statue, arms folded across her chest, apparently not ill. Nathan did his best up-chuck but had nothing to show for his effort.

"Geez, Mom, where'd you learn to drive?" I said, using a stern fatherly voice I got from watching videos. Clearing my throat, I had to spit. Tasting some of our meager breakfast, I spit again.

I gazed around the meadow. So quiet. I wondered if anyone watched us from the buildings which stood back from the road.

"Done?" asked Mom. "Ready to carry on?"

"Mom," I whined, grabbing the open door. "Can we just rest a little? There's no hurry to get to your precious beach house. If it's there, it'll be there when we arrive. If it's not there, then there's no reason to hurry."

Mom shook her head, clearly disappointed in me. "I don't care about the damn beach house."

Then Hannah sneezed. A big one. I gazed at her: stepping with knees high in the tall grass. Maybe she'd kicked up some pollen. Or some other plant material. Sneeze—a bigger one. Another.

"Hannah, get out of the grass," I called, but she was in a mood to ignore me. She wasn't having it: the plan for survival. Not with me anyway. Somehow I'd ruined it. "Stop sneezing."

"She's gotten something," said Mom in serious tone, climbing out of the truck. She went to the rear and lowered the tailgate and raised the camper shell door. All of our bags were there, plus first aid kit and a sack of other items she took from Aunt Laura.

Hannah returned to the truck, angry scowl on her face, at the edge of her patience.

"That guy was on top of you, face to face," Mom reminded her. "Breathing on you. Did he cough? Hack up his lungs?"

Hannah shook her head, refusing to speak.

Mom put her palm to Hannah's forehead. "No fever. Yet."

"It's just been an hour," I said.

"Thirty-eight minutes," Nathan proudly announced. He held up his wrist with a plastic watch on it. Then he sneezed.

"Shit." Mom covered her nose and mouth with her hand. She

stepped up on the truck's side runner and scanned the area. She pointed. "There."

"What?" I asked.

"A pond," Mom answered. "Every farm has a farm pond."

I knew what that meant. Mom would go for a bath, wash off potential viruses from her body. She gave us a stern look.

"Okay, we need to wash off. Come on." She waved us to follow. "All of us. Those were not the cleanest people. And the truck...."

"Oh my god," I muttered. "Yes! The cab is filled with all their viral breaths and whatever they coughed or sneezed. And we've been breathing it this whole time."

Mom led us over to the line of trees. We followed a cattle trail between two big trees, dry chips of manure crunching beneath our feet, up to the pond. The pond was man-made, one side a built-up wall of dirt. I mounted the rim, gave the pond a look. The placid water appeared green, reflecting the trees. Could be delicious to a cow or horse.

"You're serious?" I questioned.

"Here's what we're gonna do," said Mom, spinning around to face us. "We have to wash off. And we'll change into fresh clothes after."

"What?" Hannah practically shrieked.

"We'll take turns." Mom didn't smile; it had to be done. "Girls with girls. Boys with boys."

"Okay." I was resigned to the need for us to do as she said. No telling what viruses stuck to us. Besides, Mom was always right.

In a world where what was invisible could kill you, it was critical to stay as clean as possible. Initially Mom got on board with all the suggestions that became rules: wearing facemasks, bathing in sanitizer practically every hour, keeping apart from others. But when even top-grade medical masks wouldn't stop a virus so small it could pass through the material without bumping against any of the fibers, we could never be truly safe. The cloth masks people used were even less safe. Many people gave up on masks before vaccines were introduced. Others continued to wear masks after getting a vaccine. It became almost a custom: people wanted to show they were conscientious citizens, demonstrating they cared. Masks became fashion statements for some people. I had a mask with a Schnauzer's face. Mom's had a bar of music: Beethoven's *da-da-da-dum* of Fate.

Now, with so many waves and variants of the virus passing through communities, everyone was on their own. The man on the street with lived experience had just as good an answer for how to survive as the highly trained doctor. Everyone had to assess their own risks, do what they thought best to protect themselves. At the same time, others believed the danger had passed and tried to return to normal – until the next wave came. Mandates and edicts remained a constant source of amusement. It was safest to be outdoors, they said, away from other people. Wearing a hazmat suit with a personal ventilator attached was the ultimate in safety fashion. And no more scratching your nose or licking your fingers. Avoiding strangers was a hard-and-fast rule. So we put ourselves into voluntary confinement.

Mom regarded Hannah, then Nathan. "Okay? We have to. Or we'll get sick. We probably picked up something."

"But that pond is...yucky," said Hannah.

"Probably safer than whatever those bastards coughed out of their lungs," Mom countered.

Hannah froze, studying Mom for signs she was only joking.

"Awright." She would do it, but not enjoy it.

I was used to seeing Mom remove her clothes. She stood on the edge of the pond like she was on that nude beach. Step by step each item, mechanical, until she was naked with her back to me. Hannah did the same but much slower. She glanced back a few times to make sure we boys weren't looking. I only looked once: when she had her shirt and shorts off, standing in underwear. She looked thin in that awkward pose before stepping into the water.

"Don't peek," Nathan commanded. He hid his face against the tree trunk like we were playing hide-n-seek.

"I'm not," I said, swinging my head around.

Hearing splashes I decided it was safe now to look. Mom swam on her back, breasts rising out of the water. Hannah submerged herself until her chin grazed the surface, hit by the waves Mom sent with each stroke and kick, but she keeping her body hidden.

"Is it our turn?" called Nathan.

Hannah startled. "Stay away!"

"Five more minutes," Mom shouted, then told Hannah: "Be sure to scrub yourself. And your head and face need to go under the water."

Hannah took the instructions seriously and dunked herself. Rising again, she shook her head vigorously, letting her long hair fly in every direction, flinging water. My eyes paused the scene, made it into a slow-mo advertisement for shampoo.

Mom announced it was time to switch: girls out, boys in.

"I'll get the disinfectant," she called to us, out of the pond and shaking herself off, squeezing water out of her hair. "We need to spray each other."

"Spray?" asked Nathan, standing shyly behind a tree as Mom strode naked through the grass over to the truck, then peeked at his aunt with great interest.

"Come on," I said to him, both of us as naked as the day we were born.

Stepping out from the shade of the trees, I stopped in awe. I beheld a goddess. Standing free and natural, Hannah was lit by a ray of sunshine. Her figure was so heavenly, so regal. She held her arms out, chin up as though absorbing the sunshine.

Nathan was in awe, too.

"Don't look at your sister," I told him.

"Don't look at your cousin," he chided me.

I thought she would remain shy. I didn't care about that, but now she seemed to enjoy her time under the sunshine.

"Get in the pond," shouted Mom, approaching.

Hannah turned at Mom's command and we beheld each other's nakedness. My hand jumped automatically over my groin but she held firm in her pose, then lowered her arms to her sides, daring me to look.

As I stepped up the slope to the pond, she stepped down. We passed shoulder to shoulder, not looking at each other. I walked straight into the pond, the chilly water shocking me.

Nathan was happy to splash around but got nervous when his feet didn't reach the bottom.

By the time I got out and shook the water from my body, Mom was spraying off Hannah. Mom had her raise her arms, bend this way and that way. It was bath by spray bottle. I sent Nathan over to be sprayed next and I stood back observing, trying to not let my interest show.

"Close your eyes. Pinch your nose. Suck in your lips," Mom instructed.

For a minute my view of Hannah was blocked. In that brief night, I imagined her lazing in the grass, as natural as on her birthday, long dark hair blowing in the breeze as she chewed on a stalk of grass, gazing over the field, seeing one of many futures there, with each possibility slipping on stage to audition for the opportunity to become real.

I opened my eyes and she was no longer lazing in the grass. She'd walked back to the truck. Mom was calling me to hurry as Nathan got sprayed.

We gathered our soiled clothing and put them into a plastic bag to wash later if we found a good place.

Mom was spraying down everything inside the cab, more on the front seats and dashboard. The interior was dirty from the start, muddy with lots of sand and gravel. But we had no choice.

Hannah was pulling on a pair of torn jeans when I got to the rear of the truck to dig around for my clothes. With a towel draped over her bare shoulders, she searched for a bra in her bag, cursing that she hadn't brought more, only to have Mom say she didn't need one. Giving up, she pulled on a shirt and as her head popped out she flashed me a grimace – like she knew I saw her naked but didn't care. We had more to worry about than that.

"Don't look at me," Hannah grumbled, turning away.

"Sorry," I said automatically. "But you're beautiful."

She spun around. "That doesn't give you any right!"

"Sorry," I said again. Sometimes I wished I could just record me saying that word so I could push a button each time instead of having to speak.

"It's embarrassing." She chewed her lip. "None of this is what I want."

"Me, neither."

Mom didn't care either way, and finished her work in the cab before joining us at the tailgate.

"Here, spray me off," she said, handing the bottle to me. She held out her hands, instructing me to give them extra zaps. You could never be too careful – except for going full hazmat. Through the disinfection she complained about our situation and the men we took the truck from, how dirty they were. She pulled out new clothes, culottes and a sweater, and put them on.

Finally we were dressed again. The truck was disinfected. No more excuses. On to the beach house.

I knew she'd been driving in squares, like maneuvering pieces on a big chess board – going the long way, taking dubious detours, saying she was keeping away from high traffic areas, places that were dangerous, which I believed. But I was beginning to suspect there might be other reasons for delaying our arrival. Maybe she was afraid of arriving, scared of what the beach house meant.

I glared at Mom and she glared back, a look suggesting she was in a foul mood. Maybe having to get naked in front of her niece and nephew made her angry. Maybe not. Something else. Her tuba dented. That's probably it. But these were hard times, so I couldn't be sure what had set her off.

"Mom...?" I called, ready to ask, but she didn't respond.

We drove along, slower, Mom being more careful with chuck holes. We still hit a few.

"We're not going to talk about it," she said after one big hole. "You did what you had to do. That's how we survive."

I regarded her, checking for clues to whatever she might be referring to. The men from the truck? The gun?

"It was an accident. My finger slipped."

"Yeah, right," Mom grumbled.

"It's true. I just wanted him to get off her. I wasn't going to shoot him."

Mom was silent for a while. Until we got to a better road. She looked around for other vehicles, saw none, and pulled out onto the blacktop. The ride became a lot smoother and she went faster.

"Remember that lesson," she said, face grim and not looking at me. "Don't waste a bullet. A kick in the head would've gotten him off your cousin."

20

IN WHICH MOM RETURNS HOME

Nathan contentedly hummed a favorite tune, but his sister wasn't amused. They fought in the back seat, arguing through medical-grade facemasks Mom insisted we wear, even with the windows down to air out the truck's cab.

When Mom had enough of their bickering, she pulled over, shut off the engine, and turned in her seat to face them.

"This is going to get old real quick," she growled, "if you keep it up. We've got a lot more to worry about than what song to sing. We have more to worry about than whether they're burning coal in China or if polar bears have ice in Greenland. A lot more pressing concerns right here and now. Do we have food? Where are we going to get food? Can we protect ourselves?" Then she glared at me like I did something wrong. "And can we repopulate our corner of the world? These are the questions that matter now."

Hannah started to blame her brother again. Mom cut her off, repeating what we needed to do to survive rather than voicing our displeasure at petty irritations.

"Okay!" Hannah erupted. She crossed her arms, pouting.

Nathan snickered at his apparent victory.

Mom huffed at him. She turned in her seat and tried starting the truck. The engine groaned like it wasn't sure it wanted to turn over. Then it did. Before she could shift to Drive, it rumbled and shook and went off. Mom tried again. And again, then focused on the gauges. E for empty. The light was on, had been on for a few miles. She slapped the steering wheel and muttered swear words. She'd been too engaged in driving to look at the fuel gauge. All the bumpity-bump takes your attention away.

Sitting back, she expelled a loud sigh. "Well, it was bound to happen eventually." Glaring at me again, like I should've warned her. "Guess we're walking."

My cousins complained when they realized Mom was serious. I understood more: that Mom would insist on taking her tuba.

We piled out of the truck and gathered at the rear to get our bags. Fortunately, we didn't have that much to carry. Food items were low; that would lighten our load. Mom fished out what we needed, passing them off to the rest of us.

"How much farther is it?" I asked.

Mom shut the camper door, raised the tailgate.

"A few miles." She sniffed the air. "You smell the sea?"

I took a long draw of air through my mask but couldn't smell anything but the mask's material.

At the beginning of our journey Mom and I discussed what to do in different situations, so it took no time to divide up tasks between us. I would carry the heavy pack which had her things as well as some of mine, plus our food rations. She would carry the small pack in front and Timmy, in the soft-side case with straps, on her back. She had Officer Tanner's pistol tucked in her belt and would carry the shotgun in her hands. I would carry her pistol. There was no arguing with her, I knew, so I didn't.

She checked her precious heirloom instrument after the crash and noted the fresh dents in the upright tube and the bell's edge bent down. She feared bending it right again would weaken the old metal. The most serious dent had actually broken through the metal, causing a hissing noise when she tried to play it. She cried, then resigned herself to the tuba's age. They had been lucky for so long. But the luck had run out, all because of a pandemic.

Mom led the way, Nathan close behind her, then Hannah and me. The road remained smooth, but the shoulders were broken, and there were potholes filled with rainwater. Lots of mud to step over. Nathan enjoyed stomping in some of the puddles, much to

Mom's consternation. Hannah remained a delicate flower, and avoided anything dirty. I walked beside her but she kept getting ahead, forcing me, bearing the heaviest burden in our group, to struggle to stay with her. We had nothing to talk about. I pointed to spots on the ground for her to watch out for and she would *hmmff* at me like she already knew to be careful.

Eventually we approached a highway – a better paved country road. We paused to check each direction, but not like parents teach their kids to look both ways before crossing so they don't get hit by a car. For us, it was about concealment. We hunkered down in the brush to watch for traffic, to check for potential dangers. We waited and watched. It was good to rest, too.

Then Mom ordered us up and we continued.

We walked along the shoulder, always ready to scurry into the woods if a vehicle should come by. A vehicle coming over the hill or around the curve would see us before we could get out of sight, I figured. Then it would stop and a gang of thugs would chase us. I was constantly revising my plan for getting Hannah off the road and out of sight. That was my only thought as we walked along. I turned my head to look behind me every few steps and my ears listening for the noise of a vehicle coming upon us.

The road began to turn downward, long slopes that bent and curved to the coastal plain. We saw the blue of the sea through breaks in the trees. It was real, not just one of Mom's encouraging remarks. She'd been saying "We'll get there soon" for a couple weeks. But the sight was real and we felt it: our final destination was in view.

A truck came by and we scattered off the road, Hannah and I on the lower side of the slope, Mom and Nathan on the upper side. It was an older pickup that had seen better days, now a variety of colors where it had been patched, door panels from a different truck, one tire a donut. Red was the dominant color.

It seemed the truck's engine was off and it was just coasting, letting gravity pull it on down the slope. A man sat behind the steering wheel. It continued on down the hill, steering around the curve and out of sight.

Breaking from our hiding places, Hannah and I rejoined Mom and Nathan.

"Visitor?" I asked Mom using my sharpest voice.

"It's a tourist place," she replied, not appreciating my joke.

Probably the driver was headed to the beach – to the barrier island with the beach along its shore.

We continued down the hill, too tired to complain, and finally arrived at the bottom. We gazed along the channel that separated the island from the mainland. To our left the road turned north and ran parallel to the channel then came to a bridge, which arched high enough to allow small boats to pass under. Further north was the ferry landing, for those people who didn't want to drive so far south to cross over a bridge. Most traffic came from the north, anyway, from the cities, not from country towns to the west or south. Tourists could get to the island either way.

We were away from trees and anything that would hide us if a vehicle passed. But no other vehicles came by.

Where the road leveled out, we rested, assessing the situation. Mom pulled out a small pair of cheap binoculars. She scanned the island for signs of life: people outside, cars in motion, cyclists, dogs, boats, lights on in houses, tents on the beach – or any bodies laying about, unmoving.

"Looks like an ordinary Saturday afternoon," she said, holding the binoculars up. "Don't see anyone out. In summer the streets would be full of bicyclists, dog walkers, some out on the beach. But it's autumn."

"Could be they're all sick inside," I suggested.

"Or they left," Hannah spoke up. I turned to smile at her, now that she was speaking again, but she still had a frown.

Mom lowered the binoculars. "Listen, kids—"

"I'm not a kid," I barked.

"—there's likely only two scenarios we can expect there. One, everyone's dead and we have to be careful not to contract what they got. So we should wear hazmat till we can be sure it's safe. But we only have two suits. Or, people are alive, living in fairly normal circumstances. Yet they may be wary of visitors. Maybe a bit trigger-happy, so we need to be cautious."

"Can we go swimming?" asked Nathan, fidgeting.

Mom glared at him. "If it's safe, yes."

"What about the beach house?" I looked across the channel. "Where's it at?"

"After crossing the bridge we go right, down the island, south to the cross street. It's on the beach side there. Pastel green, last I recall. Number sixteen." She grinned.

"So that's the place...."

Mom regarded me. "Yes.... That summer...." She pondered the images flashing through her head. "Franny, Frances to her family, I never told what happened. Not 'til later, when it was obvious. Even so, she thought the same thing my family thought—"

"Where's that beach?" I asked Mom to stop her from saying too much.

"The nude beach – clothing-optional, as they call it – is on the north end of the island. Closer to the ferry landing, but it's pretty well shielded by the end of the jetty and the dunes. You can't see anything from the road. You have to pull over and hike up the dunes to get a look down at the people not wearing swimsuits. So much trouble for a cheap thrill."

I turned to Hannah to see if she was interested. A nude beach? Why, that sounded great! Besides, we had already glimpsed each other without clothes. She was attentive, I saw.

"Can we go there?" I asked Mom.

"The nude beach?" She brushed the topic aside, laughed. "Like you need to go stalking. Horny young man looking for adventure? Well, I doubt anyone's there now. You know: being autumn, not to mention it's still flu season. Not a good time for lazing on a beach, nude or not. We're here for the house. A place to stay until the pandemic's over. Then we'll see who's left and start from there. Start from scratch if we have to."

"Like repopulating the world?" I said with a chuckle.

"Exactly," Mom replied, her tone serious.

"I sure do hope there's no zombies there," said the boy.

"Nathan!" cried Hannah.

Mom's stern face silenced us. It was easy to gaze at the island, feel the sun on us, and think it was a normal day, that everything was fine. But we had to be careful of the virus, violent vagrants, and running out of food and water. It wasn't a fun holiday trip.

* * *

The beat-up red truck that rolled down the hill past us had run off the road at the bottom. Coming off the hill you had to slow to a stop and turn either left or right. But the truck had gone straight, missing the big sign pointing left and right, crossed the narrow strip of rocky shoreline into the water. The front end of the truck was half-submerged, water up to the door. The window was down and an arm hung out it. The man inside lay against the steering wheel like he'd hit his head and was knocked out.

We could see the truck as we descended the hill but we weren't sure what happened until we got closer.

Mom stood on the rocks along the shore, studying the situation – as though deciding whether to go on or to help.

Then, with a curse, Mom handed me the shotgun and set down Timmy and her pack. She put on her facemask and climbed over the rocks to the truck. Regarding the man inside, she determined if he was friend or foe, infected or not, worth saving or not.

We gathered behind the rear of the truck, watching Mom go to the driver's side. She waded knee-deep to check on the unmasked man. She showed unusual care given the hard times we live in. Using her tuba muscles, she jerked on the door, got it open with a loud creak, and took hold of the man inside and pulled him out.

Semi-conscious, his arms flailed weakly, speech incoherent. He wore a white button shirt and blue slacks, but they were dirty and torn. Mom's disgust showed, but she was in rescue mode and had to see it through. She got him onto the rocks, out of the water, and he tried to return to his truck.

"Just relax," she commanded, pushing him down.

"Gotta keep going," he said, adding swear words. "They gonna get me."

"You can't go any further. You're at the coast. You drove right into the water."

"Tried to make the turn...." He fell silent, giving up.

Mom signaled to bring a mask. I handed her one and she put it over the man's grizzled face. He didn't fight her. His chest heaved like he had to strain for each breath. That was a bad sign.

"Mom," I called, motioning for her to get away.

She wore a facemask so she just nodded.

This man didn't look any nicer than the two that crashed into us, except he was older. Mom got him out of the truck and on dry land. That was all she needed to do to be a good citizen.

"He's safe now," I told Mom. "That's enough."

Mom waved us to sit and rest while she tended to the man.

I feared Mom would get whatever he had – maybe one of the new subvariants they kept announcing every few months, always when everyone started to feel that life was getting back to normal again, when people were going out and having fun again, ignoring government decrees. The official panel of pharmaceutical bigwigs would be traipsed out on stage in front of the cameras and glumly announce that another strain had been found. But don't worry. They were working hard on yet a newer vaccine, free to you but paid by your taxes. I smiled to myself, remembering Mom's rants.

Until then we all had to go back into lockdown, as though the unwashed masses had been swimming in clouds of viruses and needed to be punished for their carelessness. It was for only two weeks, or maybe two months, then two years – long enough to see what we would do, how we would handle it, who would comply – if we would continue being gullible, as Mom said. But it was already six years since I first saw the notification on the news broadcast and asked Mom if it could be true.

I reminded Mom of that situation but she just grinned, held up a bottle of whiskey she pulled from the truck. He'd obviously been drinking. Mom was tempted, I could see, but reluctant to put her mouth to the bottle.

"I'm hungry," Nathan moaned. He repeated his complaint a few times before Mom responded.

"Then why don't you swim out there and get a fish," Mom said with a scowl on her face.

That shut him up.

The food was in my pack, so I dug out some and distributed it to Hannah and Nathan. I gave a couple crackers to Mom; she offered them to the man. One of the chocolate bars had melted and reformed, but I ate it anyway. I broke off a good-sized piece for Hannah. Her soft hand lingered against mine as she took the chocolate. Her eyes thanked me.

"So...the island...." I realized then how uncomfortable the idea felt. "I think we should go on over and find the house and settle in. I'd rather rest there than here."

Mom stood where she was, looking down at the man, then over at me. We couldn't very well carry the man with us.

"Leave him," I said. "He'll live or die on his own."

Mom climbed over the rocks back to the road, brushed herself off, shook water from her feet. I knew to get the disinfectant out. I sprayed her hands, rubbed them together, shook them dry.

"He's drunk, not sick," she said.

"But why do you care?"

"Sandy!" She acted surprised.

"Well, you're always being so cold-hearted and badass. You said we have to be so we'd survive. Then you go all soft for some drunkard who crashed his truck."

"It looks to be out of gas. He was lucky to reach the hill and let it roll down."

"Mom, we can't take him with us."

"I know." She picked up her tuba. "We did enough."

"Okay," I said with a relieved sigh.

After Mom pulled Timmy onto her shoulders, I handed her the shotgun. She glanced at Hannah and Nathan, back to me.

"Let's get on over the bridge," I said, "before anyone else comes by who needs a helping hand."

PART 2

DESTINATION

21

IN WHICH MOM BURNS THE BRIDGE

When the thinning clouds let more sunshine through, the bridge looked old, worn-out, like it had endured a million cars and trucks over the years, so many people coming to the island on vacation. The pavement had been scrubbed down to nothing, bare patches revealing the iron-rod grid that held it together. Mom doubted a car could go over it safely. It was a hundred yards, with a gentle arch to allow boats to access the piers that extended from people's backyards along the shore.

Standing beside Hannah, we gazed across the channel to the island. I wondered whether, after crossing the bridge, we would ever go back to the mainland. Maybe the world would go mad, fall into such horror that we would be happy to stay in a safe space on this island.

We turned, regarded each other awkwardly. A smile wriggled over her pretty face. Her eyes brightened. She took my hand and I liked way her hand felt in mine. We were home, or as much of a home as we were likely to find in these hard times.

"Thanks," I said.

"For what?" she spoke softly, looking away.

"For trusting me."

She returned her gaze. "Oh, it's not that. I'm just happy to get here finally. It's been like two years since we last visited."

"Two years?" I cleared my throat. "To flee the lockdowns?"

"We spent a summer here. Mother...she...."

"Oh." I watched her struggle to put words together.

"Mother hardly let us out of the house. She never—"

"Come on, kids," Mom called, with her precious tuba swaying ungainly on her back, shotgun in her hands. "Let's go. Watch your step. I see gaps in the surface. Don't fall through."

If the bridge was in such bad condition now, I wondered as we started over, how long could it have been getting worse with no repairs? Had to be long before even the first pandemic wave. Were islanders abandoning the island back then?

I carried the big pack on my sore back, a small bag in front, on my chest, for balance. Hannah pulled on her knapsack, picked up the duffel bag. Nathan carried his canvas sack in his arms, a little too much energy in his steps.

"Hey!" called someone behind us. "Don't leave me."

That man Mom pulled from the truck followed us, held up his arm, hand waving.

Mom stopped, turning to see him wobbly on the road.

Looking back, I was about to step into one of the bridge's gaps when Hannah grabbed me.

"Help me," the man moaned. "I'm not infected. Honest, I'm not. Just...just a little...drunk."

"If you're not sick, you can make it on your own," Mom called from the top of the bridge's arch.

"I need to get to the island," he said.

"We do, too," Mom responded, turning to continue across.

"Can't you help me?" he called. "Please?"

I waited for Mom to decide to go back for him or go on, but she didn't pause.

We followed Mom as the bridge rose then leveled. At the other end, as we descended, we saw a short gap between the bridge and the road. Coming up to the edge of the bridge together, we saw the beams had pulled away from the road coming from the island. No wonder people had stopped driving over the bridge: there was a three-foot span now. Storms and lack of repair had allowed the structure to tear away. Chunks of pavement had fallen below.

"You used the ferry last time, didn't you?" I asked Hannah.

"Sure did," she replied, looking north, hand to her forehead to block the sun. Memories seemed to flood through her. "And we got ice cream right after we drove off the ferry."

"Ice cream?" Nathan perked up.

"You can jump over that, can't you?" Mom asked him.

He was happy to get Mom's attention. "No problem."

"I can leap over it," said Hannah. "It's like a *jeté*. I learned it in the ballet classes Mother sent me for."

"You learned ballet?" I asked, amazed. At that news, I had to examine her lithe figure in a new light, seeing her slender legs as actually strong and limber.

"Mother made me go. She said it would make me graceful. But that all stopped with the first lockdown."

"Be careful," Mom interjected. "It's not a ballet floor."

After handing her knapsack to me, Hannah easily leaped over the gap, landing securely on the other side without losing balance, a vision of pure grace. She twirled and grinned.

"*Voila!*" she sang proudly.

I was impressed. Tossing her knapsack over to her, I got ready to hand over the big pack. And the tuba. Giving me the shotgun, Mom went next. I handed Timmy over to her, then the shotgun. Next I gave the big pack a great heave over. I took my turn leaping over but almost missed. My trailing foot caught the edge and tripped me so I landed on my knee.

Hannah rushed to me, and because she did I had to play the wounded soldier and let her massage my knee for a minute.

"Thanks," I said. "I think I can make it now."

Hannah extended her hand and helped me up. Limping a few steps, I felt silly so I walked straight.

We descended the short road from where it once connected to the bridge. Like the mainland side, the road went either left or right, not straight. A yellow sign stood to block the traffic, black double arrows pointing both ways.

Mom set down Timmy, leaned the shotgun against her hip as she scanned the rows of houses. Most were bungalows. A few were two-story with widow's watches, the perches for wives to gaze out at the angry sea and long for their sailor husbands to return.

I lowered the pack, smiling at Hannah. We were close to home. Another mile. Nathan complained he was hungry again but we ignored him. The ice cream shop was a mile in the other direction and probably closed.

"The island's shaped like a teardrop," said Mom. "Narrow at the north end, with the ferry landing, wide at the bottom. The road goes south from the ferry landing, along the channel side about half-way down, then bends to the middle. You can almost see it from here. The road takes a turn, does a bit of a jog, then forks – one road going over to the channel, down this side, and the other taking a seaward path parallel to the beach. Our house is just past the fork on the seaward side. The front of the house faces the street, the backyard goes out to the beach. In fact, you can go walking the whole beach from there with no restrictions. Only a sign saying 'Beyond here you may encounter nude bathers' – if that matters to you."

I blushed. "Not me." My eyes met Hannah's and she blushed.

"I seriously doubt anyone is enjoying the beach like they used to, what with all the viruses so rampant in the dunes. Sand fleas are a bigger problem." Mom chuckled to herself. "Last time I was here, nobody ever thought we could go mad, caught between the invisible boogeyman viruses and the jackboots of the government's 'common good'. But here we are at last. On the island."

"On the island," I echoed.

"A sanctuary from the world," Mom said with a soft sigh.

"We gonna get something to eat?" asked Nathan.

He pointed to a weathered sign advertising a burger joint by the ferry landing. Most stores on the island were clustered there.

"I wonder if they're open today," said Mom showing a wry grin. "Just waiting for us. Did anyone call ahead?"

"You think?" said Nathan with anticipation.

"She's being sarcastic," Hannah explained to her brother. "It's what grown-ups do."

"We haven't seen stores open along the way," Mom replied, her voice darker. "Nothing to stock on the shelves. No gas for trucks to deliver goods. Most stores have been looted. That's our reality."

"Only the Food Mart," I offered.

"But we got food in the bags, right?" The boy was concerned. "You gave us some before."

"Yes, some." Mom's face shifted. "We have to hope we can grow our own food. It's the only way to survive long-term. The lower pocket of the big pack has seed packets."

"Yeah, and catch fish," the boy grumbled.

"Let's hope," said Mom.

"Long-term...?" I wondered just how long Mom expected us to stay here. The image of me as an old man with a long white beard flashed through my head. But there was old Hannah, too, and our brood of grandkids around us, and I knew we would be all right, no matter how long we stayed. I glanced at her, smiling hopefully, but she was fussing with her brother.

Mom waved us on. We started to the right, heading down the road to the beach house.

"Hey!"

It was the man from the truck again. He managed to follow us over the bridge. He dragged his leg, causing him to weave as he tried to catch up.

Mom decided to wait for him. She set down the tuba but kept the shotgun in her arms. I lowered the big pack.

"Hey." He struggled to catch his breath. "Thanks for waiting." Raspy breathing. "And thanks for...pulling me outta...my truck."

"It's okay," said Mom, her tone unwelcoming.

She picked up Timmy, swung him on her back, and turned to continue the walk south.

"Wait.... Please."

I expected him to say more, but he dropped to the ground like he couldn't go on.

"Gimme a minute...."

He leaned back on his elbows, catching his breath, right in the middle of the road.

"I need help." He looked up at Mom, then at me, back to Mom. "People been chasing me. I was...well, guess I still am, mayor of a

209

small town a little west of here...." More rough breaths. "People, they rose up. Real crazy folk, like monsters.... Thought I was the monster. On account of them mandates we gotta enforce. But not my fault, see. So they come for me. To my office. Ya know, like a gang of zombies. I barely got away...."

"You were a mayor?" I asked. He sure didn't look like one, but his clothes could once have been clean enough for City Hall. His town wasn't any we passed through. Mom wanted to avoid towns. I knew it from maps: about 25,000 people before the pandemic.

"Lotta fighting between the vaxxers and antis," he said. "Got violent. And no police left. Just a free-for-all. Then they come for me. What'm I supposed to do? I ain't the police. So I locked myself in my office with them banging on the door. Then they broke in."

"Wow!" I looked at Mom. She seemed to believe him. "How did you escape?"

"Escape? Hah! They strung me up, gonna hang me from my own window, but the rope slipped loose and down I fell. Right into a dumpster. I got out and ran."

"Wow," I said again. The frightened look in his eyes made me believe him.

He pulled down his collar, showed rope marks on his neck.

"Been long time getting away, driving around to hide, finding food.... You folks the first I met since I left town. You're good folks. I can see that. Got me outta my truck."

Mom just pursed her lips, then hauled Timmy onto her back, ready to continue. "It was the right thing to do."

"Folks gotta stick together. For protection," he said. "We gotta make a new society, ya know?" He bowed his head. "But I don't wanna be mayor no more."

"That's what Mom wants to do," I spoke up, and she gave me a quizzical look. She didn't want this poor man to be part of our new society.

"Can I come with you?" His voice sounded forlorn, begging for company like his life depended on having friends. "I can do things. Like fish. I'm good at fishing. Used to come out here for fishing."

"Fishing?" asked Nathan, suddenly interested in the man.

"That's right, son. I can teach you, if you like."

"Great!"

"Well, you smell like fish already," said Mom, "so I believe you. My father liked to fish here, too."

"Sorry about the smell, ma'am. From that dumpster, I reckon. But I'm gonna wash off soon as I can."

"In one of these houses?" asked Mom.

"Yeah, my sister's got a house here. I know lots of people won't ever be coming back to this island. They're dead by now or they got no gas for cars. Maybe they'll walk here, like y'all, who knows? I got lucky finding a truck with some gas in it."

"Yeah," I sighed.

"What's your name?" asked Mom.

"Bucky's what friends call me. Buchanan officially. Kutcher. Formerly Mayor Kutcher. But Bucky's fine. Pleased to make y'all's acquaintance."

There were no handshakes. That custom went out with the first lockdown. Elbow bumps was trendy for a while, then just a head dip was enough. We kept our facemasks on with the new guy joining us.

Mom had me take the shotgun and she took the small bag I'd been carrying on my chest. I laid the gun up against my shoulder like we were on parade.

"So y'all a family?" asked Bucky. "Yeah, lotta folks kinda band together, made new families. Guess they gotta do that."

"Yeah, that's us," Hannah responded sadly.

Mom grunted, like she didn't want our status to be revealed.

"We're all related, if that's what you're asking," I explained.

"She's my aunt," said Hannah, sounding like a bold rebuke.

Bucky tried to keep up, even with us walking slower. His leg bothered him, knee still sore from his fall.

"My sister, she got a house here. Been a while but I'll know it when I see it. Address escapes me. Escape...." He snickered. "She used ta live here full-time. Not summers and holidays only. Got married. Charlotte's her name. I think she had a kid or two. But we lost contact some time back."

"Same for us," I said, "but not full-time."

"Never stayed with her when I come for fishing. Didn't want no trouble, ya know? Just slept out on the beach."

"Actually," Mom spoke, raising her voice, "I haven't been here for many years. Has bad memories for me." She shot a look at me. "Some good things happened, of course, but then not good things. So I haven't been back. Until now."

She watched Bucky. He was mulling over what she said.

"Yup. Sounds about right."

"I thought it might be the best place for us to go. Live on our own, make a new life. Wait out all this craziness."

"That's a mighty fine plan," said Bucky.

We walked down the main road under a bright sun and came to the fork. Houses stood on either side, so quiet and eerie in their silence. Most seemed intact, as though waiting for their owners to visit on the next holiday. Lawns weren't mown but hadn't gotten too out of control. Palm trees and shrubs here and there. Big ferns and flowering bushes, too. While not native to this coast people wanted it to look like they lived in the tropics. It was autumn yet on the island it seemed summer lingered.

"Thanks," said Bucky, holding back as we walked on. "Good talkin to y'all. I'm gonna go find my sister's place. I think it's over thatta way."

"Good luck," Mom called, pausing to watch him turn in a new direction. He cut across a yard, slipped between two palm frond-shrouded bungalows, and disappeared.

"Well, he seems harmless," I said.

Mom gave a smirk. "More like stupid. Or shell-shocked, on the edge of going insane."

"It might be good to have another adult to help out, if we're gonna make a new community."

We strolled down the middle of the street. The neighborhood resembled a suburb on the mainland. You might not know there was an ocean on the other side of the homes. Between them we caught glimpses of the beach and the surf rolling in. The waves made a steady roar that filled our ears, the salty air intoxicating.

"Here," said Mom, stopping in the street.

She pulled Timmy off her back, set him down gently on her feet. Gazing over the yellowed lawn to the front door, she assessed the situation.

Everything looked good – as correct as I could ever imagine it from Mom's descriptions over the years – even with the yard's grass dry and bushes wilted, the windows cloudy with sea breeze residue. The wooden door was weathered. The whole house looked weathered – what a steady sea breeze will do to wood, the salt air curing it, peeling away paint, gnarling the grain, turning a nice bungalow into an old sea captain's lodge after a few years.

Inside, however, it would be clean and comfortable, I expected. Being locked up, the interior would still be fine. I longed for a hot shower then a long nap on a big fluffy bed. Had to stretch out my sore back.

"Hannah," I called, thinking to ask if she wanted the same, but I decided not to finish my question.

"What?" she asked, sounding annoyed. She stood beside me as we looked at the front of the house.

"Just making sure you're still here," I said, adding a laugh as though it was a joke – like we really weren't running away from the world, hiding from the chaos. Not like that.

22

IN WHICH WE WELCOME THE COMMUNITY

There were other people on the island. They watched us arrive at the house. Some came out of their homes to see. Same suspicions. Were we friend or foe? Vaxxed or not? Infected or healthy? Useful to a community of survivors or just more parasites?

I lay the shotgun on front steps and set down the big pack. As I stood up with a groan, Hannah came and began massaging my shoulders – without me even asking. Her tender fingers clawed at my muscles.

"Ooo, that's good," I said.

"Yeah, you carry the heaviest load of any of us. And you never complain."

I shook out my shoulders, felt better.

Mom had set down Timmy on the porch and started looking in the windows through the gaps in the curtains.

"Is everything all right?" I asked.

She kept her hand up to her face to see in better.

The house wasn't large, not meant to be a full-time residence, just enough for a vacation. I wondered how many bedrooms it had. Probably just two. And a single bathroom.

"Everything looks fine," said Mom, coming back. "I wanted to have a look before we open the door. To make sure nobody's home who may not want to welcome us." She smiled to reassure Hannah and Nathan. "No squatters, that is. Make sure we're all accounted for. No bodies to bury. Skeletons all back in their closets."

"Mom...," I moaned, fearing she was reminding my cousins of their mother.

Mom struck a pose, a magician on stage, raised her hand then ceremoniously slid it into her pants pocket. Pulling out a key ring, she held it up like it was an ancient ritual. She selected one key and pointed it at the door. With glacial steps for dramatic effect, she extended her arm, made her hand shake as though she was nervous, and inserted the key. Pausing to look back at us, she turned the key, and feigned surprise.

The door unlocked.

We all gave sighs of relief.

"Mom, don't be so dramatic." I shook my head, so ready to be disappointed if the key hadn't worked.

"*Entre*," Mom said with a wave of her hand.

Hannah and Nathan stepped through the doorway.

"Mom...?" I called in a low voice.

From the porch I noticed a couple people had stepped outside to watch Mom's ceremony. At another house an older woman had come into the yard to watch. Two men, one older and one younger, gazed at us from the opposite house. None of them wore masks, had no late-stage rashes, looked normal – but not so friendly.

Mom and my cousins were already taking our bags inside the house. Only Timmy remained on the porch. Mom gave the house a quick tour as I remained outside, guarding the door.

She returned to the porch. "Coming in?"

"Everything okay?" I asked, sitting on the steps.

"Yes, fine. Sheets over all the furniture. They left it in good condition, whoever was here last."

She smiled brightly, like she really was happy to be here.

"That's good," I said, tilting my head toward the gathering crowd in the street. "We have neighbors."

"I still remember it," she went on. "Same furniture – all their northern climate things forced into this tropical setting. No rattan chairs like everyone else. Same vintage scent. It's remarkably the same – as if your grandma and grampa were just here."

I watched the people from up the street and across from us

observing us. Nothing unusual, folks. Just a teenage boy and his quirky mom. And her tuba. Perfectly normal.

"I must play," said Mom, her voice unexpectedly cheerful.

"What—here? Now?"

"Why not? I'm happy to finally arrive. Two weeks ago I never thought we'd be here. So I must play."

"But you're gonna call out all the neighbors."

"Might as well see who all's here."

She unzipped the soft-side case and pulled out her bent toy. Immediately sad at seeing its damage, she sat on the top step and pulled Timmy to her lap, blew a few streams through him, heard the ugly hiss from the worst wound.

She wiped a tear from her eye, then took a long breath and played. It wasn't a piece I recognized, not from the repertoire, so she must've been improvising, playing out her feelings: a gigue in a minor key – like she was pleased to be here yet recognized the hardships we'd gone through to get here. I liked how she could play two or three emotions in the same song.

I sat on the lower step, facing her, listening. She always liked when I showed interest in her playing. Ever since I was a little boy I'd happily sit as her audience. Me and Mom, happy together. I would applaud each song she played, children's songs but also the Classics. She would grin like she'd done something clever and I'd be happy, too. Clap, clap! For a few minutes I was nine again, not nineteen.

Mom came to the end of her song, held a long raspy note. Satisfied, she sat back but continued holding her tuba. She took a deep breath of sea breeze, exhaled. Then she cursed the damage to the tuba, rubbing her finger over the dents.

"All these years...." She wiped her eyes. "Everyone before me's entrusted him to me. I took him on buses in the city. I toured with him. Flew on planes. Never any trouble – only that sticky valve, but I got it fixed eventually. And now...just an unfortunate crash and *this*. You heard the hiss?"

"Yeah, air was leaking out."

"Air leaking out! He's ruined." She wiped her eyes again. "No place to repair a musical instrument, I'm pretty sure. And I don't have the right tools. Tape won't do it."

"You two've had a good run," I said, trying to be sympathetic.

"A good run?" Mom's face was red. "A good run is not what I want."

"Were you gonna pass it down to me? You always told me not to be a musician. You refused to teach me very much. Is it because I'm a boy? You wanted to pass him down to a girl, I guess."

"Not exactly." She grimaced, acting embarrassed. "Yes, my big boy, the useful scientist. A sociologist! Isn't that right? Studying people, groups of people, and how they interact. Group dynamics. How useful that will be in our post-pandemic world, where people have to stay apart." Her voice cracked. She took a breath. "Listen, Sandy, you don't have to play music *for a living*. That was just my good fortune. You need to play music *for yourself* – for your sanity, for your soul – to *save* your soul. Especially now, in these hard times we live in. It's the last vestige of civilization. You must keep it going."

Her words struck my heart – although she'd said it before.

"I will, Mom. I promise."

"Well, you've made lots of promises in your life. At least keep this one. Okay?"

I got teary, nodded. Then she slid Timmy down onto the steps and we hugged, Mom and me – as we'd done when I was a little boy and she was my entire world.

"I love you, Sandy."

"Love you, Mom."

"You guys coming in?" asked Hannah from the doorway.

I wiped my eyes, parting from Mom. "Sure."

"Aunt Pauline?" called Hannah in alarm.

"It's Polly," Mom responded, looking out across the yard.

The street in front of the house was occupied by a couple dozen people, staring with the intensity of hungry people deciding what to eat first at a buffet.

"It seems like you've called out everyone." It wasn't funny any more. "Was that your plan?"

An older man, balding and pot-bellied, stepped forward, taking it upon himself to speak for the crowd.

"Mighty fine playing," he said, patting his belly as though he'd just eaten. His voice sounded croaky like he hadn't spoken in a few days and had to recall how to do it. "Ain't heard nothin like that in long time. Got no power on the island, so can't play no music."

"Live music is best," said Mom, thumbing back at Timmy. "I'm afraid he's gotten some damage. He doesn't sound good now."

"No, it's good. Even from a tuba."

"Hey!" Mom feigned anger.

The man held up his hands. "Ma'am, no offense intended. I used to play trumpet in school band long time ago."

"Okay, you're forgiven." Mom chuckled. "Where's your trumpet now?"

"It was a school rental so I don't have it now."

"Too bad."

"Yeah, we coulda formed a band."

Mom regarded the people standing at the edge of the yard, many appeared in a daze. I became wary. The shotgun lay nearby on the porch. Mom thought they were merely transfixed by her impromptu recital. She'd seen people affected that way by music. A great performance was like a drug.

"And how about you?" she asked of the people gathered there. "What's your instrument? And you? What's yours? Can we make a band on this island?"

"I got an alto sax," one woman replied.

"I have a guitar," said another.

"No, ma'am," said the fat man, nonplussed. "I'm Owen, by the way. I'm not like any kind of village potentate, but they seem to look to me to do the talking. You see...." He casually flipped his hand at the people who'd gathered. "A lot of us here are still kinda traumatized by situations they gone through. Pay 'em no mind. I mean, they're harmless, but they won't talk to ya. Got conditioned to not speak, gone 'mask mute'. See, we don't get visitors, so they being careful, don't know what to say."

"We're not exactly visitors," said Mom, hands on her hips. "My family owns this house. It's our vacation home."

"Oh, yeah?" He smiled like it was good news. "So you're one of them Braun sisters?"

That shook Mom. Her face shifted into fight mode.

"I suppose I am. But it's not Braun. It's Baumann. Close, but *nein zigarre. Ja,* one of the notorious Baumann girls. But am I the one who went off to a fancy university and married a rich man? Or am I the shy artist who married the art dealer? Or just maybe I'm the baby sister who snuck down to the nude beach when she was underage? Who knows? Who can tell? And does it matter?"

"Sure don't know any of that." He fumbled with his hands in his pockets, looking embarrassed. "My parents knew the family in this house. Nothing about the girls, only that there *was* some girls here. Mama just said to leave'em alone. Guess we were all young back then, huh? Times've changed. Sorry. No offense."

"None taken."

Mom stood and took relaxed steps down the walk, cut across the grass to meet the stout man standing at the curb. Owen's belly stretched over the curb into our yard.

She extended her hand.

"You still do that?" asked Owen.

"Shake hands?" Mom chuckled. "Of course we do. It's how we show we're not carrying any weapons."

Owen laughed, raised both hands, palms out. "I guess so."

They warily shook hands.

Releasing their hands, Owen called for 'sani' and a woman in the crowd held out a plastic bottle from which she squirted a blue liquid onto his hands. He wiped his hands together. The woman offered some to Mom and she accepted.

"By the way," said Owen, "you being from off the island, what variant is it nowadays?"

Mom shook her hands to dry them.

"They went through the alphabet and started over again. Then added numbers to identify subvariants."

"Subvariants," he moaned, then scratched his head.

"It's more like what kind of apple do you want when the store has fifteen varieties. They're each a little bit different. Main thing is how much can you get people to pay for each of them? Here's our newest apple. Try it. Can we sell more of this kind than that kind?"

Owen chuckled. "Last news we got before power went off was Theta." He got serious, sanitized hands back on his hips. "Omega was a real bitch, that's fer sure. Knocked off half the folks in my neighborhood. Came down from the city. Schools never reopened. I got us here to the island, me and my brother's kid, Jackson. Been here five years. Everyone else, they all died."

"I'm sorry," said Mom. "Deaths in our family, too."

Other people came in closer, tightening the cluster, half in the street and half in the yard, entertained.

"Well, we ain't got no apples here," said Owen. "None on the island. We try growing some vegetables. We got some fruit trees, tangerines mostly. Most of all we ain't got no virus here. That's really our main thing."

The people around them echoed his sentiment. A few of them shook their fists at the damn virus or the authorities who imposed restrictions because of the virus. On the island they could live free of both problems.

I could hear them well enough from the porch, sitting next to Timmy. Hannah came out, sat beside me. She'd changed into a baggy pair of Bermudas. Her long, bare legs stretched out over the steps. Leaving her shoes inside, she wiggled her toes.

"What's she telling them?" asked Hannah.

"Setting the rules, I guess. You know how Mom is."

I started to relax, able to believe that everything was going to work out. Just like Mom always said. We were the lucky ones, the ones who would survive this extra long flu season.

Hannah pulled up a leg, set her foot on the step, and began picking at a blister, complaining about our hike.

"We're all islanders," said Owen with an air of pride, "either original stock or been here since the first pandemic wave and got stuck here."

"I guess the ferry's not running," said Mom.

"Not for a few years." He narrowed his eyes. "You musta come 'cross the bridge. Kinda dangerous. At least it stops vehicles from crossing." Shaking his bald head, he turned to a guy in the crowd. "Bill, we gotta make sure we get only the right kind of people here. Shoulda blown the damn thing up when we had the chance."

He regarded Mom again, blinking like a secret signal.

"Oh, I don't racial types or what-not but people who ain't got the virus. Hell, we got the Johnsons and they're Black. And the Garcias are Hispanic." A man in back raised his hand. A woman nodded. "Heck, I got some Seminole on my mama's side." He pointed to a short man. "And Charlie Sato there was born over in Okinawa. And little Amira.... Where is she? Can't see her. She got adopted from somewhere in the Middle East by the Leibowitzes." He regarded Mom again. "So we got plenty of diversity awright — if that concerns you."

"Well...." Mom waved her hand to indicate us. Everyone gazed at Hannah and me on the porch. Mom smiled. "We're all healthy."

"And y'all got vaxxed?"

Mom cocked her head. "Does that still matter? If a person is 'fully vaxxed', all seven official shots plus dubious boosters, then no need to worry about unvaxxed people. Right? It's the unvaxxed who should worry about other unvaxxed. But I see nobody here is wearing masks. Thank goodness. We had to put on hazmat suits to get through one area."

"Is that right?" Owen turned, explained the rules again to the crowd as a reminder: a teachable moment. "Well, now that you've touched my hand, I gotta wait and see if I develop any symptoms."

"Please." Mom spoke louder so everyone could hear. "We only want to live here in peace, in our family's house. But we're willing to help you, any of you, with any task that needs doing. We want to be part of the community. Heck, I can play a recital every night, if you like."

Owen was nodding his head, thinking. A few others seemed to approve of Mom's offer.

A younger man with a scraggily beard came up, nudged Owen,

spoke a few words to him.

"How about her?" asked Owen. "She spoken for?"

"What do you mean?" asked Mom in a wary voice, turning to following Owen's hand pointing to the porch where Hannah and I were sitting.

"She looks old enough for impregnation," he said. "If we're gonna grow our community, we need that. Not many females here the right age. Either too young or too old. See, we got some fellas need wives, need to make more sons and daughters." He scanned Mom up and down. "You don't look so bad yerself. Still fit enough. Could probably push out a couple more kids."

Mom's face froze, half-grin stuck there. "Oh—I see what you're saying." She coughed twice, a signal for us to get inside the house.

"Coughing? You sure you're safe?"

"Oh, I just drank some soda, got caught in my throat. Nothing to worry about." Mom cleared her throat, part of the act. "Yes, she's spoken for. You see, that young man there is my son and she's his wife. Got married just before we left the city."

"That's fine," said Owen, hand brushing over the village logo on the upper corner of his shirt like it was a badge of authority. "Gotta check, y'all understand. It may still be necessary – in order to spread our genes, ya know – for her to take on extra husbands. For her second, maybe third baby. Or fourth, ideally. For genetic diversity, ya know. Mother Nature demands that."

Mom chewed her lip, looking the man in the eye. "She's still young. Let's she how she does with that first baby. Okay?"

"That seems fair."

The crowd agreed with him.

"See, we've got our rules here," said Owen in apologetic tone, "so if y'all wanna stay on the island y'all gotta follow'em, just like everybody else here."

223

23

IN WHICH WE SETTLE INTO A NEW NORMAL

Inside the house, the living room, dinin area, and kitchen were all one room, with a bar separating the kitchen from the rest of the room. Open concept, Mom called it, perfect for a summer home. She told stories of how her family would gather in this one large space and bicker about everything.

Of course, there was cleaning that needed to be done, but we were hindered by a lack of water. Although the tap ran, the water was slow and not so clear. Owen said the water plant up north continued to pump but it was no longer purified so we needed to boil the water. Making a small fire in the barbeque pit out back was the only way to boil it. But no electricity to turn the stove on. Had to use the fire pit in the backyard. We were given a plastic jug to store our boiled water in – as well as a big bottle of the blue sanitizer. Candles were a welcome gift from the community.

I thought everyone was being nice to us.

"They're currying favor," said Mom, giving a glance over at Hannah. "Don't let any of them near her."

"I won't," I assured both of them.

We gathered around the coffee table in front of the couch for a make-shift dinner. Someone donated a small pink fish because we were newbies. It was about the size of my hand. We grilled it over the fire pit. Divided between us, we were still hungry so we added some of our junk food. We also split two tangerines and a lemon. Later, alone out back, I shared the last chocolate with Hannah.

"Now listen up," said Mom as we sat back from the low table, pretending our bellies felt satisfied. "We must be careful what we say and do here. It's not quite as I expected – or maybe it is how I expected it to be but hoped it wouldn't be. This is not a vacation resort. Oh, don't look so confused."

"They helped us," I said.

Mom snapped her fingers. "They are not our friends. Just nosy neighbors. They want something from us."

"Yeah, I know," I cut in stupidly, having no clue. "Our help. Do our fair share. Be part of the community. I'll work hard, don't you worry."

"No, Sandy," Mom grumbled. "It's not your labor they want. No, they want..." She regarded Hannah. "...her."

"Me?" My cousin practically jumped up. "What for?"

"Because, dear niece, you are a young female and they aim to breed you."

Hannah was aghast. "Breed me?"

"What are you saying, Mom?" I demanded.

"What's breed mean?" asked Nathan.

"You didn't hear what they said when I was talking with that Owen at the curb? He explained how their community works. He asked if our 'girl' was taken, 'spoken for' – meaning you, Hannah. So I said you were Sandy's wife."

"What?" shrieked Hannah.

I stared at her, not sure what I should feel. Really, I was fine with it. Her eyes were on me, angry like it was all my fault.

"Sorry," I mumbled, bowing my head.

"It's just pretend." Mom gave each of us her most serious look. "You just have to act like you're married. So be lovey-dovey. Or else they're gonna take her and pair her with one of the men on the island."

"That's crazy," I said. "They can't do that."

"Who's going to stop them? The police? There's no police here." Mom turned to Hannah. "You be sure to call me 'Mom' or 'Polly' like I'm your mother-in-law. And you, Nathan, you should call me 'Mom', too. Not 'Aunt'. Got it?"

"Okay, *Mom*," said Nathan, giggling.

"No, I won't," Hannah growled. "I have a mother. *My* mother – and she's dead. I won't forget her. And you can't replace her. Not ever!"

"I know," said Mom, reaching out to hug her but getting a cold shoulder. "I'm not trying to replace Jackie. But you must go along with this. It's about our survival. At least for a while – until I can figure out what to do. Or we could find ourselves in a dangerous situation."

"I think it already is a dangerous situation," I surmised.

"Can't we just leave?" asked Hannah.

"But we just got here," Nathan grumbled.

"Anywhere we might go, we'll be walking." Mom held up her hand. "There's a council meeting. I plan to go and see what's up, hopefully get a better idea how to deal with all their ridiculous, antiquated ways."

"Yeah, ridiculous," said Hannah with a grunt.

"Yeah, and anti-qua...." Nathan tried to add.

I tried to console her, but she shook off my hand. "Sorry."

It was for our own survival. We had to go along with Mom's plan for now, but Hannah kept complaining. I tried to interject my thoughts but only made it worse. Nathan got fussy.

Mom waved us to silence.

"Isolated here, they think the world's ended. That they need to remake society. They haven't seen life off the island for a while. They don't know the truth."

She glared at me, to make sure I was paying attention.

"Yes, Sandy, it's like I've been saying. About repopulating the world. But my idea was further into the future than what they're thinking. To them, it's over already. Not a thing left of civilization on the mainland, just a wilderness of crumbled cities. Like in the apocalyptic movies that were banned. No more civilization. Swept away. I can try to correct them but...maybe it's better not to say too much about our journey getting here."

"No, you don't wanna give them any ideas," I said. "Or ruin our reputation."

"Anyway," Mom went on, "there aren't many women of child-bearing age on the island, apparently, so they're interested in – to put it politely – increasing the population."

"But they can barely feed themselves as it is," I had to say.

"And us visitors," said Nathan, pointing around the table. "I'm still hungry."

"It's like some dystopian movie," I said, my gut rumbling. It couldn't be real. "No way I'm giving her up to some stranger. No way!" I turned to Hannah. "I'm sorry, but I won't let them take you. Besides—"

"Besides, she's too young for that." Mom's face was stern.

"For what?" asked Nathan.

"For sex," Hannah answered.

We all shut up. What a storm of thoughts she must've been fighting through: the kind of upbringing she had, talks with her mother, awkward experiences at school before going virtual. Who knew what she'd been through? I worried she had a lover back in that town – a boyfriend she hadn't mentioned. Or a girlfriend.

"I know all about that, Aunt Polly," said Hannah. "I mean, *Mom*. I know what to do. I've seen some porn. I see what they do."

Mom muttered a curse, shaking her head. "That's certainly not the way – *shouldn't* be that way. If done right, it's...." She waved her hand to dismiss her words but they lingered in the air like silent gas. "It's supposed to be pleasant."

"You don't have to worry," said Hannah. "I already know what to do, yeah, when it's time. Mother told me the whole stupid birds and bees story. Also I had the lessons in school. Human Sexuality class."

Her sweet chuckles at that moment helped me stay calm even though I guessed she'd forced them.

"Yeah, our virtual class was quite graphic, if ya know what I mean. We had to watch lotsa content. Yeah, actual porn. Our sex teacher had subs to a lot of streaming services and he just played the vids for us. He told us what each step was."

I tried to laugh but it sounded fake. "Yeah, I know. Same for us, but ours were scientific. Drawings, animation, not live action."

"Being in lockdown so much," she went on, "I guess we weren't expected to actually have sex with anybody, so our lessons focused on masturbation. We had to try it at home – on cam, so he could grade us on our technique."

"What? Total perv!" I grunted. "My class didn't do that."

"I only got a C on the exam. He was gonna let me try again for a better grade, but I said I was okay with a C."

"He shoulda been arrested," I cursed and Mom agreed.

"Teachers do anything with virtual classes. Nobody checks. He was showing the boys how to do it, and made us girls watch him."

"He can't do that," I protested.

"But if we failed his course we wouldn't graduate." She pouted. "Doesn't matter now. We can't even get online for classes now. The internet's down. Guess I'll never graduate."

"Kids! Listen to me," said Mom. She took Hannah's hand. "We will protect you. Forget everything you saw on those vids. Forget your creepy teacher. This isn't the time for that. Believe me, it's definitely not the right way to treat you – or any woman."

Mom let out a sigh like she had to hold herself together.

"In the end, it must *always* be your choice, your decision, when and where, and with whom to have sex. If you even want to. And every time after that first time. Not all of us get to make those decisions for ourselves. Instead, it's forced on us."

Mom shot me a glance to check that I was listening.

"And when you might be ready to get pregnant...if you're even willing to.... I wouldn't think now is the best time, anyway. Not until this pandemic is over. And maybe not here, either. They've turned this island into some kind of.... I'm not really sure what to call it. A patriarchal paradise, maybe."

"Relax, Mom." I'd put on my confident smile that felt a little more sincere. After all, I was a man now but I wasn't part of any patriarchal paradise. "I know she has to get older. Everything at her pace. So no hurry, okay? I'm willing to wait. I want everything to be right—"

"Willing to wait? For what? Geez, Sandy! I never agreed to do or be anything with you." Hannah calmed herself. "Yeah, okay, I

229

know you wanna, but don't be such a perv about it, okay? All I said was I'm glad you're here. I like you, sure, but, geez, I'm only sixteen. That's not even what I'm thinking about now. I'm just trying to get to seventeen." She put her hand to her belly, feeling it gurgle, dinner falling short.

My mouth tightened. "Well, Mom was sixteen."

✳ ✳ ✳

Sometimes I say stupid things. I don't mean any harm. The words just come out. It's part of my Aspie traits, Mom said. I apologized and explained it later when we sat on the back porch, Hannah and me, watching the stars twinkling out over the sea. The yard had patches of grass but after about forty feet a low wall of bricks made a border. Below that wall the beach spread to the surf, sixty feet at high tide and more at low tide. We tried to count the waves rolling in but lost count.

Hannah let out a long sigh, and I thought I could hear all her regrets streaming there, a rough set of rapids.

"I guess I gotta fuck somebody," she said in a mournful tone as she played with her fingers. "Even my mother said that. I'm sure she meant after I get married, of course."

"Actually," I started, thinking to ease her mind, "you don't."

"Mother always said when I was little: 'God's got a purpose for every part of your body'. And she'd point down there whenever she was bathing me and said 'It'll hafta be used one day'."

"Well, boys, umm...." I smiled. "At least we can do two things with one part." But she didn't laugh with me.

"Yeah, before virtual school I wasn't so interested, too young to care, then during our virtual school I got turned off completely. Except...there was one girl in my class kept sending me love notes, always saying she wanted to be my girlfriend."

I took a deep breath, never getting any love notes.

"She was nice and all, kinda pretty...but...we couldn't ever get together anyway. Virtual school, ya know. But I wondered what it would be like, ya know, if we did get together. I kinda wanted to explore, ya know? Figure out things, get another point of view."

I tried to picture that scene. "Yeah...."

She tilted her head. "You ever have any boyfriend?"

"I never had *friends*." I chuckled to cover my confession. "No, I never wanted to be friends with another boy. Not like that. Boys are disgusting."

She gazed at me. "Not all boys." A grin flittered over her face, almost before I could notice, turned into a frown. "I don't wanna, but if it'll save the whole world. In the future maybe everybody will worship me. Ya know? The great holy goddess or something," and she laughed.

More breeze, more twinkles from the stars.

I heard her sniffling, then she wiped her eyes.

"No, you don't. You don't have to do that," I offered, hoping to be supportive. "I didn't mean to pressure you."

"It's not that I mind getting big and fat, and then have all that pain to push a baby out. Believe me, the vids we had to watch for class weren't pretty. I don't mind doing any of that. Gazillions of women did it. My mother did it. Your mother did it. I could do it, too. If it's gonna, like, save the world."

"That's not what Mom meant." Right then I wanted to put my arm around her but feared her rejection.

"It sure is what she meant." She gave me a hard look, like she'd been condemned to death. "I don't wanna do that. I've seen the porn vids. Guys like that. But it sure doesn't seem like very much fun for the woman, lemme tell ya."

"Well, that's not real." I watched her for a moment, hoping she might see how sympathetic my eyes were but it was dark. "Pretty sure. There's different kinds, so maybe you saw the bad stuff."

"In regular movies it's fake, but for porn it's real."

"Yeah, okay...."

She took a long breat, let it out. "I bet you wanna." It sounded like a challenge, daring me to deny it. "All guys wanna. You wouldn't be normal if you didn't wanna do it."

"Well, I think I'm normal. But Mom says I—"

"You know what I mean."

Sometimes my younger cousin seemed older than me, and a lot smarter, able to see things I couldn't. I knew then that I had to stick with her. I had to be nice so she'd stick with me.

"Okay, then...uh, honestly...I want to. Yeah, sure. Cannot lie. But, also honestly, I...I never did any of that before." My chest felt tight and I had to take a deep breath. "Don't laugh, okay? I never met anybody, so I never got the chance. Then the pandemic. Same as you? Besides, I only know what they showed in class. Just lots of diagrams. Tab A goes in slot B, kinda."

Hannah repressed a laugh. "I ain't done it neither."

That made me feel a lot better. We were in this together. We could figure it out with nobody being the expert. I wouldn't mind looking stupid if she was my partner.

"Mom caught me looking at some online one time," I confessed. "She gave me the big lecture. Then she dared me to...uh.... She said if I was 'so damn horny' she was there for me. That scared the shit right outta me."

Hannah laughed. "Yeah, my mother, too. I mean, getting the big lecture. What good girls should do and not do." She fell quiet. "I miss her. If only she coulda held on a little longer. She could be here and get better. Fix her head and all. I don't know what to do now. She would always tell me what to do – the *right thing* to do. Now I'm stuck with your mother."

"Well, my mom knows the right thing to do...."

In the darkness I sensed tears in her eyes. She brought a hand up to her face. I wanted to put my arm around her again, moved it but stopped.

"I'm real sorry," I said. "I never knew her, so I gotta rely on what Mom said. They were sisters, after all. They had stronger ties than us, I guess."

"Stronger than mother and daughter?" Hannah turned to me with her teary face. "Or mother and son?"

"But your mother had two other daughters, right? She lost both of them. And went crazy."

"She gave up on me." Hannah chewed her lip. "Like she was preparing to lose me to more violence. She shut down in advance.

But I took care of her anyway. What else could I do? It was so bad, I guess I'm good she's at peace now."

"I'm sure she was glad you were taking care of her. I guess it's not uncommon in these hard times. People dying from all sorts of things other than the virus. That's the tragedy of what's happened the past few years." I listened to myself, hearing Mom's words coming out of my mouth again. "We get forced into these difficult situations, have to make difficult decisions."

Hannah let out a big sigh like she'd been waiting for just the right moment. "Now it's every girl's fate to be forced into sex. To save the fucking world. Nature's cruel joke."

The surf's constant moan blocked my response.

Shaking my head, I couldn't decide what to say. "It's wrong. In principle it's wrong. But if we look at it from a purely biological perspective, women are the only ones that can save the world. Sorry you were chosen to be the girl, but you're really a pretty good one. A pretty one."

I smiled as brightly as I could, satisfied with my words, but it couldn't come close to the twinkle of the stars over the sea.

"Mother said I should get with some man just as soon as I turn eighteen, so I'll be protected. Ya know, he'll protect me. And feed me. I dunno, go hunting or some shit. And I just stay home having babies, and cooking, cleaning, shit like that."

"I'd go hunting for you," I said. "Or some shit."

She laughed, a dry sound that cut through the humidity.

"I don't mean Mother was like a 'trad wife' or anything, but she musta thought it was the best way for a girl to survive in a post-pandemic world."

"Yeah. I get it. Gotta survive another flu season, Mom says."

"You know 'Laughter' by the Wu Crew? It's 'Xiào shēng' in Chinese – they sing in Chinese, but you know Chinese music was banned, which only made it more popular, so everybody listened to all the streams. Anyway, I looked up the lyrics and translated them. The song's about survival skills. Laughter is one of'em."

Before I could respond she started singing: "'Drag your ass outta bed / Got some hunting in your head / Better aim straight and

true / Or they'll make a meal outta you' – but sung in Chinese."
She tapped her hands on her thighs in rhythm. "And then a bunch
of drums and Willie Chung screams over it: 'Kill'em all! / Kill'em
all! / From jungle cat / To the rich and fat!' That part's in English.
Great song. Yeah, it's coming true now."

"They were ahead of their time," I offered.

"You know it. But their time is our time."

"Our time." I let that idea hover in the air, date-stamping this
moment with Hannah in my mind's history.

Then she turned to me, scooted up against me, hip to hip, and
reached for my hand.

"Sandy?"

"Hannah...."

"I never met any men. Boys, yeah, okay, but not a man. You're
my first man. Officially. You're a *young* man but it still counts.
You have a good look. A good body. Remember: I saw you at that
pond, washing off. And you saw me, too. All of me. So we know
something about each other, right?"

"Right. But I...uh...."

"You don't have to worry. If they make me do it, I'd rather do it
with you than some stranger here. I mean, if I really have to...."

I didn't know what to say. But I wanted to assure her I wasn't
going to force her to do anything, most of all *that*. I would never
pressure her, even with words, to do anything she didn't want to
do. I would be a good man – like Mom always taught me to be. She
raised me right, whatever that meant. But Mom forgot to teach
me the practical skills I would need to survive in a crisis like this.
I tried to remember what I learned in Scouts.

"Sandy?" she called again so softly.

I broke out of my trance. "Yes, Hannah?"

"I think it's still okay to kiss."

My breath stopped. "Kiss?"

She nodded. "Yes, kiss. I mean, if you wanna. I'm asking this
time. Don't wanna force you or anything."

"Okay," I replied, barely able to breathe.

"We should practice. Ya know, in case we meet someone."

Nodding, I said: "Makes sense."

We leaned in slowly, our lips pushing against each other's and pinching. Her tongue slipped into my mouth and it startled me so much I almost bit it. I stayed calm. It was so erotic that I felt hot electricity streak through my body – and I guess the same for her. Her hands held my face as she rose up on her knees to press harder. I put my hands on each side of her, feeling her ribs.

But me thinking about how she hadn't been eating enough ruined the experience. She noticed when I lost my focus. Leaning back, she pulled her lips away with a soft puff of breath.

"Probably need to practice more," I said. "Sorry."

"Yeah, definite."

She sat back, not looking at me. Eventually our eyes settled on the same pair of stars twinkling above the ocean as the roar of the surf covered our sighs. It was our time.

24

IN WHICH MOM CHALLENGES TRADITION

The next few days were a confusing mix of settling in and holding off boredom. Mom gave us tasks and we did them, usually without complaint because we wanted something to do but, of course, we could never tell her that. Then we sat around doing nothing but wondering whether we did the right thing in coming here. People seemed tolerant of us, but not so friendly, always guarded. There was an ominous shadow to our existence on this sunny shore.

Mom went around checking out the community, looking for ways she could make life better. She went to the council meeting, thinking to offer what help she could. After all, we had to fit in if they were going to allow us to stay. It was *their* island, it seemed, even though we owned a house on it.

Sitting with Hannah out back in the evening, we heard Mom return from the council meeting. She dressed in clothes suitable for life on a sub-tropical island: a basic pair of shorts and tanktop, which she looked good in. But returning, she was disheveled and sweaty, like she had worked out at a gym.

"Mom? You okay?"

She waved off my look of concern.

"Okay, here's the deal," she said, sitting down with a loud exhale. She straightened her hair, ran her fingers through it as she spoke. "They're all men on the council, of course, seven of them, led by that fat Owen character. I counted fifteen other men my age or older. Twelve women my age or older. There weren't many younger than me. I don't know if they exist and just stayed home or if there really aren't many here. That makes you two very special."

She stared at each of us, her eyes warning us.

"So it's a nice community," I said. "Better than Pineville."

Mom shook her head, obviously disappointed in me.

"They're making a *new* community here," she said. "Just as I figured from our earlier conversation. I did my best to convince them it's not that bad elsewhere, in the outside world. I said we came to the island not because it was the *only* place left to survive but to get away from the chaos of the city. We had a house here, so why shouldn't we come here? But they believe the world really has collapsed." She looked down, shook her head. "People don't think of repopulating the world unless they think the world has ended. Or it's their latest role-playing game. Not sure if they believe it or if they're pretending. They wouldn't listen to me. Big difference between their twisted ideas and what's actually happening, but they're panicking. They're worried about tomorrow. That's big T tomorrow. I still believe this pandemic will end soon enough and everything will gradually return to normal – the old normal."

"Really, Mom?" I grinned, encouraged. "You think so?"

"Not at all." She rubbed her face in her hands. "I'm not sure of anything. I said that to get along. They have these crazy ideas...." She regarded Hannah. "The reason I did that is to save you. Both of you. These guys are quite serious."

"What do you mean serious?" I asked.

"They're like my pervert teacher," said Hannah coolly.

Mom sat back, more breaths. "You're not far off."

"What do you mean by that?" I had to ask, confused.

"Because we're original residents, have property here, showed my old residence card, they let me speak. I tried to be clear. They seem to be trying to run this island like one of those dystopian patriarchal societies you see in sci-fi movies, where they repress the women. The movies that were banned."

"But they were nice to us. They gave us things we needed," I said, not at all understanding; I hoped Mom was wrong.

"So what you're saying is all the men want wives?" Hannah got it right, kept her frown on. "Don't they have wives?"

"Some do. Some of the wives are older," Mom said. "What they really want is children to carry on after them. Or the opportunity to make children. Some have children but they either grew up, moved away, or they died in one wave or another. Remember the third wave targeted kids under twelve. The men want wives or, maybe more accurately, sex partners. And they're even willing to share. In fact, sharing seems to be a big thing here. They use the word a lot. A different kind of 'common good'. Like with food. And sex."

"Food and sex," I muttered. "That's all they think about."

"It's food *for* sex," said Mom.

"You mean sex for food?" asked Hannah quietly.

I thought of Aunt Laura and suddenly I understood why my mom looked so rough.

Mom flashed a smile, something calculated to reassure us.

"I put them off a while," said Mom, taking a breath. "They're willing to wait for you two, the happily married couple, to have your first child."

"Our first child?" I asked, feeling nervous.

"What happens then?" asked Hannah, glaring at Mom.

"They pass you on to another man for your next baby."

"What?" I practically shrieked.

"And if I don't have a baby?" asked Hannah, keeping her cool.

"Same. If you're not pregnant, then.... According to their rules, they'll assign another man to father your child."

"They can't do that!" I roared, jumping up.

"After your first birth," Mom continued, "they're expecting to share you anyway. To spread their genes."

"Spread their genes?" I tried to chuckle; it couldn't be real. "That's weird. Then everybody's cousins."

Mom pointed at Hannah, then me. "You, too, Sandy. You're expected to share your 'seed' with the women of child-bearing age. Lucky you. I think there are six now – and kids who will grow up in coming years." She turned to Hannah: "The men are already deciding which of them goes after Sandy. And the older ones want their turn. They claim senior's rights."

"No," I said with a grunt. "I won't let them."

Hannah put her hand on my arm.

"I know," Mom responded. "We obviously can't stay here." She lowered her head, looking more tired than I'd ever seen her. "But we don't have any other place to go now. And no car."

"Back to Aunt Laura's. We can go there," I offered.

"Or my house," Hannah mumbled.

"Possibly." Mom wet her lips. "I wanted to get here first, check out the situation. Then go get Laura, bring her and Bootsy here. But now we know it's not a good place."

"But she...." I stopped, unsure what to say about my aunt with Hannah present.

"I haven't seen Aunt Laura in years, or those cousins," said Hannah. "Mother never had anything good to say about her."

"She is a type," Mom agreed.

I stared at my mom, imagining the meeting she'd attended. A meeting for what? To sort out our status? Divide up their tasks? Make to-do lists? Assign work crews? Obviously they explained the rules of the community to her.

"So...what happened?" I dared ask.

Mom looked me straight in the eyes. "You've never been to a school board meeting, have you? Lots of bickering. Lots of gavel banging. Supposedly have an agenda but don't keep to it. Overall an unpleasant experience. Oh, and I met Bucky there. Remember him?"

"Old Man Kutcher?" I said with a lame snicker.

"Yes. But not so old. Looks about forty-five all cleaned up. He cleans up nicely, washed and shaved. He spoke up for me, tried to help."

"That's good," I said, feeling there was more than Mom was sharing. "Did he find his sister's house?"

"Oh, yes. Charlotte, older sister. She wasn't in good shape, he said. Wheelchair-bound, some injury. Paralyzed below the waist. He found her fallen beside her chair inside the house. Couldn't get up. Dead for a few months."

"Ew," Hannah squealed.

I bowed my head. "Sorry to hear that."

"I guess with no power, and the cell towers off, she couldn't call for help."

"That's awful," I said.

"So anyway, kids—"

"I'm an adult now, Mom."

"So kids...after their preliminary business, they got to voting on us. Like it was up to them and not our right. Statements for and against, pro and con. Which was mostly, you can guess, about me and Hannah – how useful we could be to their long-term plans. The men determined that I fit the right categories. Hannah, well, obviously she was acceptable to all the curmudgeons. Sandy could work for the community, also supply his 'seed' to the 'womenfolk' to help 'propagate' the 'species' – their words. They expect Hannah to pop out no less than four babies, five or six would be ideal, they said, preferably with four different fathers – including you, Sandy. Apparently they understand how 'diversity' works. That Owen guy was a high school Biology teacher before the pandemic. Kept tapping on an old paperback novel on the table like it was the Bible. He kept reminding everyone of the rules and *tap tap tap* on his book. Men demanded their rights. Practically started a fight, crazy over who gets chosen to be with you next."

"Did they choose?" asked my cousin, a quiver in her voice.

My gut exploded as realization swept through me.

"Not yet." Mom looked at me. "They're willing to wait for you to have your first child. With your *husband*. They're giving you a year to 'pop one out' – which, of course, means you've got to get pregnant soon."

Hannah expelled a long sigh. "Okay.... I get it."

"And I'm her husband," I needed to confirm, glancing between Mom and Hannah. "Right?"

"Yes, of course." Mom looked at Hannah. "Listen, I know we're just playing the roles. We have some time, so don't worry. I'll fix things."

"What things can you fix?" Hannah barked back.

Mom shook her head. "They talked about me next – like I was on an auction block, talking about my 'attributes' like I was a prime heifer, asking all kinds of personal questions to determine my 'fitness'. My fitness for 'duty'. They mean conjugal duty. 'What men need', one fellow put it. And that Owen tapped on his book."

"But that's crazy!" I exclaimed. "How can they?"

"They grab you and hold you down, use you all they want," said my lovely Hannah nonplussed. "Because there's no cops here to stop them. Because it's the new normal."

"Or the cops join in," I muttered, thinking of Officer Tanner, then stopped myself from saying more.

"One council member's a doctor. Doc Rick. Chiropractor. They had him inspect me. He played along. At first they figured I could watch kids they already have, be a nanny. Or teach older kids since I was a professor. Then Bucky, bless his heart, said I was still young enough I should 'get in the pool'."

"Pool?" I asked stupidly.

"He meant the 'gene' pool."

"The what?" I was angry at that idea. "Gene pool?"

Hannah laughed awkwardly.

"I told you before," said Mom. "We may need to repopulate the world. Or at least an island. We just chose the wrong island. Can't have it both ways: either I'm 'of child-bearing age' with certain rights and responsibilities, or I'm not. Very cut and dried with these fools."

I was shaking with fear. "So what happened?"

"They agreed I was in the child-bearing category. I have a son, so I've proven my good genes. I'm ready right now, they decided. I had to accept their invitation, join their little game. Or else we'd have to leave. But it's just a lot of talk, I'm sure. I can deal with that. Buys us some time, anyway, time to figure out what to do, where to go—"

"You what?" I was shaking. "What does that even mean?"

"It's just for now. We'll see how things go. Got a few weeks before anything's going to happen. We're granted settling-in time.

Meanwhile, we'll plan what to do. We'll be okay."

Mom cleared her throat, like she was choked up but hiding it. She looked up, a perfect fake smile on her face. She tried to laugh. I'd seen that before and knew it wasn't good.

"So then, just to confirm what the council decided, one asked if I was prepared to 'host' the men. I laughed at their idea. 'Couldn't I just play recitals for everyone?' I answered. He said something crude and I knew they had no sense of humor."

"What did he say?" asked Hannah in a dark tone.

Mom made an ugly face. "He said: 'If you kin put yer mouth to that big tube, there's plenty other tubes you kin putcher mouth to.'"

Mom chuckled, imitating the way the guy talked, but we didn't join in her humor.

"Yes, that was crude." My response didn't seem strong enough so I added: "That's disgusting."

I thought that would end Mom's report. Thanks to Bucky, at least she got home safely.

"So did you?" Hannah asked. She seemed not so eager to hear the details as wanting to confirm how far the men would go.

"What?" asked Mom, unsure what she referred to.

"*That*," Hannah replied with angry shading.

Mom seemed to blush, for her a rare thing, hard to see in the firelight but I caught it.

"Yep, they all laughed at what he said. Then they got quiet. I never felt more afraid than at that moment. I knew the women wouldn't do anything. They dared not intervene. After discussion among the men, they had a vote. They decided if we follow their rules we can share in all the community's resources, or else we have to leave."

She fell silent. Hannah and I regarded each other.

"What did they do?" I asked Mom, afraid of the answer.

Mom looked up. "They said they'd be gentle. Never wanted to hurt anyone. It was for the good of the community. They wanted to 'give her a try' right there."

"Right there?" I erupted. "In front of everybody?"

"Then Bucky got up."

"Bucky?" asked Hannah. "The drunk man?"

"Old Man Kutcher," I said.

"Yes, him." Mom flashed a smile. "They must have known each other. He said he went often for fishing. Told them to think about who they were, what they were representing. He asked who they had become in this pandemic world. Whether they were thinking of the community or just themselves. He asked if what they were proposing was how they believed we should be treating people. He said: 'You want your daughters treated like you're treating this woman?'"

"That's what I would've told them," I blurted out.

"Good for him," said Hannah.

"He gave them a stern lecture – and I finally could believe he'd been a mayor. Talked like a politician. Now that he was clean and sober, he was impressive." She chuckled. "Country, maybe, but impressive. Made those council boys feel ashamed, made'em back off. He told them how I helped him when he crashed his truck, that I was a good woman – a good *person*. An asset to the island."

"Wow," I muttered.

"Yes, it's good he was there." Mom *whew*ed. "Can't imagine the way things might've gone were he not there. I guess I was lucky."

Lucky? Anger had been building in me as I listened to Mom's account, rage seething through me. I was ready to fight anyone who would try to hurt my mom. But I doubted my ability to fight, to really fight someone. Pulling the trigger of a pistol was easy – and cowardly. The thought of fighting with my hands made me sick to my stomach – not for any pain I'd suffer but for how my lack of skills would cause me a lot of embarrassment.

"And if they forced you?" asked Hannah solemnly.

Her question caught me by surprise. Why would she ask that? Was she curious about that scenario? Or did she want to know what she should expect as a girl on this island? Maybe she needed to prepare herself for when they might force her to do something. That put me more on edge.

"Well," said Mom with an exhale, "I guess I'd have to lay back and let it happen. Then it's done." And she glanced at me. "Kind of like being on a towel on the beach. You close your eyes and count seagulls." She held her fake smile too long. "Anyway, kids...as I said, we're okay for now. A month, at least. Or three. That will get us through winter. Maybe flu season will be over by then. Maybe society will be back to normal. Then we can leave."

"And if it's not done in a month or two?" I asked.

"Then I'll have to do my part," Mom replied with a sigh, "so we can share their resources, and make some kind of life here."

"Here?" My mind was a storm. "It's a terrible place."

"But it's the only place we have for a while," said Mom.

With an exhausted huff Mom got up, went in the house.

"I think she must've thanked him," said Hannah with a wink half-lost in the darkness. "Because he stood up for her, and helped keep them off her. Ya think?"

"Yeah," I replied, "think you're right."

After a minute we heard water running. Mom was taking a shower. After a few minutes, the water off, she called out to us: "Where's Nathan?"

25

IN WHICH MOM DIVES INTO THE POOL

Like any boy, Nathan had the urge to explore, especially being in a new place. Hannah and I thought he was in the house. Last we saw, he was playing with a set of toy cars he found in a box, happy to direct traffic across the coffee table. We thought it would be fine to go out back and talk – or practice our kissing.

But Mom didn't find him in the house.

So we split up. Mom walked down Seaside Drive, calling out his name. Hannah and I went along the beach, looking for him in the dark. We didn't call out, not wanting to bother anyone. We looked over at each house as we passed, then glanced at the surf. Nobody was outside.

"Nathan," I called finally, no longer worried about disturbing the neighbors.

"Nathan!" Hannah cried out but got no response.

I hoped he would come racing right out from between houses, maybe chasing after someone's pet dog. Or he'd come up behind us and shout "Boo!" like it was all a game to him.

Being a boy, he was free, no responsibilities until he reached 'child-bearing age', as Mom said. I smiled at that realization but I couldn't laugh. It was too ridiculous. On the other hand it made perfect sense for a community in survival mode. Things couldn't really be that bad, could they? After getting food, they could only think of sex.

I told Hannah more about leaving the city, the way life was by the time Mom decided we should leave.

Hannah took my hand as though reassuring me, just like Mom did when I was little. We continued hand in hand up the beach, talking on a safe subject: the collapse of society. I felt we were making our own plan. Food and water. Then shelter. We had all that on this island – but with conditions, rules. Thank goodness we were property owners.

"Are you okay?" she asked, sensing me lost in thought.

"I'm with you." I bit my tongue to keep from saying something stupid.

"Me, too," she responded. She drew close, gave my shoulder a deliberate bump with hers.

We gazed at the stars, forgetting we were searching for her brother. The constellations we saw were also seen by generations past, and would be seen by generations to come. Life goes on, no matter what happens to the desperate people below, so fearful of a pandemic. I told her my idea, thinking it was profound and she would think I was smart.

She drew close again, stopped me. She stretched up and we kissed. I wrapped my arms around her slender body. I wanted her to feel how strong I was. I could lift her up without much effort. I hoped she believed I could protect her. She was my pretend wife.

After another kiss, we parted but kept our hands clasped.

"Mother said if two people're together long enough they might as well be considered married," said Hannah. "It's called Common Law Marriage."

"I think that applies if you've been together for lots of years, not a couple weeks."

"Feels like years, Sandy. Like you've always been in my life."

I looked deep into her eyes, though the darkness prevented me from seeing her soul.

"Hannah, I will protect you always. I wanna be your guardian. But I worry I'm not prepared. Mom only taught me how to be kind and gentle. That's sissy stuff. I don't know how to be tough and mean, to be a violent man."

"But I don't want a violent man. I want you as you are."

"I may have to be violent to protect you. What about the other men on this island?"

"You shot that man attacking me. After the crash."

"Yes, but that was an accident."

"But your mother relies on you to be her guardian."

"Yes, but I'm not able to do that. I want to...to...."

"When you and me are together, I don't feel violence in you, Sandy. I feel only kindness. That's why I like you. I feel safe with you. I know you'd never hurt me—"

"Hannah, you don't know what I've done."

She pressed against me. Her hand slid deliberately down over my belly. My whole body tensed.

"I know what you've done, Sandy."

"Do you?" I felt her hand down there but, thinking of what I'd done, it didn't make any difference. "When we were at Grandma and Grampa's house, some vagrants broke in. They found Mom and they...they were...hurting her. I didn't know what to do. They didn't see me. I took the pistol we had and shot them. Killed them. Two of them. And Mom shot a third guy."

"You told me." She brought her hand up to my chest, pressed it over my heart. "Then you were a violent man. But you had to be. You were protecting your mother."

"But I don't wanna be that man."

"You needed to be that man." She looked me straight in the eye. "You can turn it off when you're done. You can stop yourself. That's the difference. You can turn it on and off as you need to. That's what a good man does. Some men are stuck one way or the other."

Her hand warmed my chest. "Okay, I get it. A time to fight and a time to love. So I fight when it's time to fight. And I love when it's time to love."

"That's it." She hummed a tune, then burst into the lyrics: "'Do your own shit / Make the fatal hit / You gotta stay true / To the Wu Crew' – yeah, funny how the Coronas mention the Wu Crew in their song."

"They sure had their thumb on the turntable," I laughed.

"Turntable?" she asked. "What's that?"

"Oh, Mom's got these disks, about this big...." I held up my hands to mark the width. "She's got a big collection of them. You put them on this turning platform – the turntable – and they go round and round as a needle runs along a groove. That picks up the music embedded in there. It can sound scratchy after a while, but Mom likes them."

"Oh, that's weird." She giggled, took my arm in her hands. "It must be fun to be old like your mom. So many crazy old things to remember."

"Yeah, I wonder if she thinks so. She's got Timmy, and he's plenty old."

We had been strolling down the beach under the starry sky. I put my arm around her shoulders, she acting as though she felt chilly. She nuzzled against me. It was great, but I remembered we were looking for Nathan, the curious kid.

Hannah seemed to realize that too, and looked up at me.

"He might have gone back to the house," I said.

"If he got bored, he'd return," she echoed. "Makes sense."

"Maybe Mom's found him by now."

Hannah laughed. "Then she'll be looking for us."

I saw something in the dark, way ahead, standing up. I had to squint but it became no clearer. It could be a person but no way to be sure. I stopped us.

"What's that?" I asked.

Hannah gazed up the beach, then laughed. "Looks like a sign."

"What sign?"

"You know." She patted her chest. "The sign you're afraid of: 'Beyond this point you may encounter nude bathers'. That sign."

"Oh." I continued to stare into the darkness. "That's it, huh?"

I shook my head, not believing. I imagined Mom going beyond that sign, her and her teen friend. I pictured them frolicking on the sand, enjoying themselves, then needing to rest.

"You okay?" asked Hannah, taking my arm again.

I cleared my head. "Yeah."

"Let's go back."

* * *

A light was on inside the house when we returned. It turned out to be an oil lantern. As we stepped through the front door, we saw Mom sitting on the couch with a man standing near her holding the lantern. Nathan was asleep on the couch, his head resting on Mom's lap.

"Found him," she spoke softly, seeing us. She put her finger to her lips. We heard a low mew. "Rather, he found us. Came home on his own. Seems he went out and found this kitten."

A tiny ball of yellow and brown fur tumbled off the couch, then scratched at threads of the rug on the floor.

"A kitten?" I stared at the tiny thing. "Where'd he find it?"

"In a yard down the street." Mom brushed his hair. "He got upset when he came home and nobody was here. So when I came in he was crying, poor baby." She looked down at him. "But he's safe now."

"No harm done," said the man, dressed in coveralls without a shirt, someone I didn't know but had seen a few times. "I seen the mama around, always got a mouse in her teeth. Or fish scraps."

Mom smiled at the man, then regarded Hannah and me. "How about you? Find anything interesting?" Her sly smile accused us.

"No, nothing," I responded. "Just a lot of sand."

Hannah broke into a grin. "Lots of sand."

"I see," said Mom. I expected her to wink knowingly at me, but she didn't.

"Well, good thing he come home, ma'am," said the man who had to be over fifty.

"This is Joe. He lives next door," said Mom. "What used to be the Wilsons' house."

"Pleased ta make yer 'quaintance." He raised his hand as if to tip a hat that wasn't there. As he did, his eyes fixed on Hannah. "Yer right, ma'am. Shore's a looker. Gonna have y'all some pretty young'uns."

None of us liked that remark; the room fell silent.

"Well, then. Be seein ya," he said and turned to go, taking the lantern with him. Then he paused. "I'm...well, I'm scheduled to be seein ya purdy soon, ma'am. See, I got the first draw. You being in the pool n all...on the list. Thought ya wanna know. But I'll clean up, don't you fret." He gave Mom a grin. "G'night."

"Goodnight," said Mom in a weary voice. Her smile fell off.

"Ooo," said Hannah. "Seriously?"

We sat in shock – despite being relieved to find my cousin. Our candles burned on the coffee table as we looked at each other. Joe exited, but not without a loud hack and spit from the porch. Mom seemed amused.

"I was looking for Nathan," she said. "He came out, helped me look. That's all."

With all the dangers we were finding, she appeared too calm. I should've been with her – but I should've been with Hannah, too. I felt myself getting overwhelmed with decisions, my heart beating faster. I had to take deep breaths to hold off a meltdown.

"In the pool?" I grunted. "On the list?"

Hannah gave me a look like she recognized something I could not. I was jealous of men taking an interest in Mom. And Hannah. I was ready to fight them. Everyone was my enemy. I could feel a meltdown coming.

"Sandy? You okay?" asked Mom.

"So, Mom," I spoke gruffly, "how come you came back from the council meeting all messed up like you were?" I tried to speak in a nice tone but couldn't control it, feeling betrayed. "You looked like you were in a fight or something."

Mom tried to hide a grimace. "That was hours ago. You're still concerned?" She paused as if replaying a memory. "Okay, after the meeting, I was coming home – actually we weren't too far from the community center – and Bucky caught up to me."

"Did he attack you?" I was angry and Hannah tried to take my hand to calm me.

"Not at all," said Mom. "Just.... Just a little fooling around. He had a little bottle of vodka, like we used to get on airplanes or in hotel rooms. He asked if I wanted to share a drink – because of all the stress of the meeting. I really felt it, so I said 'sure'. That's all. Then we made out a little."

"Made out? What does that mean?"

"It's a Boomer term," Hannah jumped in, "for what you and me did. Just the kissing part, but not any sex."

"Not sex, right?" I found myself standing, my fists clenched at my sides. Like I was the parent.

"Oh, no, Sandy. Not even close." She giggled like a school girl. "He did run his hands through my hair, though. Said it was nice."

"So that man...Bucky...."

"Old Man Kutcher," Hannah laughed.

"Huh? What?" Nathan grumbled, waking.

"Are you like his girlfriend now?" I demanded.

Mom dismissed my accusation with a wave of her hand. "I've never seen you act this way before. What's wrong? You worried about your mom? That's sweet. Thank you, but I'm fine. I've been taking care of myself since you were born – and taking care of you, too, let's not forget."

"But you...you were...kissing that drunk?"

"He wasn't drunk, or *a drunk*. He's actually rather...nice. I guess that's the best word. Not the best, not the worst, but in the middle. A step up from good enough." She put her finger to her lips as though smoothing lipstick. "Yes, very nice." She regarded me. "Isn't it all right for your mom, who isn't married, by the way, to spend time kissing a man?"

I had to use all my strength to hold back my rage. I knew what it was, had read about it: the monster awakening inside me. Mom had always been there for me. She'd even teased me, done things for me when I was younger, like we would be together forever.

"Sandy, calm down. Bucky's not your dad, and he's not going to be, not any time soon."

Hannah got up, flicked her hand for me to go with her. I went willingly, but anger rattled through my muscles. It hurt. I could only relieve the pain by exercising my urge to fight.

"Come on, Sandy," Hannah cooed, taking my hand.

In the bedroom, she sat me down on the bed, held my hands.

After my breathing relaxed, she pushed me down, then joined me, side by side. We lay in the dark, her arm over my chest, my hand holding her other hand.

"You did it," she said after a while.

"Did what?"

"You got violent there, but you kept yourself under control. See? Like we talked about on the beach."

"I did?"

"You did." She put her hands up to my face. "See? I told you. You're a good man." She kissed me.

I rolled against her, wanting more, but she pushed me back. Sitting up, she pulled off her top over her head. She lay beside me again. Her hands took my hands, placed them where she wanted them, and taught me what she liked.

✳ ✳ ✳

In the morning, Mom caught us: undressed, face to face on the bed. We were innocent, just some touching and kissing, learning about each other, but afraid to go further.

"Okay, kids," called Mom, a smirk on her face at the sight of us on the bed. "Up and at'em. Lots to do today."

We sat up. Hannah pulled the sheet over herself.

"And you hated me kissing someone," Mom snickered.

I shook the sleep from my head, muttered: "We're supposed to be married, you said."

Hannah giggled. She slid off the bed, pulling the sheet with her, leaving me exposed to Mom's judgment.

"Don't be shy." Mom dropped on the bed beside me. "I've seen you naked since the day you were born. No secrets between us." She gave me a once-over. "Yessir, you're looking good, but thin."

She gazed at Hannah getting dressed in shorts and t-shirt, her back toward us. Mom got up with a huff.

"None of us is eating very well." She smiled at me, judging. "You both need to gain some weight if you're going to have healthy babies."

"Mom!"

Hannah spun around, her t-shirt tail swinging like a tutu. "I'm not ready yet!"

"I know." Mom looked at each of us, pity in her eyes. "We have a few months to work on that. But it starts today."

26

IN WHICH MOM WISHES FOR LOVE

When we arrived on the island, we had to get checked out. What they called a clinic was just a side room in the community center. Doc Rick sat on a folding chair beside his 'desk', which was just a folding table. Wearing a white lab coat, he looked official. He had a bright smile, was clean-shaven, and appeared about Mom's age, with dark curly hair. As the only medical person on the island, he was an honorary member of the council, tasked with testing every new arrival.

On the end of the table he used as his desk stood a stack of test kits he must've snatched from his real clinic on the mainland when the pandemic started, hoarding them, maybe buying his way onto the island with them. He was thinking ahead, for sure. He would run out if there were too many visitors. It was 'standard procedure', they said and Mom agreed to it. She knew we weren't infected but she wanted to put them at ease.

Mom sat on the chair beside the 'desk' and Doc Rick, gloved and masked, inserted the swab. Mom made a face, then forced a smile so we wouldn't think it hurt. Into the plastic bag went the swab to be tested later. "When the power's on again," he said, and explained how the portable solar panels he had needed most of the day to charge.

I went next. It felt weird but didn't hurt. The school nurse was worse. Doc Rick tried to keep me relaxed by talking softly. His jokes were better than Mom's. There weren't any current sports to discuss – too many players had died – so he asked what sports I played. He played soccer in school. Video games, I had to admit, but that was a while ago. Mom didn't want me getting hurt by any 'roughhousing' but then she did show me some boxing moves she learned from her grandfather.

Hannah went next, immediately shied away from the swab up her nose. Based on what people we met said, the first symptoms were in the throat, not the nose. Better to take a sample from the throat, I suggested, rather than the 'brain wall', as Doc Rick called it. If a person has no sense of smell, he said, then it's going to be up the nose where he should test.

"It's all right, folks," he said. "We chiropractors study the same biology and chemistry the other kinds of doctors do. But probably more anatomy and nutrition than other doctors." He gazed at Mom. "On the island I mostly set bones and stitch up cuts. Nobody thinks about needing adjustments. A few of the ladies come in for massage, but let's call it physical therapy. Sometimes I need to console a resident when they're overcome by the stresses of our dire situation. Fortunately, I had a few psychology courses, so I'm good. Good listener, anyway."

"I hear you," Mom responded, nonplussed.

"My wife, Sue Ann – God rest her soul – she was a nurse. She worked double shifts at the beginning. Then she was a patient."

"Oh, I'm sorry," said Mom. "Sorry for your loss."

"Thanks. ...And your husband? Did he pass, too?"

"Me? Never married." She looked at me. "Just lucky."

"Oh. Well, that's a fine looking young man," said Doc Rick. The way he gazed at me made me blush. "Do you know Bobby? You two would get along." He turned to Mom: "Bobby's my partner. We met when I arrived. He's actually Sue Ann's second-cousin. They have a house here, but I never visited until...." He turned to me: "We should kick a ball around sometime."

"Sure," I replied.

"Sometimes Bobby and I ride the stationary bike to charge up the generator. If there's a lot of lab work."

Nathan was fussy, refused to be examined. Hannah took some

time to calm him, and we got it done.

Doc Rick examined us for signs of infection like rashes or other skin anomalies. We had to strip down behind a curtain. He looked us over, poked around. Mom quizzed him about island politics as he checked her. Hannah complained when he had the females get up on another table for a pelvic exam. He asked lots of personal questions like about their menses. Mom asked why it mattered. He said some women reported problems after getting vaccines so it was important to assess any issues.

"You would not believe the things I saw before I came down here," he said with a groan.

"Yes, I would," Mom responded.

Then it was Hannah's turn to hop up on the table, put her feet flat, knees up. He *hmm*ed a lot when examining her, then stepped back and pulled off his gloves. He motioned her off the table and she got dressed.

Sweeping the curtain back, he had a strange grimace.

"You said these two are married?" he asked Mom, not Hannah. "She seems to be a virgin still."

Mom didn't blink. "I'm just the mother-in-law. Don't know why they haven't consummated by now. Is it anybody's business?"

"We need to know these two are actually wedded. Trying, you know. It's a rule here."

"A rule, huh? Can't we keep this our little secret? Think of how much stress they've been under traveling here. Also, no privacy. No doubt they'll get on it now that we've settled in."

"Absolutely. I can do that. If you can keep our little secret that I agreed to keep your little secret. They check my reports. They're kinda strict on the island, if you know what I mean."

Mom gave a nod. Her face remained wary as Doc Rick, smiling like he'd completed a successful surgery, pronounced both women normal. They were fit and eligible to be in the pool.

"Hurray," Hannah grumbled.

"This information has to be noted in the community register," said Doc Rick. "Then you'll be good to go."

Nathan was happy to show off muscles he thought he had. He

wanted to be a wrestler someday. He liked leaping off the couch to grapple with an invisible opponent on the floor. Doc Rick knew wrestling, told him about Greco-Roman style he did in college.

I stood calmly when it was my turn, waiting for the him to be done. Everyone was dressed when he finished with me – including examination of my genitals and prostate. He needed to check the motility of my sperm, too, and asked for a sample.

I asked him why. He said: "The by-laws state 'he shall giveth of his seed freely that the chosen woman shall be made fruitful'. So we need to be sure the little guys can swim. If you want to be included on the list, we need to check."

"Do I have to be on the list?"

"A young man like you?" He grinned. "Of course you want to be on the list. All the men here are."

"Mom? Do I have to?" I called from behind the curtain.

"Just do it," she responded, then chuckled. "You need help?"

So I gave him my sample. Standing behind the curtain, I could only think of Hannah, sitting steps away, and tried to be quiet. Later, using a microscope, Doc Rick would determine whether I was fit for the list.

After all the testing, we were suppose to wait at the house for the results, about 24 hours. As expected, none of us had the virus or its variants. The results were reported to the council and put into the public register so everyone in the community would know our health status. My motility was pretty good: 85 percent, and in my 3.5 milliliter sample I had 160 million little guys, the report said. When we looked later at the register, someone had put a red star beside my name. Hannah had a green circle, indicating to everyone she was on the pregnancy track, to be colored in when pregnancy was confirmed. Mom had the blue checkmark of being in the pool. Nathan didn't have any mark yet.

Leaving Doc Rick's office, we took the long way home, going out to the beach. The slope was gentle and waves rolled in like water spilling over a tile floor. Walking barefoot, carrying our shoes, we watched the morning sun rise. It seemed like we were in a paradise – if we didn't think too much about the rules.

"That guy was creepy," said Nathan, saying aloud what we all thought.

"He better not post those pics anywhere," Hannah grumbled.

"There's no internet here," I reminded them.

"But they're in our medical files now," said Mom.

Nathan skipped ahead, ready to forget his unpleasant visit.

Hannah took my hand off and on, matching her mood. One moment I was her lover, another I was just a boy she knew.

Mom walked the slowest. She seemed happy to walk a beach on a breezy morning, having no worries. I was simply happy to have Hannah in my life, especially if I had to endure a six-year flu season that wasn't ending anytime soon.

We borrowed a neighbor's portable solar-powered generator, charged from sunlight. We were able to vacuum the floors and use other devices a while. Hannah got her MP3 charged. Mom found a gasoline-powered generator in a storage shed. She suggested this house might be our home for a couple years, so we might as well make it livable, not do only enough to get by like for a two-week vacation.

Also, we realized we were four people with two beds.

"So who's sleeping with me?" Mom asked that first night when we arrived, giving me a wink.

"Not me," said Hannah, shaking her head.

"Uh...me neither," I responded a moment later.

"Nathan?"

"Huh-uh," he grunted. "I'm not sleeping with my *aunt*."

"So no girls with girls and boys with boys?" asked Mom.

"No," I snickered.

Nathan pointed to the living room. "I can sleep on the couch."

"Then you two'll have to share a bed," said Mom, meaning me and Hannah. "Hope you don't mind."

"It's...." I tried thinking of an excuse, just to please Hannah, so she wouldn't think I was perving on her, but no words came to me.

"It's okay, I guess," she said with a sigh. "But you stay on your side."

With only two bedrooms, and one double bed in each room, the beds old and soft, we decided Mom would take the smaller room which had windows on the front of the house. It was the same room shared with her sisters as a teen. That had to be triggering. Hannah and I took the larger bedroom, the one meant for parents, and it didn't seem ironic to us. Nathan was happy to camp out in the living room. He made a fort from the couch cushions and a pair of blankets.

Later, standing in the doorway of our new bedroom, shoulder to shoulder, our hearts beating together, the future unfolded and spread out before us like a blossoming flower.

"After you," I said, gesturing like a butler. Then I thought of the ritual of carrying a bride over a threshold. But before I could share my joke, she pushed ahead.

"You better be nice," she muttered, squeezing past with a little sashay to tease me.

We sat on the edge of the bed, the other side against the wall. Knee to knee, hands on our thighs, we seemed to be waiting for instructions. We were just two shy kids.

"Are you okay?" I asked after a while. "I mean, okay with this arrangement?"

"I guess. What else is there?"

"It's just sleeping arrangements. And I don't snore."

She giggled. "That's good to know."

"I can't sleep with Mom. And I bet you don't wanna sleep with her either. She sleeps nude. So...."

"I get it." She tilted her chin up, hummed a tune, then broke into lyrics: "'It'll matter in the morning / Dreams that claw your brain / Leave you with a warning / That you're gonna go insane.' That's a Viral Dark song."

"Never heard of 'em," I had to admit, but in a nice way, wishing Mom could take out Timmy for some decent music.

I was surprised Mom was okay with Hannah and me sleeping together. We understood no hanky-panky, just sleeping. I wouldn't 'try anything', as Mom would say, nothing 'naughty' or 'untoward'. Hannah sure wasn't going to let me do anything she didn't want. If Hannah 'tried something', I told myself not to resist much.

* * *

It seemed a long time ago that we arrived. Now, however, as we tried to drift to sleep, face to face as we said 'goodnight', we held each other on the bed. Rather like being with Mom when I was a little boy, my puckered lips around her fat nipple. Now the other person was a girl about my age – my lover, my everything.

Her small breasts pressed against my chest. Our lips touched lightly, as though afraid to meet. She reached down my abdomen.

"Hmm," she whispered, "that *is* you."

"Can't help it."

"Because of me?"

I snickered. "Yeah – sorry."

"Don't be."

Without another word, she tugged at my undies, got them down over my hips and took hold of me, like she was grabbing a hammer, ready to pound nails. At first she just held on, then she began moving her hand. We were eye to eye in the darkness. I lost my breath, then felt afraid – afraid of feeling guilty – and put my hand over hers to stop it.

"What's wrong?" she whispered. "Not doing it right?"

"I...love you," I mumbled.

"You can't say that." She released her grip. "Not yet."

"Why not? I do."

"It's too soon."

"No, it isn't. It's what I feel."

Her lips pursed. "Isn't it what you want?" she asked, meaning what she did with her hand. "Boys like it, right?"

"Yes...eventually."

"When?"

I couldn't answer.

And then, deep in the silence of the house, I heard a sound, a strange noise I hadn't heard before.

"Listen," I whispered. Hannah had given up on me and rolled onto her back. "Sounds like crying."

"Nathan?"

"No. I think it's Mom."

I got up. Standing naked, listening, I glanced back at Hannah in the dark. I wanted to join her, but I was afraid of what I would do. Thankfully I had to check on Mom.

Padding to the other bedroom, I leaned against the wall by the open door. Mom mumbled to herself in the dark, sniffling between phrases, breaths between sentences.

"What've you done, crazy girl? What were you thinking? Think you're so tough. You can do damn near anything. Now look at you. You made it to the damn beach house, but for what? Live out the rest of your life?" She sobbed. "And the kids? Okay, so you're in charge. Exactly what're you supposed to do? Huh? Bucky's right. You defy each side, can't make up your mind which way to go. What should we do? Stay? Go? Which? When? Is it time? The right time? Fucking pandemic fucking up everything."

It was like she was praying, asking God to give her advice.

"Sandy?" she called from the bed. "Is that you?"

I went in, stood beside the bed. In the dark she reached for me, bumping my crotch. I took her hand and held it away as I knelt beside the bed, against the mattress. Mom lay stretched out atop the sheet, nude as usual.

"Come here, my sweet boy." She pulled my hand.

I followed her directions to lay beside her on the bed.

"Come to Mama," she cooed.

She rolled me into her arms, hugging me tight. Loosening her hug, she turned to face me. She kissed my cheek, then suddenly my mouth. I pulled back.

"Mom, don't." I knew she was upset but we were different now. Whenever she'd been this way before, she'd find comfort with me: a hug, sometimes more. And I didn't know where the line was.

Her hands caressed my shoulders, went down my back. Then she fell back, pulling me with her, on top of her. Her legs fell open, thighs cradling my hips. With her arms around me, holding me, I felt engulfed. Her breath was hot on my neck.

"No, Mom."

She must know what she's doing, I decided, not just acting in a dream, in her half-sleep. She knows it's me.

I pushed away, breaking out of her arms' hold, raising up on my arms like a perfect gym class push-up, trying to keep out of the way.

"Sandy?" Hannah appeared in the doorway. A loud gasp, then: "What are you *doing?*"

I jumped off the bed, stood before my cousin.

She stormed out.

"Wait," I called. I couldn't see well in the dark, but she had to be angry and tearful as she ran away.

"Let her go," Mom muttered from the bed. She sat up half-way, laying on her side, braced on her arm. "She won't understand."

I spun around to face her. "Mom! Why did you...? This...."

She shook her head, mumbled words I couldn't make out.

"I've teased you far too long," she said in a clearer voice. "Yes, I know I shouldn't." A sigh, a moment of silence. "It was cute when you were little. And when you hit puberty – boy, howdy. The way you'd get excited. One word or a glance and *sproing*. But now.... Okay, now it's pathetic. I'm sorry, Sandy. Forgive me?"

I still couldn't speak, my throat clenched so tight it hurt.

She lay back with a groan. "A mother's love. Eventually it has to end."

"I'm sorry," I finally said. I didn't know what for, but the words tumbled out unchecked.

"I'm still here for you. I love you. You know that, right? If you ever want...or need...*anything*." She sniffled, wiped her eyes. "But I won't, you know...be the one to start anything."

Standing in the middle of the dark room, lost and naked, my mind exploded. I had no idea what words should come out of my mouth next.

"Mom?" I spun around, a light flicking on in my head. That's it, the right words: "You're my mom."

"I said I'm sorry, Sandy." Again she sobbed. "I'm just...just so overwhelmed by everything."

"I get it, but...not *that*."

"You wanted it. I could tell." She seemed to be smiling in the dark. "You were right to refuse." A clearing of her throat. "There's some things.... Well, old normal or new normal, some things just can't be."

She was my mom. She cared about me. The only person who cared about me. I had to be nice to her.

"Until it's just you and me," I said to meet her half-way, "the last two people in the world. The only two people left."

"And we have to repopulate the damn world." Her attempt at a chuckle fell flat.

"Yes, then." I took a breath. "I think then it would be okay."

"I may be too old." Her voice was dark, spilling out like a quote from the Bible. "Promise me."

"I did." Confused and frustrated, all I could do was breathe. "Mom, are you drunk? Were you drinking?"

"Promise me, when it's my time to go...."

I took a breath. "I'm sure not gonna do that when you're old."

"If I'm dying...?"

"Mom, stop it." I stepped to the door. "I'm going now."

"Wait," she called.

"Try to relax, Mom. Think of some good times, not hard times. Count sheep. I won't come back tonight." And I left.

I waited in the hallway, listening for Hannah. She made no sound – no weeping, no heavy breathing, no cursing.

Stepping over to the bed, feeling my way, I sensed she was there, on her side, facing the wall – my spot. I pulled on my shorts and lay beside her, balanced on the edge.

"I'm sorry," I whispered. "Mom's drunk.... She just grabbed me. Like I was someone she used to know."

Hannah grumbled something, but I thought it best not to ask for clarification.

"She's sad, worried," I whispered. "She's always been strong."

I listened to Hannah breathing.

"Nobody can be strong forever," she said after a while.

And that was the last she spoke to me.

27

IN WHICH OUR FAMILY GROWS

"So here's our situation," said Mom plainly.

We all sat around the table, a plate of granola bars and cut-up tangerines, and cups of freshly boiled water for our breakfast. A few pieces of crackers remained from our previous dinner.

"Another day in paradise," I muttered, not happy.

Mom flashed a smile like it was going to be a good situation she would tell us.

"We have a house, have shelter over our heads." She waved to the window behind her, indicating the rain falling outside. "And we have *some* food. Some." She looked at Nathan. "And we'll get some fish, too, thanks to Bucky teaching you how to catch fish."

Nathan's mood brightened. "Yay!" The tawny kitten stirred in his lap.

"Enough fruit. Spinach, carrots, broccoli growing. Potatoes and sweet potatoes will take time. And tomatoes and peppers. Green beans, lettuce, and onions are coming along. Hopefully, we can eat those in a few weeks. Got water from the tap, but have to boil it, and a few cans and bottles from the community center's hoard. No electricity, but plenty of candles."

"And Old Man Kutcher's lantern," Nathan spoke.

"He's not an old man," Mom corrected.

"He's older than you, Aunt Polly."

"Remember, Nathan, I'm you're mother now. Call me 'Mom' or else people will get suspicious."

"You want a cracker?" asked Hannah absently, holding up a small broken piece from the plate.

"Old joke, dear," Mom sneered, holding her smile.

Nathan ran with it: "Polly wanna cracker?"

"Stop it, kids!" Mom had no patience with that joke.

Hannah grinned but refused to laugh. I looked at her and she turned away, denying me her pretty face.

"People," I called out. "Let's have order. We're not vax cops."

Mom laughed at my act. Everyone settled down.

"So...we can stay here and maybe get by," said Mom, repairing her smile. "But the rules they've got here...not so good if we stay. We can be part of their New Weird Order, but we have to follow their rules. Or we leave, fend for ourselves. I don't know what's north other than the city most tourists come down from. Can't be a good place to live now. And the ferry isn't running so we'd have to go across that old bridge again. We'll be walking. Carrying our belongings. Foraging for food in nature and looted stores. Not an easy thing to do. Watching for vagrants, too."

"And zombies?" asked Nathan.

"Not zombies, just crazy desperate survivors."

"Mom?" I called out to get her to pause.

She went on: "They think the world's ended. They think we're all alone so we have to rebuild society. I tried to describe what we went through. It's bad, okay, but it's not the end of the world. It'll pass. My plan's always been to wait it out. Let the bad pass. Like Passover. Just hunker down for a while. Then everything will be returning to normal again – the old normal or some variation but not a new normal. Not the normal they want to make here. They got strange ideas, right out of B-movies. Or old church revivals."

"Mom?" I tried again.

"Yes, *son?*"

I shot Hannah a look at hearing Mom's new name for me, but she had no expression. I was a dog house occupant again, forever tormented, seeing my Love but never acknowledged by her.

"What about Aunt Laura and Bootsy?"

Mom bowed her head. "Well, I did want to go back for them. I wanted to check the house situation here first. And now? What do I think? Given how Laura is getting on, she may actually fit in. Food for sex, as they say."

Hannah's attention piqued; she glanced at me like it was my fault they had such rules on the island.

"But getting back to her," Mom continued, "that's going to be difficult now that we don't have a car. It's a long hike. Then the hike back. Do we all go? Only me? Me and Sandy? What would happen to you two while we're gone? No, I don't think that's going to be possible. The four of us need to stick together, watch out for each other."

"But if the city's gonna return to some kind of normal," I said, my hand up like I was in class, "we can head back that direction and get her on the way."

"Okay," said Mom. "How will we know when everything's back to normal? Got any kind of communication?"

Hannah and I instinctively reached for our phones, forgetting they didn't get any signal so we no longer carried them with us. Mom chuckled at our stupidity.

"Sometimes," Hannah spoke, "when I'm near the lighthouse, I almost get a signal. Too weak for anything."

"Maybe they have an antenna there," I said. "For ships coming into the harbor."

"I'll have to check," said Mom. "You may be right."

"May be?" I sneered at her.

"When we get a signal, I guess it means everything is back to normal," she suggested. "Someone will fix the equipment."

"If the last electrician hasn't died," Hannah muttered.

"We need to recharge the phones," I said. "Somehow. But it's low priority for using their generators."

"So what do we do here?" Hannah spoke up. "I mean while we wait. Laying on the beach is boring."

Mom thought a moment, not for an answer but for the right answer, and the right answer had to be clever. I learned that over the years. Like the way she practiced her tuba, playing the same passage over and over until it was perfect – then over and over again perfectly.

"We just live," she said.

I expected more, but it made sense. The plan was to wait. On this island, in this council-driven community, waiting really was a misnomer. You had to be doing something. Getting food, mostly. They didn't like idleness. It was the devil's playground and thus forbidden. That was in the by-laws.

"Just live?" I mumbled.

Gathering in the community center after we had time to settle in, we were assigned tasks by Olivia, the short but sturdy woman a bit older than Mom who was the council secretary while having an affair with Owen, the council leader. She read from papers on a clipboard.

Nathan was assigned to fishing duty, working with Old Man Kutcher, learning the fine art of casting the line into the water to entice a fish to bite. They worked mostly from the end of the pier. Turned out Bucky was a good teacher, showing a lot of patience with the boy. They regularly brought fish to the community center for distribution. A few crabs were captured on the beach, too, and put to the boil pot. There were plans to net shrimp using one of the boats.

Each day I would go work in the garden beside Mom. It once was a decorative flower bed at the front of the community center but now transformed into a vegetable garden. We followed a basic routine: prepare the soil, plant seeds, water them, care for the plants as they grow, harvest vegetables as they ripen. Same with the fruit trees. I went around yard to yard at people's houses and picked lemons and tangerines. One house had a cherry tree, another a few raspberry bushes. I carried baskets back and forth, gathering fruit then delivering it to the community center.

Hannah was assigned the task of minding the kids while the parents worked. She could learn how to care for babies was the idea of island elders. They penciled her in on their calendar as birthing her first baby by next year, planning her next pregnancy with another partner the following year. A lottery would decide who the lucky guy was. However, we were a long way from that.

Even the thought of sex made her shut down. And with her being tired from her work every day, she sure wasn't in the mood even for flirting.

Mom reminded us of our tasks at home. Despite our work for the community during the day, we had to keep the house neat. With rain outside and being a Sunday, we stayed in and rested, however. Some people on the island gathered to pray and sing at the community center. I went once. They thanked God for saving them from the deadly virus, promising to work hard to show Him that He made the right decision in picking them as His survivors. They felt special, blessed. They would be fruitful and multiply. Mom was invited to play her tuba at the service and she promised someday she'd join them.

Each morning, we headed to our daily chores. Like a regular job, but without any pay. Well, food was our pay. Do our fair share of work and we could share the community's food. I remembered learning in school about the *Mayflower Compact*: everyone worked for the common good, sharing everything. But Mom, talking while she worked the plot opposite me, told me of the French commune and how it got out of hand, so crazy that Monsieur Guillotine had to invent a device for getting rid of the slackers. So it could go either way, Mom explained with a wink to me and a nod at Owen who was walking by then, always checking out Mom's rear.

Nathan reported another fun day with Old Man Kutcher. My cousin had caught a large fish, half his size, but it had to go to the community hoard, not brought home. It was divided between six families. He looked forward to each day of fishing, except when the weather was bad. Bucky took him out to the end of the pier that stretched 100 feet out over the water. Nathan said when he was older, they would try surf casting.

Hannah usually came home exhausted each day with her shirt dirty from food the babies spit up and other out-pourings from her little charges. Her boss was an older woman named Victoria who had no kind words for her and ordered her around. She criticized everything Hannah did. She even questioned her fitness to be a mother, saying she was too thin. The babies cried when Hannah held them, eliciting more complaints from Victoria, who lost her own children, ten and seven, when the pandemic swept through her town, forcing her to flee to this island where her in-laws had a house. Her husband, a medical technician, had stayed in the city. He became infected and died or so she presumed, never hearing from him again.

But worst of all, Hannah reported, were men who stopped by, just to look at her. They didn't have any kids in the nursery. They stared as she did her work. They complimented her. Others made remarks which she couldn't shrug off. They knew where she lived, where she worked, and her route between. Somehow I didn't think the by-laws would protect her, so I started escorting her.

When Victoria wasn't around Hannah could sing to the babies and toddlers. They didn't understand the lyrics, so there wasn't any harm to their moral development.

Mom continued to complain about the dirt that got under her fingernails. The worn-out gloves she tried to use made it worse. There wasn't enough water to waste with daily showers so Mom tried sponge baths but she never felt clean. We were all a little grimy. That left her grumpy. Playing Timmy helped a little. She played a song she made up when I was a little boy that she called 'Sandy's Song', but played it in a minor key with a bluesy beat. Her playing wasn't as wonderful as before. She got frustrated and just blasted loud and long until she ran out of breath.

And life went on, day after day, until we began to forget what day it was and no longer cared.

28

IN WHICH MOM CUTS LOOSE

There were dates to remember on the island, dates to celebrate or at least acknowledge if they happened to be sad things. Someone found fireworks in the community center and they shot a few out over the sea when we gathered for a kind of festival. Everyone was glad to forget whatever people off the island might be facing — the outerlanders, they called them.

Mom was dancing with several men on the beach, taking turns with them, as a couple of women played jazzy music with guitar and saxophone. Everyone was happy. When Mom's shirt slipped open, the last button popping off, nobody said a word. She whirled and spun without missing a beat. Others wore much less. It was a chance to cut loose after so many weeks on the island.

Hannah and I sat on a breakwall that ran from the top of the beach by the street straight down into the water, intended to slow beach erosion. It went out another twenty yards, forming a jetty. People sat on the sand in front of us. A few stood behind us, watching members of the community dancing and acting crazy. Some of them were smoking sour-smelling weeds they'd grown.

I took Hannah's hand — or maybe she took mine, I couldn't be sure. We worked out our issues, and I swore never to put anyone ahead of her. She was my wife, after all, and I was her husband according to Mom and community by-laws. We were required to be pregnant soon, by the anniversary of our coming to the island. But we hadn't even done that act yet.

"Is that good?" she asked me at night, putting her hand down between my legs. "What you like?"

"Yes, I like it." I likewise slipped my hand between her thighs. "Is this okay?"

She nodded but in the dark I only could sense it.

"I heard sometimes two people turn around so one of them is reversed over the other," I whispered into her ear. "That way they can do things for each other at the same time."

"There's a number for that," she giggled, then stopped. "By the way, Sandy: I think I'm seventeen now."

"Seventeen?" Her age hadn't been on my mind.

"Yeah. A few days ago," she whispered. "But I guess nobody remembered."

"Oh – sorry. I'll never forget again. Promise."

We carefully maneuvered around so she was on top of me, just like in porn vids. She was so marvelous, figuring out what to do as I tried my best to please her—

A voice broke my trance, shattering the replay of the night's enjoyment: "Anyone sitting here?"

It was Jackson, Owen's nephew, 25 or so, blond and somewhat muscular, a surfer type. I hadn't interacted with him much but I had no reason to welcome him into our bubble.

He sat on the breakwall beside Hannah; I was on her other side, my hand on the breakwall by her hip.

"How's it going?" he asked Hannah, not me. "I see you around from time to time. You're probably the hottest girl on the island, ya know? That's why I signed up for your lottery. I might get to be your next husband."

She tried not to look at him, eyes forward.

"Hey," I called him out. "She's my wife."

"Just giving her a compliment," said the jerk. "Nothing wrong with that. It's a free island. She can speak for herself. We ain't that kinda society where women gotta shut up." He laughed, but we didn't. "My uncle says we're way more liberal here."

Jackson pointed to a couple on a blanket on the sand, by the breakwall, half in shadow. They were having sex, the man laying over the girl. Looked like Marcus, older than Mom, with Sara, a little older than Hannah. I saw others paired up on the beach, and a group of three, enjoying the evening in their own way.

"Look at'em," said Jackson with a chuckle, "the old pervs." He gave Hannah a leer, pushing his knee against hers. "That's what we should be doing, ya know? Liven things up around here."

"We're fine," I said, an edge to my voice. I gripped Hannah's hand tighter. "We're okay watching."

"Figures," he said, almost a snarl. "Typical sissy." He turned to Hannah: "How about you and me give it a go? Sissy boy here can watch, since that's what he likes."

"I don't think so," I responded.

"Lighten up, kid. She can speak for herself."

He took Hannah's hand from her lap and caressed it, rubbing his thumb over her palm. She tried to pull her hand back. I kept protesting but he ignored me.

"You can do whatever you like here," he said to Hannah. "So what if this boy is your husband? Just means you go home with him. But you can do whatever you like with anybody you like. It's in the by-laws." His big toothy smile reminded me of a shark. "So let's go. Come on, Hanny. I'll show ya some real fun."

"Get your hands off her," I demanded.

"You have to share," he said, chuckling. "Not enough girls to go around. You're just her husband, so you get her first. That's fair. But she can do what she wants." He gazed lustfully at Hannah. "So how's about it? Ready for something new and different?"

"Stop it," I growled, jumping off the breakwall and standing before him.

"She's not saying no," he said, laughing. He turned, asking a couple sitting nearby if he could borrow their beach towel.

"Leave her alone," I commanded.

"So what's it gonna be, Hanny?" he asked her. "We need to get this train outta the station."

"I said don't bother her." I struck a fighting stance, fists up.

"Sandy! Don't!" Hannah exclaimed, standing.

"Yeah, don't get in our way," Jackson laughed. "She wants to be with someone new. Don'tcha, Hanny?"

"She belongs to me!" I shouted back.

"Stop it!" Hannah exploded. "I don't belong *to anyone.*"

People around us were watching our drama and more turned at her outburst.

She took a breath. "I belong to me. Myself." She turned to me. "I *choose* to be with you, Sandy. I *want* to be with you. But you don't own me. There's a big difference."

"See? She's free to be with who she wants," said Jackson. "So how about it, Hanny? Ready for bigger and better?"

Before she could answer, I stepped between them, arm raised. I swung my fist into Jackson's jaw. At the last instant I noticed my elbow going back had smacked Hannah's chest. With my elbow bash, she fell back against the breakwall.

Jackson righted himself, brought up his fists. We boxed for a minute, each of us landing punches, face and belly.

"You're pretty good," he said, circling. "Who taught you?"

"My mom did," I responded, not hesitant to say it.

"Your mommy?" he teased.

That made me explode in rage. I charged at him, brought him down hard on the sand. We wrestled, tumbling over and over, with sand spraying. I tried to get my hand free to throw another punch but we stayed entangled.

A few men came up and ordered us to stop fighting. Two men pulled us to our feet and separated us. I had managed to make his nose bleed, which got him mad. I felt soreness on my cheek and in my gut but I was full of rage and eager to keep fighting.

"You two gotta settle down," said Owen, community leader. He wore a hideous red thong and nothing else, with his belly hanging out. Olivia stood behind him wrapped in a beach towel. "We're supposed to be having fun tonight. It's Make-a-Date night, ya dang fools."

"I know," Jackson tried to explain. "That's why I'm asking her. Besides, I'm in her lottery pool—"

"He was harassing my wife!" I exclaimed.

"He's had his turn," said Jackson.

"You know the rules," said Owen, rubbing his big belly. "Read the by-laws. She's got till after her first birth before she takes on a new suitor." He gave Hannah the once-over. "That's not gonna be anytime tonight, son."

Jackson remained angry but he got the message.

"Make-a-Date night's for y'all to get with somebody new, that ain't yer spouse," said Owen, "but y'all gonna need permission of yer new partner anyhow."

"I asked her."

"And she said 'okay'?"

Jackson shook his head. "She didn't say 'no'."

"But did she say 'yes'?"

"No."

Owen clapped Jackson's shoulder. "Then yer off-limits, boy." He gave Hannah a grin. "Course now, little lady, if ya don't get a bun in the oven after being here a year, then yer gonna hafta switch it up, take another fella for a run, see if you can getter going."

With chiding from the men around us, Owen's sulking nephew stalked off, humiliated. I won! The men patted my shoulders like I was one of them now. Then they excused themselves. The beach was calling. Partners called. The night was young, their mindsets young, and love was being made.

Hannah hugged me. She examined my face, bruised and puffy. My cheek had been scraped and bled a little.

"You really looked tough," she said, which were about the most delightful words I ever heard her say. "Now let's take care of that pretty face."

In my whole life I'd never felt better. I felt heroic as we left the beach, returning to the house.

Hannah dabbed some ointment on my face to soothe the rough spots. Her fingers were so gentle, her touch so kind, I could let her caress my sore face forever.

We went straight to our bed, stripping ourselves as we hurried down the hallway. We slipped into a new position we learned from porn streams, but when we were ready, I hesitated.

"I'm sorry," I whispered.

She held my face in her hands and kissed my unhurt cheek to reassure me.

"We're okay, Sandy."

We kissed a while, then heard noises from Mom's room. I put my hand over Hannah's mouth just as she started to speak. We listened but were unable to make out the words. I got up. Taking her hand, Hannah rose also. I wasn't about to go alone to Mom's room like last time. We stepped naked into the hallway.

Obviously it was Mom's voice. We heard the rustle of sheets, the squeaking of the mattress. The night was filled with heavy breathing, gasps, grunts, and muffled giggles. Then the sounds I feared most: "Oh! Oh! Oh!" from Mom and "Jesus! Jesus!" from a man.

I turned to Hannah, beside me in the hallway. My lips were pursed in embarrassment. Hannah repressed giggles. I shook my head like we shouldn't bother them. I just wondered who Mom was with – and if she was okay.

Back in our room, I put my mouth to Hannah's ear. "I can't believe Mom is fucking somebody. All my life I never saw her have any interest in that. But she was always teasing me."

Hannah shifted to put her mouth to my ear. "Don't worry. It's what mothers do. My mother dated a couple guys after Dad left, but she never let them sleep over."

"They have no choice here," I whispered back.

"Neither do we," she said.

We lay together, caressing, playing the happy married couple despite our skin sticking together.

A little later, we heard the shower running. Mom's giggles were clear. A man's muffled laugh followed.

"Might I join you, ma'am?" It sounded like Bucky.

"Why yes, sir, you may," Mom replied.

Hannah snickered, tapped my face. "And you were so worried about your mother."

"I'm responsible for her."

"Now you're responsible for me, don'tcha forget."

Her hands slid down my belly. She knew what she was doing. She knew what I liked. I touched her, too, my fingers massaging her until she was ready. I moved over her. I tried to be gentle but she tensed at the first discomfort. I paused.

"There's no hurry," I told her.

She wrapped her arms around me. "They want us to get on with it. We have to."

"Not tonight."

"Then when?"

"When everything is right."

"It'll never be right," she whimpered.

✳   ✳   ✳

In the morning Mom and Bucky were standing in the kitchen, his arm lazing across her shoulders. Her arm rested around his waist. Neither wore clothes. They shared tangerines and had fried some eggs. Two more eggs sat in a dish.

Mom greeted me in a manner suggesting everything was quite normal, nothing to be shocked at. But I had to focus on the most interesting aspect of the scene.

"Eggs?" I adjusted my shorts, ran a hand through my hair.

"Looks like someone got lucky last night," said Mom, happy to let her breasts hang free.

"You?" I asked, making a frown, glaring at Bucky.

"No, Sandy – you."

"Me?"

"We heard you and your *wife* grinding away last night." Mom's smirk was sharp. "Was it beautiful?"

"We heard you two fucking," I rebutted.

"Sandy, be polite," said Mom with fake shock. "You know it's been quite a while. For Bucky, too." She grinned lovingly at him. "Just having fun. Two adults having fun. We can do as we please. Besides, I've devoted my life to raising you. No time for dalliances. But you're an adult now – as you like to remind me. So I'm cutting you loose, son. You're free. On your own now. Happy trails."

"Mom," I whined like I remained her little boy.

She pointed out how I still had certain mannerisms that were not appropriate for an adult. Thankfully Bucky spoke up to stop the argument:

"Them eggs come from chickens we got from a family arrived by boat while back. They rescued a whole farm. That's where we got the cow and pigs. But Maybelle ain't for barbequing. She's strictly for milk. For the kids. The pigs, they're making fertilizer. The chickens finally got to laying eggs, so it's a special treat."

"What family?" I asked.

"That'd be those Carpenters. Come down from up north on a raft." He scratched his head. "Dad is Joseph, and Christina and Peter the kids. She's about twelve, I'm guessing. She's coming along fine, be a real asset in a few years."

"Already sizing her up?" Mom made a face.

"She's gonna grow up sooner or later, ain't she? Sooner or later she's gonna need a husband, make some babies for the island."

"I haven't seen them yet," said Mom.

"They're staying at Miss Anabelle's place."

He meant the Seaside Inn down from the community center, a ten-unit motel that had seen better days. Some people who didn't have a house on the island stayed there. Other people made use of abandoned cars on the street as their homes, but those bedraggled people tended not to associate with regular community members.

"How about the mother?" I asked.

"No mama. Mary was lost to the virus."

"Too bad," I said, feeling sad for them. How many families had lost someone? Every day came reminders of why we were here on the island: a village of survivors, escaping a pandemic.

My mind flashed back to when we first arrived at Grandma and Grampa's farm thinking we would stay a week or two. At that time we didn't know anyone directly who'd lost someone. We didn't associate with people after the first lockdown. We kept to ourselves. Just me and Mom, and her tuba.

This island community was my first experience mingling with other people since the pandemic first began. The sixty or so people on the island seemed like a crowd. It was both unsettling and gave me a sense of hope, that we had people to do things, to help each other. Yes, there might be underlying threats if we didn't follow the by-laws – especially for females.

"Hey there, little missy," said Bucky, eyes wide.

I turned to find Hannah coming up to me, putting her arms around me from behind and planting a kiss on my cheek in full view of Mom and Bucky.

"Oh dear," Mom gasped, surprised at the sight of her niece without a stitch on. "Why Hannah May Whistler, whatever are you doing?"

Hannah yawned, just rolling out of bed, forgetting she was nude. "I smelled eggs."

Nathan, who was sleeping within a fortress of couch cushions and blankets with his kitten, popped up at the talking. He peered over the top of the couch, gasped at the sight of his sister.

"Ooo! I can see your titties."

"Nathan Lee Whistler!" exclaimed Hannah in a shocked voice like Mom, "you naughty boy you!" And she swung an arm across her chest, lowered her other hand to cover below. "Stop looking at me."

The kitten scurried at the noise, knocked a lamp over. Hannah went to pick it up as Mom waved her arms madly.

"Calm down everyone." Mom hopped off the stool. She poured a cup of freshly boiled water. "Not a thing to be ashamed of, kids. You've never gone to a beach before? You never felt the tropical breeze on your dainty skin? Never wanted to get rid of scratchy, itchy clothing? Dance *au naturale* under the light of the moon?"

Bucky roared with laughter. "Oh naturally? The hell you say!"

"Dance under the sunshine? Like a wild animal?"

"Ya shore are a wild thang, sweetcakes," Bucky sang, taking Mom's hand and twirling her around. "In bed, hell, yer a real wildcat. *Guhrrrowl!*"

I caught on. I knew what he meant but my feelings conflicted. I was happy for Mom in my head, but in my heart I felt betrayed. She was supposed to take care of me. And I was supposed to take care of her. Confusion filled me.

"Come on, Sandy," called Hannah, taking my hand.

She insisted I twirl her around, too. But she broke away, did her own dance, in her ballerina figure rising up on her toes, arms in a bow over her head.

"Yay, Hannah!" Nathan applauded. Our eyes met, sharing a thought. He gave me a thumbs up, like Bucky always did.

Hannah ended her dance and rushed to me, out of breath, her arms swinging around me. I wrapped my arms around her, too – like she was my lifebuoy, knowing for sure that she was my life now, not Mom. We kissed – right in front of everyone.

"Ew, yuck," Nathan sneered.

"Quiet," Mom ordered. "Your turn will come."

Nathan pouted, complained that he would never like girls and Mom tried to convince him otherwise.

"So is Old Man Kutcher gonna live here now?"

Mom blushed, shot the man a questioning look. "Maybe."

"Is he gonna be my new dad?" asked Nathan.

"Would that be so bad?" Mom replied.

"Already go fishin together, don't we?" said Bucky. "That's dad stuff, ain't it? My pops taught me how ta fish."

"I guess he's gonna leave the fishing gear here," said Nathan. "Easier to take to the pier, anyway."

"What a clever boy!" Hannah ruffled the hair on his head, and he tried to slap away her hand.

"He shore is," said Bucky, grinning.

Mom clapped her hands to get everyone's attention. "Then it's decided. Bucky's part of our family now. So Mister Kutcher is now Dad. In our bubble. Agreed?"

"Okay," I said, not excited, but I doubted anybody heard me, thrilled as they were.

"Are we gonna have a ceremony," asked Bucky, "like at the community center? Make it official-like?" He took Mom's hand, raising it as he acted out the placing of an invisible ring onto her finger. "How 'bout it, milady?"

"We could." Mom blinked. "We should. Let everybody know. It

would affect my position on the list."

"That goddamn list!" Bucky grunted. "Yep, that'll shore put off fellas making claim on ya. If yer paired with me, you'd be off the damn list." He gave Hannah a look, like it was a warning. "How y'all coming along?"

"We're fine," I said on her behalf and Hannah elbowed me.

Mom must've thought I was speaking about her and Bucky's decision, not about our own attempts to get pregnant.

Bucky got it, though. "Well, you two keep at it. If you ask me, it's the practicing that's the best part. You'll get lucky one day." He smiled at Mom. "Like me n yer mama."

Mom held up a nearly-empty bottle of whiskey. "I'll drink to that."

She took a long draw and handed the bottle to Bucky who also drank. He turned the bottle upside-down, tapped the bottom until the bottle was truly empty. He coaxed down the final drop.

"To new families!" Mom cheered.

My eyes met Hannah's at that moment and we both smiled. I hugged her. Our family was getting bigger.

29

IN WHICH LOVE IS MADE

One night Hannah and I sat out on the back porch, shoulder to shoulder, watching the stars together. The beach lay out there somewhere; we could hear the surf rolling in but couldn't see it in the dark. The air was cool for the island but people from up north would call it mild. We put on jackets, but Hannah still insisted on wearing her usual cutoff shorts and flip-flops.

She wiggled her toes, drawing my attention from the stars. I had painted her toenails earlier, at her request, and she'd put her feet in my lap as we sat on the front porch. I used hot pink polish she found in a dresser drawer.

"You think it's about Christmas?" I asked after a long silence, gazing up again.

She kept her eyes on the ocean of stars. "They don't even know there's a pandemic going on down here."

Well, stars aren't too smart, I thought, deciding whether to say it as a joke or forget it.

"Haven't looked at a calendar for months," I said instead, with a chuckle. "I don't even have any calendar."

She took my arm, pulled it around her shoulders, like she was chilly or she wanted a pillow.

"What will you get me?" she said.

"For Christmas?" I studied her face: grinning but sad. "Stores are all closed."

She nodded, but I had to look away, unable to stay gazing into her eyes for long. She had developed that ability to read my soul and it was unnerving.

Mom said I did that – not meeting people's eyes – because I had autism, even the high-functioning kind named after the Nazi scientist who first put the set of traits together and called it a syndrome. It's the reason Mom was so protective. She worried I might be taken away when the pandemic came. There would be no need to vax the 'undesirables', she expected them to decree. Save the useful members of society first. That meant no musicians. I understood, but I still wasn't sure what it meant for me. I just did what Mom told me and knew she would always be there.

Now we were on an island with its own weird society and its own strict rules. And Mom seemed far away.

"No store to buy anything," I said after a while, looking down, glad to get the words out. "I could make something from a piece of driftwood, I guess."

"You're funny." She giggled and patted my leg.

"I could catch a really big fish for you. Make you a great feast. Put some meat on those bones, like Mom says."

"Let's not talk about your mother."

"Your mom, too."

She turned to me and I met her eyes for as long as I could, really trying, then had to look down.

"Yeah, you're right," she said. "Aunt Polly makes a good mom. She looks out for us. But not so strict."

I knew Hannah noticed my quirk, but she never said anything about it, just went on with her thoughts.

"Nothing to buy, huh? So I guess we have to do something for each other. That's just as good."

"Like what?" I asked, totally innocent.

She let out a big sigh, like she'd been holding it in for days.

"I'm ready," she said.

"Ready...? For what?"

"For you."

"Me?"

"Oh, don't act so stupid, Sandy." Then she saw my expression.

"I'm sorry. I didn't mean it."

I flashed a grin. "It's okay. Usually Mom's with me, protecting me. I never get to be on my own. Sometimes I don't know how to act or what to say."

"So I'm like your mom now, huh? Telling you what to do?" She laughed, I'm sure intending to be sarcastic, but with her voice so sweet I didn't mind.

"No...."

She stood suddenly, grabbing my hand and pulling me up.

"Come on," she commanded.

"Where?"

"You'll see."

She rolled up the towel and we strolled up the beach, the surf to our right, houses on the left, all the lights out. No way to know if anyone watched us. A strip of moonlight marked our path.

We passed the first breakwall that ran down to the water.

Now we were entering uncharted territory, going into the wild zone between the community on the south end and the north end with the ferry landing and shops, art galleries, tourist traps. The middle had yet to be developed; signs encouraged people to build a hotel or condo. Sand dunes and wild palms rose in a few spots. A lagoon formed where water collected during low tides. Cranes and egrets swooping in by day. Lots of sand. A beautiful place in both sunrise and sunset photos I'd seen.

Hannah paused to slip off her flip-flops, continued barefoot as she carried them in her hand. I worried – Mom raised me to worry – about Hannah stepping on something in the dark. But I didn't want to be Mom so I pulled off my sneakers and walked barefoot, too. We slowed to be more careful where we stepped.

Then we came to the sign.

> *BEYOND THIS POINT YOU MAY*
> *ENCOUNTER NUDE BATHERS*

It was a monument. A warning and an enticement. A way to mark the passage of our lives: youth on this side of it, adulthood beyond. We had come to it before but shied away. Here at night, nobody would be on the other side. Suddenly I felt we were really the last people on Earth and it was our duty to repopulate the world.

"Well...?" Hannah grinned at me. "Ready?"

Smiling at her, I pulled off my jacket, felt the cool air. But I didn't balk. Off came my t-shirt. Then I unsnapped, unzipped my jeans, let them drop to my ankles, stepped out of them. Undies rolled down. I made a neat pile of my clothes.

When I looked up, Hannah was watching, acting giddy, like I was doing a strip show for her.

"Caught you looking," I snickered and stood up.

"I caught you looking, too," she said with a childish frown.

"Sorry." I looked down.

"Don't say that." She came up to me, put her hands on my face and gave me a quick kiss. "Nothing to be sorry for."

She stood apart, removing her clothes as a performance. When she was in her birthday suit she struck a dramatic pose, arms up in the air triumphantly as though she'd finished a dance and the audience applauded. She wanted me to gaze at her, so I did. She was beautiful – even in the night with only a faint moon. I knew her best in the dark, of course, when we were planning our future, assigning it to our dreams.

She took my hand and pulled me along, past the sign and into the danger zone. We left our clothes in piles by the sign. There wouldn't be anyone to bother them. We were free.

Free like Adam and Eve – but with a beach.

"You wouldn't even know there was a pandemic going on," she said, daring to laugh.

"It's far away from us," I responded. "It's like we're the only two people on Earth."

"Tonight we are."

We walked leisurely, then raced a little bit here and there over the moist beach, teasing each other, until we were deep into the clothing-optional section, far from our clothes. We saw no one else. We did see a hare scurry away, but he likely had no opinion about our behavior. Crazy humans!

We chased each other, playing tag, tickling each other when caught. We stepped into the cool surf, getting our feet wet, kicking the water like children. I could understand Mom's attraction to being nude on the beach. We hugged and kissed, skin to skin, as waves rolled in around our ankles.

Hand in hand we strolled the hard-packed sand, gazing at the dunes, listening to the surf rolling in.

"Here," my lover announced.

I stopped beside her. With a survey of the dunes, checking for spies, I felt the breeze on my skin. Hannah shook a bit, remained determined. I held her in my arms to warm her, and she warmed me. We kissed with passion.

She stretched the towel open on the sand and sat on it, waved me down. We continued kissing, adding caresses that ignited our fire. When she was ready, giving me a smile and a nod, she pulled me on top of her and welcomed me. We were slow and careful. I followed her instructions until we were completely merged as one.

"I love you, Sandy," she moaned during and sighed after.

"I love you, too."

"Merry Christmas."

"And it'll sure be a happy New Year."

30

IN WHICH MOM TAKES ON THE COUNCIL

It was a rainy winter, with storms blowing in from both land and sea lashing the island, keeping everyone indoors. Work didn't get done, food not gathered, and no fishing. We grew hungry and thin. But being indoors did have some advantage: Hannah and I spent a lot of time in bed, fooling around – if you know what I mean. Mom knew what I meant, and she had to check on us from time to time, certain we were doing it wrong. I worried we were doing it too much, but Hannah kept dragging me to bed early each evening like she couldn't get enough. And first thing in the morning. And sometimes in the afternoons.

Mom was settling into island life, adopting the island ways, by-laws and all. If we were going to make the island our home for the foreseeable future, some things needed to be changed. She ranted about the stupidity of the council members, most of them fat old men (the others were her age and thin), and how she could run the island a lot better. It wasn't just the ridiculous rules about pairing up she objected to, it was how to increase food yields.

"Awrighty," said Owen, getting flustered by her interruptions at the meetings, "if ya wanna join the council, show us yer ready to serve the island's needs. Then we can have a vote."

Mom took their challenge as winter gave way to spring – took it too far. Once dared she wanted to shove it back in their faces, make them see their corrupt humanity and weep in shame. Maybe not. Maybe she liked her new lifestyle, finally free from having to look after me. Bucky encouraged her. He would stand up for her with the council. There was a lot of alcohol available, too, thanks to another boat arriving, people trading goods along the coast, the things they'd looted from stores in the cities.

The rain eventually ceased and the sun shone, turning the island into a humid, tropical garden. Everything blossomed. By then, no one could remember winter – except Hannah and me; it was special to us. Everyone knew the summer would be hot and steamy, and I predicted that would bring out the worst of the islanders. They would give up doing their tasks, want to laze in the shade or swim in the sea, and at night gather for their *soirees*, as Owen called them.

Mom did her best to follow the rules, attentive to every detail, like the government had cameras pointed at her all the time. She did her tasks with care and participated more in community life. Urged on with increasing harassment from Rhonda, Toni, and Danielle, three council members' wives who wanted to be sure Mom stayed in her place, she gradually gave in. She let herself get swept along with the whims of the people around her. I tried to help, but the most I could do was be sure she didn't get hurt.

Now that she was trying to fit in more, the council would vote to make her a member – which she very much wanted – as long as she demonstrated her willingness to serve the community.

"You wanna be on the council, ya gotta show you honor the spirit of our community," Owen was always telling her, with the worn pages of his favorite futuristic book never far. "I ain't no 'commander'. Not like that. My late wife Betsy, she did everything right but never could get pregnant. But we still gotta be practical. Like the 'good book' says: You gotta put out or get shut out."

Another spring evening's gathering, the air thick and hardly any breeze, I realized how low we had fallen. This *soiree* was held in our backyard; it was our turn to host. Sitting with Hannah, we were getting used to the way adults behaved. Everyone had a job to do, but after work they really cut loose and misbehaved without restraint. So did Mom. Part of it might be genuine enjoyment, but part of it had to be only an act.

"Mom, put some clothes on," I had to say again.

Before she dared to jump naked over the barbeque pit just to show us how crazy she was, there wasn't a pair of days that went by when I didn't have to tell her. She loved the sun on her skin.

"But it's too damn hot tonight."

Mom lounged on a bench taken from a nearby house which no owners had claimed since the pandemic began. In the firelight I could see sweat running in rivulets over her body. Now she never hesitated stripping down to cool off. She looked better than other woman going half-naked at community events. She was an easy target for a grab or spank. She would punish random gropes with colorful words and laughs.

"Old Man Jones said he got a hare." I tried to use a country accent like many islanders, just for fun. Phrases got stuck in my head and I found myself repeating them. It made Hannah laugh. "Said he'd share it with us if you let him lay with you."

"Lay with me?" Mom laughed, like a scrape of metal. "But he takes too long. No, the fool can't get it up, can't keep it up, and in the end got nothing to show for it. A waste of time."

"Even so, if he'll share the hare he trapped...."

She snorted, drunkenly amused. "Is my boy so hungry he'd sell his mama?"

In our group, we were less than a tribe of strangers yet more than random pairs. Each person had special needs, had particular ways of surviving, and if we could borrow from each other then we could keep going using the new economy: barter system. I studied this new normal. No matter their age or condition, women always had something to trade. Mom learned that and used it. By then our community was down to getting food and passing the time with sex.

"She gonna?" Jones asked me, his eyes wild with lust. His grayish beard fluttered in the breeze, hands patting his bare belly, tattoos of exotic women covering him.

"She'll think about it."

"When she smells it smelling good," he said, "then she'll be givin' in."

I just nodded; no words were worth speaking.

He was right, though: with the rabbit skewered, roasting over the fire, grease dripping down, the crackle of fat melting from the meat...it was tempting.

A couple of lonelies came out of the shadows, stood near the flames. We didn't know their names, maybe arriving by boat or else they'd always been on the island. Maybe they lived in one of the island's abandoned vehicles. They seemed too wasted to speak, too traumatized for normal interactions. Maybe they were 'mask mute': wearing facemasks so long they shunned speaking. Music that Mom played on her tuba seemed to calm them.

One of them grabbed at the hare, a bare hand grasping the slippery meat, drew back at the heat. Tried again but only managed to knock it down into the fire. Old Man Jones grabbed the end of the skewer and saved the meat from being burned. He cursed at them, tried to shoo them away.

"It's ready, I'd say." Jones grinned, hand combing through his beard, pulling out some debris. "She ready?"

I turned where I sat with Hannah. "Mom?"

She stepped forward, out from the shadows with Hollis, her latest partner. He took a seat by the fire while she stood. A layer of sweat covered her body, soot and dirt and oil staining her, quite a mess, with her hair stringy, face tense and unashamed. If she could get a good shower....

"Well, ain't she purdy," said Old Man Jones.

"You sure, Mom?" I glanced at Bucky. He wasn't paying any attention, too busy smooching with Portia across the circle from us. It seemed he and Mom had an open relationship. It was the island way: share and share alike.

Mom sniffed the air, smiled. Pointing at me, then the hare, she waved Jones to follow her back into the shadowy enclave. We couldn't hear anything with the fire crackling and people talking, half of them crazy in the head, drinking and smoking their weed.

Bucky and Portia, who lost her husband out fishing in an old boat that took on water and went down, finally engaged in sexual amusement. Some people needed privacy, some didn't.

"I think yer mama's gonna exceed her quota," said Owen with a bawdy chuckle. "I swear, maybe I better take my turn, move up the list, trade places with Randy."

Olivia lifted her head from between his fat thighs. "Huh?"

"Nothing yew need ta concern yerself with, Livvy," grunted Owen and gently pressed her head down. "Keep going."

Jackson, Owen's jerk of a nephew, laughed. "She'll earn a seat on the council in no time." He glanced over at me, hoping to see me react but I gave him nothing.

"Damn tootin." Owen winced. "Easy now." He relaxed after a minute. "That's it. Just like that, Livvy."

Seeing Olivia working hard, Kurt slid over to us brusquely, asking if Hannah might want to play. She shook her head as I spoke a firm "No". He asked again, even displayed his goods as enticement. Again we told him to go away and he did. I didn't have to fight him like some of the men did to win a wife here – a new addition to the by-laws. You could challenge another guy's spot in line for a particular girl: either pay him off or fight him. Jackson had been fighting his way up the line for Mom's list.

Then Ana Maria scooted next to me, batting her eyes, hand on my knee. "You wanna?" she asked. The woman was almost as old as Mom. I said "No, thanks." She got up and left.

Hannah snuggled against me to signal her loyalty. She was almost shivering, not from chill but from fear. So many wanted us – wanted to coax us away from each other. We might've been the only faithful couple on the island.

Eventually Mom and Jones returned, arms around each other and laughing.

"It looks ready," I said, not wanting to regard them.

The hare was divided between us with the lonelies squatting nearby, watching intently. I tossed a small scrap to them and they jumped at it, nibbled it up like starving dogs.

"Don't give'em that," Owen cursed. He fed a morsel to Olivia, kneeling before him, her mouth open like a baby bird's. "Only makes'em hang around. Don't wanna encourage wild ones."

I nodded, then flipped another bite to the lonelies.

Sometimes Owen acted like he was my father, glad to offer advice. Old Man Jones wasn't my father, either – never could be. Nor Bucky. Or any man who visited Mom. But someday I would be like them, just Old Man Baumann looking for a bit of pleasure, the only thing left in this hard world, the last act of humanity: the dopamine rush.

And what was done to an innocent island hare reminded me of a bunny I once knew before we moved to the apartment, back in the salad days of green grass, shade trees, fragrant flowers, especially clover which drew the bunnies to our yard, back when we easily defeated viruses. I marveled at the bunnies, watching how they munched, their eyes darting around, always watchful of danger. How cute! Eventually the bunny never returned. Mom sat me in her lap and explained how the lives of bunnies typically go. I cried and she consoled me.

"Everything is a lesson," Mom used to tell me. "Some lessons simply cannot be taught. They must be lived."

As she emerged from the shadows again, taking a cloth and wiping herself off, I realized I had another lesson. People will do anything to survive, to get a bit of food, to maybe see another day, and do it all again.

She sat down with Old Man Jones. He gave an enthusiastic thumbs up to Bucky who thumbed back. Mom caught that: the deal between them, the sharing of a prize.

Mom and Jones leaned against each other, his arm around her, his other hand cupping a breast. I watched them smooching on the opposite side of the fire pit. Mom grinned like she was happy. That was good enough for me. I held my own partner, safely pregnant, her new bump clear to everyone.

31

IN WHICH MOM PLAYS A RECITAL

It was on a Saturday evening, or a Friday, that Mom played her first official recital on the island. People argued over what day it was, not having any calendar, but they agreed it was summer. It was held inside the community center where the acoustics were better. Almost everyone on the island attended because live music was a passion most islanders enjoyed.

To open, she played Ralph Vaughan Williams' *Six Studies in English Folksong*. Next was the *Sonata for Tuba and Piano* by Trygve Madsen. Then came Henning Christiansen's *Lettres de Tuba* from 1984 followed by the challenging Penderecki *Capriccio* (1980) and Carter Benson's *Scenes from the West*, but without the harmonica part – obviously. (Go figure: Not one harmonica to be found on the entire island.) Finally, to bring the recital to a close, she played the popular *Sonate for Bass Tuba and Piano* by Paul Hindemith. Karen did a decent job with Mom's reconstruction of the piano part on the community center's aged instrument despite missing two keys.

The applause was great and went on long enough for Mom to agree to encores. At Hannah's urging, she played a fair rendition of the Wu Crew's *Chinabound*. Most of the audience never heard of it before. (Later, Hannah explained the lyrics were about being tied up with China economically, not taking a trip to China.) To please the elders, Mom played an up-tempo version of *Down In the River to Pray* and the bluesy *Reflections on the Mississippi*, as well as a couple songs my grandmother had liked. More applause.

The event was made possible only because of the careful work by Rusty's Repair Shop – actually Dale and Hank, the repairmen who ran the shop after Rusty passed away pre-pandemic. Usually they worked on boats but Mom ran into Dale and they talked metal, he being a former trombonist. So Mom brought her beloved tuba in to see what could be done. The two men worked on it a couple weeks. Dale, who never liked wearing shirts but had a long white beard and bald head, and his best buddy Hank, clean-shaven but a stout fellow with long white hair falling from his head, took a liking to Timmy, handling him with the same care Mom did. She stood by to supervise, and they chatted about music through all the hours of work. Eventually, repaired and freshly polished, they declared Mom's tuba whole and renewed. To thank them, since there wasn't any money on the island, she offered to perform her repertoire. They suggested having a concert for the community and Mom happily agreed.

Toward the end of the recital some of the men had to run out to meet a yacht arriving in the darkness, a different kind of horn being blown to let the harbor master – whoever it was that night – know a ship was docking. Turned out it was Hollis on duty, and he knew next to nothing about docking a ship of that size, so others had to go help.

We didn't get the full details until later the next day. Mom was tired and wanted to go straight home. I carried her well-used tuba down the dark street to our house as she talked about her performance. Nathan praised her. So did Hannah, saying she was surprised that Mom was that good. Mom was so pleased with her concert she couldn't stop talking about it. She was now ready to return to the city and perform, even get the band back together: Lucy (second tuba), Carina (euphonium), Velvet (keyboards), C.J. (electric guitar), Babs (drums), and Mom (lead tuba) – Tubafonics reborn!

Hannah and I were eager to resume our relationship in bed as Mom and Bucky sat conversing in the living room, Mom trying to get Nathan to go off to sleep inside his couch cushion fort with him complaining about the adults talking too loudly for him and his kitten to fall asleep. Hannah and I snickered off and on as we lay together, listening to life going on despite the swirling clouds of invisible deadly viruses all around us – at least, as news reports picked up from Mike's ham radio said. People were dropping like flies across the mainland, yet another new wave of variants. It seemed the world off the island was eating itself alive, going mad, but we were safe.

Every now and then a boat or raft would come down the coast. Usually it was somebody not seeking protection from government tyranny but looking for a village to rob. The island men would send them away: "No room here, private island, keep moving." Or we had to put them down if they tried to fight us. One invasion, I hit one of the pirates over the head with my garden shovel, split it open. I got stuck with graveyard duty, but swinging a shovel built up my muscles, made me strong.

After her recital, Mom got more attention. It seemed that some of the men hadn't known she was actually in the pool, thinking she was too old. Men started coming by the house, hoping to catch a glimpse of her trotting around in next to nothing for the price of some food. Mom always treated them like long lost cousins.

It had been a struggle for everyone during the spring weeks, with storms keeping anyone from going out fishing in the boats we had. There wasn't much luck fishing from shore, either. Chickens got spooked, stopped laying. Maybelle's milk lessened and people talked about butchering her for one final barbeque feast. Yet Mom held them off, certain that more milk would come.

In late spring, probably May, a boat arrived with crates of fruit and vegetables, sacks of flour and sugar, cases of canned beer, and boxes of women's sundries. The men were traders, asked us what they could get for their wares. Not much, it seemed, as our island's products weren't enough to allow extra for trading. So the women joined together to pay them. Mom got shamed into participating, but she thought getting the beer was worth it. And in that way we managed to survive the harsh winter to welcome the warm, rainy spring and another hot, steamy summer.

* * *

It seemed that a yacht arriving at the end of Mom's concert was symbolic, an act meant to restore order to the island. At least Mom thought so. She realized the island way wasn't going to work for her, not long-term. She felt foolish, like she'd been tricked. But she got on the council at last and that made her happy. She could run the island her way now.

The yacht was captained by a sailor named Giovanni. He had a winning smile, waving to the people who gathered to admire his boat. Many of them seemed to know him, welcomed him, asking where he'd been during the past few years. More interestingly, he arrived with three young women, one of them very pregnant. He was returning to his 'home port' hoping to find a safe place for the birth.

As the feckless men gathered around to listen to his tales of adventure on the high seas and in foreign ports, it seemed he was a popular guy. Tan and fit, he had a bright grin. An old captain's cap settled back on his head, dirt-blond curls slipping out from under the cap as though trying to hold on to the last of his youth. Now he was maybe sixty. He could pass for fifty and probably best anyone younger in a fair fight.

The women also gathered, in awe of the handsome gentleman: so charismatic, his accented English so charming, seductive when his voice slipped down from baritone to bass. He was an intriguing figure. The more you listened to him, saw the twinkle in his eyes, the more you were drawn to him – the more you wanted to be his friend. Or lover.

Mom stopped by to see who our newest visitor was, because everybody was talking about his arrival. The women on the boat were his harem, Mom said with a sneer, but with the pregnant one also being the youngest – perhaps too young – the story went deeper, or was lost on ocean waves. Mom had a way of talking by then that was influenced by the salty banter of island men. She could curse with the best of them.

"This Lavitalebela yacht, it is enough for me," the captain mused with his circle of admirers. "I can pilot it myself, yes? Yet it can sail also much on its own, if you have enough sea."

Being away, he had no idea there was a pandemic. Far from land, he hadn't been impacted by it. On the ocean everything was the same. Only when he tried to dock had he been fended off, told there was a plague, that he should try elsewhere or have to accept a forty-day quarantine – adding a story how 'quarantine' actually meant a forty-day wait, a custom dating back to the Black Death. With enough provisions dropped aboard, he could sail on.

But he apparently had a stowaway: fifteen-year-old Eliza, who was charmed by the manly sailor. He taught her how to handle the yacht. She proved a quick learner. They developed a healthy friendship. You could see him blushing through his tan façade as he spoke about her.

"I only purchased the yacht for, mmm, to sail around with the nude girls on board, for they can be tanning," he said with a warm smile, "and to make me look like a king, yes? It's common wish for young man with a rich papa."

Carlotta he took aboard in Genoa, intending to sail around the Mediterranean for pleasure. Eliza became jealous. He called her his 'little cabin girl' to put Carlotta at ease, but he secretly kept up relations with Eliza. Then out through the Strait of Gibraltar they sailed and the ocean swept them far. They found Penelope on the Canary Islands, also looking for adventure, and welcomed her aboard. In time his three ladies got along well enough, he told his audience.

"And so it is easy to see how I can become King of the Sea," he said with a barely modest laugh. "Crew and yet lovers, too. What a happy life, yes?"

When they arrived on the other side of the world, however, they found the pandemic once more. Negotiations at every harbor for supplies. Sailing down the coast, trying every port. He recalled a lovely island he previously visited. He didn't recognize it in the darkness, the harbor unlit. Only the lighthouse gave any clue.

"So again we visit your fine isle, for a little rest. And a doctor for Eliza, if there is one among you. She is due very soon. I recall a doctor here named Baumann. He used to take holiday here...?"

The murmur of voices rose so no one noticed Mom falling faint at the rear of the crowd. I caught her, set her gently on a chair. While she recovered, I buttoned up her shirt, which she liked to leave open in the hot weather. Must be the heat, I thought. The main hall of the community center was stuffy.

I stayed with Mom but returned my attention to the debonair gentleman commanding attention with his infectious smile. It was easy to like him. Even questioning the relationship he had with the girl didn't hurt anyone's impression of him. I thought I might go to the front once Mom was back on her feet. I might offer him a traditional handshake – unless he'd also switched to fist pumps.

I watched and listened. I gazed with doe-eyes, feeling my heart quicken. His voice was seductive – just as Mom had said. A charm that could melt any girl's heart, that could open any girl's legs. Especially when on a nude beach. Especially—

Take away the tan and remove his cap, add some hair, and you would have...me!

I almost fainted beside where Mom sat.

"Mom?" I called to her. "Is that...? Is he the one...?"

She fanned herself, looking away.

He absolutely reeked of celebrity. I couldn't take my eyes off him – not even when Carlotta pranced about in her thong, topless and jiggling, as she came inside from tanning on the community center's veranda. And I hardly noticed when Penelope sauntered in wearing a modest two-piece suit as though down a fashion show runway. Sure, I gave her a glance, who wouldn't? But I've seen women like them online. This man, Mr. Giovanni, also gave the ladies a glance and a knowing grin, his mark of approval. Victor was his name, someone said. Vittorio, another name someone called him. Victor Giovanni: entrepreneur, seafood magnate, son, sailor, captain, lover of women – perhaps also known as Dad.

32

IN WHICH MOM FLASHES BACK

"Listen, Sandy," said Mom as I helped her back to the house after her shock, "you know I love you. I've always tried my best to look after you. To raise you right. And protect you from the cruelties of the world. You know that, don't you?"

Mom looped her arm around mine. I didn't know what to say, so I mumbled: "Of course."

"I would never hurt you. You do know that, right? I've always told you the truth. Maybe too much sometimes. But sometimes I just don't say something, which isn't exactly lying. Well, not by my definition, anyway. It's...."

She paused in the middle of the street, her hand pointing to a pelican flying overhead, looking for a place to land.

"Someday I'll be gone and you will be on your own. I want to know you'll be okay. So I've tried to train you how to survive. Not like my grandfather taught me, certainly. Not like knife fighting. I thought you'd be in an urban environment, so you needed to know how to get along in that situation, with technology and so on. But everything is different. And I just don't know if you're ready."

"Ready for what, Mom?"

"The future."

In the community center she'd grabbed my arm, pulled herself to her feet, and ushered me out. No words. She looked weak so I put my arm around her as we headed out. I wanted to ask lots of questions but I held back, seeing how she wasn't in any condition to answer. She knew I suddenly understood everything.

As I handled Mom fainting, I overheard people telling Vittorio that his Dr. Baumann hadn't been seen on the island in years and probably succumbed to the pandemic. He expressed his concern, gave his sincere condolences, then asked if there might be other doctors who were on the island.

Doc Rick was the only one. Vittorio would go see him at once. His entourage accompanied him.

I asked people what they knew of Dr. Baumann.

"He and Vittorio was best buds," said Olivia, who'd been on the island forever. "Used to go out sport fishing together. Got a huge marlin one time, I remember."

I thought of that as Mom and I reached the house.

Inside, she was happy to drop down on the couch, even free of cushions. Nathan refused to take his fort down. I got Mom a glass of boiled water, now room temperature.

"Wish it was beer," she grumbled, accepting it.

"You obviously know him," I spoke up before she had finished drinking. She almost choked. "Who is he? Seems everyone knows him."

"H-he's just...," Mom sputtered, lowering the glass, "just some foreigner who visits from time to time. A bit of a lush, in my opinion."

"I heard he knew Grampa. Is it true?"

"Yes." She gave me a long look – until I had to look down. "They went out fishing together. That's all. He had the boat – a different boat back then. Dad knew the best places. Sometimes they would go out for days. He always had girls on board. Bikinis or less, lazing on the decks, working hard on their tans. Tough work being eye-candy. But Dad liked that."

"Grampa? Never thought he would be that way."

"Every old person once had a young life, remember."

"But he was so nice to me."

"And they mellow in their old age, their sins forgotten."

We regarded each other: me loading the next question and Mom preparing to answer whatever came at her.

"So Grampa.... What did he do?"

I lowered my head, sensing I was about to feel ashamed even more for my family. Wasn't it enough that we were all trying to survive a pandemic and the harsh life around us? No, we had to deal with family drama, too. Maybe it would be better to simply get the virus and die, no questions asked. Then our family drama would end.

"Best as I can tell, he enjoyed some time with one of those eye-candy girls. I doubt she was related to him – your yacht friend. Maybe his girlfriend, but not his daughter. Anyway, Dad got her in trouble. I should say they *both* got in trouble. But as a doctor he could take care of that sort of problem in private. Except he didn't have his tools with him. Too awkward to drive back to his office and get them, not with the family watching. So that girl stayed on the island, then disappeared. Left on another boat probably. Dad kept the baby, however. And your dear Grandma, bless her soul, after much swearing at him, accepted the baby, agreeing to raise the girl as their own. And they decided to name her Pauline, after her grandmother from the old country."

I about dropped my glass. I had to sit, but I almost missed the couch, stumbling, catching myself, pulling my butt onto the couch while feeling that I wanted to vomit.

"You, Mom?"

It seemed the house was about to explode.

"Yes." A faint smile slid slyly across her face and continued, sliding off. "That explains the gap between your aunts and me, doesn't it? I'm an accident, in the truest sense of the word. From your grampa's accident. Don't even know my mother's name. Your grandma was always my mother."

I just sat in stony silence.

"And you're an accident, too. But a happy one, for sure." Her eyebrows relaxed a bit. "So now you know. Happy? You and me, we're one of a kind. I like that. But, well, nobody gets to choose their parents. You have to work with what you're given. I've tried my best raising you, Sandy, my lovely boy."

I was still in mid-gasp.

"Take a breath," said Mom.

"But then...." I took a deep breath. "So then...Hannah and me? We're not as close as we thought."

Mom smiled softly, as though she was glad she no longer had to hold it all inside.

"Oh, I'm not sure how it's calculated. Half-cousins? Is that it? Another degree of separation."

"But we're—"

She held up her hand, index finger extended as if to signal me to pay attention.

"And then, sixteen years later, the favor was returned. Dad dallied and then his buddy seduced. I was the prize. Even steven. Everything back in balance. And here we are: living through a pandemic, but stuck on this shitty patriarchal island, a so-called sanctuary."

Whew! I exhaled, ignoring her last words, staying focused on the most important part:

"But that's good, isn't it? I mean, me and Hannah. Me with her? We can go on being a couple, right?"

She seemed angry. "That's what concerns you most?"

"Sorry," I said, refocusing. "I mean—"

"Yes, I suppose you can stay a couple. Besides, would anything stop you? Who cares? Guess you'd be called 'kissing cousins' – but you've done more than kiss. That's obvious. You make a good couple. Enjoy each other. Stay together. We're in hard times so can't be too picky. Be comfort for each other. Make a sanctuary together from the world. Love each other."

"We do, Mom. We...." With a hard swallow, I wasn't sure what to say. "We sure have a lot of sex. But don't worry. She's okay. I'm okay, too. But it sure does feel great, I gotta say."

Mom unleashed her sharpest smirk, almost cutting her lip. "I know. I can hear you two at night."

The biggest grin I'd ever had suddenly erupted upon my face.

"It's so wonderful! And she's so perfect."

"Now you can repopulate the world." Her tone was darker. "I'm happy for you. You have my blessing. Save us. Make a new family.

After this pandemic you can start over."

She tried to pull herself up, saying she wanted to get her tuba and play. When emotions overwhelmed her, she let them escape out through that 18-foot pipe, calming her with every phrase from her imagination or from the repertoire. I always liked hearing her play although I often worried what made her feel the need to play. This time I knew.

I helped her up and she moved to the straight-back chair in the corner. I brought Timmy to her, lowered him to her lap, and she wrapped her arms around his metal girth, settled her fingers on his valves, and with a long draw of breath, pressed her lips softly against his hard mouthpiece and let loose everything that had built up in her heart over the years.

33

IN WHICH TRUTH RAISES ITS UGLY HEAD

For the next few days I tried to avoid the community center as much as possible. But I still had to move the seed trays from where they grew on the back veranda, overlooking the harbor, to the garden on the opposite side. That meant I had to pass through the main hall. Thankfully hardly anyone was ever there during daytime hours, only Olivia or Doc Rick.

Olivia told me that Vittorio and his ladies were staying aboard his yacht but they also took a room at the Seaside Inn. Eliza, the pregnant girl, preferred being on land, which was easier on her stomach. So that was another place to avoid.

My curiosity drew me down the seaward street to the shabby inn. I pretended to stroll by, out for a walk, taking in summer breezes. I saw them sometimes, the three women sitting outside their door, chatting. The two older ones spoke in a mix of Italian and Spanish. I could understand a little because I took a Spanish class before virtual school. They seemed to be discussing what to do about Vittorio. They didn't like being put in such poor lodging. But it was fitting for a girl like Eliza, the older women said.

I wanted to look their way, to see reactions, but I knew to keep my eyes focused ahead.

"What were you even doing down there?" Hannah accused me, cornering me one evening. "You wanna be with them? Do you? They're way too sexy for you."

"No, no, no," I responded, but thinking: *Too sexy?* Hannah was the sexy one, in my opinion.

I took her out back, sat her down, and told her the story Mom had divulged.

"So we're actually farther apart than regular cousins," I said. "But Mom gives us her blessing. We're free to go on being Mister and Missus Islander."

"Yay," she intoned in fake joy. "Like it's just to keep the other boys from messing with me." She shifted on the porch step, put her hand to her belly as though feeling something there.

"Everything okay?" I asked.

"You knock me up, then go looking for more pussy some other place," she grumbled. "I don't like that."

"No, I wasn't. Only your pussy. Only you." My heart quivered, fear gripping me. "This ship's only got one harbor. Only you, my dear sweet Hannah May Whistler."

"I'm a Baumann now, thank ya very much. Don't ya know? No matter how bad that is. It's a lotta fuckin responsibility."

"I do know." I grinned at my wife. "I do."

"Make sure you do. It's a real big sacrifice, ya know." Then she sang one of the songs playing in her head: "'Jab me, baby, one more time / Oo, it hurts, hurts me real good.'" She grinned at me. "That's the Coronas' 'Needle Fuck' and, yeah, I know you never heard it before."

"None of your favorite bands ever wrote any love songs?"

"Love of the vax, maybe. 'Alone Together' is kinduva love song. Like, if you wouldn't stand maskless close to each other you sure wouldn't kiss, much less fuck. It's a sad song."

All I could do was smile, feeling bad that she wasn't able to have her career as a rockstar. She had a good voice. And she loved to sing. Later she made up a song she called 'Mystery Man' which went a little like this: 'Mystery man, where you from? / You gonna make me moan and come? / Dock your big yacht till my harbor's full / There's plenty of fish in the sea / Besides li'l ol' me....'

✳   ✳   ✳

I still wanted to meet him. I wanted to ask him what the hell he was thinking that day? Seducing a girl? Why? Just because they were on a clothing-optional beach didn't meant sex was permitted. I was thinking too much. Getting fixated. Mom always called me out when I did that, but now I was on my own. Yes, with Hannah, but she didn't know how to stop me. I had to catch myself.

I suppose some people on a nudist beach might be excited by what they saw and want to have sex right away and couldn't stop themselves. I could understand that. After all, Hannah and I had done it. But we went at night. And nobody else was there due to the pandemic – probably nobody in daytime either.

Besides, fresh air and a good distance apart was the recipe the health officials advised. It was clothing that captured and held the virus, just like the cloth masks we were supposed to wear over our faces. So why not shed them and walk naked under the sunshine? Vitamin D from sunshine was also a defense against the virus, they said. Why not lay out on your towel on the sand, and read a fat paperback or just nap as you tan?

Even now Hannah and I would take a walk up to the nude section of the beach once in a while, find ourselves alone, and set out our towels to relax, ignoring the history of the place, talking about our future. We made plans for returning to the city, what I'd show to her there. We would need to get our own place, not live with Mom and her tuba. That meant getting a job again.

Seeing the mystery man, I stopped thinking, straightened up from leaning against the railing.

"Hello," I called to him as he climbing down the ladder from his yacht, strolled up the landing beside the community center.

He looked around for who called him, saw me and gave a wave but kept walking. When he got up to the plaza, I stood blocking his path.

"Good day," he spoke in a cheery voice, his baritone vibrating through me. When I didn't move, he seemed annoyed, intent on side-stepping me, but he remained polite. "How are you?"

It wasn't a sincere question, just a routine greeting. But I gave him an honest answer.

"I'm searching for someone," I said. "You're Vittorio who also goes by Victor."

"Yes, it is I." He flashed his famous smile, teeth so white. "May I help you?"

"I'm looking for someone...."

"Yes?"

"Someone who was visiting here, on this island, like you are. But about nineteen years ago."

"Nineteen? So much is past." He lifted his captain's cap and ran his hand over his balding head. "Are you certain you can find that person?"

"Well, I've heard so much about you, I wondered if you maybe know him – *knew* him."

His face flashed concern. "Who is he, this man you seek?"

"As I said, he was visiting here nineteen years ago."

"Nineteen years, mmm."

Vittorio took notice of me, scanning my face, perhaps deciding whether to take me seriously.

"Or twenty." I remembered I had to account for the months of pregnancy. "You knew Doctor Baumann, I heard."

"Yes.... We were friends."

Yeah, friends! I almost snickered. Accomplices, actually.

"I hear he has sadly passed. *Riposa in pace.*"

Mom's late night rambling barged into my head, telling me all sorts of things. About her being introduced to Grampa's friend in the very house we were living in now. Mom coming out dressed for the beach in a bikini and suddenly confronted by her dad and a handsome stranger. She blushed and after introductions excused herself. How rude! Grampa had to apologize for his daughter. But his friend said, she overheard from the hallway, that she wasn't being rude; it was simply a young nymph's delicate innocence that prevented her from acknowledging the true power she had over grown men, power which she hadn't yet noticed but which would come into ample use as she matured.

"Yes?" he called back my attention.

I shook off Mom's talk. "Do you remember meeting a girl at

your friend's house? About twenty years ago?"

"My friend?"

"Doctor Baumann."

His face tightened as though he was struggling to pull out one particular moment from a haystack of memories.

"Ah, so many years. How can I sort them all?" He laughed, feigning embarrassment. "Is there a special one you refer to?"

"Did you even know her name?" My tone turned rough, but I couldn't stop. "Or didn't it matter?"

"Matter?" His grin was fake now.

"Don't you know? Can't you guess?" I began to rage.

"What is it you are talking about?"

"I'm talking about my mother!"

It was difficult to maintain control of my emotions – boiling up from a place I didn't know existed. I felt so tense, so ready to fight. It was like one of my meltdowns when I felt overwhelmed: sudden rage I couldn't control, usually over nothing at all. But this was something.

"Ah! Your mother...." He nodded, understanding.

"Yes, my mother...." Tears collected in my eyes but did not fall. "You were with my mother."

He blinked a few times. "Your mother?"

"You had sex with her. On the beach." I pointed north.

He turned to look north. "On the beach...?"

"Yes, there. On the nude beach. So you...." I didn't bat an eye. "You're probably my father."

"What?" He seemed shocked but tried to chuckle. "How can you say that?"

I was determined to force a confession from him. "Because it's true. Isn't it?"

So I told him the story Mom had told me so many times in my life. How I got my name.

"Yes, yes." He rubbed his head, looking past me. "It does seem a memory I have." Then he broke into a grin. "There were four, you say? So...could be one of them, yes?"

"Only one looks like me!" I put my fingers to my eyes, pulled them open wide. "See? Do you see? Look at me. Look! Do you see someone you recognize?"

His eyes narrowed. "I'm looking...."

Staring into my eyes, he eventually blinked.

A long breeze blew between us, ruffling his shirt, shifting his cap, while I held steady.

"Am I going to get bald, too?" I asked calmly.

He stared at me a while.

"Yes," he said sadly and took a long breath. "Yes, I suppose you will also lose your hair. Like me. It started after I turned forty, so be prepared." He grimaced like he'd been caught at last. "Do not let yourself be fooled by the advertisements for medicines or surgical procedures to reverse it. No. They don't work. None of them."

34

IN WHICH MOM TEACHES HISTORY

We awoke one morning and the news was worse than before. So Mom decided we should leave, wait it out at the farm, but danger followed us, north and south, to the east, to the coast, trying to find safety with family members who, instead, needed our help more than we needed theirs. Finally arriving at our destination, the last place we could go, the edge of the continent, on an island separated from the world, only to find the past catching up to us after years of sneaking around the shadowy corners of our lives.

"Helluva journey," said Mom, her voice weary as she sipped another warm beer. "Yessiree, I did my part. Got us here. Got you and your cousins here to safety. Well, safety of a kind. But always stay alert."

"I will, Mom."

"Someday we'll leave. Don't know where we'll go, but gotta be somewhere better than here. That's for damn sure. But what's left for us in the city? We ran away, left everything there, and the rent unpaid. Let them track us down, if they want. Anyway, can't stay here. I really can't stand the way they run this island."

She had been playing Timmy, a few happier songs of her own invention, and expressed a desire for some staff paper to write them down. I promised to see if Olivia could print out something. There was a big stack of paper reams in the office. Some of the island's guests were writers who used holidays for concentrated writing sessions. They would run out of paper.

"James Farley use ta come down ev'ry winter," said Olivia, big toothy smile appearing, like she'd known him personally and some of his fame had rubbed off on her. "He wouldn't leave till he got another one o' his manuscripts done. Once he stayed a whole year working on one. Crime thriller. He even named the heroine's dead sister after me. Typed out ever'thing on one o' those old typing machines."

I drew out staff lines on a piece of paper, then had Olivia print several sheets while we had a few minutes of electricity. Mom was so happy when I gave them to her.

"Thanks, Sandy." But she didn't start scribbling notes right away as I expected.

Hannah popped into the living room to wish us "goodnight" and wink at me. That was to remind me to join her in bed. These days she was so tired from her work at the nursery. But instead of having sex I massaged her shoulders. Working in the nursery was good for her, everyone said. She would learn how to care for babies for when ours was born. Nathan joked about her getting fat, like she'd eaten more than her fair share.

"Everything'll work out fine," said Mom. "I know it will. Just stay outta harm's way." She finished the can, belched. "My work here is done."

"Geez, Mom, take it easy."

Laughing, she started in again on her standard lecture about responsibility – what mine was. That talk dovetailed into what her responsibilities were, what they'd been and may possibly be in coming years. For one thing, she hated the idea of becoming a grandparent but was willing to do whatever needed to be done, like watching the kids while we worked.

"It does have an odd kind of symmetry. Me at sixteen. Now your cousin at sixteen. Like bookends. And you at sixteen: all you knew was how to jerk yourself. And this house: number sixteen. Now we have to wait for Nathan to turn sixteen and meet a nice island girl. Ah, time flows, even during a pandemic. Everything's going to work out fine."

"Uh, Mom...? She's seventeen. We forgot her birthday."

"Oh." Mom frowned. "Okay, next year we'll do something for her. Her and the baby."

"But we celebrated it anyway, her and me, on the beach."

Mom smiled as though a warm memory blossomed in her.

"Was it special?" she asked.

"Yes, very special. And we saw a bunny run by."

Mom smirked. "That's what was special about it?"

I stopped, realizing I was being stupid again, thoughts going everywhere at once. "No, being with her was the special part."

She studied the ceiling, then measured the walls for a time, waiting for the shadows to come together.

"I welcomed him, I want you to know. It wasn't anything like rape. Just to be clear. I wanted it. I knew he was the same man at the house I was introduced to. He followed me. But I blame your grampa."

The room got real quiet.

"Grampa? Why?"

"I always felt like he sent him after me, like they made a deal, tit for tat. Your grampa's daughter for...for *his* so-called daughter, that girl on the yacht your grampa fooled around with. Mom. Now they were even."

My head dropped, had to catch it in my hands.

"Mom, you don't have to say anymore. It's done now. I'm here. And Grampa's dead. You're here. That guy from the yacht is here, too. I don't think he's gonna do anything. Cause trouble, I mean. What's there for him to do? What do you want him to do, huh? Apologize? Is it enough? We're in a pandemic. The old rules don't apply, you said."

"So upset!" She chuckled at my consternation. "A pandemic is the excuse for everything. But you need to relax. You need to put things in perspective."

"There is only one perspective, Mom!"

I didn't know where my outburst came from. I felt helpless, like the facts of my life were rocks in a fast-running stream and I kept hitting them, hurting with each crash.

Mom was crying. A sob got loose and she acted like I couldn't hear it.

"You okay?" I asked softly.

She shook her head. "Everything's so fucked up."

"Language," Nathan called inside his couch cushion fortress.

* * *

Perhaps feeling guilty, Victor showed me his yacht, the complete tour. He introduced me to his ladies and they dutifully smiled at me, greeted me in bored voices. They didn't mind me seeing them skimpily clad. Victor didn't seem to mind me seeing them either. I wondered if he might be tempting me, getting me interested in them as payback, a distraction from my inquiries.

"I told her to put on clothes, we have guest," Victor explained after chiding Carlotta in Italian. She got up curtly, stormed off. Penelope laughed like they were sisters and she'd won the fight. "You, too," he said to her.

"It's okay," I said, just glad to be treated as a man instead of a boy. It was hard for me to pull on a mask and play a role like that, exhausting if it went too long. "I've seen plenty of naked women in my life, especially online. Now on the island. They can get pretty crazy sometimes."

"Yes, so many beauties," Victor confirmed. "Like a paradise. Specially your mother, yes?" He put his hands up, gesturing like he was squeezing invisible breasts. "My memory is good."

"Of course she's a lot older now."

"But still, she is...how you say? ...hot?"

"Some of the men here think so. Me? Well, she's just Mom to me." I did a quick reassessment: if I were her age, I'd fall for her easily. "She's always been tough and strong. Not slim and sexy like your ladies."

Victor was listening intently, something I didn't get very often. Nobody gives a shit about young men until they're fully adult and can do some work. Or they cause trouble.

"Go on," he said.

"I guess she was slimmer when she was young."

"I remember she was mature for her age, had a good chest."

"What I meant was...."

"Yes?"

"I always thought I look more like her. She never told me much about my father – *fathers*, all of you – so he never appears on my face when I look in the mirror. I just see Mom."

He crossed his muscular arms over his bare chest, tanned and a little hairy, virile. His shorts allowed his athletic legs to tan also. We had to go on the gangway single-file and he went first. He moved with confidence and determination.

"So why...." I waited for him to step off the gangway onto the wharf and turn around. "Why did you...? After you were with her, why...why did you invite other guys to...to join you?"

His eyes widened, brows raising. "I don't know. It's a man's sport, so perhaps it was in the sporting spirit? I thought he would enjoy what I enjoyed. A recommendation. Such as: 'Hey, come see this girl, isn't she beautiful, what do you think?' – like that."

"Like *that*? Just like that?" Then I understood like a kick to my head. Mom wasn't his; he didn't care who she was. There was no love. She was only a moment's pleasure, something fun to try and then walk away from. Anger ignited in me.

"I suppose that is what happened," he said so casually.

"So you get these other guys, not even friends of yours but complete strangers, to take advantage of her? How could you?"

He stopped and faced me, just like father to son and I'd been caught in the lie, not him.

"Beauty," he said wistfully, gazing up at the sun. "Have you ever seen something so beautiful you had to possess it? Even if you never look at it again? Like an art collector?" He focused on me. "Or is it better to create beauty? Like an artist? Or better to be a curator of beautiful works, like for the museum? If I make something beautiful, I want to show it to everyone. Yet if I only discover something beautiful, I still want to let the world know of my discovery. Like that. I did not create your mother, yet I found her, a beautiful work of art. I wanted to possess this art, then I wanted to let the world know what I discovered."

My face tensed as I fought to hold back my anger. I wanted to punch him in the face. I made fists at my sides but couldn't raise my arms. He had to get some punishment, I decided. If I got in a fist fight with him, I knew I'd lose. Maybe better to make a trap, get back at him that way.

"So I should apologize, yes?" He tried to smile, acting sincere, but I saw right through. "It was wrong thing to do. I understand. It is different world now. Yet, in that moment...in the ecstasy...I was filled with such joy. I wanted to share my joy with the whole world. It was ecstasy. Yes! And a man was passing by, so I waved to him. He came to us, saw opportunity, and she never refused. And, like me, he also wished to share his joy with others – other men who would be amazed at the beauty of this girl laying there, so free and open to the world and all its possibilities."

His words hurt – like power drills whirring into my head. Standing on the wharf, I got dizzy as I listened to him talk, with the glare off the water striking my eyes. I could imagine a sunny day on the beach, not seeing who was over you, just accepting him – maybe thinking they were all the same man. What would her thoughts be? Get it over with? Or give me more?

I felt sick as we continued, going into the community center overlooking the harbor. He slipped into Italian as his thoughts became inner-directed. Then he stopped and faced me.

"I must apologize," he said, voice strained. "It is the right thing to do. I apologize also to you. It must be a difficult life being the son of a whore. Even a beautiful whore. Yet we all must find our way through life, yes?"

A shadow approached and he turned to greet his shipmate, Eliza, who'd come out of Doc Rick's clinic, another wellness check for her baby. She reported on the check-up: her baby boy was fine, developing normally. Victor smiled warmly, then remembered I was there and lost his smile. The ever-returning theme seemed to become apparent to him.

"Eliza, my sweet. She is a very beautiful mother," he said, hesitation in his voice. "A safe birth. It is good we could make landfall to this island." He put his finger against the cheek of the baby, stroked it. "Antonio is a handsome boy, already looks like me. No hair."

"It's good to be here if you have to give birth," I said. "My wife is pregnant. She's due soon."

"Oh, then congratulations! You the papa, yes? So you're a man now, certainly."

At his praise, I did feel like a man. I was old enough, I had a wife, and we had a child coming. I worked for my community and shared its resources. It was the beginning of a new life for me, childhood and youth discarded. I was ready to take my place and finally be a man, a husband and father.

I stared at the baby in Eliza's arms, suddenly realizing he was actually my brother—half-brother. How many others did I have as siblings because of this man?

Feeling another presence as Victor released Eliza from their embrace, I turned to see who approached. I knew it was going to be devastating, but I could not avoid the crash.

"Oh, hi...*Mom*."

35

IN WHICH MOM WEIGHS THE WORLD

If this had been a movie, romantic music would swell over the scene as two past lovers rushed headlong into a tight embrace, overjoyed to see each other once more. But this wasn't a romantic movie. In a flash I knew it was a Western and guns were being drawn on a dusty street as townsfolk scurried out of harm's way.

Eliza stepped back, sensing danger. I took a step to the side, clearing a path for the bullet Mom surely had loaded with his name on it.

Mom wasn't expecting him to be there, I decided. She hadn't planned anything, just entered the community center to tend to whatever business she had. His presence caught her by surprise as much as her arrival did for him. They regarded each other a minute.

"Mom," I said, "this is Victor."

She gave a nod, acknowledging she heard me, not that she approved.

"Victor," I continued, ready to jump between them, "this is my mother. Her name's Pauline. But everyone calls her Polly — if you ever did know her name."

He pulled on a grimace, cobbled together from equal parts embarrassment and delight. Brushing his head, he extended his hand. But he quickly withdrew it as he remembered that we no longer shook hands due to the change of customs in the pandemic era. He made a fist, instead, intending to fist-bump a greeting.

Mom wasn't moved and kept her hands down at her sides. Her knit pullover was soaked from sweat, a little dirty from working in the garden, and her shorts had some former period stains that wouldn't wash out.

"I'm happy to make your acquaintance," said Victor with a chuckle. I wasn't sure if he was being ironic or if he believed it was the proper expression for the situation. "I had no idea you were here." His frozen smile melted a little. "So long ago, yes? So many years apart, I cannot remember.... I...I must apologize...." He wiped his eyes as though he'd been emotionally struck, but to me it seemed an act. "Please forgive me. I meant no harm to you."

I watched Mom become invested in this man's act. She took a step toward him. As she did, I saw Eliza in the corner of my eye move further away, moving to a bench, holding her baby close. It was a good spot to view the drama.

Mom took another step, as though deciding if this man was the same man from the beach, and then, deciding he was, instead of rushing him with her fists pounding and giving him a good kick between his legs, she ran to him, tried to leap into his arms. But not knowing if he would catch her or considering whether she might be too heavy for that kind of movie moment, she ceased up.

They embraced. I crumpled on the plaza pavement, mind blown. My knee hit, hurt. What was happening? I looked over at Eliza for another opinion. She looked angry, of course. Here was her man hugging this other woman and they appeared to like each other, an odd situation which left her where exactly?

Eliza got up awkwardly, regained her balance, toddled over to Victor and Mom. Her words were angry and she beat her hand on his back and shoulder, her curses coming loud and quick, as she juggled her baby in her other arm.

Mom fell back from the girl's onslaught but her anger was all for the man, not the woman.

"No, wait! Stop!" Victor cried out. "We are old friends." He repeated his words and Eliza paused, getting tired. "We have not seen each other for nineteen years. It is miracle, yes?"

I couldn't read Mom. Either she really did like seeing this man again, even knowing he had arrived but avoiding him, or else she was luring him into a devious plot to exact revenge on him. I searched desperately for a clue in her face, her body language, her behavior, and got nothing.

"Mom, what is this?" I was confused. All my life I'd assumed she would hate the man who seduced her — raped her. But here she was, hugging him like they were old friends.

"So you've met?" Mom asked me, knowing the answer.

"Yes, he is a fine boy," said Victor, putting his hand on my shoulder. "A fine young man. You have done well."

"And Rosa?" asked Mom. "How is she these days? Probably she has a family?" Mom turned to me. "Rosa is his daughter. My age. She was—"

"Ah, she.... Sadly she has already passed. The virus caught her and...same story for many people. Yes, she married, had children, a boy and a girl. She worked in a hospital in Milan, the first to be overrun with cases, and then...she must join them."

He wiped his eyes — maybe an act, who knew?

"Are you in touch with her husband and children? You must be happy to be a grandfather."

"Ah, yes...they are fine, I believe. As for being this kind of person called grandfather, I...." He gave Eliza a glance. "It is not so much for me. I will try. Yet I do my part to maintain a healthy society...by staying away, staying at sea."

"That must be a satisfying life," said Mom, winsome like she wished she had gone with him when he finally sailed away that summer's day long ago. "You must come for dinner some evening. Although we don't have much to eat or share. So bring your own ration and we'll just eat together."

"Ah, but I have much luck today." His grin widened, like he was glad to change the topic. "I have two good fish...the, uh, what is it called?"

"Red snapper," I said.

"Yes, two of these fish. Good size. Plenty for all."

He told the story of catching them, full of nautical details, and Mom listened attentively.

"You have to add them to the community hoard," I reminded them. "It's in the by-laws."

"I am not a member of this community, they like to tell me," said Victor with a frown, "so I keep what I catch, share it as I like. Until they let us stay as members."

"We have some fruit, too." I turned to Mom. "My extra work earned us extra ration. I made up for Hannah's break time. She needs to rest now."

"You see? He is a good man," said Mom to Victor, adding a chuckle. "That's all from me, of course. You were far away, and you never knew he was born. Away living your wild, carefree life as you please. I imagine with you seducing girls left and right, you must have other children scattered from port to port."

"I do not know of them, if they exist," he countered, acting humble. "Only this man do I know."

I liked that they were calling me a man.

A few more pleasantries, easy questions and polite responses. Everything they said made my mind storm through one scenario after another, each running to its end in a flash. My life had come to this: these two people on a beach, not even thinking of me or imagining anything I've done in my life.

Then we parted, Victor helping Eliza and the baby off to the Seaside Inn and Mom and I returning to our house.

Half-way she took my arm and held it for the remainder of the walk, leaning her head against my shoulder. I liked that; she was Mom again. She remembered the tangible things that come from intangible thoughts.

"So you like him? Even now?" I asked when we sat on the back porch, gazing out at the beach. "Even after what he did?"

"After what he did...?" Mom echoed. She pulled her feet up, set her chin on her knees. "It was a long time ago. The details slip away but the story remains."

"And...?"

"You saw him. He's a handsome man. Easy for a girl to be seduced. I wanted him, sure. It's not hard to admit. I know it may be hard for you to think of your mom that way, a girl lost in full lust. When he appeared on the beach – standing over me, with his interest so obvious – I couldn't resist. I wanted him, and he...."

She gazed upward, pondering.

"What, Mom?"

"He was so gentle and loving. A perfect intercourse. Not my first, as I told you before, but the best. And we met a few more times that summer before he had to sail away. So, I don't know, I might've named you 'Palm' or 'Cabana' instead of 'Sandy' – or perhaps 'Bungalow'. Bungalow Baumann. Has a ring to it—"

"You had an affair with him? It wasn't a one-time thing?"

"That's right." She looked at me, her expression like she was surprised she'd forgotten to tell me this important detail. "Even if you think it's wrong."

My heart raced, feeling betrayed. I always trusted Mom to be honest with me. I didn't know what to do. She was the only person in my life, after all. She could do anything and I would stay with her. She was my home, my guardian.

"So you've been lying to me." I felt my face reddened. "All these years, nothing but lies."

She reached over and gave me a hug. "No, I haven't. All the details are the same." Long sigh. "I certainly don't want to glorify older men seducing teen girls. Not at all. But what happened to me, to him and me, was special, not a mark on a crime report. I definitely don't recommend other girls do it. But in my case – *only* my case, which is all I can know – it was something special. It was a girl's crazy love for this...this Adonis. And getting to experience one great moment against which she would measure all others. Not even what happened next darkened that afternoon in my memory. One, that was great, perfect. Two, okay. And two more, well, yeah, too much and not so good, to be honest."

"Mom, stop."

She saw how she'd upset me. "Well, you wanted the truth."

I was choked up, but I forced myself to speak. "He said I was.... He called me the son of a whore. Yeah, he said that. And he said I should be glad I turned out okay anyway."

"That's mean." Her voice remained mellow, like she'd settled into the comfort of the memory. "But not wrong."

"Not wrong?"

"You have turned out okay. Better than just okay. You're a wonderful man, a loving husband in our pretend world. You will survive this crisis and be a leader in post-pandemic society. I'm sure of it."

I gave Mom a hug. Tears welled in my eyes. One dropped onto her neck and she raised her hand to wipe it away, stayed to brush my cheek as she used to do when I was little and got upset by minor things that stoked me into full-scale rage.

"What're y'all talking about?" a man asked.

Looking back through the house to the front door, we saw it was Bucky returning from his day's work. He had a big cooler with his catch in it.

"Got dinner right here," he announced.

Nathan entered after Bucky, his arms full of fishing gear. He maneuvered through the house to the back yard, set everything down there.

"Better go get Hannah," I declared, realizing the hour and jumping up. Every day I escorted her to and from her work.

"And I need to play," said Mom, lifting her hand for a boost up. "I feel like playing.... Let's see.... Maybe the *Tuba Suite* by Morton Gould would be just right. Rewritten version, that is, without the three horns, transcription by...well, by me."

As I hurried up the street I could hear the mournful siren song echoing among the houses.

36

IN WHICH TRUTH HURTS

With a sloppy kiss to her sweet forehead, I greeted my dear wife. Hannah sat inside the community center while a handful of guys kept her company, asking questions they hoped would indicate who she would choose to be her next partner after her baby was born – even though Jackson had won her lottery. The discussion made her uncomfortable, but rules Mom insisted be added to the by-laws prevented anyone from initiating intimate acts without the other's consent. It was good having Mom on the council. They really couldn't keep her off it, given the force of her personality, the way she could beat them down. Besides, she'd worked hard to get their votes. Of course, someone could break the consent rule, but that would mean exile from the island and certain death in the outerlands.

I helped Hannah up, my hand at her elbow, as those jealous guys watched. She hugged me, all for show. Her belly bowed out. Blushing at their lustful looks, she gladly turned to go home, with my arm around her.

"It's what Mom would call 'complicated'," I told Hannah as we walked home. "All this time she's been – what's that word? Yeah, *deflecting*...whenever I wanted a straight answer, ya know? But I think I finally figured it out."

"How you got your name?" Hannah laughed – but the laughter made her clench her belly. "Ooo, he doesn't like that."

We smiled at each other, guessing but unable to know for sure if the baby would be a boy or girl. Nathan had done a trick Old Man Kutcher taught him and said the new addition would be a boy. Mom, using her great intuition and a few rubs of Hannah's belly, measuring here and there, was sure it was a girl. Mom was happy there would be a female to play Timmy.

We heard shouting before we got to the house. Neighbors were out, too, alarmed at the contest. As we arrived, we saw Mom and Bucky arguing. I'd never seen Mom so worked up. She slapped him and as he fell back from the steps, she threw one of the empty flower pots sitting on the porch at him. I'm sure she deliberately missed.

"Mom!" I shouted and she halted, cloud of fury boiling around her. "What's going on?"

Bucky got to his feet. "Yer mama's gone plum insane is what's going on."

"I have not!" shouted Mom. To Bucky: "Get out now. Go home."

"But...this is my home. We sleep together, goshdarnit. I bring you fish, don't I?"

Mom cursed under her breath, waving Hannah and me to step behind her to enter the house. She stayed to block Bucky.

"If you're going to be such a...a jerk, you better find yourself another house to sack out in. Try your sister's house. I don't care, just go away."

"I can't go there," he shouted back. "There's two families living there now. Nine people stuffed into that house. No room for me."

"Then try the Seaside Inn."

"But they's full, too."

"Then try out back. By the dumpster."

"I was s'pose ta talk you outta joining the council," he shouted. "Cuz you'd only cause trouble. But I stood up fer yew. They only agreed to vote you in to keep on abusing you. I told'em ain't right. I spoke up for you. Told'em you were the best dang person on this island to run the council. I told'em that—"

"You didn't stand up, you played along!"

"Not playing along – guiding! Like a goddamn shepherd."

Mom stood defiant again, then entered the house with a slam

of the door. A minute later she tossed his clothing out the door as Bucky stood dumbfounded, hands on his hips, a scowl on his face and curse words flying.

"That's lotta bad words," said Nathan, putting his hands over his ears. He still crouched by the porch railing.

"Well, that's what you get when you deal with that kind of bastard," Mom responded.

"An' she deserve ev'ry one of'em," said Bucky with a sneer and an upright finger. "I stood up fer you. Again!"

He gathered up his clothes and stalked away, muttering more curse words.

Mom flipped a switch, instantly becoming gentle, caring, calm Mom again. She cheerfully asked Hannah about her day. Nothing special, no baby was sick, played with the toddlers, liked how they giggled, taught them some words. Made up a new song.

"That's good," said Mom. She urged us to go prepare dinner – whatever we had in our rations that could be shared among us. No fish tonight, the catch going to the community hoard. But we had two kinds of vegetables and fruit. Mom cooked some wild rice that grew on the island and, with some butter made from the milk of Maybelle, it wasn't bad.

"So, Mom," I asked as we finished eating, "are you going to tell us what happened with Bucky?"

Mom's face didn't ive away anything as she took the dishes to the kitchen sink.

"We had a disagreement. That's all."

"But a big one," I said.

"Really big," Nathan said with a mean face.

Mom chose another face. "Yep. Sometimes misunderstandings can become big ones. He was being an ass. A traitor. And then has the audacity to presume things that are none of his business."

"Oh, I get it." I smiled but I felt bad.

"Get what?" asked Hannah.

"You told him about Victor, didn't you? Or he found out on his own. He worries you'll go back to him." I glanced at Hannah, who showed concern. "Typical reaction to the ex returning—"

"That's not it!" Mom barked. Her face changed again; I knew I had to be correct. "I told him he was back. He knew it already. Everyone knows. That big yacht, fashion models on board – who wouldn't know? Then he starts in with his interrogation – like he has any right!"

"But, Mom, he's been good to us." I thought back to the day she rescued him from that truck. "Besides, isn't it normal to ask questions, just to get your bearings? To know how to react to things that happen."

"Is that right?" Mom was momentarily caught off-guard by my sharp observation. I always observe people, and listen, mostly so I can borrow their scripts for interacting with the world.

"Yes. I guess. Maybe," I conceded.

Mom smiled, pleased. "You've learned so much."

"It's in my Sociology book."

"Well, you act like a decent fellow, not an ass."

I refocused. "What did he do?"

"You mean after admitting he led me on, kept the damn vote going so they could keep having their fun? to trick me? You mean all that?"

"I kinda thought that's what he was—"

"Then he gets jealous. Well, I could handle that. But then he begins accusing me of doing things behind his back. Like what? In the three hours I was at the community center? With people all around me? He's just plain crazy. I don't know which is worse, his jealousy or his betrayal."

"You told him there's nothing between you and Victor?"

"Exactly. But like an jackass he hee-hawed and didn't believe anything, wouldn't accept anything I said. Got himself worked up and kept coming at me so I had to slap his face to stop him. Then he punched me. Can you believe it? Just pulled his arm back and pop!" She put her hand up to her face.

The shadows behind the candlelight kept me from seeing the mark on Mom's cheek where Bucky's fist had landed.

"Wow." I couldn't believe he would do that, especially if he had not been drinking. "Was he drinking?"

"No, clean as a baby's bottom."

Hannah laughed at that remark.

"After a diaper change," Mom finished.

"Ew," Nathan snickered. "That stinks."

"So he's no longer living here?" I asked quietly. "Or is this just temporary? Until you calm down?"

"I am calm!" she exploded, and we all froze.

"I mean," I continued, taking a softer approach, "is he going to be banished from this house forever or only a short time?"

"Am I going fishing with him any more?" asked Nathan.

"What'll we do for food?" asked Hannah, hands over her belly. "Baby needs protein."

"You got eggs," Mom replied in a voice strained from shouting. "And you can fish on your own, Nathan. Same as fishing without an ass standing by you. And you, Sandy, you can take care of your wife and let your mom make her own decisions about her own life. You're not the government demanding I get fourteen jabs and stay indoors for ninety-five days."

Mom stormed out of the living room. When she slammed the bedroom door, the whole house shook.

"Wow," I muttered at the scene. So dramatic.

Hannah came over to me, hugged me as best she could, our bellies pressed together. She didn't have to speak; we both had the same thoughts. We learned to communicate with only our minds, like we were two halves of the same person.

Later that night, we resumed our conversation in whispers. Usually we talked about all kinds of things, many that didn't have anything to do with life on the island or our future plans. She shared her new song, then we discussed Mom.

"I dunno, maybe she's going through the change," Hannah suggested. "Mother was very cranky when it started with her."

"She's not that old. Unless all the stress she's under makes it start sooner."

"Or its the effects of all the virus variants floating around. She maybe picked up something here or there. Sub-clinical, but still affecting her. Could trigger it to start sooner. It's possible, makes

333

the body react that way. Early menopause, they say.'"

"No," I countered. "I heard it's a side-effect of some of the older vaccines. If you get the shots too close together and you're at the wrong age, or something."

"That's so creepy." She thought a moment, brightened. "That must be where the Coronas got the idea for their song 'Over the Hill'. Ya think? ...'She's up in age and drying out / Lost her mojo and her clout / Gotta call it quits / It's the shits / Too old for the dirty deed' ...well, anyhoo. I heard a lot of girls were no longer fertile after getting all the jabs."

"Yeah, maybe. I really don't know. Mother never let us get any jabs, so I'm plenty fertile as you can see. Maybe your mother just got mad at what he did to her and that's all there is to it."

"Simple answer is the best, huh?"

Hannah stretched over and we kissed.

"Still can't believe he punched her like that," I said. "Not after the way they came together. I mean, finding each other. Weird. I really thought they were good for each other. Mom stopped flirting with me.... Then he gets mad enough to hit her? Something's off."

She snuggled against me. "Would you ever hit me?"

"What? Heck no. Never." I couldn't believe that my dear wife would ask me that.

"You wouldn't ever get mad enough to whop me?"

"No, never."

"I could do anything and you wouldn't never get that mad and haul off and punch me, knock the shit outta me?"

"I swear, Hannah. I will never hit you."

We gazed at each other a moment in the dark.

"Okay," she said with a strange giggle. "I believe you."

37

IN WHICH AUGUSTINE ARRIVES

It was appropriate Mom selected Bruce Broughton's *Turbulence* to play away her anger, although she made a mess of it. She started over, couldn't get in the right mood, and eventually gave up. She blasted the loudest notes she could.

We heard her clearly from the beach behind the house, where we lay out on towels under a hot sun, just Hannah and me and her huge belly, the three of us. She smiled, grimaced, then smiled again. She was getting close. I leaned over to kiss up and down that glorious curve. She said my lips tickled and play-slapped me away.

Mom played *Rock'n'Rave* and *Ballad for the Girls of Buchanan* from her Tubafonics days. They sounded better. The baby calmed. Then she played *The Fart Song*, my favorite when I was a kid, all the low notes for my childish amusement. I had to tell Hannah the story how she composed that song: I was at that age when farts were funny.

She switched to the Sousa marches *Fairest of the Fair* and *Hands Across the Sea*, playing the melody, not just the tuba part. The lively tunes lifted us out of our bad mood. The drama between Mom and Bucky was so exhausting. I needed time to recover, and I was only an observer. Thankfully, Hannah kept out of it to keep the baby at peace.

One problem we realized was Bucky was no longer providing us with fish he caught. Nathan continued to go to the pier where

Bucky fished, but the boy reported it was all silence, no more casual chatter between him and his father-figure. Nathan brought home his usual catch, sometimes a good-sized fish, other times a fish no larger than his hand which Bucky'd say "weren't enough worth cutting for bait."

"Looks like we'll need to cut back," said Mom at dinner, the small sea bass laying in a sauce on a plate before us. "Nathan and I will skip tonight. It's Hannah who needs to eat. And you, too, Sandy, if you're going to stay strong enough to protect her."

"But I'm hungry," Nathan moaned. "And I caught the damn fish."

"Watch your mouth," Mom snapped at him.

"Bucky says 'damn' all the time. And other words."

"No more about Bucky!"

"But Bucky says—"

"I have part of a chocolate bar you can have," said Mom.

Giving most of the fish to Hannah, I took a bite to make Mom happy. She feared a ship might come to our island and we would be taken hostage. The island men with their pot bellies and the skinny nerd boys would be no match for any kind of invasion. She talked so negatively, thinking of worst-case scenarios – like she wanted something bad to happen just to liven her routine.

Perhaps she was right, I considered, observing the men while doing my chores. The boys – young men like me who were quick to choose which girls they wanted to pair with – young women like Hannah – spent their days tossing around disks and footballs on the beach. It was hard to get them to work. I understood Owen's frustration. One group of boys was supposed to repair the wharf, another pair had to build a new coop for the chickens. More of the guys were assigned fishing duty but they tended to nap and miss tugs on their lines. But, once they had wives, matched by lottery, they began taking their duties more seriously.

Once Mom was on the council, she suggested the men should have training in how to fight. Owen balked at that, saying we didn't want to become like the cities we'd left, the way the police had terrorized everyone, arresting anybody on the streets during lockdowns no matter how innocent. Or coming to your house and arresting you if you posted a comment online against anything. He gave lots of examples, and repeated his often-told tale of how he was beaten and put in jail a few weeks when his face mask slipped down off his nose while he was out in public. It wasn't a slipping mask, another council member corrected, it was his back-talking to the police.

"It was him acting like he's the dang World Health Org's top scientist," said another council member, "spouting his righteous indignation just cuz he taught Biology to kids, and too stupid ta know ya cain't say none o that shit without getting thrown in the slammer."

Mom described how a boat could sail in and off jumps a gang of pirates to ravage and rape.

"Who would be able to stop them? Who could fight them?"

The men of the council became afraid. Instead of asking her how they would form such a militia, they quizzed her about how she might know there was a pirate ship coming. Flabbergasted, Mom explained in exhaustive detail, as though she was speaking to a child, that it was only a possibility. She didn't have any foreknowledge of an attack actually happening or being planned. But they accused her of sneaking on the island to infiltrate, doing reconnaissance for pirates. She dismissed them with a hand flick, a few curse words, and told them they'd better be ready.

Then she'd gone to Victor, found him lazing in a Speedo on his yacht, met the half-naked ladies aboard, and told him what the damn council had said.

"She was hoping he could talk to them," I told Hannah as we relaxed on the beach. "You know, give'em some perspective on the dangers of being an unarmed island. He didn't have any military experience, she said, just cadet school his dad sent him to when he was young. But everybody would listen to Victor. He would take Mom's side, of course. But then...."

"Then what?" asked Hannah, rolling on her side, belly toward me, like the turning of a great whale.

"Then Bucky showed up, stood on the wharf watching for Mom

to get off the yacht. When she did, he made a big scene about her going aboard to see Victor – like they'd been fooling around."

"Were they?" Hannah paused at another kick from inside. "She coulda been seeing him, ya know, for sex. Your mother's like that. It's a lot like Viral Dark's 'Boat Babes', ya know?"

"No, not like a Viral Dark song," I laughed. "I believe Mom when she says she only went there to talk. But you know how Bucky can be: sees betrayal in every facial tic and throat rumble."

Hannah laughed, then stopped as the baby objected.

"I keep telling Mom to just apologize, even though he's the one that's wrong. Then he'll share his catch with us."

"So what's the problem? I mean, other than your mother's bad attitude. Geez, grown-ups! Never can just hang loose, let things lay. Like that Jabbers' song 'Laying Loose'."

"He started it, is what she says. He tricked her with getting the council vote. Then accuses *her* of being unfaithful – like that's a thing here on this island. I mean, it's everybody with everybody here. It's a fucking orgy."

"I think 'orgy' includes 'fucking', so it's kinda redundant."

"Yeah, well, we're not part of that scene."

"Not us," Hannah cooed. "We are so trad it hurts. Pregnant before I even finish high school, thank you very much."

"Nothing wrong with making a family. It's how we all got here, isn't it? It's how we'll survive."

"Okay, maybe, but it's not exactly how I saw my life going."

"Me, neither. Nobody saw it coming. I was supposed to go off to college. Maybe become a professor like Mom. But here comes a big pandemic."

"I wanted singing lessons. Maybe form a band with Leslie and Cindy, my friends up the street. Really needed guitar lessons, too. Leslie was the one with the guitar. Cindy played drums. I was gonna play bass or keyboards, and be lead singer."

"You still could do that," I said, sounding hopeful.

"Not now." Her hand slipped down over her bare belly. "It was supposed to be me going with Dad to the store that day. But I was hanging out with them. So Kristen went. After that, Mother never let me go out. She got groceries, made me hide in the closet till she got home. Didn't want me to get raped, ya know."

"Oh," was all I could say, staring at her belly. "Did you have a name for your band?"

She laughed like it was a pleasant memory. "We were gonna be Loose Girls." She smiled to herself. "Originally we were the E-Street Bitches. That was Cindy's idea."

"That'd work," I responded with a chuckle.

"Leslie wanted it to be our initials: H-L-C. She got 'Halcyon' from our initials, thought it was a cool word, but Cindy said it didn't sound badass."

"Yeah, I can see that. I like Loose Girls."

"We made some songs during the lockdown. 'Candy Store' and 'Street Girls' were pretty good. Wanna hear'em? 'Jab Equals Love' was maybe our best. That's 'Jab' with an equal sign, then 'Love'. Get it? You show your love by getting the jab? Not that you love getting the jab. Yeah, we liked hanging out, singing and making up songs. Especially the Wu Crew and the Coronas. We did covers of Callie Odem and Jewel Rhee. Yeah, good times. Maybe I could be a doctor, like on TV. A TV doctor, I mean, not a real one."

"So an actress...."

I regarded her, transfixed by her sweet voice, her stories of life before we met. I also loved the way her small breasts had swollen during pregnancy, nipples dark under the sunshine.

She caught me looking. "Geez, Sandy. You're like a pervy old man."

"But they are right there! Staring at me."

"You want me to put on a shirt?"

"No...."

"I'll put a shirt on if you can't control yourself."

"Okay, I'm under control."

A frown pushed back on my face as I returned to reality.

"I told Mom to say she's sorry, even if she's not, just so we can get food. Everything's about getting food. I know there's no way for Bucky to believe her, or her to accept him back. That's just who they are."

"She's changed since we got to the island."

"I guess so. Switched from a cool, calculating warrior bitch to a hissy-fit council member."

"That escalated quickly," she laughed, winced.

"Probably because of meeting Bucky. She was happy to get sex. I guess. I dunno. Never saw that side of her – I mean, being a woman, not as Mom. Maybe that's what made her change. Things became real."

"And they weren't even officially paired."

"Not like us?" I smiled big for her.

"We got married before we got to the island, don't you recall? That's what everybody thinks," said Hannah, with a frown for my forgetfulness. "You want Owen to bless our union like he did for Sara and Marcus? Tie a red ribbon around their wrists, wave the island flag over their heads? Drink the old, flat wine, everybody clapping?"

"Yeah, we shoulda had a ceremony," I said sheepishly.

"Everybody knows you're mine and I'm yours, and better leave us alone so we can do our baby thing." She patted her big belly, waited, got a kicked message back. "We worked damn hard for that green circle of fertility. Now we can repopulate this island."

I guess she expected me to respond, but I continued smiling at her, lost in wonder at this beautiful mother. Beautiful even when she seemed annoyed. She tried to sit up on the towel but it was awkward. When she declared she was ready to go back, I helped her up. It was a struggle to get her to her feet, but when she was fully upright, we noticed the liquid that flowed down her legs.

"Oh, no! It's time," she panted. "I think it's time. It's what your mother said to expect."

"We gotta get you into the house. I'll send Nathan to get Mom. She'll know what to do."

"Not Doc Rick?"

"He's a chiropractor."

"But he has medical training."

"For delivering babies?"

"He delivered Marcus and Sara's baby."

"He mostly just caught the baby when she pushed her out. And clipped the cord. Even Nathan could do that much."

"What're we gonna do?" asked Hannah.

"I'll get Mom."

✳ ✳ ✳

We named her Augustine because she was born in the month of August – early but welcomed nevertheless. We thought the name was appropriate. After all, Aunt Laura was actually Lauraline. Jackie was, of course, Jacqueline, and Mom was Pauline. Mom didn't like the name and suggested that since she was born on an island she should be named Isla – silent s. So our little daughter was Isla Augustine Baumann, the great hope of the island, and officially registered in the community ledger, the next one in the Baumann line, no matter how twisted that line might be.

Mom was delighted and so proud of me. Hannah had grown into a wonderful woman and mother – taking to baby care like a fish to water, Owen said, as though she was his daughter, thanks to her work in the community nursery.

"Someone has to," Hannah would say. "Besides, it's better than working in the garden" – like I did. She never talked much about what she wanted to do other than sing, but we had few options in our pandemic world. Medical school was out of the question. No more dreams of being a doctor like in the TV shows. No more wishing to be a rockstar either. Maybe she would follow in Mom's footsteps and become a leader in the island community. But next for her, Owen enjoyed reminding us, was to have a second baby with a different father. I hated that idea, but we didn't need to be concerned until Isla's first birthday. That's what the by-laws said.

Victor's so-called stowaway, Eliza, had her baby a few weeks before us. She didn't count, being an outsider, but being born on the island made her baby son an islander. Antonio and Isla shared the nursery; some people thought they might make a fine couple one day and produce the next generation of islanders – not caring that Antonio's father and Isla's grandfather were the same. Lots of talk like that on the island: planning the future, matching this boy with that girl, checking the list to see who was next to partner with so-and-so. Mom was crafting rules to manage it, trying to be fair yet practical: one year between giving birth and the next partnering, for example. She thought we'd leave before then, the pandemic done. As it stood, six months to get acquainted, then six months of trying, and if no success by the one-year anniversary then they go to the next name on the list. The men on the council agreed.

To many it seemed Mom was taking over the island and some didn't like that. Besides being on the council, she took it upon herself to teach the kids. She started school again. Older kids had missed so many lessons Mom had her work cut out for her. When she proposed the idea, the council agreed without debate. It would keep kids out of trouble. And her idea to have the men train to defend the island was accepted with little resistance. She would lead that, too, they agreed after hearing her Marine grandfather's harrowing stories of Vietnam.

It all started with Isla, however. Not having any Ob/Gyn on the island, Mom went to the library in a room of the community center and flipped through pages of a medical book. People had been using the books for kindling, so little by little the shelves were becoming bare. I popped in a few times to grab a book just for fun. I found a Scout manual, all about surviving in the wild. Hannah and I often read a novel together, like *East of Eden*, taking turns speaking the words to each other, as though we were the last generation that knew how to read and the words on the pages were sacred, pronounced with reverence.

Mom got enough information from the book to help deliver the baby. With no epidural, there was a lot of screaming. I wanted to stay, no matter how much it hurt to hear her in pain. Mom tried to send me out, but Hannah insisted I remain.

"No – let him stay," she grunted. "I want him to see what I go through. So he'll never ever complain about anything ever again!"

I promised right then and there I would never complain about anything, seeing how she fought through the birthing.

Looking for the medical book, Mom found other books in the library and set up a classroom in the community center. A dozen kids under fourteen were required to attend for three hours every day. Then they would go do their usual tasks on the island. Mom taught them reading, writing, and arithmetic. One of the men came over to teach history, geography, and oceanography. Even Owen liked teaching Biology lessons. After all, kids would grow up to be fishers and farmers or in other ways serve the community.

"You don't *have to* work," Mom would tell the kids, "you *get* to work." She managed a balance between authority and kindness. "You need some purpose to make a good life. Learn a skill, share it, teach it to others. If you get bored, help someone."

Maria, thirteen and not yet old enough for the list, was going to be my next partner, according to the list. She shadowed Mom to train as the next teacher. If the kids were diligent in their studies, Mom might finish the class by playing her tuba. They particularly enjoyed the *Effie Suite*, a set of songs following the adventures of a young elephant.

It was good that Mom had the men drilling. A bit of exercise was good for aging physiques and for the development of manly manhood for the younger males. She had us line up, rank and file, run through calisthenics. We trained with the weapons we had. Council members took an inventory and found we had plenty of guns but not much ammo. We crafted a lot of spears. Randy had a hunting bow and some arrows he used to pick off sea birds that landed to snip at fish scraps. The older men just went through the motions, their bellies not allowing much freedom of movement. For them it was for show, to inspire the younger men who would actually defend the island.

And that day came.

Once in a while a boat or raft would drift down from the north, following the current, and find our island. There was a boat with two men in it, Burt and Kirk. They were happy to find a village, but within two days they assaulted Olivia. They ripped half her clothes off by the time we got there. We confronted them and it was James, holding the .22 rifle, who shot Kirk. Burt ran but was captured and beaten, then sent on in his boat with instructions never to return. Kirk was buried at the far end of the island, in the old church yard near the ferry landing, safe among the old sailors from long ago.

As the council made new by-laws for fighting invaders versus fighting between islanders, other boats arrived without incidents. There was a boat with two women, haggard and hungry. Priscilla and Maddy were already paired, past child-bearing age anyway, so Mom made them off-limits. Nursed back to health, they were given tasks in exchange for food rations.

Roberto and Amara, little boy Lenny and daughter Ayomide, arrived one foggy morning, begging to dock, just another family escaping chaos in a city up north. They told of the horrors there. They'd lost another daughter to violence and a grandmother to the virus. They checked out clean by Doc Rick and allowed to stay. They brought a pair of goats, male and female, from a children's petting zoo, to add to our resources.

George and his three young sons arrived with their provisions. Austin and Becky made it. Larry and Fred, too. An unmanned barn door floating like a raft with a few rabbits on it also landed. Then a guy named Dixon in orange coveralls, insisting he'd done nothing wrong, got a second chance on the island. And Vivian and daughter Alicia came. Then came Zeke, his cousin Jed, and their other-side cousin Wade, all hoping to find wives. But they'd have to work a year before they could get on the list.

In this way the island community grew.

Occasionally it diminished. An older woman, always quiet like she'd been traumatized by past events, one day began shouting at phantoms. She got a knife, waved it around. She grabbed a boy coming out of school lessons, put the knife to him, shouting that kids were devils, carried viruses, had to be killed. A crowd formed, begging her to let the boy go. Mom arrived, decided the situation demanded action, and shot the woman. The council voted to make Mom the sheriff – in addition to her other duties.

With her extra duties, Mom no longer worked in the garden with me, so I had a couple new people to train. I was becoming proficient in getting vegetables to grow in the soil we cultivated. Tomatoes, peppers, and zucchini grew the best. I had to wash off thoroughly, of course, before Hannah would let me play with our little girl. Isla, despite being born early, quickly regained proper development. Mom thought Isla seemed normal but I worried she might be like me.

"You'll know later, if at all," said Mom. "You were maybe five before I suspected anything. And I knew for sure when you were ten. I took you to a specialist, did some tests."

Mom didn't like being a grandmother. Oh, she enjoyed Isla as much as any of us, but that status made Mom feel old, even though she was still on the list. In fact, following the by-laws, she met with someone once a month when the timing was just right. She did her duty but never expected anything to result. For Mom it was pure recreation. It also made Bucky mad – which she liked.

"I stood up fer yew," Bucky kept reminding Mom.

Then Mom went out one day on Victor's yacht. They hoped to catch some big game fish to stock the community rations for the winter. They managed to hook a marlin, five feet long, and a small shark, as well as snappers, groupers, and sea bass – a successful outing to everyone who saw the off-loading of the catch.

Except for Bucky, who remained jealous of Mom's renewed relationship with the foreign yachtsman, and stood rigidly on the wharf watching the unloading, his arms crossed angrily over his chest, pouting through his beard.

"I stood up fer her," he had to remind anyone who had ears. "But she done betrayed me."

38

IN WHICH MOM GETS OFF THE LIST

"Out again, ain'tcha? Sleazy whore bitch!" Bucky called out from the wharf. People there, off-loading the fish, turned at his call. Just Bucky, nothing for concern. "Whatcha doing fer eight damn hours beside catching fish, huh? Crazy whore bitch!"

I took his arm, pulled him aside. He resisted a moment, then resigned himself to go with me. By the entrance of the community center, I halted us.

"What are you doing? That's my mom," I chided.

"Just letting her know I know what she's doing, is all."

"Doing what?"

"Cheating on me with that foreigner!"

"No, she isn't." I glared at him. "Probably not. Anyway, none of your concern now. She's got a lot of things on her plate, you know. Can't be bothered with you all the time. You gotta let her go. Time to move on." It was weird how the lines from videos played back for me when I needed to say something. "You hear me?"

"Yeah, maybe, but she's still a cold-hearted bitch," he said with an angry grunt.

"Hey! That's my mom you're calling a bitch."

"Yeah, well, you're calling my bitch your mom so it's even out."

Defeated, he dropped himself on a bench to the side of the plaza in front of the community center.

"I am so stupid. I was wrong. I shouldn't be jealous. Yeah, I know she's doing her duty, on the list and all, can't count that.

But *him*.... No way. Bastard's not eligible. He's not no islander. Ah, hell, I miss her. Miss being with her, you know? Like in bed. Man, she was wild in bed. Like a tiger. And she tearing me apart. Yessiree, couldn't ever get enough, and I sure couldn't keep up. Ya know? No, she's more a bear. Smothers ya, keeps you in her nest and plays you to death. Pushes them titties in yer face and ya can't breathe – and can't get away neither."

"I'm sorry."

I didn't know how I should feel. Bucky had been good to us. He still took Nathan out fishing despite Mom. They had to be sneaky.

"Hey! Nate!" he would call from the side of the house in the morning. "Let's go fishin."

Nathan would rush off before Mom could see Bucky.

"Yessir, I know," he moaned, head hanging. "Same thing with my ex back in town, way back when. She left me, too. You coulda guessed that. She said it were cuz I's always acting jealous. Every damn guy she e'er spoke to made me hoppin mad. I couldn't never trust her. The more she talked to'em, the less she treated me good at home, ya know?"

"I'm sorry to hear that," was all I could say.

"And you know what the killer was?"

"What?"

"She *did* have men friends on the side. So it weren't me being jealous, it was me having a sharp nose snooping out her betrayals. Can't stand betrayals, not at all."

"So you were right?" I wanted to laugh, but held back.

"Then I met yer mama. She saved me, goshdarnit. Pulled me from the truck. Got me sober here, treated me good. Man, she was a bear in bed, though. Ah. Loved her sitting on me, bouncing up and down, those titties bobbing! And her mouth! Oh, man—"

"Okay, I don't need all the details."

"Yeah, you're right. It's stuff for my memories. But either way, I miss her, really miss being with her." He jumped up, enraged again. "Except that foreigner! He took her from me. Ain't right. Not him! Never *him*. I know he's got that big yacht, that female crew. He's a handsome sonuvagun, but, hell.... Ain't right."

I watched him torturing himself, needing to fight to get his pain out, but he was unable to throw himself into action.

"Maybe you should have a drink, just calm yourself down a bit. You can have my beer ration for today, if you want it."

"What? You get a beer ration? How old're ya?"

"I'm twenty now," I replied proudly. "And Hannah is eighteen. We're full adults."

"Well, that's mighty kind of you."

He swaggered into the community center, hoping to pick up a can of warm beer from the hoard. It was closed during the day, I knew, a way to keep everyone at work. At least he was away from the wharf.

✳   ✳   ✳

When Mom returned to the classroom, she was still a little fresh from the outing, sunburnt and fishy. The kids didn't mind. Some of them saw her hefting groupers off the yacht, her tuba-trained arms strong and agile, and were impressed.

"It's not so bad here," I said, sitting with Mom on the back porch, sunset fading over the rooftops behind us. Hannah was inside nursing a fussy baby. "I sure had doubts when we arrived, but with you in charge, it's a lot better."

"Takes a woman's touch," Mom chuckled.

"Making those old men give in.... That's badass."

Mom laughed openly. "Badass?"

"It's a word."

"And you know so many, huh?" She sat back, felt a pang in her back. "Eventually even the badass gets a bad back. Yes...so much to do. But it's working out. We might as well stay. We're making a safe place to live, away from the world, on our little island. Let the rest of the world go to shit, I don't care."

I regarded Mom like she was a different person now.

"Do you think we'll ever return home to the city?"

She shook her head. "You want that? It's hard to get off the island now, anyway."

The previous week there were explosions in the morning. It turned out that some men had blasted the bridge once and for all, letting it fall into the channel. Now there was no way on or off the island except by boat.

"If we could increase our livestock," Mom went on.

We had enough chickens now that we could afford to roast a few and still have enough for producing eggs. She listed things she needed to do – that the island folks needed to do. I was afraid she would give me a checklist, too.

Hannah brought Isla out, thankfully, and sat down with us. She handed our daughter over to me for burping.

"Come on, Isla, let it out," I cooed.

"You're good at that," said Hannah. She always had me do the burping after she did the feeding. We traded the diaper changes, too. Cloth, rewashed, reused was all we had.

Mom regarded us, like a queen scrutinizing her knights for their loyalty. I could see in her face the litany of changes she had accepted. Now she was an island leader, an educator, not just my mom but also 'grandmother'. The matriarch presiding over the island. I felt so proud she was my mom.

Isla let the air out and I handed her back to Hannah.

"Damn," Mom grumbled. She glanced down, holding her belly. "Another visit from dear Aunt Flo seems imminent."

"I get it now: 'flow' like in a river." I chuckled.

"I hope not a river," said Mom. "But I wonder, when I get this sick feeling. It's hard enough to get food, so I don't want to waste any by throwing it up. Either it's the change coming – hah, now that I'm a grandma – or else I'm pregnant."

Hannah gasped.

"You women are always talking about your periods," I said.

"Speak for yourself, Sandy," Hannah responded.

"What do you men talk about every month?" asked Mom.

"I suppose we talk about why women are always talking about their periods."

"Typical," Hannah moaned.

"Except, well, I haven't had one in a couple months." Mom

grimaced like she felt embarrassed. "Too much grandmother work wearing me down. I'm getting old. I mean, you can only open your legs so many times."

"Mom!" I gasped. Although it was well-known, no one spoke so baldly of being on the list.

"You're only a year older than last year," said Hannah.

I agreed, and patted Mom's back.

"So which is it?" I asked, not quite sure what I was asking.

Mom pinched her lips, holding back what seemed like a long stream of words. She looked uncomfortable.

"Either it's the change – I'm not that old – or I'm pregnant."

"Wait, how old are you?" asked Hannah, her eyes bright with excitement. She was trying to rock Isla asleep but her exclamation awoke the baby.

"Not that old," Mom snapped. She turned to me. "Remember how we talked of having to repopulate the world? How I would get too old for that eventually? Well, I wasn't trying at all. Perhaps it's happened anyway."

"But...it...." I couldn't put my words together.

"Who's the dad?" asked Hannah bluntly.

"You sure?" I couldn't breathe. "Shouldn't we wait some more? It could still be menopause."

"Nope. I'm thinking it's the other way." A smile rushed across Mom's face and fled quickly in fear. "One more thing I do for the island: repopulate it. I'm going to need a raise. I hope we keep expanding our food resources to match our population growth. Eventually we'll reach some kind of equilibrium."

"Could be anybody," Hannah explained to stupid me. "She's been on the list more than a year."

"No birth control pills on the island. No condoms. Stores have been looted out for a few years. So it's up to God. That's who I blame. But I'm pretty sure we've been on auto-pilot for some time now." Mom had a serious frown. "And the council. I blame them, too. I shouldn't have compromised on the by-laws, not with regard to the list. Let things happen of their own accord, I say. No need to formalize a protocol. That Owen and his damn book! It's not a how-to manual; it's a novel. Let people get together on their own – like ordinary date night. It's worked well for thousands of years."

"Actually," I said, launching a stream of facts from my special interest, "they had arranged marriages a lot more in history than love matches. It's in my Sociology book. They matched up people based on the good of the community, not the wishes of the couple."

"Is that so, my little professor?" Mom responded.

"Yes," I replied, watching her gently rubbing her belly.

She stared at her belly as though determining whether it was larger than before.

"So it's true?" I asked.

Hannah shot me a disapproving glare; I should've known the answer already.

"I'm going to go ahead and act as though it is," said Mom. "But we shouldn't go telling people. Not yet. They'll see soon enough. I'll answer questions then."

39

IN WHICH MOM TAKES ONE FOR THE TEAM

The best thing about having Victor's yacht docked alongside the community center was the solar panels which generated power for the boat. He could run the motor, navigation instruments, and a small refrigerator, even a radio – although there was little traffic, mostly dire messages like "Don't land here, don't want you here" and "Don't land there, they eat outsiders" and so on. With a cable, power could run machines in the community center, like Olivia's computer. It worked better than portable generators and folding solar panels a few people contributed. We had power by the end of the day. Doc Rick could run his lab. Hannah charged her MP3 player. We filled the fridge with fish and other perishables, put Darrel in charge of giving out rations according to tickets issued by Olivia which were printed off the computer she ran for a few minutes a day. The tickets looked like new paper money, with the island's flag waving at the center.

A few of the houses on the island had similar solar panels on their roofs, but the link to get electricity from the panels to the light switches inside didn't work and nobody knew how to repair it. Several families had emergency generators but they ran on gasoline. Jason had portable solar panels so he could charge his generator, but it ran down too fast for powering his whole house. Having Victor's yacht docked almost powered the whole village. But we had to unplug it a couple days to let him charge enough for a fishing trip.

"There you are!" called red-faced Bucky, seeing Mom at the office in the community center and walking right in. His clothes were dirty, like he hadn't bathed in days. And he'd been drinking. "Always hanging out with yer buds stead of me. Whud I eva do ta hurt you, huh? I stood up fer ya."

Mom turned to address him, setting down the papers in her hand, the food stock inventory. On the council meeting agenda was her plan to improve the island's gardens by shifting to more nutrient-dense vegetables using hybrid 'survival' seeds Vivian had brought from up north.

Mom was getting used to Bucky coming by to harass her.

"What do you want now?" she asked, trying to be as polite as she could be while maintaining an edge to her voice, letting him know he really wasn't welcome.

"I want you, ya dumb whore!" He grinned, showing the gap in his teeth, a new development.

"Well, you can't *have* me. I'm not possessable. I'm free, a free woman. Besides, I'm too busy running this island. And you're not clean and sober enough for me to even give consideration to your wants and needs."

"But *he* can? That it? The foreigner? Wha you been doing with him? I know you go board his big-ass yacht, ride those waves. That it? You like riding them waves?"

"Drop it, Bucky," Mom snapped. "You really stink."

"It was you told me to go live in the dumpster behind the Seaside Inn!"

"By it, not in it." Mom pinched her nose.

I'd arrived from the garden at Bucky's loud cursing.

The way Mom stood there didn't encourage him. She had a defiant air. By then it was apparent to everyone she had gained weight, her belly spreading. Olivia saw the curve and with a nod from Mom recorded her new status in the register. She was off the list until after the birth.

"Wha's that?" Bucky exclaimed, pointing at Mom.

"What's what?" Mom shot back.

"*That*." He walked up to her, still pointing his finger at her belly. "You got a kid? Already? Who's it from?"

Mom frowned, looking annoyed, like she'd expected everyone knew already. Counting the weeks, it could be from Bucky's final visit. We quizzed Mom for days until she confessed. She had been with Victor again, out on the yacht, as people suspected. For old time's sake: on the yacht, making love on the foredeck under the hot sun while out fishing. Something about the sailor had always intrigued her, going back to that summer.

"That foreigner? He the one got you pregnated?"

"You're drunk, Bucky," said Mom with a dismissive flip of her hand. She stepped out of the office, heading across the main hall to the tables Darrel had set up for the meeting. "Go home. Sleep it off. I've got a meeting to prepare for."

Mom was facing the table, setting out papers. Olivia had come to the opposite side, helping organize the papers for the council meeting happening soon. Mom dressed nice for the meeting, a pair of khaki culottes and a snug white blouse. A band of skin showed between the top of the culottes and the bottom of the shirt. Her belly had a curve to it.

Olivia gasped and I spun around to find what alarmed her.

I saw Mom collapse: grabbing the table but falling, hitting the floor, then her head hitting, as blood ran from her. A knife stood out from her belly.

I rushed to her, dropped beside her, looking for what to do. It didn't seem too bad: I could just pull it out. Like a cut on a finger, it would heal, the two sides coming together, mending, like new.

But not this wound. It went in deep. The handle of the fish skinning knife was down to the surface of her belly, the long blade maybe going through her baby inside.

I was mad with confusion.

Olivia was screaming. Doc Rick ran out of his office, joined us. But he didn't know what to do, either.

"Mom, what do we do?" I asked the only expert in the room.

She tried to take a breath, couldn't. Her grimace told me it wasn't going to happen. And she knew it.

"Get Victor," I shouted, and Doc Rick ran out.

A few others had arrived early for the meeting, others came at Olivia's scream, but they had no idea what to do, debating among themselves. A couple voices among them seemed glad she'd been wounded, which would keep her out of the council meeting. She was a lot of trouble anyway.

"It's my mom!" I shouted at them. "She's done more for this island than all of you combined."

They shut up – but didn't help us.

A hand gripped my arm, pulled me down.

"Sandy," Mom groaned, one hand on her belly, the other grabbing me. "Remember how we were going to repopulate the world? You and me? Last two people in the world? Well...it's not gonna happen...so you take care of your wife and child. Make a plan...trust yourself...and trust Hannah. Rely on her."

"Mom!" Tears flooded my eyes. "No!"

"And keep Timmy close.... He's the link between you and me... and everyone before us...."

"Wait, Mom – please!"

"If you pull it out, I'll lose a bucket of blood. I'm bleeding inside. No way to fix this."

"There's gotta be." I looked around desperately, my eyes wet, pleading. Where was an ambulance? Where was a hospital? A surgeon? Even a medic? Where? All gone in this pandemic world.

A long exhale. "I wish...."

"Stay with me, Mom."

Her eyes closed and her breathing became shallow.

"Mom, don't go. I love you. I need you, Mom."

With eyes fluttering open, she smiled up at me. "I love you, Sandy, my sweet boy."

Then she was gone.

Really gone.

My whole world destroyed.

The pool of blood had spread out around her, seeping out from underneath where the knife tip exited. It must have clipped an artery on its path through her. Even so, I lifted her head and shoulders, held her in my arms, as people gathered around to watch. No one helped, not one of them.

Victor split the crowd like a god descending from Heaven, and stood beside me, over me and Mom. He could see what happened so no need to ask.

"Where the criminal go?" he called to the crowd.

Some pointed to the entrance doors. He had fled, of course. So he must be on the island, not far down the street. Victor called a few men and they ran as a group out the doors.

Amara brought a blanket from Doc Rick's office, laid it over Mom, pulled it over her face. Then she and Olivia began mopping up the blood, cleaning the floor. The council meeting was due to start soon.

✳ ✳ ✳

The gang of island men led by Victor cornered Bucky outside our house. The way I heard it later, he begged for forgiveness, acting meek and innocent, saying he didn't know what he was doing, it all happened so fast. When Victor went up to him on the porch, to take him into custody – not that we had any jail – Bucky tried to fight him.

Of course, the small town mayor, his belly full of alcohol, was no match for Victor who was much more fit. The men didn't know what to do; the book with the by-laws was back in the community center. What was the proper protocol? A punch to the face by Victor knocked out the criminal before they could decide.

But Bucky rose again, tried to hobble away on weak legs – grumbling something about Nathan and how he'd left the boy at the pier, hanging from a rope, more vengeance directed at Mom. He'd wanted to take a hammer to her beloved tuba, too, but the men caught up to him before he could break into the house.

They waited for Bucky to fall again, which he did a moment later. But then he stumbled up again, limping along the street, dragging his bum leg, headed toward the ferry landing. He wasn't getting away too fast so they didn't pursue him.

By then I'd caught up with them. Although startled by all the blood on my shirt, they knew the reason for it. There was nothing I could do for Mom now but be sure her attacker was dealt with.

I waited with the men, watching Bucky stumble up the street as though he thought he could get away. They told me what he'd said about Nathan and I sent Jackson to check.

"Aren't you going to do anything?" I asked the men.

"He is not going anywhere," said Victor.

"That dude was real trouble from the get-go," said Randy.

"Sorry 'bout yer mama," said Joe. "She was mean as heck, but she was fair. Gonna miss her."

"Yeah. I'll miss her, too," said Darrel with a wry chuckle. "She was the best on the list, really put some effort into it."

"Shut up," I growled at them.

Eventually Victor went after Bucky, walked behind him a few paces, then shoved him down, waited for the man to get up but he didn't this time. Bucky was done, finished, exhausted. Taking him by the arm, Victor dragged him up the street to us. The former mayor was a rag doll, but still flailed his arms and kicked his feet in protest.

"Here is criminal," said Victor, throwing the man down on the pavement. "Is there going to be justice?"

"What should we do with him?" asked Joe, hands on hips, trying to look tough.

"Yer mama," said Darrel. "She was the sheriff."

"The council will act as judges," said Victor.

They discussed options but I didn't hear them. My head was a storm of emotion and I couldn't think straight. But through the clouds a path cleared. Like an eagle soaring straight and true, I saw the way, the only way, and the sun was so brilliant.

I raised my hand, pointing at Bucky crumpled forlornly on the street like a pile of shit, and squeezed the trigger of Mom's pistol.

40

IN WHICH MOM GOES HER OWN WAY

In that first instant they didn't know what to do. They stared at me, looked down at the body, back at me in disbelief. They weren't afraid of me. But they did step back.

"Dude," Darrel mumbled.

"She was my mom," I muttered.

I lowered my hand, held the pistol by my side, the safety on again.

"But...dude...."

I didn't resist. Handing the pistol to Victor, I let the guys lead me back to the community center.

The council meeting was in chaos, everyone shouting about what had happened and what to do about it, what new laws they needed to make, because saying you couldn't do something would keep someone from doing it again. They considered what space could be used as a jail and who would take over as sheriff.

Everyone fell silent when we entered. They seemed shocked at the blood on my clothes, as though I'd been the one to wield the knife. Mom's blood had soaked through my clothes, seeped into the pores of my skin, and we were one again, just as when I grew inside her, attached to her.

Owen got up, cleared his throat, looking over the crowd. He clenched and unclenched his fists.

"We all know what happened here," he stammered behind the table, then spoke in a stronger voice. "Nothing like we expected.

This's a peaceful island, see. I mean, we're all neighbors. We have to work together for the common good. Love thy neighbor, we say. We're s'posed to take care o' one another. None can stand apart... and act against another. That's basic to our by-laws."

"Fuck your by-laws," I said with a grunt.

"What's that, son?" asked Owen, safe behind his table.

"She did more for you," I spoke out, "than all of you combined, and you never appreciated her."

"No, we appreciated her...and all she's done for the island. That's why we let her on the council. Needed a woman's voice."

"She was more than a woman's voice," I shouted.

"Agreed," said Owen. A few of the council members nodded. "But let's not forget we saved her and all y'all's family from the deadly pathogens rampant on the mainland. You helped Kutcher come on the island, too, so—"

"We aren't responsible for him."

"Ain't ya?"

"Each man is responsible for himself, what he does. Not the people who try to help him, and fail."

"Well said, son." Owen looked among the council members, as if wishing someone else would get up and speak. But he was met with blank faces. "This here's a safe place...here on the island, our island, separate from the world. Here we are virus-free—"

"She didn't die from a virus," I said, shaking off the hands that grasped my arms. "She died from the violence that comes from people held captive too long by circumstances imposed by tyranny, by propaganda, by constant petty impositions, inconveniences that pile up to become mountains that cannot be moved."

I turned and met the eyes of several people in the crowd, and they looked down or turned away.

"In the end none of us can endure it – and we lash out. Like wild animals set free, striking at the closest enemy we find, even if the other isn't our enemy. It's all a big misunderstanding, and we're sorry for what happens. We dare ask for forgiveness. But in a world without law and order, without even the idea of freedom that goes with it, without an expectation of peace or the right to feel safe, secure in our homes, and in our own bodies, what have we got? A set of by-laws that're just for show? That serve some fat old men's perversions? Trying to impose a minority's desires on the majority? Without freedom what is there to fight for? To stay alive for?"

Everyone was stunned. Victor, standing behind me, put his hands on my shoulders as though thanking me for what I said.

"Fair enough, son." Owen took a quick poll of council members. "But now, umm, we...we need to see justice done in this matter. The matter of your violent actions."

"My actions?" I raged.

"This is my son," Victor spoke out. "From long ago. I knew his mother then." He looked around the crowd, all eyes on him. "It's true. Maybe you guess before now. Yet, she is gone, so I will claim him and be his parent."

"That's mighty kind o' you, Cap'n Vic," said Owen. "But we here are trying to see justice done."

Victor shook his head. "I know this. So I ask you to forgive him for what he did."

"But he shot a man, killed him in cold blood."

"The man who murdered his mother."

"But it's not—"

"To kill a murderer is what we call a righteous act, and is not punished. I will supervise him. There will be no more trouble."

The row of council members squirmed behind their table, low voices deciding. Then Owen stood up, shifted his belly, and rubbed his hands together.

"The by-laws clearly state.... The rule is.... See, we ain't got no jail and no police, as y'all know. And so we've decided.... Because killing is outlawed on the island and one killer is already dead.... We decree that this one before us, Sandy Baumann, be sentenced. The council all agrees. He should be banished."

The crowd gasped, but some cheered.

"No, it is not fair," Victor cried out, stepping in front of me. "He did nothing wrong. He did only what anyone would do."

The murmuring of the crowd drowned him out.

"It is not right," cried Victor.

"There's no telling who he might shoot next," said one council member. "The boy's learned to kill. Someone be messing with his wife? Or fighting over food? Who's next?"

"He's got a quick temper," said another member.

"No, he's not reliable," shouted another.

"He's got vengeance in his heart now," one insisted.

"No!" Victor shouted back.

Owen waved at the crowd to be silent, but got them to quiet only a little.

"It's settled then. Sentence is effective immediately," spoke Owen, raising his voice. He looked around for his gavel.

Another council member tugged at his arm, spoke to him.

"Effective by dawn tomorrow," Owen corrected. "You have time to pack."

"And in other matters," Larry said, standing up as Owen sat, "we'll lay the body of Polly Baumann in a place of honor in the community cemetery. Tyler's agreed to make a headstone."

"Let me dig her grave," I called out, as men held my arms.

The council members nodded. "Fair enough."

"And let me play a song for her," I spoke so all could hear. "It's what she would want."

I was led outside where the sunshine hit my face, blinding me, making me feel alone in the world – alone without Mom to teach me, care for me, protect me, love me. She was my best friend. She was my entire world.

Hannah joined me outside and handed Isla to me. We cried, foreheads together. I kissed our baby, hoping she would remember me. What was I going to do? Sent off the island, sent into the outerlands? I would face a hard journey to nowhere, countless dangers along the way, and likely a gruesome end.

"The outerlands is no place for a young woman," I told her when Hannah insisted she would come with me. And the baby, too? Impossible. "It's too dangerous. Better you stay here."

"I sure know what we went through to get here," said Hannah, gathering Isla back in her arms. "It wasn't so bad."

"It's been almost two years. Everything's gotta be worse now. I don't want you to go—"

"But I'm your wife," she stammered tearfully. "I hafta go with you. Your mother told me to take care of you."

"Yeah, I know she said that. But I depended on her way too much. That's over now. Now I'm on my own. I have to be."

I gave her the choice. People would look after them, I knew. Hannah would likely pair up with another of the island's men. I recommended Greg or Tyler. Heck, even Jackson might do since he'd turned into a decent fellow after our fight. And he'd won her lottery, after all. One of them would protect her.

She swung her arm around me, Isla in her other arm.

"I need you, too. *We* need you. We are a family."

"But it's safer for you to stay here."

I hugged Hannah and our baby, and drew strength from them, strength for whatever lay ahead.

✳ ✳ ✳

I dug the grave, made it as deep as the island water table allowed, working all day – late enough that they postponed my departure another day. Tyler dug Nathan's grave right next to Mom's while Bucky's body was taken out to sea and left to sink with a stone tied to his feet.

I stood on the beach, my last night on the island. I found the moon staring at me. I picked up fistfuls of sand, threw them at the moon, got half of it blown back in my face.

"Mom!" I shouted as loud as I could to the sea. I repeated my shouts until I could voice nothing more and dropped to my knees.

Hannah came out of the house with Isla, coming up behind me. She knelt, put her hand on my shoulder, shouted "Mother!" for me. Again. And again.

I slowly shook my head. "What am I going to do without my mom?"

Hannah lay her head on my shoulder, her arm across my back. "You have me."

I heard her but couldn't believe it.

In the morning we had the ceremony. Most of the islanders attended. Good words were said. And other words more about themselves and their memories of Mom.

"She was a fine-looking woman."

"Helluva woman."

"One of the best I've ever had."

"A pretty good tuba player."

"She always put out, never just went through the motions."

"She really cared about the island."

"We'll miss her – but not her big mouth, never would shut up in council meetings."

"A loss for our community. A loss for Saturday *soirees*."

"She went her own way and she often got lost, but she always found her way home again."

"What a bitch. Shoulda gone sooner."

"Full of spitfire."

"A real pistol."

"...that slow-witted boy's poor mama."

After the words I played the songs she wanted – did a poor job of it but I'm sure she would hear them correctly rendered.

A line of islanders filed by me, shook my hand or did a fist bump. There were a few hugs, claps on my back or shoulders, words of condolence, winks and nods from lovers, real and fake smiles. Others just offered a solemn nod, acknowledging I had lost someone dear to me – as many of us had in our pandemic world.

Later, as we gathered at the cross street, ready to make the trek north to the ferry landing, Hannah arrived. She wore her pair of ripped jeans and a jacket despite being a warm day. With boots on her feet, a pack on her back, she carried Isla in her arms.

The men parted for her and she stepped through them to join me. We kissed. She took my hand. I was surprised, but glad she'd come to see me off. I didn't know why she bore a pack, though. More supplies for me to carry?

Holding my hand, she tugged me ahead, like she was going to walk with me.

"Wait," said Owen, standing with his belly hanging out, hands on his hips, like a sunburnt Buddha. "What're you doing there?"

Hannah stopped, turning back. "I'm going with him."

"But it's dangerous out there," said Owen in fatherly tone.

"I know," she said. "That's why I'm going. Because he needs me. I hafta go."

"But we need you," Owen insisted, stepping toward us. "We need you to help build our community. You and your little girl, both. You have to stay."

"You gonna stop me?" She handed Isla to me, took a stance, fists raised. "I never had no fighting lessons but I got a whole lotta energy. I could outlast a fat old man like you. You'd probably have a heart attack."

Owen's tan face paled. He licked his lips, looked down, then after a moment looked up.

"Well, don't know if we can let you go. We need you. You're an asset to the community. We'll lighten your load. My nephew'll be happy to take care of you. You won't want for anything, I swear."

"No thanks." She dropped her fists, stood straight.

Owen's face tensed. "Fellas, I think you better grab her."

I pulled Mom's pistol from my belt, pointing it at Owen. He knew I wouldn't hesitate to use it. The council debated whether I should get it back. Victor convinced them I needed it for protection in the outerlands.

The others took a step and I aimed at each of them.

Joe stopped, hands up. "I ain't gonna grab her. Ain't right."

Owen grunted, spit. "You just lost your pool privileges for two months." He stared down the others.

I lowered the pistol, tucked it away in its holster.

My eyes met Hannah's, then Isla's. We were together, ready at last to face the outerlands.

"Awright, awright, go on!" Owen cursed. "Y'all are gonna die out there anyway." He stood numb, a fat slob who'd run out of his hoard of pills. Embarrassed, he gave us a flick of his hand and started back to the village.

Victor and the other men gathered our bags and walked us to

the ferry landing.

A few small boats were tied up there. After selecting a sound one, we got in. They rowed us across the channel to the mainland, helped us unload our bags. Then handshakes, fist bumps, nods.

"Here, take this," said Victor, handing me a canvas pouch, its strap torn off. "Maybe helps, maybe not."

I looked inside and saw two bundles of dollar bills in bands and some gold coins in a clear plastic bag.

"*Buona fortuna*," said Victor, offering me an awkward smile, something forged through years of regrets now raging at him like a hurricane. "I wish you well...my son."

I hugged him as tight as I could, holding it a long time. We released each other with back slaps and sad faces.

The boatmen called to him and he joined them.

They rowed back across the channel as I stood on the shore with my wife and child, gazing south, seeing the island awash in the afternoon glare as it slipped from my view, and from my memories. Mom's island – where my life began and hers ended. Behind us lay the road ahead, and we would walk it as best we could. A new life in a new world awaited us – and I shook as I thought of all the responsibilities Mom had passed to me.

I swung Timmy, snug in his soft-side case, onto my back and we started off on a new journey.

In the end some of us would survive.

It wasn't so much the conveyor belt of viruses and variants that killed us but ourselves. Trained month after month to be suspicious of each other, we eventually unleashed our pent-up fury, driving hate into everything around us, without mercy, and that was our end.

That was also our beginning.

ACKNOWLEDGMENTS

As typically happens when writing a novel, a lot of influences come together randomly to initiate a story idea and then propel the writing forward.

I can determine some of these influences, such as the film *A Boy and His Dog* (1975), a sardonic adventure set in a post-apocalyptic landscape, based on Harlan Ellison's short story. I would have done it differently, of course, but I gave my novel the working title of "A Boy and his Mom and her tuba" – perhaps a little too obvious. It was a what-if exercise, after all.

At the start of the SARS-CoV2 ("covid-19") pandemic, I sought to write a novel on this end-of-the-world theme. However, I wanted to focus on the initial days, when everything was immediate and real, not the far future aftereffects. While preparing for it, I read a few post-apocalyptic novels. *Earth Abides* (1949) by George R. Stewart, was definitely ahead of its time. While the hero finds himself alone at the start of the novel, with not much mentioned about the cause of humanity's demise, his construction of a new society became a helpful manual and I leaned on that for the second half of this book.

Other works with a near-future or post-apocalyptic setting were well-known to me (e.g., *The Handmaid's Tale* by Margaret Atwood). I tried to avoid any resemblance to them as much as possible. The trick, I quickly realized, was not to portray what I *might want* to happen in the future but, rather, what I *believed* would be the way things would likely go given the way they were now. (Alternatively, suppose a character in a novel used a book such as Atwood's as the basis for a society?) Therefore, I consciously tried to keep to the realistic, the probable versus the plausible, and away from the more fantastic.

My own experiences during these two years also could not help but influence this novel. The story told by the man in the pine woods, for example, is based on my experiences with the virus in its earliest days. As usual, I tend to put some of my own life into a story I'm telling. I am a tuba player – used to be. However, my mother is in no way like the mom in this book. Neither is my father. I did have a Schnauzer and lost him in a similar way. My parents did have a home on a barrier island but only upon their retirement.

Finally, I always select music to help create an appropriate emotive soundscape for my writing and revision time. The aural support is crucial to unlocking my muse. I was lucky to find right away the ideal soundtrack in the music of Gavin Luke, from several albums and EPs, which I played over and over during the months of this project. For example, the song "Notes to Self" fits perfectly with the final scene of this novel.

I would certainly be remiss if I did not include a list of the tuba music mentioned in the novel – and listened to during parts of the writing. I've actually played some of them. Thanks, forever, to all the music composers and performers who continue to keep hold of our humanity through difficult times.

A special thanks must go to those who worked the front lines during the pandemic, some of whom lost their lives alongside their patients. Our gratitude is immeasurable.

Musical Works Mentioned

Alec Wilder - *Suite #1 for Tuba and Piano ("Effie Suite")*
Bruce Broughton - *Turbulence*
Carter Benson - *Scenes from the West**
George Gershwin - *Rhapsody in Blue* (not known for tuba)
Gordon Jacob - *Tuba Suite*
Gustav Mahler - 10th Symphony (4th Movement)
Hector Berlioz - *Sinfonie Fantastique*
Henning Christiansen - *Lettres de Tuba*
John Philip Sousa - *Fairest of the Fair, Hands Across the Sea, The Thunderer*
John Williams – *Concerto for Tuba and Orchestra* (referenced but not named)
Krzysztof Penderecki - *Capriccio*
Michael Daugherty - *Reflections on the Mississippi*
Morton Gould - *Tuba Suite*
Paul Hindemith - *Sonate for Bass Tuba and Piano*
Pauline Baumann - *Rock'n'Rave**; *Ballad for the Girls of Buchanan**; *The Fart Song**
Ralph Vaughan Williams - *Concerto for Tuba and Orchestra*; *Six Studies in English Folksong*
Stefan Schweiz - *Lamentations on the Occasion of a Stillbirth**
Trygve Madsen - *Sonata for Tuba and Piano*
(Traditional) - *Down in the River to Pray*

*Music which, as of the publication of this novel, has not actually been composed; therefore, a product of the Author's imagination. Anyone is welcome to compose a work with this title; please notify the Author when available.

Tubafonics songs mentioned:

'Bullets' (a.k.a. 'Bullets Over Babylon')
'Rock'n'Rave'
'Ballad for the Girls of Buchanan'

Pandemic Pop singers/bands (songs mentioned)

Buddy D
Callie Odem
Jewel Rhee
JuJu Beans
Maddy Fink and the Pink Lezzos
Perfectly Sane
Red Velvet
The Coronas ('Over the Hill', 'Needle Fuck', 'Alone Together')
The Jabbers ('Laying Loose')
The War Chix
The Wu Crew ('Petty Grooves', 'Laughter', 'Chinabound')
Viral Dark ('Boat Babes')
Wang-Chang
Wuhan Wave

As of the publication date of this novel, none of these bands are known to actually exist; they are products of the Author's imagination. If any of them should exist somewhere, apologies are offered.

www.ingramcontent.com/pod-product-compliance
Lightning Source LLC
Chambersburg PA
CBHW060154260626
47160CB00001B/261